from Guy aug 09

Alan Brownjohn is author of three previous novels. *The Way You Tell Them* won the Authors' Club prize for most promising debut novel, 1990. *The Long Shadows*, 1997, was chosen by Jonathan Coe as a book of the year in the *New Statesman*, and was followed in 2001 by *A Funny Old Year*. He is a leading poet who has published twelve individual and three collected editions, the most recent in 2006. In 2007 he received a lifetime achievement award from the Books Committee of the Writers' Guild of Great Britain. He has edited poetry collections with Seamus Heaney and Maureen Duffy, and produced versions of classic dramas by Goethe and Corneille for the National Theatre, BBC Radio 3 and the Lyric, Hammersmith.

Windows on the Moon

Windows on the Moon

Alan Brownjohn

BLACK
SPRING
PRESS

Published in 2009 by Black Spring Press Ltd
Curtain House
134–146 Curtain Road
London EC2A 3AR

www.blackspringpress.co.uk

ISBN Hardback 978-0-948238-41-3
Paperback 978-0-948238-42-0

A full CIP record for this book is available from the British Library

Cover design Ken Leeder
Front cover photograph © Harry Todd (Getty Images)

Typeset in Caslon by Dexter Haven Associates Ltd, London
Printed and bound in Great Britain by CPI Mackays, Chatham

for John McCormick

Prologue

A woman enters a room for the very first time, invited by the man following her. There is a rule in this situation that she goes over to the window, immediately, curious about the view but also looking for assurance that she could escape to freedom if she needed to.

On a late July afternoon at five, fourteen months after the end of the Second World War, Maureen Hollard walked slowly into one of the rooms above Bob Spillar's Rio Café. Spillar stood courteously aside to let her go first, and because the room was darkened by the dropped venetian blind he switched on the light. But even before he could do that Maureen was parting two of the worn and stained slats of the blind with cautious fingers, and looking through.

Then she took the liberty, as she thought she might, of raising the whole old contraption with a tired clatter by pulling down one of the strings at the side. She wound the string round a painted metal hook when the blind was about two-thirds of the way up. The view revealed—what else?—was of the side exits of the Empire across the road, and to the right the forecourt of the second-hand car dealer's, with its Ford 8s and Morrises and several Austins (black 10s and 14s), and the Buick, and even an Alvis, very well polished; all of these pre-war, of course. Beyond that forecourt the road joined the High Street, and Maureen looked first that way and then in the other direction up towards home, ten minutes' walk away. Below, cars and buses passed by occasionally, two or three every minute.

'Do you like it?' Spillar asked her. But he had not brought her up here to let her look at the view. He wanted to show her the new 'rest room', as he called it, recently repainted and provided with a double bed. He had high hopes of it.

She did not reply at once. It was a sunny but humid July day and very hot in this rest room, even though the blind was down. She was permitted to open windows downstairs in the café, where she had been working for two months, so she took a further liberty and lifted up the stiff lower half of the sash window for fresh air, rested her hands on the ledge, and then for a few seconds leaned out and looked. But then she turned away quite quickly and pulled the window down again, and released the string, and let the blind drop fast.

In looking down over the street she had seen her husband, Perce Hollard, and their son Jack, turning the corner. Perce had said he might be home early, and Jack often stayed late at school, and they had met on the same bus; which had probably just changed its destination for lack of a replacement driver. 'All off if you don't want the garage!' had caused everyone, grumbling, to get down and walk or wait. Perce and Jack were walking the last stretch home.

'I must go home now,' Maureen said to the disappointed Spillar. But in a tone that suggested a necessity she might not like, and a deferral of something until another day. Or that was how Bob Spillar chose to interpret it. Without knowing it, she had also seen in the street two other people who would be sitting in the darkness of the Empire one evening in the following January, with her and Perce and Jack: fifteen-year-old Sylvia Freeman, a fast-growing pupil from the Junior Technical College, who was walking towards the High Street along the side wall of the Empire; and Claude Derrichet, who was using the name Pierre-Henri Mallinot. 'Pierre-Henri' was a thirty-seven-year-old citizen of France who was beginning, this summer, to put together an uncertain living from private teaching in London.

One other person walking by, Cyril Baxton, fifty years old at least, had intended to go to the Empire that same night but stayed in the Black Horse and Harrow and did not make it. Maureen did not know Cyril, nor did she recognise a seventeen-year-old someone walking past towards the High Street immediately below. He would also not be in the Stalls in the Empire in January, but was well known to Jack: he was his former classmate Ronnie Walston, who cultivated the personality of a sophisticated rogue.

Ronnie did happen to see Maureen leaning out of a first-floor window above the Rio Café for a moment, and he remembered her later. Mother saw father and son, but preferred not to let them see her. Father was talking seriously to son, a sixth-former (which he had never been himself). Jack was profoundly distracted from what his father was saying because he saw Sylvia, with whom he was in love, on the opposite pavement, with Ronnie walking along some way behind her. He couldn't greet Sylvia, because they had never spoken. But he did wave to Ronnie, who grinned and called out something Jack failed to hear because two cars went by at the same time. It gave Jack pain to think that the beautiful girl was within ten yards of such a boy. But that was unnecessary because they never met and spoke.

There was no reason why Jack should feel pain at the sight of Cyril, who was completely unknown to him. But that would have been more to the point.

1

But then, one week into the following January—

Snow fell heavily on the Monday. It was cold, though a thaw followed after about forty-eight hours. The end of the month was to be colder again, much colder and for much longer. The cold was to become a lasting memory, a legend.

None of the people shuffling along Row R in the Stalls at the Empire on this early January night are going to shed their outdoor coats during the entertainment.

'Pierre-Henri Mallinot', who is really Claude Derrichet, arrives first. Pierre-Henri, thin, and of low-medium height, neatly suited, trim and inconspicuous, the sort of foreigner who in no way stands out for any quirks of appearance, is early. He has little to do tonight; his second and last pupil left at six-fifteen. The usherette leads him down the slope to his seat, R21, the first in the row to the left of the centre aisle. He pushes its frayed and faded velvet bulk down with his left hand, but there is spring in it and it jerks back into a vertical position so that he has to sit firmly to keep it down.

He begins to look at his programme, but almost immediately has to stand again to allow more early people, Sylvia Freeman and her parents, Tom and Rebecca, to pass him and take R20, R19 and R18. He does it with a dapper charm, without any smiling but with Gallic courtesy, so that the gesture is noticed. Rebecca Freeman, a thin grey-haired woman old for her forties, notices; and later says to Tom and Sylvia, 'I wonder who was that foreigner sitting next to us? He seemed a bit nervy.' Tom, a resigned man who does not see as many things as his wife, shrugs. Their daughter Sylvia, tallish and mature-looking for her age, fifteen, hardly remembers anyone at all when her mother mentions Pierre-Henri later.

For about five minutes there is an echoing thump and snap of seats pushed down or springing back in this high hall. But then it's absorbed into the general crowd noise and the murmurs of anticipation, also the coughing that people are getting over before the show. Meanwhile, the orchestra under maestro Leonard Canthorpe has begun to tune up in its lighted cave in the front, below the edge of the stage with its scarlet curtain trembling in the draught.

Perce and Maureen Hollard, with their son Jack unusually joining them for this night out, have arrived late. The slight and attractive usherette Jack believed to be years younger than himself, and he was almost eighteen. But he saw that she had thickly applied lipstick, bright when her torchlight caught it and her full lips moved to murmur the seat numbers as she read them on the tickets. Her eyes flashed up at this tall, lithe boy with the severe parting in his brown hair, but dropped again as she decided she would not take them all the way round to the centre aisle and guided them to the wall end of Row R, that being nearer to their destination. The beam that revealed their vacant seats also revealed to Jack the face of Sylvia Freeman several places further on. His heart jumped with excitement and something like fear.

'We came in by the wrong door,' Perce muttered with impatience, mentally blaming Maureen for it. Jack hoped that, after the argument with his mother, his father would now let matters rest. The overture crashed to an end and the curtain was rising with a quick switch of melody in the orchestra pit. Seats went up noisily along the row as the Hollards pushed along with apologies. There was precious little space for them to pass with everyone's overcoats on in the chilly dark.

Yes, it was Sylvia all right, four or five seats farther along, her face illuminated from the stage and visible in clear profile, fixed on the popular tenor. Timothy O'Dwyer was standing dangerously downstage, for greater intimacy with his audience. Did he realise it showed him to be older than the photographs, rougher and more lined in feature than he used to be? Not the draw he once was, though a few women in the audience had come mainly for him. There had been a drink problem, it was said.

'Timothy O'Dwyer first on the bill indeed!' Perce Hollard, still in his office clothes, said to his wife Maureen, who had changed and brightened herself up after her day's work at the Rio Café. The implication of his remark was accurate. O'Dwyer had been one of the mighty and had fallen—until they revived his reputation long after his death with a CD of 'The Great Lost Voices'. Tom Freeman had come for a young woman singer appearing much later, whose voice he almost worshipped on the radio: Sandra Brean, soprano, billed as 'The Songbird from Southampton'. But then Tom, Rebecca and Sylvia Freeman and sometimes also (though not tonight) Sylvia's older sister Eileen, were regulars at the Empire, where Rebecca would end up working. The Hollards were not regulars.

What had brought Perce and Maureen Hollard? At the end of a bad day at Perce's work (he had long feared and resented the attitude of one particular colleague in the office, William Luddon) he and Jack's mother had had a row out in the scullery. It continued as she came back into the kitchen and tried to poke life into the fire, and Jack had no idea what it was about. He had come into the kitchen to see his mother turn away from the grate, and stand up poker-in-hand, and there was something in her strong, angry good looks (which Jack was proud of, contrasting her with other people's mothers) that suggested she could have been about to hit his dad with it. If so, it would have been utterly exceptional and very frightening because Jack had only ever seen joking physical tussles between his parents, never anything violent.

There had been a verbal row going on in the scullery, but it was not any words his father had uttered that produced Maureen's angry and ambiguous gesture with the poker. It was rather a gesture he had made with a hand, perhaps even just a finger, Jack saw as he himself came in, something private which Jack guessed might have stretched far back into his parents' lives. It was a sign intended as a final gesture in the row, and although it was nothing obscene or aggressive it caused this furious raising of the fire poker. Maureen lowered it again and then seemed to have been tearfully upset by Perce's action. Perce went out through into the hall with an unpleasant smile on his smooth features.

A minute or two later he came back into the kitchen where Maureen had sat down at the table next to the bewildered Jack and continued to dry her eyes with a handkerchief. The poker rested in the grate. Grey flameless smoke still drifted up the chimney over the coals of the fire, which still gave out no heat. Perce said, 'Sorry, dear. Put your hat and coat on. We'll go to the Empire. You coming with us, lad?' It was a proven method of calling off rows, used more than once before, though there had never been a row quite like this, so inscrutable in its character and disturbing in its intensity. That, or 'Let's go to the pictures.' He decided he should join them. He didn't much want to go to the Empire, but his presence might help to keep a further outbreak at bay.

What had brought Pierre-Henri Mallinot, from the department of the Charente in southwest France, to the Empire? He knew he would be watching coarse, inferior entertainment, but if pressed he would have had to admit that simple loneliness drove him there. His pupils for private French lessons at his lodgings with Mrs Orlop in Benford Street were no kind of company for him. He had formed no friendships with any of their parents. And he absolutely did not want to seek out any French compatriots in London.

The signs in red lights at each side of the large Empire stage had changed from '2' for Timothy O'Dwyer to '3' for a man, wife and child acrobat team. But didn't the 'child' look too old? With such a lined little face, was he a child at all? Perhaps he was an adult dwarf performer pretending to be a child, no relation at all to his parents? Nevertheless he played the comic, obstreperous infant to perfection, doing his own acrobatics yet nearly ruining several moments of dexterity or poise as the fully grown couple leaped, somersaulted, spun, and stopped to pose for applause. To enjoy this act you had to ignore the possible age of the boy and just appreciate the skill and comedy. When Jack leaned forward and looked along to Sylvia, who had not noticed him, she was smiling happily in profile and clapping her hands.

'I wonder what we're in for now,' said Tom Freeman, who liked to make murmured comments.

In truth he knew. And an element of curiosity had also lodged in Perce Hollard's mind during that week, as he passed the Empire and its prominent posters on his bus to work. Because, low down on the bills, in one long row of small but eye-catching crimson letters came 'The Nine International Nudes'.

The family of acrobats bowed, were applauded again, and seen off with a fast and merry little tune done by the Empire Variety Orchestra at full speed. The scarlet halves of the high curtain met, a well-timed very short silence let the audience clear its throats and resettle itself, and then Leonard Canthorpe in his conductor's spotlight raised his hands, extended his baton towards his orchestra, and paused.

Who knows, he may have winked at his musicians before nodding once, raising his baton, leading them into a quiet, respectful few bars of a little classical melody many in the hall would have recognised but not been able to name. Jack, listener to major classics on his portable battery radio in his bedroom, and popular classics on his parents' valve wireless downstairs, knew it only as 'Boccherini's Minuet'.

Along from stage right, in front of the curtain, slowly paced 'Madame Marguerite' in an evening dress of lavish length, patterned with flowers in blue and green, one of the two she had for professional use, silky, low at the neck above extremely white, cold skin. Her hair was permanently waved and glossy, worn high and dark to allow her ears to be seen and her earrings to sparkle and glow in the footlights; as did various silver bracelets and gold rings when she moved her hands with deliberate French expressiveness.

The gentle, tripping minuet was hushed by Leonard Canthorpe as Madame Marguerite acknowledged a small clatter of uncertain clapping from an audience unsure whether it was appropriate to give it already to someone who had no recognisable reputation and had not yet done anything.

'Ladies and gentlemen, I am Madame Marguerite. It says in your programme we give an Artistic Performance. In your honour—as true lovers of great art—my young ladies present to you tonight five great paintings or sculpt-ewers'—she said it that way—'featuring the female form in all the beauty of nudity, which has never ceased to inspire immortal artists down the ages.'

Her voice was clear and confident and sounded 'learned', as Tom Freeman said later. The accent, despite Madame Marguerite's name, was not exactly French, but neither was it London, or English regional. It was not aristocratic-pretentious, or Mayfair-posh. Jack even believed it had a kind of educated style. He wondered if he himself, in the sixth form at Crofton Boys' County Grammar was, at the moment anyway, actually less educated than Madame Marguerite?

As she spoke there was movement behind the curtains, signifying that persons and props were being put in place; there would have to be no movement whatsoever when the curtains parted again.

Madame paused, and looked at the curtain, and listened, and satisfied herself that she could begin to introduce the first work of art.

'First, ladies and gentlemen, the lovely Natalya and the charming little Renée offer you *The Toilet of Venus* by Diego Velazquez'—here Pierre-Henri Mallinot did notice the anglicised 'z' in the name—'from the National Gallery here in London, better known to you all, I know, as "the Rokeby Venus".'

Swiftly but with dignity Madame Marguerite resumed the wings at stage right as the curtains began to draw slowly aside. The orchestra stayed silent. The two figures revealed on the stage were utterly still, except when they shivered involuntarily in their pose. They were on a 'bed', probably an easily lifted camp bed, with an off-white sheet on it topped by a shiny coverlet somewhere between dark blue and silver. On top of the coverlet reclined a nude woman with her back to the audience, propping up her head of brown hair with her right hand, her right arm resting on a pillow or cushion, or perhaps even on a box or suitcase because the hidden articles seemed square in shape. She gazed into a mirror held up for her at the foot of the bed by a much smaller woman, or a very young but pubescent girl, got up as Cupid with extremely small feathery wings, who knelt with one slim leg bent and one arm concealing her breasts. What silenced the coughing, imposing on everyone a stillness to match the immobility of the two figures, was that prominent, fully extended length of Venus's upper leg, the round buttock, the wide bareness of the goddess's back. Her entire nakedness was only implied, but authentic nudity it was. The postures were held, though the smaller girl holding up the mirror to the recumbent Venus was seen by Jack to shake rather in her hard-to-sustain position, and the scene lasted for about twenty seconds. Then the curtains slowly closed again.

It was not very clear, there being no traditional response to exhibitions of this kind in a theatre like the Empire, what the audience should now do. Some few did clap, desultorily, too little applause for it to catch on. Sylvia later wondered whether she should have clapped herself because (though she was not to know it at that point) this opening display meant more to her than anything else in the evening. She had used mirrors to look deeply into her inner self as shown by her eyes, and wonder what she really was, as well as trying to see whether she was, or she could be, beautiful.

How authoritative Madame was, Jack thought. In a way, how flattering she was to an audience with enough knowledge to sense that this was a genuinely Artistic Performance. Though he certainly saw that this was much more about stage nudity than about pure art, he wondered whether there was not some genuine sincerity in Madame's purpose? Turning it round, perhaps Madame told herself that if she had to earn a living by presenting static nude shows she'd at least stir a bit of interest in art at the same time; because she did not patronise, and she did not hint that her tableaux had any other design on the audience.

'And now,' Madame continued, 'to show that artists revere female beauty at all periods in the history of art, we come quickly down to our own century and to a famous work by the great French sculptor Aristide Maillol, *Les Trois Nymphes*, *The Three Nymphs*. Allow me to introduce Bianca, Gudrun and Doris. You may have seen the original in the Tate Gallery here in London, but I know you will find these young ladies just as lovely.'

A small platform, perhaps hexagonal, raised the three nude young women slightly above the level of the stage for better viewing. A clever coloured spotlight played on them making them look burnished, but it was clear that underneath it their poor winter bodies would look pale. That was something that Perce Hollard hadn't noticed with Venus, because the interest of the mirror and the presence of the blue coverlet material, also the simple surprise of the bare flesh in public, drew attention away from Natalya's and Renée's whiteness.

The poses of the three standing nymphs were not strained or unnatural, but holding them for even those few seconds on the draughty stage was difficult. Naked flesh quivered, the nymph with her left hand raised in appeal to another nymph was shaking. The three were presented in profile to most of the audience and Maureen wondered what you might see looking from the side, from a box for example. But the boxes looked empty. She knew she could never expose herself like this, but then who would ask her?

These nymphs had a much stronger effect on Perce because the tallest, on the left, standing with calm arms at her sides, vividly reminded him of the way the younger Maureen would stand in the bedroom when they were first married. The more he looked, in the moments available, the more moving and frightening it was. Maureen never stood deliberately like that these days. Their sharpest emotional connection now came in the kind of row they had this evening; when dredging up past jealousies was all that they did with passion.

Jack believed that he was catching sight of the farther nymph's vaginal hair, but he wasn't sure. If that was what he was seeing, then it was the first time in the flesh, and he was almost shocked to think it didn't matter, or it didn't stir you very much. No more than the hair on the tribeswomen in the geographical magazines. But suddenly he felt awkward about being in the sixth form and not knowing these works of art (if he unquestionably knew some others, Picasso's *Guernica*, say) which some sort of music hall entertainer on this stage knew perfectly well. Perhaps, unsuspected by him, lots of other, quite ordinary people in this freezing auditorium tonight did know these famous representations of nudity.

'And now six of our beautiful ladies take you back again to the period of that heavenly Venus and present *The Judgement of Paris* by the great Peter Paul Rubens. Which one will be the lucky lady? This wonderful painting is in our National Gallery. Presented by Ingrid, Gretchen, Bianca, Natalya, Renée, Lucia.'

Madame Marguerite slowed up her delivery of this announcement because it was apparent that something more complicated had to be done behind the closed curtains. After she withdrew, making an elegantly slow exit, it was a full fifteen seconds before the curtains parted again. Even then it was a second too soon, because some human movement was seen on the right of the group of six women, someone coming into place late behind a prop, a narrow cardboard tree-trunk that shook as it was brushed by this clothed figure, a girl with bare legs and midriff certainly, but wearing a man's hat with a wing on it (borrowed from Cupid?) and a loose reddish cloak of some flimsy stuff over her shoulders.

In front of her, on a stool at the foot of the tree, though a garment wrapped round her waist hid it, sat a big girl with an even more masculine look, leaning earnestly forward and offering to someone in a group of three girls in the centre downstage an apple. Down on the ground to the left crouched Venus's Cupid without wings, the slimmest, smallest girl in the group, with her back to them. All were utterly naked except for wisps of airy fabric held over parts of themselves. But two girls had their backs to the audience, thus offering, like Venus, only the implication of complete nakedness.

When the curtain slowly opened on the third of the three downstage girls, the one on the left of the trio, there was a small intake of breath from parts of the audience at the sight of a girl naked from head to foot with her hands raised and clasped behind her head. What she did was stand and face everyone in the long rows of seats in the darkness, and smile. Her hands held a loose wisp of fabric which she may have just removed, but they held it behind her head and back, and all the front of her white body was exposed. Except for some of her pubic area, which the end of the wisp partly covered.

To the boy, Jack Hollard, who had helped pass the magazines round at school, this was the shadow-crossed black-and-white world of *Lilliput*, *London Opinion*, or *Men Only*. Or of the pin-up magazines which the barber, Mr Redford, deterred him from browsing in his shop—'Not for you, boy!' It was the same flesh, but in a palely coloured natural way, in the weak yellow stage sunshine. It struck Jack, who had never before seen living female nakedness, with its insignificance, its vulnerability, its pathos. This was not about beauty, not about lust. It was about girls with nothing on.

'What's the "judgement", then?' Tom Freeman wondered in a low but audible voice, mostly to himself, a man who had once been in the courts for a very minor offence, never repeated. Perce, Jack's father, considered that he himself was being judged daily, at work; that was what he felt at the moment, and he feared the result, he had a determined and obnoxious rival. His smoke went up to join the shifting blue beds and layers of it above their heads.

'Now we return to England and Victorian times,' Madame Marguerite was announcing. 'Three more of our beautiful young ladies—Katrina, Masha and Gretchen—will be *The Three Graces* by the wonderful Edward Burne-Jones.'

Jack believed his suspicions were fully confirmed when he saw these three figures, chosen no doubt as the tallest of the nine. They stood there patently trembling now, surely arranged to create sexual desire? The audience could see almost every feature of the bodies of two of them. The three made an interlocking group, each risen to her full height except where the bending of a leg and the downward inclination of its hip took away an inch, preventing a girl standing with rigid, unrelieved stiffness. The middle Grace had her bare back to the audience. To her right stood a girl whose left shoulder was clutched by the right hand of the middle girl coming up from almost behind her. Her left arm was resting on the bent right arm of the second figure, whose left arm rested on her bent right arm. The left arm of the middle figure met the hand of the figure on the right on the right shoulder of the girl on the left, whose two hands were clasped on the bent right arm of the middle girl. Jack gasped in silence to see two genital areas fully revealed. But they were virtually without hair: it had either not grown or been cut or shaved.

The complexity of this arrangement at first drew Maureen's eyes away from the girls' faces, but when she did look she wondered whether she herself could still be said to look anywhere near as young as that? What would it look like if three middle-aged women like herself, her friend Patsy Partridge and Millie Foster next door posed like that? She gave a bitter smile in the dark at the thought. One day a man would try to get her opinions on this; but not yet. The audience had even less opportunity to take in this group than the one before. When the curtains drifted together again there were sounds of restlessness up in the cheaper seats, perhaps at the front of the Balcony. Someone considered he had not been allowed enough time to develop his artistic appraisal of the breasts and pudenda statically displayed down on the stage, in a curious reddish light this time, for what—about ten seconds?

'Finally I have great pleasure, ladies and gentlemen, in presenting to you all nine of our international ladies in one of their own favourite Great Works of Art, a bathing scene by the famous French painter Paul Cézanne. *Les Grandes Baigneuses. The Open-air Bathers.*'

'True enough, but would I translate it like that?' Pierre-Henri Mallinot was thinking. And which of the Cézanne bathing scenes, or variations on the same kind of scene, was this to be? Madame's accent was far from perfect, but you could probably guess that she had learnt French somewhere, and applied it efficiently to her peculiar task. Of course the young women did not look in any way 'international', certainly not French—with possibly one exception, the 'Renée' small enough to represent Cupid or a child. They were unalterably English, whatever poses they might adopt. But as they had clearly been told by Madame to be 'artistes', and it was their living—or part of it—they did take it seriously.

Englishness...Pierre-Henri sometimes wondered whether he might eventually have to become English. For all his safe solitude, so far at least, he had enough close contact with Englishness in this obscure suburb, through his private lessons for children and his contacts with their parents and with shopkeepers and librarians and café proprietors, to absorb a few English attitudes and conventions. He felt, for a few moments a degree of shock he would not have felt even in provincial France at seeing this generous array of young women in the nude in a respectable working-class district of London. In Paris, or Marseilles, or even in Périgueux or Angoulême, it would not have been nearly so outrageous. Pierre-Henri was, as it were, feeling shock with, and for, the English. But he did quietly share the feeling of disappointment that was becoming evident upstairs. That feeling reminded him of his own deep lack of a female body to look at privately, and hold. In that Rubens scene the girl Paris holding out the apple reminded him, in the way she sat, of Marcelle Grenier (or Levine) reaching out to take something from him from the armchair she always occupied in his home in La Tignelle.

What could he call home now? Where was Marcelle now? Sitting naked and reaching from some other chair or bed to something offered her by someone else?

The performance had so far taken no more than five or six minutes, though in that time it had driven what had gone before altogether out of the minds of the people in the Empire. After Madame's words in praise of Cézanne now came a quicker opening of the drapes, swishing clearly in the silence which had preceded every tableau after it was announced; a sound you had never heard before in this high scarlet cavern: the rustle of fabric and the creak of strings pulling it you could pick up, eerily, as high in the theatre as the threepenny seats at the back of the Balcony.

The tree supporting Paris and Mercury in the Rubens had gone to stage left for Cézanne, whose girl bathers stood, knelt or lolled, this time in a greeny-bluey light. They nearly all had their backs to the audience, their lower regions occasionally covered by towels, though a large girl (one of the Three Nymphs?) was stepping energetically over something on the ground. What was clear again was that there was really very little blatant nudity, only the audience's discerning that the girls must be wearing nothing at all, without question.

All these women seemed frozen into statues that looked awkward about maintaining an existence in stone; that longed to use the suppleness of their naked bodies in movement and activity and truly outright shivering. But now the curtains were tugged together again, this time much too rapidly for some of the people in the Balcony, who found the liberty to be cheeky and emit a low long sarcastic 'Aaah!' of disappointment. A clear male voice from up there even called down 'Encore!' His friends laughed, and added other remarks not easy to pick up in the Stalls, and that encouraged more laughter. The Cézanne being the last tableau there was general, though rather tentative, clapping; whereupon Madame Marguerite appeared again, smiled, and blew kisses from the three middle fingers of each hand to the entire house.

And what was this? She was extending an arm to those closed curtains and they were quickly opening again. Was there in fact to be an encore? Would they now all walk back onto the stage and take a bow with nothing on? The stage was bare except for the cardboard tree, but Madame was beckoning into the wings on both sides while the applause went on and increased in volume, with some cheering from the Balcony.

All nine girls did emerge, in smiling ones and twos, one pair holding hands. But each International Lady was in a thin pastel-coloured dressing-gown, happy to be even that much warmer, waving to the audience very briefly before turning and exiting, the curtains shutting them off again. In the thirty seconds only taken by all of this farewell, Leonard Canthorpe had conducted the Empire Variety Orchestra in a jauntier, faster, less reverential version of the tasteful minuet item they had started with. He brought it to an end abruptly when the applause died down, switching to a louder, recognisably vulgar tune for the pair of broad male comedians who came next on the programme as the red signs changed to a '5' on either side of the stage. This was Wheeler and Cole, who made much, though not in a derogatory or hurtful way (they were thoroughly professional and loyal) of the act preceding them.

2

But early in the next week Sylvia Freeman stood accused in their bedroom by her sister Eileen.

'You won't tell me anything more?'

It was a dark teatime. Eileen worked only ten minutes away from their home in this long, twisting and turning, uphill thoroughfare, in a women's garments store in one of the short parades of shops between the long shabby terraces of three-storey houses. It was a drab little premises, run by Mr Collinger with more hope than success; he had another similar shop on the other side of the borough and was said by Tom Freeman to have 'irons in other fires as well'. Sylvia's family lived in another such parade, in a two-bedroom flat two floors above a one-room printing works on the ground floor. Two doors along there was a small cork factory.

Sylvia was saying nothing beyond the fact that the 'older boy' whom her mother had spoken to Eileen about only today, the 'young man' her younger daughter had chatted with in the interval at the Empire (that was how her mum had described him) was 'a friend'. When Eileen had walked in angry at having to call her young sister in for tea the second time, Sylvia was lying on their shared small double bed. The mirror that was usually propped up against the wall on top of the chest of drawers was on her stomach, glass-side down, hugged there as soon as she heard her sister coming. Sylvia had been found out.

Her father, mother, and brother of eighteen years old, soon to be called up into the army, named Frank because it was his father's second name, were waiting around the table in the living room; and Sylvia, the youngest, was refusing to join them.

Tea would be on the table in two minutes, but she was not coming, and Eileen, who was twenty, began to use this tiny stretch of spare time to ask personal questions. Lately she had started to take on the role their mother was too gentle to take, or not feeling well enough for it. Mum was also too tired from her cleaning work in the mornings to prevent Eileen doing that, and protect her youngest from her. Eileen knew what was right and what was wrong for a fifteen-year-old sister.

Yet really she had little else to interest her, unless you counted the advances of Mr Collinger when he deigned to visit his staff, just her and Lesley, in this less promising of his two shops. One day, for example, she had been standing on the display surface in the window of the store arranging a blouse on a dummy when he put out a hand and felt her leg. Anyone passing in the street and looking into the window could have seen what he was doing.

Still Sylvia said nothing. So Eileen went out and slammed the bedroom door. This action upset Sylvia, but she did not cry at that point. With the door slammed by an older sister ugly enough for two ugly sisters, and the sound of the living-room door closing on her family and their horrible tea, she simply sat up, turned onto her side, and resumed what she wanted to do. This involved stretching out full length, propping up the mirror with her pillow at the top of the bed, and looking into it to see how much of herself was reflected.

In the cold bedroom she had all her clothes still on, even the Technical College blazer over the pullover and her white blouse, and she still shivered. She could see her face and her clothed shoulders, and the bulge of the pullover, and down almost to her waist, and she was pleased by it. Her medium-length very black hair, mostly cut or trimmed by her mother, half-covered her ears and her neck, and she thought it looked quite nice. She sometimes tied some of it in a quick loose knot at the back of her head, which lifted it away from the nape of her neck, and that was even better.

She had been warned against pride in Religious Instruction, and thought she was intensely wary about becoming a victim of it. So she was careful to be modest among friends, and reserved her vanity—if she had to admit to it now—for the dreams. These had begun one afternoon when she was thirteen, alone at home after school and suddenly trying herself out in every mirror the household owned. The bathroom mirror, the door of the cabinet above the washbasin, cracked in one corner, was blunt and brutal. It shamed the pimples and the tiny mole. The wide mirror over the living-room mantelpiece left her face too much in shadow, even in artificial light. Not enough light ever came into the room, facing as it did the wall of the next house five feet away across the narrow back entry. She opened the wardrobe in her parents' bedroom for the body-length mirror and quite liked fixing herself in that, in her increasing tallness.

But the best mirror for flattering her was the one in the coat-stand out in the cramped hallway beside the front door. She thought that one was particularly clear and accurate. It caught sufficient daylight if she opened her bedroom door, but not too much and not too strong. This mirror gave her face not only a freshness but also a mysterious look which she started to think about.

One thought she had was that mystery was important. When she opened her mouth a little and looked at herself steadily, she believed she had mystery. In her sleeping dreams she mixed with impressive strangers who whispered to each other, in the future, that she was a famous beauty. It had confirmed some of her dreaming when, last August (she then still being fourteen-and-a-half) an older boy she had been seeing on the bus without ever speaking with him had spoken to her in the park. They had looked at each other regularly, every day for months, in the bus, but it had remained the kind of looking everyone did with each other around the age of thirteen, something automatic you couldn't help. Except that in this case it had become an expected ritual.

She and Marian always sat together halfway down the upper deck on the left, the pavement side of the bus. Jack always passed them and went on to a front seat if he could get one, glancing back at Sylvia on his way. Leaving the bus well before they did, the Technical College being five stops on from the side road that he walked up to get to Crofton County Grammar School, he invariably looked at her intently as he passed along the aisle towards the stairs at the back. And since he made sure he was first off the bus he was always walking quickly past it before it resumed its journey. He could look up as it went by, and Sylvia would invariably look down. A bond had been established, of daily glances exchanged in silence.

He wondered about her name, and then one day the only seat available was behind these two girls from the Technical College on the upper deck, and he had a piece of wonderful good fortune. The dark girl had been holding her school travel card open for the conductor to inspect it, and he could read the name: Sylvia Freeman. But still they did not speak, and it went on like this until the summer evening in the park, an August evening when all the schools were on holiday.

It was fortuitous. One evening they both happened to take walks alone in the park, arriving from different directions. And that night's sighting gave Jack the hope that he might see Sylvia again the next night. Sylvia began to take brief rests alone on park seats, looking at the view across to where Crystal Palace had stood before the fires. One evening Jack dared to sit down on the other end of the same seat; and still they did not greet each other. She looked round at him with slightly open mouth. But she could not say anything, there was no reason for speaking.

Then she got up and walked casually out of the nearest gate, and was going in a direction that meant she would pass a farther gate round the corner.

That was not the direction of her home, the address on her travel card, so Jack assumed Sylvia Freeman was not yet making her way back. At once he rose and walked away fast towards that second gate, and strode out of it, and turned so that they came face to face with each other on the pavement. Now they did speak. Or rather, Jack Hollard spoke, and said 'Hullo' in a choked voice. He had been sixteen for six weeks, and this happened after about fifteen months of wordless love.

She put the mirror down on her bed, hearing renewed tea noises out in the living room, ignoring them, and thinking about the meetings with Jack that began with that August greeting five months ago; because on the next evening in the park they spoke again and exchanged names properly, and agreed they would arrange meetings instead of leaving it to accident. On Saturdays through the autumn they met regularly, and she soon discovered that he liked to walk. They would go on buses (and he would fully pay for her because this was out of term and no bus travel at a reduced price was available), but walking and talking seemed to be what they mostly did. She told him things about herself, but not many things because he did not question her that much. He talked about their surroundings as they walked, and radio programmes, and films like the one he had just seen one Saturday, *Anna Karenina*. It made Jack think, he said, with the possibility of a cold winter ahead, of beautiful, dark-haired, remote Sylvia sitting muffled in firs in a train watching mile upon mile of a snowbound landscape passing, and thinking of her lover. He described all this to her on one cold walk when, unseen by him, Ronnie Walston had spotted the two of them from the upper deck of a passing bus.

Sylvia understood in a general way what he was saying about a lovely dark woman in a film, and it suggested to her that her scheme to be pale and enigmatic was working. But she did not actually want to be a filmstar. She had never acted in the Technical College plays, despite the attempts of fierce little Mr Osric Evans, the music master who produced them, to get her to audition as a tall bellows-mender in Shakespeare. But she had read about a girl born to a poor Jewish shoe-repairer in New York who became a famous society beauty. Her own father, Tom, worked in a factory making machines for rolling your own cigarettes, and her mother, Rebecca, cleaned offices up in town, so Sylvia was not precluded. He told her his father was called Percival and worked in a shipping office, and that his mother was called Maureen; but he did not mention his mother's job at the Rio Café.

One dark afternoon Jack enthused about *Huis Clos*. He had heard the play on the radio several months before, but only now found the courage to say his piece about it to Sylvia. Describing how it presented Hell as 'other people', describing the room in which people without eyelids were condemned to frustrate each other for eternity, he ended by telling Sylvia—partly as a sort of complimentary joke—that he could think of 'one person it would definitely not be hell to live with in a room for ever'. She gave him a profound and flattered smile for that, a smile that appeared to show she had grown older and more mature since their first timid meetings last summer. At that moment they were sitting together in their thickest coats on a frost-covered bench in another, more distant park, looking at orange-beaked moorhens walking on the ice on its ornamental lake.

When he suggested, 'Shall we go back?' Sylvia got up very eagerly. As they walked away Jack put his left arm round her waist to guide her along the first few yards, but only as far as that. This was the only physical contact he ever had with Sylvia Freeman.

Suddenly Eileen was at the bedroom door again, throwing it open with an abrupt squeal of the loose brass handle; and Sylvia was caught in the mirror-gazing position because she hadn't heard her coming. 'Mum says you were smiling and chatting with this boy for quite some time in the interval that night at the Empire. He looked much older than you. Goodness knows what you think you're doing at the moment. And tea's ready, for the third time!' (In fact it was only the second). 'What on earth do you think you are doing?'

Sylvia sat up with the mirror hugged to her breast again, feeling tears but also feeling defiant.

'Nothing to do with you.' It was that emphasis that insulted her sister.

'Who's this boy who's such a lovely secret then?'

Her answer came in a rush of anger intended to keep back the tears, but it failed to do that. If anything it brought more tears.

'He said he'd go to Hell with me if he had to.'

'He said what? He said—*what*?'

'I bet it's more than any boy's ever said to you.'

The first remark frightened Eileen, who experienced a flood of bewildered thoughts about what her young sister and this older boy could have been doing. The second hurt her very badly, as Sylvia knew it would. She was incapable of giving Eileen any further answer, even if she had been able to devise one. More and more tears came, she couldn't as much as open her mouth to speak.

'If you could see yourself,' Eileen declared to the weeping girl, hands on hips, concluding (she hoped) that Sylvia was indulging some kind of fantasy; though she would not have put it that way. If it had ended there, Sylvia would have come out quietly to the tea-table after another five minutes. But her sister, wounded by the second remark, did a bad thing. She reached out and wrested the mirror away from her, and showed Sylvia herself in it, wet-faced and despairing. Sylvia turned onto her front. She clenched her teeth, she clenched her fists, clenched them so that the tendons showed in her thin wrists, and pushed her face into the other pillow, Eileen's, at the top of the bed, and said something she had never said before. She did not think beautiful and mysterious women swore, but now Sylvia did. She said, 'Bloody go away!'

Later she ate all her tea alone at a corner of the half-cleared table when everyone else had finished, avoiding anyone's look, especially Eileen's. Eileen's silence for the rest of the evening was contemptuous and unforgiving.

When Ronnie Walston, who had left school at the end of the fifth year eighteen months before this, stopped Jack in the High Street on the first heavily snowing day near the end of January, his opening gambit was characteristic, because any casual encounter with Ronnie involved talk on sexual matters.

'I see you're going around with a piece of totty from the Technical College. Not bad, either.' It was congratulation, envy even, not an accusation. Coming from Ronnie, working in an office and moving in worldlier places than school, it was something to be pleased with.

'What about yourself? Found any more photographs?'

Their three terms in the fifth form had been marked by the discovery (in each case, it was maintained, in a father's bedroom drawer) of small sets of pornographic snaps: Baxter's Spanish pictures in the autumn, Edwards's Italian in the spring, and Walston's French, voted the best, in the summer.

'I concentrate on *doing* these days,' Ronnie assured him.

Jack smiled at the idea, but later Ronnie's observation of him with Sylvia became painful to remember. It was not out of any unreasonable fear of Ronnie's appreciation of Sylvia, but because his meeting with her suddenly stopped.

Sylvia and her school friend Marian were failing to appear on the morning bus. This was puzzling and disappointing to Jack, but then these were winter conditions, producing problems in people's homes, and bus breakdowns, and unpunctuality. After a week of not seeing them (though he still noticed younger girls from the same school) Jack caught an earlier bus, and there they were. But Sylvia was not acknowledging his greeting, and her friend Marian also turned away.

This was repeated on the same earlier bus for another week, so he wrote her a letter. Two letters, and she answered neither. He sent her a box of chocolates which she parcelled up again and sent back; he ate them himself in bed the same night. One Saturday Jack was certain he had seen her boarding a bus in Greenstead Road in the heavy warm blue coat she had worn when they had sat and watched the moorhens on the ice in that different, faraway park; also when he had met her in the Empire and managed to speak to her while they thought neither set of parents was watching. He ran after the bus, it accelerated, he threw himself at the platform while the conductor appropriately left him to take his chance, grabbed the rail, got a foothold, boarded it, climbed the stairs—it was the same coat but another girl. When he got down at the next stop, professing he had made a mistake (and not paying a fare for this journey) he walked disconsolately back along the High Street and straight into her, wearing her own authentic coat. She tried to ignore him. He turned and walked alongside her. She swivelled her head away when he spoke.

'You must listen to me,' he said. Sylvia said nothing, looking enigmatic and hurt, even insulted. She kept her head down. 'Why aren't you speaking to me on the bus?'

They were walking in the direction of her home. She did not want him to pursue her all the way back. So she suddenly burst out with, 'My sister says I'm too young to be meeting a boy.'

'But we've been meeting for months. And I love you. You do love me, don't you?'

She shook her head and told him not to follow her; so he stood and watched her stride purposefully away. All of which now made Ronnie Walston's implied compliment grievous to him, because if he met Ronnie again, and Ronnie mentioned it again, he would have to inform him that it was apparently all off. Possibly Ronnie might not remember who he was talking about.

The pain was a little lessened by the knowledge that Ronnie, whenever they met, talked about sexual activity and not love. Jack was convinced that there was very little connection between the two, indeed sex was often a mere vulgarity, a debasement of love or a profanation of it. From the second form in the wartime emergency secondary school, Ronnie, who sat next to him at that time, had been the class authority on sex—in the makeshift showers after gym in their school in evacuation in Herefordshire, Walston had been the first boy to be able to show pubic hair. Part of his status as an expert derived from a kind of knowing reticence—you just took it that he knew everything. Your own ignorance or naivety, or your attempts to keep up with him, or impress him with what you had found out, invoked nothing more than a tolerant, kind, long-suffering smile. Jack had asked him once about any known method of curbing sexual desire. Ronnie smiled and said, 'During the war they used to give the Yanks bromides in their coffee.' Whatever 'bromides' were, their use by 'the Yanks' certified their effectiveness. Anything 'the Yanks' did or used was superior to anything done or produced by the British.

Ronnie could also flatter and favour you by letting you in on something. Jack felt proud, considered himself admitted to a furtive brotherhood of the wicked, when one afternoon in the fourth form during maths Ronnie quietly passed forward to him an opened copy of *Men Only*. There was a passage of print marked in red pencil in the margin, and Jack read of an ample belly-dancer moving from table to table in a Cairo nightclub. When she reached a group of British army officers sitting at a table, and she launched her rotating midriff at the company, one of the officers picked up an olive from a bowl and adroitly fixed it into her navel.

Jack need not have feared pain about Sylvia when he ran into Ronnie again quite soon after that last meeting, exactly a week later when the snow lay thickly on all of the streets. Today they began almost at once, for some reason, to exchange theories of general interest to broadminded young men, whether they worked in sophisticated offices or were still at school pursuing Higher School Certificate.

'Knocking shops? Oh you'll find them anywhere.'

Jack did not believe him.

'Round here?'

'Oh you'll certainly find them round here—if you know how to spot them.'

'So how would you spot a brothel round here?'

Jack's laugh became troubled, and Ronnie thought Jack deserved a small shock to punish his innocence.

'You'd find one not one hundred yards from where we stand on this sunny day,' he said. Snowflakes settled on Ronnie's lapel, on his chin, on what might have been the deliberate commencement of a moustache on his upper lip. 'Round that corner in Greenstead Road, not far from where it joins this High Street, next to the second-hand car dealer's?' Jack listened uncomfortably. Ronnie grinned. 'The Rio Café!' he said. 'Upstairs. They keep the blinds down most of the time, that's a usual sign. I saw a first-floor window open one sweltering day last summer—and this ravaged-looking blonde leaned out, and gazed up and down the road looking for customers.'

Jack gasped and nodded and stayed silent. He did not know whether any other women apart from his mother worked at the Rio, but he thought not. His mother had fair hair, often well-waved and attractive, he supposed. It could only have been her that Ronnie had converted into a tart, couldn't it? It shook his confidence in Ronnie's worldliness; but it also appalled him to think that anyone could have made such a mistake about his mother.

In the cold, with barely enough fuel for the daytime fire, Eileen was sleeping badly, and began to come to bed earlier and lie awake; so she and Sylvia talked more, huddled together, warming each other. It took real courage to penetrate the freezing sheets at the foot of the bed, which still froze even though the hot-water bottle had been rubbed on them before it was pushed to the bottom to console the girls' icy feet. This meant that they felt closer, and Sylvia felt more able to confide.

Gradually she revealed everything about her secret meetings and walks with Jack, and Eileen satisfied herself that there had been nothing to worry about so far. But it was nevertheless true that things could happen with older boys if you went on encouraging them. She informed Sylvia of the sort of thing she meant. She persuaded Sylvia that the best thing for her would be to put a stop to this little adventure right away if she had any doubts about it.

Eileen digressed during this particular conversation, and began to weep about her own lack of luck with men. Only Collinger at the shop had ever approached her, in any way. Was she really so very ugly? So fat and dumpy, Sylvia having grown almost three inches taller already? No, of course she wasn't, she was rather good-looking, Sylvia assured her. She could tell her own sister fibs in a good cause. In return she could listen to her and take her advice. She decided she would stop these meetings with Jack Hollard by changing the time she caught the bus to school, and ask Marian to catch the earlier bus with her so that she had some protection.

Their talk ended in good humour. While the bottle was still hot you could not touch it. When it lost some of its heat they laughed and competed for it, grabbing it between the soles of their feet and manoeuvring it to their own side of the bed. The raw warmth of the rubber lapped their ankles as the cooling water sloshed around inside it, and when it was no longer very hot they tired of the game and were sleepy anyway. The last thing that Sylvia thought was that her dreams of beauty and mystery did not contain a somewhat ordinary-looking brown-haired boy from Crofton County, and that Eileen might be right to tell her that at fifteen she had plenty of time to wait for the right kind of boy. Probably someone nearer her own age.

At some point in the night she or Eileen were dreaming, and one of them kicked out and pushed the hot-water bottle from under the sheets and blankets, and coverlets and coats, and onto the lino. Sylvia awoke next morning after this conversation, after her sister had already gone, and saw the grey flowers the frost had woven on the outside of the window. She was cold, and felt with her foot to find the bottle, just in case there was any heat still left in it. Then she realised it lay on the floor on her side of the bed. When she picked it up she felt thin pieces of ice breaking inside it.

3

And of course the pipes froze in the Rio Café. At the end of January. The sink in the kitchen, and upstairs the washbasin and the bath (where Maureen had taken baths) yielded no water, from either tap. Only the lavatories worked. Bob Spillar was desperate. He was on good terms with the second-hand motor man next door, whose Alvis had been sold, although the big Buick already on display last July was still there, now a bulky snow-and-ice sculpture on his forecourt. Snow covered all the prices written in large white letters on the windscreens.

On the other side from the Rio was Redford's the barber's, with its red-and-white pole, and Spillar felt unsure of that man. Redford gave out a suspicious air. He never spoke to Spillar when opening up his shop. Redford's didn't, to Spiller's knowledge, share any customers with him because the Rio's clientele were a changing lot, no one was regular. They were performers or cleaners dropping in from the Empire after rehearsals, or between matinées and evening shows. They were workers still clearing up local bomb sites for rebuilding purposes, toiling for a fortnight or so when the weather allowed it, and then gone. There were also a few of the poor, and shifty, and drunk-by-dinnertime people (sometimes all three in one old man, or old woman with a bundle) who shuffled from here to the library, or any other available warm space. Some respectable customers did drop in very occasionally, like the very trim foreigner (he looked

French to Spillar and Maureen) who invariably ordered only a cup of tea and sat with his face behind a newspaper as if he didn't wish to be seen. But those were outnumbered by the shabby gamblers who favoured the Rio if they had fallen out with the workmen's 'Luncheon Rooms' farther up the street, and sat there marking the morning editions before they left to seek out street bet-collectors lingering in heavy overcoats outside one or other High Street or sidestreet pub, the Black Horse and Harrow perhaps, or the Spotted Cow.

Beyond the barber's was an empty shop, beyond that the double-fronted furniture store which only opened irregularly, and then the small grocer's providing no competition for the South Suburban Co-operative Society on the other side, and the Labour Party offices. Spillar would not want to be seen crossing the road with jugs from the Rio to beg water from the Co-op, and certainly not from the Luncheon Rooms, a commercial rival.

'Oh, I'll go to Redford's,' Maureen said resolutely, after Spillar had run through, and rejected, all the other options. She lifted her coat from its peg for even this short expedition and took the two big enamel jugs, chipped in unsightly blue scars in places, to the door, one in each hand. One jug she lodged under her left arm awkwardly, opened the door with her free hand, and kept it open with her foot. Its bell rang dismally as a wall of freezing air barged in. But Spillar came over to hold it open for her.

Should he really keep the café open today? Would anyone come? He had a thought. He went upstairs and switched on the small electric bowl fire in his rest room. It did heat a room very effectively, this fire, a good glow was reflected off its curving brass surface.

Redford's (late Mellish's) the barber's, was very warm compared with the Rio. It was only ten-fifteen, but the small and stocky, bald-headed Redford already had customers in each of his two chairs, and two more waiting. At this moment one of his wash-basin taps was running water that steamed, an enviable sight. As Maureen released the catch on his door and pushed in, he paused in what he was doing and turned to her, cut-throat razor in his hand, lather cooling on the left side of the face of an elderly client. He gave Maureen what people disliked about him, a look of (quite unintended) hostility—as if anyone entering his shop was an intruder. His eyes looked over his glasses so as to see Maureen, this frown of suspicion continuing until he had adjusted his vision. His assistant, Colin, rumoured to be his illegitimate son, also looked up. If you wanted to, you could see a family resemblance in his face and in the simultaneity of this action, repeated by both men each time somebody entered the shop.

'Mr Redford, is there any chance that—?'

She tilted the two enamel jugs forward in a little mime of collecting water from a tap, hoping the men watching her would not realise where she came from (but how would Redford himself not know?). There was no dignity in a café asking a barber's for the favour of some water.

'So you're in trouble?'

'I'm afraid we are. If I—?'

'Through the door. In the corner on the right.' A curt permission as he connected again with the lathered face in the wall mirror.

When Maureen had half-filled the first jug from the brown brass tap in the corridor with something like half a gallon (it was already becoming heavy to carry) she knew that it would need four journeys or more, and wondered if it was not ridiculous to imagine the Rio could remain open in this weather. Spillar opened his own door quickly on her return, so that as few passersby as possible would see these actions. Everyone was suffering in this cold but it would not help the Rio if people saw that his plumbing had let him down.

'What did Redford say? Did you ask him or his assistant?'

'I saw Redford. Nothing,' she told him.

What had struck her as she passed through the smoky silence of Redford's shop was a male atmosphere in which she did, in fact, feel she was intruding. It had become more evident and more crude since the days when the Mellish brothers owned the shop, and she used to take Jack, her only child, to Mellish's for haircuts. The Mellishes worked in white coats, snipped, clipped, conversed, cut men's eyebrows and the hair in their ears and nostrils by request, applied lotions, were polite and deferential. But Redford's grey coat belonged in an ironmonger's, his wireless on a cluttered ledge played dance music while he worked, as if he needed the rhythms in the way workers on a conveyor belt needed them. He gave a short-back-and-sides in ten minutes and yet his customers seemed to have to wait a very long time (his young colleague, or son, was slower and more meticulous). The bill for the Empire on his wall was out of date, still advertising the show that had featured the 'Nine International Nudes' four weeks before. The tatty magazines on the chairs were ones known to include pin-up pictures. Slotted between the glass and the frame of each mirror was a small, vivid mauve envelope containing contraceptives, blatantly drawing the attention of the occupant of each of the two chairs if they looked up at themselves and at the barber working behind them.

Spillar busily decanted the precious supply of water into jugs and bottles and basins in the grimy kitchen, Maureen helping. Then she repeated the journey, Redford remarking, 'So you do hope to open today?' All the time she had a familiar premonition. It was that Spillar would say what he soon did say. She wondered whether he insisted on a supply of water for this reason alone, so they at least could have a cup of something as a preliminary.

'I think we deserve a break for a cup of coffee,' he duly said, with a smile straight into her eyes.

She did not respond, just left the kitchen and went over to the chair she always sat in to wait until customers appeared.

There was an irrelevant single electric-bar fire on the wall above her head, which might have warmed the ceiling a little. Through the hatch she could not see Spillar's face, but she saw his heavy hands pouring a liquid coffee-and-chicory mixture into a dessert spoon from one of the big trade bottles on which there was a picture of a turbaned Indian bringing a cup of it on a tray deferentially to a British army officer in khaki shorts.

Maureen's passage through Redford's barber's shop past inquisitive old men's eyes had made her less eager to continue with this intimate 'coffee' ritual, usually confined to a small span of time after they closed at the end of the day. Beyond the window it was snowing in the street, muffling all external sounds and turning down, as if with a volume knob on a wireless, the broad distant roar of the metropolis. The entire country had been slowed or stopped in what was becoming the worst winter of their lives, with its privations, economies, exhortations and appeals, a winter in which Jack Hollard was in love with Sylvia Freeman and his mother Maureen went with Bob Spillar to his rest room in the Rio Café, where she worked five days a week to earn a little extra to keep the house going and provide just a few shillings for herself.

Today she went very reluctantly, but she still went. Spillar turned the notice in the door round from Open to Closed, and turned the key. A quarter of an hour later Pierre-Henri Mallinot tried the locked door before seeing what the notice said, turned away again, and went to the more public Lyons's in the High Street, where he hid his face even more deeply in his English newspaper.

In the office where Perce Hollard worked, not far from Victoria, they had the best coal available, from somewhere or other, and no pipes were frozen. It was not the office of one of the coal companies taken over by the government, but a large shipping office next door to a civil service block on one side and a former coal company on the other. So perhaps a deal had been struck by the chairman, Sir Rigby Armstrong, upstairs. People said that during this winter in Sir Rigby's top floor office there was an altogether amazing fire.

The room had a floor of varnished and polished pinewood you could see your face in, a mahogany desk with crystal paperweights on it but no papers under them, and a monumental swivel chair in which the Old Man sat doing nothing. Around the walls were antique chairs and sofas, and on the walls pictures of liners, old sailing vessels and framed historical marine documents. But above all, there was always this fire, a fire you would only expect to find in heaven. This remark came from Alan Carstairs, the most prominent of Perce Hollard's younger colleagues, who had been to the chairman's 'palatial boudoir', as he called it, and seen it for himself, blazing in the world's worst winter when a new ice age was surely about to begin. Such a fire, keeping one plutocratic chairman happy for a day, could have warmed a whole street in shivering Southwark for a week, Carstairs said.

And Perce Hollard could confirm this story, because while his wife Maureen was collecting water in jugs from the barber's shop next door to the Rio Café he had been required to convey personally a message from his department boss, Mr Arthur Jedleigh, to Sir Rigby himself. It was in an envelope severely marked 'Private'.

He was allowed to go past the smart secretary in the front office and enter this grand and legendary room, where he stood for the first time face-to-face with the chairman. Perce wagered that the fire he saw was probably maintained for the Old Man's comfort by day and night from at least September to May. Behind the elaborately-tiled hearth with its shining brass fender that looked like an artefact created in gold, was an immense, broad grate with a vast cargo of glowing bright orange coals.

This layered, almost castellated, structure looked so steady and unshifting that it might have been able to retain its shape and warm the entire room and the office outside for up to a whole day without replenishment. Zealous flames immediately lighted any small exploding effusion of smoke from its dark, arranged blocks of coal. The clean cave of the great chimney carried any other smoke and fumes invisibly up and away to be laid down in the skies on settling swathes of what would later come to be called 'smog'; you could see how the white of the snow-blankets in parks and gardens would be black with smuts, just as the shovelled-out streetside banks of snow were yellowed by the urine of the roundsmen's horses.

Perce Hollard was asked courteously by Sir Rigby Armstrong, to Sit Down, and it seemed to him that when the chairman had opened and read Jedleigh's note he looked across the polished tabletop at Perce with particular scrutiny and curiosity, leaning forward and applying a hand to his chin. It went on for several long seconds, long enough for Perce to worry about this deep, almost suspicious, scrutiny. Could the letter contain something critical about himself? It would have been mean of Jedleigh, if that was so, to ask him to deliver it. That would have been utterly unlike the prim but pleasant Jedleigh with his discreetly crimson ties and neat waistcoats.

Then suddenly the chairman briskly folded the piece of paper in his hand, fitted it back into its envelope, and smiled.

'That's all very clear, then. Mr Hollard.' (He added the name after another look at the letter.) 'Thank you. Now—how long have you been with Fitch & Armstrong, Mr Hollard?'

'Eight years, sir.'

'Happy years, Mr Hollard?'

'Yes—very largely, sir.'

Perce was an honest man, so that he could not reply emphatically that he had been delighted with every minute of the experience; but he could not go so far as to reveal that at the moment he was having a miserable and uncertain time. He felt everything he did was subject to a process of amiable yet watchful judgement from Jedleigh, and vigilance on the part of his slightly younger colleague William Luddon in case there was anything in which the latter could catch him out. He knew that only he or Luddon could receive the apple of promotion when Jedleigh retired. If he ever did retire...

'Right through the war, then...The war was none too easy, was it!'

One reason why there had been little opportunity to meet Sir Rigby before this was his residence in the country during the blitz and the V1 raids.

'No sir, it wasn't.'

'Good...' The chairman did not give the impression of being a man for much smalltalk. 'Good. Er, well—thank you, Mr Hollard.'

At which point Perce believed it correct to stand up again. But Sir Rigby was staring down thoughtfully at his mahogany tabletop and the letter, and for a moment appeared to have forgotten Perce was there. A few more extremely long seconds went by. Something spurted and roared for a moment among the coals of his fire.

'Thank you, sir,' said Perce.

'What? Oh yes...G'bye.'

It was a curious moment, as if either Sir Rigby was about to fall asleep, or was thinking very deeply about something or other. Perce went back down to the narrowness of his own desk in one of the rooms heated by ineffective hot-water radiators and not by coal fires. The radiators failed for much longer periods in desperate weather like this, and today they had not been working at all. So Perce's account of the fire was something the others were eager to hear. Alan Carstairs and the three juniors, the very pretty Dora, Doreen (always confusing) and Terry, appreciated his description. But Perce's close colleague William Luddon kept his face bent down over the papers spread out in front of him and appeared not to be listening. Perce was proud of being able to tell his story, in particular describe the fire; but Luddon, a thickly built man with a determined manner, in a very formal but distinctly ill-fitting suit, made him feel gossipy and frivolous by his lack of response.

Their immediate chief, Jedleigh, came out of his own small inner office, smiled briefly at the young Carstairs, crossed the room to Perce and asked, 'Everything all right?' almost as if it might not be.

'Yes, sir.'

Then Luddon looked up from whatever he was doing and gave Jedleigh an obsequious smile that suggested an air of superiority, coming as it did so quickly after Perce's acknowledgement of Jedleigh's enquiry. 'May I possibly see you for a couple of minutes, sir?'

Jedleigh raised his eyebrows slightly, but agreed, nodded, turned away and surveyed the room as if there should be something more to do to justify his coming out; and returned to his 'inner sanctum', as everyone in the outer office referred to it, with Luddon following and closing the door for him.

These two senior clerks, Perce and William Luddon, shared equally a small range of responsibilities either closely or loosely related to record-keeping—sailings, arrivals, consignments of goods, licences, and the spotting of straightforward errors or puzzling discrepancies in relevant documents received. Their province was responding to information arriving by letter, telegraph, tape machine, or verbally on the phone, or sometimes in messages conveyed by couriers turning up on the doorstep.

Jedleigh would probably retire in the summer. He had been allowed to pass the usual limit. He was sixty-seven already, and was said to be looking forward to an active retirement; but then he had hinted he was feeling that way at sixty-five, and sixty-six, and was still here denying promotion to either Perce or William Luddon. Jedleigh was not resented, indeed he was rather liked. There were far worse departmental bosses in Fitch & Armstrong Ltd than old Arthur Jedleigh. It was William (never Bill) Luddon who was giving Perce Hollard his uncertain and miserable time.

Perce had resolved to make the chairman's fire his story for this evening at home with Maureen (and with his son Jack, if he was there and wanted to listen), but Luddon's behaviour meant that he entered the house with a frown. Jack was home and in the kitchen, but didn't notice anything wrong about his father; Maureen on the other hand did notice. She was eager to forestall any enquiry about her own day; so, 'It's Luddon, isn't it!' she exclaimed when she saw her husband's face.

'Of course it is.'

'What is it now?'

'He spent forty-five minutes today—forty-five, I timed it—in Jedleigh's room. Trying to prove to him that something I'd done on my own initiative wasn't accurate. He could have taken it up with me, but he went to Jedleigh.'

'*Wasn't* it accurate?'

Maureen's least wisp of doubt, or failure to understand, upset him.

'Of course it was bloody accurate. I'd checked it over three times. Three times.'

'No need to shout at me. If I were you, I'd go and see Jedleigh myself.'

'Jedleigh called me in when Luddon had left. That's how I know.'

'What did he say to you?'

'He didn't say anything outright. He had his funny little smile on, and just said, "Mr Luddon appears to think we should go over some things to be 110 per cent sure we're all getting them right".'

'Not just your things?'

Why, he wondered, was Maureen taking a persistent interest in all this? She could have told him, but naturally did nothing of the sort. It was about trying not to feel the pain she had in remembering her own morning, not least the fact that today she had deserted her reluctance to let it ever happen again.

'It was mainly my work.'

'Can't you take some of Luddon's work in to Jedleigh?'

'No.'

How could Perce possibly explain to Maureen that such an action would be the merest reprisal tactic, and start a petty war of nerves, and undermine his relationship with Jedleigh? But Maureen's look still questioned him, so he added, 'That would make me look as malicious as Luddon...But I'll have to do something while it goes on like this.'

'Like what?'

Oh, he'd have to set about explaining. He noticed that Jack was listening, but was no doubt bored by it. Luddon had got in first with the expensive new badly fitting suit and a new smart manner he had brought to work in the last couple of weeks; and now he had tried to get the advantage on a question of ordinary routine efficiency. Then he had begun to linger in the corridor after coffee and lunch breaks. On any excuse—for example examining the staff notices on the green baize board—so that he could find a chance to greet Jedleigh and leave the thought in his mind that he was becoming an essential aid in day-to-day affairs.

He wanted to be regarded as the man-in-waiting for Jedleigh's job, the obvious replacement. Hollard's merits, his experience, his punctiliousness, his courtesy, would be disregarded or forgotten. Luddon frequently spoke of his intelligent wife. Perce had only met Mrs Luddon once, at a company social gathering, but it rankled with him that she too was smart and officious, and helping Luddon all the way. A contrast with Maureen came to mind, came to haunt Perce. It came out of a part of himself of which he felt ashamed, because he did love her.

'That wife of his is just as ambitious,' he ventured to say now, which was ill-advised, because Maureen's face showed a pained look. He forestalled any trouble by immediately going on, 'But how was your own day?'

'Oh, we were frozen up. Completely frozen up. The lavatories were all that was working. Spillar sent me to the barber's with jugs to get water in so we could stay open. I went about three times. You know what those big enamel jugs are like when they're full! There I was, having to have the doors held open for me and the water slopping on the pavement and freezing, and him filling kettles and basins with it and sending me back again. That barber's is a dirty place these days, it's gone properly downhill since the Mellishes sold it. You're better off going to barbers up in town. Redford looks so suspicious of a woman coming in. And hardly anyone came in the café anyway, well only the odd cleaner from the Empire. We closed at one. There was no point in staying open.'

Why was Maureen going on like this, in one of what he secretly called her 'gabbling sessions'?

Jack did care. He believed that nothing would persuade him into the kind of work his father did to keep the home going and buy the coal for the fire which they reduced in cubic capacity with bricks in the grate, so as to lessen the quantity of fuel they consumed; a stratagem begun in wartime and resumed in this cold peace.

Yes, Jack cared about these peculiar reverses his father felt were inflicted on him by his colleague's behaviour, and cared about his father, though he would never bring himself to say so; and knew he would never let himself end up working in an atmosphere like that, year upon year trundling daily to an underheated office in an Edwardian block in Victoria. He cared only too much about his mother working in the Rio Café, and went on telling himself that it could not have been her whom Ronnie Walston had seen leaning out of an upstairs window, thus confirming his suspicion that the Rio was a brothel in thin disguise—and Ronnie missing out Beryl's Milk Bar round the corner, which the police did raid two months later. Jack had never called in to see Maureen at the Rio because he didn't want anyone to see him doing it, or even suspect that his mother worked there. He preferred to forget that she did, and never asked her about it.

He could recognise Bob Spillar, who employed his mother, but had never been introduced to him. He vowed to himself that he would never speak to the man. Sylvia had told him once that her mother was an office cleaner and that her father made roll-your-own cigarette machines in a factory, and their jobs were sanctified for him by Sylvia being their daughter. Though he had never met Tom and Rebecca Freeman, he crowned them with his respect because they were Sylvia's parents.

Perce and Maureen had not asked him about his day at school, though they were proud of having a clever boy, Maureen especially, and Maureen was proud of Perce having a respectable job with good pay. Jack supposed he loved his mother, but that also was difficult to admit—although he had felt sure he did love her during a peculiar conversation he had had with Clive Garner that morning.

Clive had been in his form all the way up the school, and they were now together in the Sixth, two of a group of six: Arkley, Clissold, Edwards, Elmborough, Garner, Hollard. He and Clive had for a long time been informal, slightly distant, friends, but school friends only, and had only recently visited each other's homes for the first time, producing a connection between their fathers, who began to recognise each other at the shops and talk about cricket.

Today Jack had been looking up in case Sylvia was visible in an upper-deck window and returned his gaze (she was, but she did not) when Clive stepped off another bus and caught him up. They set out on the last hundred yards talking, unusually, about parents, beginning with Clive's sense of the frustration his father felt for the greater part of the year outside the cricket season. They spoke in a serious but defensive way. You did not admit devotion to parents at seventeen, whereas it was never discussed in childhood because it was implicit.

Clive confessed that he regarded his own mother as beautiful, though not so beautiful as in her youth, in the photograph albums; particularly in the posed studio photographs everyone seemed to go in for in the 1920s. Jack let himself say that he considered his own mother attractive. Clive's mother had leisure pursuits of her own which his father categorically did not share. 'He has the cricket in the summer and nothing in the winter. She does her infernal whist drives in the winter and nothing in the summer. But she has her job all the time.' Jack did not ask what kind of job Mrs Garner did in case Clive asked about his own mother.

For his own part he wished his parents could be closer, could either share more interesting activities, or divide and each do something more venturesome, like the Garners. Jack knew his father had been quite a good cricketer before he had been born—team photographs filled the albums—but he had not kept it up. He took an interest in Jack's promising progress to the 1st XI at school, yes. But only a casual interest.

'I must get my dad to work on him,' said Clive. Mr Garner had captained the Parents' cricket XI against the School last year, and might be doing it again this year. Jack agreed without thinking what might come of that.

There was something incongruous and plain peculiar about trudging through uncleared snow along the residential sidestreets on the way to school while talking about mothers and fathers and cricket. Yet when they turned in, crossed the yard to the front steps, and entered the school through the special grand door up the front steps entered only by the sixth form and the masters, they were still keeping the subject of parents going. It had even become humorous and animated as they pushed through the swing doors of the library, along the corridor on the left, which served as Sixth Arts form room. Here the six people in the form each had his locker and customary chair for lessons around the library table, three each side. They were: Garner, Edwards and Elmborough with their backs to the window, Arkley, Hollard and Clissold facing it. No Christian names were used until after they left school.

'You are deep into some personal converse, I think,' observed the comedian of the group, Arkley, coming into the room behind them. Clissold, already at his locker unloading books studied at home the night before and brought in for the day's work, turned round and listened, but did not join in.

'On the topic of mothers and their social range,' said Clive Garner. 'I'm deploring my mother's narrow range and her obsession with the game of whist.'

Clissold's face remained blank and he still said nothing. But Arkley raised his eyebrows.

'And I can say that my mother's range is non-existent,' Jack Hollard added; too quickly, so that he felt a touch of shame.

'My mother's range is only intermittent,' Garner explained. 'It's in full evidence at the moment when she can get to whist drives through the blizzards, but it stops for the summer.'

Arkley smiled, a little strangely.

'My mother has to have assistance to have any social life at all,' he said, smiling ruefully. Of the others, only Edwards, entering now and catching that remark, knew what he was referring to. Jack could not see Arkley's face.

'*National* Assistance?' he surmised, with a laugh. A little joking about homes and families was allowed, but this reference to what had replaced 'the dole' for the unemployed was unfortunate. It was an unguarded, inappropriate quip.

'Yes, entirely,' said Arkley, with a smile that absolved Jack of any unintentional slur or cruelty, passing by the joke as if it had not been made. 'But mainly physical assistance. She has to be assisted out of bed and assisted out of her chair to cross the room,

I'm afraid. She had infantile paralysis in her twenties—when I was three.'

'Well—I didn't know,' Jack replied quietly.

'That's all right,' Arkley grinned.

'A bad moment, I think,' said Clive Garner to Jack as soon as Arkley was unable to hear him. Jack nodded, but could not have spoken. He was too near to tears of embarrassed anger with himself.

4

And yet there was a man living round the corner from Sylvia's who had forgotten almost entirely about his parents, though he now earned his only living from dealing with other people's.

Pierre-Henri Mallinot, admirer of Madame Marguerite's representation of Cézanne's nude bathers despite himself, sat, two-and-a-half weeks after Jack Hollard and Clive Garner had that conversation, on a dark and very cold mid-afternoon waiting for his first pupil of the day. She would be dropped off for her lesson by her mother, who drove a Lea Francis, and would be collected later after her mother had spent an hour in the Ladies' section of Mandelston's, one of the better clothes emporia in this unpromising part of the world.

Looking round at the situation in which he had deposited himself, Pierre-Henri began yet again to retrace in his mind the events in his life that had brought him here. The man still needed to come to grips with his own story, and if possible to exorcise it, and adopt a normal-looking, inconspicuous life in England. Settle down here? Only time would allow him to decide that; time which would alternatively tell him when or whether he might return to France. It could be, he sometimes thought, that he was already fixed in his new identity and vocation for ever—if you could call it a vocation. It could be irreversible…

He sometimes found it difficult himself to think exactly how he had come to be sealed in the tedious privacy of this upstairs back parlour, looking out onto nothing but a yard with dustbins and flowerpots and a coalshed, all now draped with frozen snow. He was sitting at home, 'home' consisting of most of the small first floor of Mrs Lettie Orlop's house in Benford Street, No 78. In this forgotten inner outskirt of London, Pierre-Henri measured safety by the degree of boredom he felt. His pupils came in certain limited stretches of the day, after school and at weekends, so he had plenty of time to go out before that, and in the mid- or later evening after tea. But most of his forays were cautious—and boring.

In the daytime he walked the streets and parks to keep fit, but he did it fearfully. In this early February he even wondered how fast and far he could run on the ice and snow if he had to, if anyone were pursuing him. He feared that seeking public entertainment might expose him to observation, and therefore danger; though the darkness of the Empire and the anonymity of the crowds in the picture-houses, the smoke-filled Plaza or the Gaumont, or even the nearby little Park Cinema, seemed secure enough. Not that he enjoyed films or 'music hall'.

He felt most vulnerable, most likely to be spotted, if he went into town, where there were better, French films. So he did that only rarely. He reasoned it this way: his absence would have been noticed very soon back in La Tignelle. People might have sighted him on the way to Paris and in Paris, then on the journey by train to Calais, and (because half the boat passengers were French) even crossing the English Channel. There were potentially hostile French people in London, and some expatriates that would notice another French person for the simple fact that he was French. When he left La Tignelle for England last summer he knew that his money would not last, and that he would have to find a way, or ways, of quietly earning a living there. The method he believed he could risk was to employ his knowledge of his native tongue, teaching it to private pupils whose parents would entrust them to him as a tutor for exams.

To his surprise and relief the cards he displayed for a few pence a week in newsagents' windows in the more affluent-seeming stretches of these South London suburbs (and the advertisement he put, with a box number, in one local newspaper) actually produced results. From mid-August onwards there came a small but steady flow of written enquiries (Mrs Orlop was not on the phone), and then meetings with parents and children whom he usually charmed and reassured in the clean, tidy, business-like bareness of his modest sitting room (which Lettie Orlop cleaned as part of his deal with her). Mrs Orlop let Pierre-Henri put his graduation certificate, on which he had carefully replaced 'Claude Derrichet' with his present name, on a wall, lending him a frame for it and removing a picture of the cliffs at Hunstanton to make space.

These anxious parents had the money for it, apparently, though they complained about the taxation inflicted by 'the Socialists'. Pupils began to come singly or in pairs for hour-long sessions after school, and he taught for several hours at the weekend. The Christmas holiday had meant more teaching hours in the daytime, less of his wandering circumspectly round the streets and parks and libraries and cafés trying not to be noticed.

Sometimes Pierre-Henri Mallinot had slightly more ambitious thoughts, and translating them into action might bring in a little more income. His teaching was elementary stuff, far below the level he was capable of. He did not propose to apply for any kind of permanent school post, that would be hazardous. But it was possible that the role of an examiner in more advanced French might suit him, and be comparatively lucrative?

The beginning of all this was now so very far away, in his own country during the war, among people he knew in a community he understood. It was in Marshal Pétain's France, when the future appeared to offer quite another prospect. To think back to that beginning would require a jump over a huge waste of intervening time, but Pierre-Henri wanted to wind back the entire experience into himself. He had plenty of opportunity to do it while he lived, in a dull, stable way, the life of a polite, unobtrusive, frightened exile, giving respectable French lessons to middle-class English children mostly dropped by car in this backstreet in a tract of southeast London never in the news.

To start with his choice of this city rather than another, or some small English town more on the scale of La Tignelle, or Angoulême, or Périgueux: Pierre-Henri believed London was the best option because it was somewhere to melt away into, be submerged in. During the war not so long ended it had been a city of foreigners, of civilian exiles and foreign forces. Walk the streets, he had heard, and you would see countless men and women in uniform with labels on their shoulders denoting their country of origin: Poland, Norway, Jugoslavia, France. In the final months of the war it had been quite common, as Mrs Orlop averred, to see penniless German prisoners, garbed in blue, killing the time they were allowed to spend out of their local camp by wandering the streets alone, not permitted to speak to anyone, grim and thoughtful pariahs.

Now the war was over. But the presence of foreigners was still natural. Many had remained in England, some had married, they were slowly becoming familiar traders, workers in factories, where their labour was gratefully accepted. If Pierre-Henri kept his head down, encountered bureaucratic authority as infrequently as possible, made sure he never lost his French passport and other documents, he should remain safely invisible. If any uninformed English people ever questioned his credentials—which was unlikely—he could talk hypocritically about the maquis activity in his region of France, the links with the Free French forces in England, any number of brave and dangerous exploits he knew about.

His weakest link was his utter lack of any contact back in France who would keep him in touch, or perhaps testify for him. He had no references to show (unless the school and university certificates he had been careful to bring with him proved sufficient). But by this time he was at least assembling a small file of appreciative notes from the parents of children whose prospects for Public School Common Entrance or General School Certificate seemed to be visibly improving under his tuition. One day he had felt bold enough to go out and telephone the number, obtained from a reference book in the public library, of the University Schools Examinations Board.

But this was later.

When you reach England, he had said to himself originally, when setting out from La Tignelle, look wholly undisturbed if you are detained by officials at the port and are asked questions. No hauteur, no angry impatience, no restlessness. Above all no display of temperament. Be like a normal visitor obviously expecting to be allowed through. Nowadays dozens of other foreigners daily would be entering the country. Change just enough money on the boat, or at Dover, to buy a third-class single ticket to Victoria, then seek out quiet, reliable and discreet places to make further small exchanges of saved-up francs to cover the first couple of months of modest lodging in this city.

Apart from the mundane but correct 'clothes he stood up in' (he knew the English phrase) he had one further clean suit in his luggage. And the green coat. He thought he was going to have to get rid of the coat somewhere, without looking suspicious about it. Sell it? If so, how and where? A second-hand clothes shop? A garment so obviously foreign and unusual? It would stir suspicions if he even tried.

The train from Dover to Victoria, once he was through the customs without trouble and had successfully bought a ticket, was not unduly full. But that was not an advantage. Pierre-Henri did not want to be noticeable as the sole occupant of one of those eight-person third-class compartments, nor did he care to share one with just one or two strangers who might be bored, and start looking at him, and even talking and showing curiosity.

Let alone other French people. Thus he looked for a fairly full compartment where he could sit in a corner by a window onto the corridor, and say or do nothing at all.

People with children were less of a risk. He had noticed on the train from Paris to Calais that children who stared or pointed were actually protective! Their actions embarrassed their parents and focused attention on their misbehaviour rather than on its victim in the corner. Twice he was apologised to. The second offending child was repeatedly smacked. He said good-bye to the tired mother with a brief, gracious smile at the station in Calais and they did not turn up on the boat.

His schemes for finding accommodation were as well worked out as they could be by someone who had only visited London once before, as a twelve-year-old with his parents in 1921. It had shown him post-war conditions following the Great War, the war people now ruefully called 'the First War'. But that was different, because although London had been frequently bombed it was not a city still considering what to do with many thousands (not just dozens) of bomb sites, cleared or half-cleared, and how to pay for it. Pierre-Henri could not afford to think of the tourist hotel his parents had taken him to, though he remembered it with affection. It was somewhere along a central London underground line near a famous park, or parks...He might not be able to recognise it now, he really couldn't recall its name, it would certainly be costly.

He would try first to find somewhere not in the immediate vicinity of the station, which would mean either paying too much for such luxury as there was in post-war London or resorting to one-night squalor. He would look for somewhere dingy but decent, and camp out in it for a day or two until he found permanent lodging in a place of even greater obscurity. Once outside Victoria Station he began to walk with his heavy suitcase in a completely unsuitable direction, passing blocks of offices—government departments, insurance companies, shipping enterprises.

From one of those Perce Hollard emerged to catch his bus home during this rush-hour. He stepped considerately aside to allow space for this foreigner with the luggage to pass.

Pierre-Henri doubled back, and realised that if you went to the right quarters adjacent to famous stations you found nothing but small shops and cheap but acceptable hotels. Out of some bottomless well of petty entrepreneurial aspiration came the desire to make a living by nothing more than the running of places such as these. He looked at shabby boards outside them, or off-white notices propped up in the windows, offering VACANCIES for BED AND BREAKFAST, an English custom which he believed could sometimes be expanded to include EVENING MEAL in seaside towns, or cities or their suburbs.

He picked a small, cleanish, impersonal business-and-tourist hotel in Belgrave Road, dropped his bag with some relief on the floor in his allotted room, and stretched himself out on the bed to think. Immediately and harrowingly this place, simply because it was a single room in a building with thin walls (and forgotten pictures on them, except they were English and not French) brought back to Pierre-Henri the room of the same size and quality not far from the station in Périgueux. But he had to drive the memory of that room from his mind and concentrate on what exactly he would do next.

Yes, this hotel would provide him with some kind of evening meal in an hour's time, although his anxiety in these strange surroundings, and the drinks taken with his tedious, unwanted English companion on the cross-channel boat, did not enhance his appetite. Well, first he would not go out this evening, he would retire early, take the English breakfast early, and then make his way to the side of Victoria Station where trains left for anonymous southern and southeastern suburbs.

He believed that quiet private lodging-houses might be found near small suburban stations; places not too large and with not too many people constantly arriving and leaving, but on the other hand not providing, as company, entrenched guests who had settled in them to die. He wanted a place where he would probably not be simply 'lodging', but taken on as an unobtrusive resident for months perhaps. He had imagined correctly (his observation from yesterday's train) that the first three or four stations on this line only served inner industrial quarters, where no one wanted to stay who did not already live and work there.

He calculated that the fifth station, for which he had bought a ticket, would offer a more likely area, and yet the eligible establishments he saw were like more genteel versions of the ones around the railway terminus in town. The curtains looked fresher, the brass on the front doors had been polished, but they were essentially miniature suburban hotels which would be expensive for longer stays. They looked like the regular resorts of very small-scale commercial travellers. 'Gentlemen' were offered 'Accommodation' on fading boards set in neat front gardens, those words not carrying implications of dubious opportunities.

The weather was exceptionally good, the kind of day that suggested summer had come and was indestructible. Pierre-Henri bought the *Evening Standard* and the *Star* and scanned the advertisements for 'Accommodation', but quickly realised that although his newly purchased road map of London, opened clumsily on his lap, gave him his location, there was no clue as to the kind of area in which 'Small apartment to let' would be situated. In this calm park, on a seat near an ornamental lake where grown moorhens swam and dipped in the sunshine, he felt safe but lost. Two stops further down the line was a region that disdained even smart small hotels, let alone lodging-houses. Here there were just wide and silent avenues, big individual residences with drives and garages, and lamps by the front doors. Occasionally a woman would appear at a door and shake a duster, but she would not be the owner. Everywhere lacked paint and bore other signs of wartime deprivation, but it claimed smartness with conviction. In mid-afternoon here there were no passers-by. Pierre-Henri began to feel stranded in English bourgeois territory where boundaries were drawn against foreigners, against the lower middle class, the upper working class, the manual working class, the poor. Places where the destitute would be arrested. Such as Witham Grove, where Perce Hollard's immediate boss, Arthur Jedleigh, lived.

One station back, then. He had seen from the map that this would be a place with fewer green patches, no broad long streets, just a crowding together in chunks of smaller streets, no doubt a poorer but still a reasonably clean place. If he failed altogether here he would return by train to his base in Belgrave Road and tomorrow try north London instead.

Again his guess was accurate. Five minutes from the station and the dingier streets around it, across a High Street of busy shops, past a large palace of light entertainment, and he was into a complex of small stores (no big retail chains represented), an 'off licence', a butcher's, a post office combined with a baker's. It looked very like a self-respecting upper-working-class district where clerks were slowly and deliberately buying, on mortgages, small bay-windowed houses with tiny, tidy front gardens. Once they would all have had protective railings to emphasise their security and privacy, he guessed: along the low garden walls were the holes, or sometimes the stumps, where the metal had been sawn away to provide material for munitions.

For several minutes Pierre-Henri saw no sign of a café or pub, which he took to be a good sign. Nothing went on here except quiet, unobtrusive living. Probably no one rented out rooms either, but he would take a look at this display of cards outside a newsagent's just in case. And here was a chance. One card spoke in neat, misspelt blue handwriting of providing a 'nice upstairs flat for a respecktable gentleman or lady. Write or call on Mrs L. Orlop at 78, Benford Street, S.E.6.'

The map took him there after several minutes spent trying to determine where he stood at any given moment from small street signs, high on brick walls, that badly needed painting or cleaning. Benford was a notch or two down from its neighbouring streets. The red-tiled front steps were shorter, and the gardens narrower, but there was a cared-for atmosphere about this one long terrace of red-brick cottages. As for Mrs Orlop—she was, he guessed, in her fifties, slight and wiry, bright-eyed with a mixture of welcome and reasonable curiosity for anyone taking up her advertisement.

'I've generally had some very nice English gentlemen,' she told him when he made it clear that he came from France, and wanted to spend some time in London to see England and pay his way by giving private lessons—if that was something he might do in Mrs Orlop's house? Her emphasis on 'English' was something she thought later might have offended him, but she wanted to tell him the truth and let him know that she was making an exception in taking a gentleman from abroad and expected no foreign habits. From somewhere she had heard that you needed to make your own position clear from the start if you were taking foreign lodgers—that was the way one of her friends in the lodgings game had managed to have no problems whatsoever with her Indian. Not that Mr Mollie-knot, as she pronounced him, was not respectable in appearance and charming in manner; but you never knew, and you needed to be firm from the start...

She showed him the upstairs of the house, and he seemed very appreciative, praising the comfortable look of this sitting room where he had a table to teach at if he took pupils, and a three-piece suite, and even a radio to himself. He would be asked to come downstairs for breakfast, and for his evening meal if and when he wanted to take one (which would of course be extra). She would like two weeks' rent in advance, if that was all right; and suddenly Lettie Orlop realised that in the course of showing the flat to this gentleman she had more or less assumed he would want it, and she was offering it to him.

The last gentleman she had here was a worker at the hospital across the road, which had provided her with a number of lodgers over the years. But they had moved him…Pierre-Henri's laconic charm had worked on Mrs Orlop, and she felt sure she would get used to having a Frenchman in time, as long as the neighbours didn't mind. It might be pleasant to have children coming to the house if he was really going to have pupils here to teach them.

First impressions are always the most reliable, she believed, and in this business of letting rooms you had to be good at summing people up and asking the right questions in the first couple of minutes. References mattered, but to trust your own first impressions was much more important. (When she asked this gentleman about references he smiled and asked her whether she could understand French, so she did not insist.)

Pierre-Henri turned out to be the quietest lodger she ever had, the street hardly noticed his arrival or (in the end) registered that he had disappeared.

5

But Sylvia—

Although she lived only three minutes away from 78 Benford Street, at 274 Oaktree Lane, an inner suburban thoroughfare and not a rural route for a long time by the 1940s, she rarely passed Mrs Orlop's door, and had not recognised Pierre-Henri Mallinot in the Empire as someone she may have seen in the street. Any more than her parents had. It was a measure of the Frenchman's wish to be a private, unnoticed person.

Pierre-Henri did not want his face to be known locally, and did not frequent the nearest small shops. When he dispatched letters and accounts to pupils' parents he bought the stamps from a larger post office farther away, and not always the same one. So he had not met Eileen and Sylvia in the small local branch when they posted a parcel together because Eileen wanted to be sure Sylvia had actually sent it.

Eileen had also helped Sylvia wrap up the parcel to send back these chocolates that the 'older boy' had sent her in the attempt to set up further meetings. They turned inside out the same brown paper in which it had been received, and there was hardly any space for the name and address. By cramping the letters Sylvia managed it, but she made a peculiar error. Instead of 'Hollard' she wrote 'Hollman', using the end of her own name. It was as if she was partly addressing to herself the punishment involved in renouncing Jack Hollard's heartbroken gift. She liked chocolates, and would have eaten them if Eileen had not absolutely insisted she send them back. Accepting presents from a strange young man was not right, she had said.

Sylvia's schoolfriend Marian, companion on the morning bus, was in on the conspiracy to elude Jack by going out earlier, even though she had to get up ten minutes before her usual time. Sylvia wanted to be sure that she would never be alone on the bus to school, and Marian kept her promise to be ready when Sylvia called for her. But Marian grew somewhat tired of making the effort, and she said to herself that she could not see why Sylvia had decided 'to play the tragic queen about all this'. One day their friend Ginger, in the same class, told Sylvia outright that she ought to have gone on seeing Jack if underneath she really wanted to. It was her own life to lead, not her sister's.

'My sister wouldn't dare treat me like that,' she declared, loudly, on the bus. But no heads turned. People were tired on these cold mornings. They just dozed, or sat and read the papers, and drew on their cigarettes or pipes. The upper decks were travelling chambers of sour smoke.

'Oh but your sister Joy is not Eileen's age,' Sylvia countered.

'My sister's older than your Eileen.'

'You don't know Eileen. She can bully like some big child.'

This was Sylvia finding a reason for accepting Eileen's advice when she had begun to think it had been weak to give in to her. Her old resentment of Eileen's interference had begun to well up again, though she could not now reverse a decision about Jack that she had, after all, taken for herself in the end. She remembered that a vicar on the radio in a church service for youth had said that girls must be careful not to lead boys on because it might encourage a boy to follow impulses he could not control.

'Sounds to me you don't really think she should be allowed to bully you,' Ginger said. Once Ginger had got going on something like this there was no stopping her. 'The way to stop it, Syl, is to stand up for yourself and do what you want. I wouldn't let my sister dictate to me like that if she *tried*. And she wouldn't try.' All this was said now in quite an urgent tone as they neared the college on the last yards from the bus, the breath gushing from her mouth in frozen clouds on this mid-February Wednesday.

Sylvia was tugged in two directions, in one by her pride at having had a boyfriend, an older boy at that, and in the other by her blushing embarrassment at having it debated by her friends. She was on the edge of tears now, and when the bitter air caused tears of cold to form, she let real tears follow them.

It stopped there, but it resumed in the lunch hour with another girl from their class, Maria Sorel. Maria was the daughter of Spanish Civil War refugees, and seemed older than the others because of what had happened to drive the family out of Spain. She seemed to all her friends to be blessed with more knowledge of life, and of love, and of wisdom about the mystery of love than any of them. When they met her in the icy playground in the sunshine of the break Marian and Ginger, almost together, pulled Sylvia in front of her and said, 'She's let her sister make her ditch her first boyfriend. Because he's two years older than her. What do you think, Maria?'

Maria had large and generous brown eyes. They could widen and flash. When she dispensed wisdoms she touched a listener on the hand briefly, and people felt she spoke with both affection and authority.

'What I think is—' Maria hesitated, and put out a mittened hand to take Sylvia's gloved one while she decided what she really thought. 'What I think is, let your heart speak for everything you have done.'

Then Maria pushed the bare tips of her fingers into the back of Sylvia's hand, and let it go. None of the other girls at school ever spoke like this. To Sylvia, Maria sounded like a girl of fifteen speaking with the maturity of a woman, and out of the depths of a romantic country, Spain. To Maria Sorel, flattered to be consulted, her own words resembled something she had heard as a child from adults or big girls, and was now repeated without her completely understanding what it meant. For Sylvia, Maria's wide-eyed, friendly gaze would not leave her for many minutes, right through the bell for afternoon school.

During the first afternoon lesson, which was needlework, Maria kept looking across at Sylvia, half-smiling. Sylvia's heart finally spoke for her when she and Maria left their seats in the cold classroom and went over to the one functioning radiator; with permission, and after other pairs of girls had done this, complaining that they needed to warm their fingers if they were going to be able to handle the needles. She explained to Maria what her heart had told her, if not in exactly these words then in phrases very like them. (She felt very adult about having worked it out like this.) 'You have done it now, stopped seeing Jack of your own accord because you know you could have defied Eileen if you really wanted to. There can't be any turning back. You are not meeting Jack any more, you do not reply to any letters he sends, you sent his chocolates back. He was never going to be a proper boyfriend. But—in future you will decide for yourself, you will let your heart speak for what you want to do according to your own wishes entirely. If your heart says you can go out with an older boy, go out with an older boy.'

On the Saturday soon after this Marian, who was several months younger than her friends, and one year junior to them in school, gave a party for her fifteenth birthday. It lasted from four in the afternoon to eight-thirty in the evening, and Sylvia went. It only occurred afterwards to Marian's father, Mr Richardson, that the idea of a children's party for his eldest child had been misjudged. He supposed that he had been influenced by the fact that he had Marian's three younger siblings to cater for. They liked parties, and wouldn't understand if Marian had no party this year. But he knew also that he did not want Marian to grow up, and while she was content to be feted like a child he would do that for one last time.

He, Marian's mother, and an auntie would organise and supervise the party. The younger siblings were allowed just one guest between them (they would have their own turn with their own parties in due course) and it turned out to be an eleven-year-old pal of Marian's ten-year-old brother Peter. Marian could have six guests, and an equal division between the sexes was suggested. Sylvia and Ginger, both fifteen for months already, were on the list, and there was fourteen-year-old flighty Anne. All these girls attended girls' schools (Anne was the only one at the Girls' Grammar and not the Technical College) the boys were street neighbours, or known from junior school: Donald and Owen, both still fourteen, who had played street games with Marian from an early age, and John, who was only twelve but had outgrown the other two. Marian and Ginger had joked somewhat cruelly to Sylvia that they might invite Jack, but Sylvia knew that apart from anything else his age made it impossible, and ignored the threat.

Despite the persisting extreme cold the small house, No 6, at the bottom of Benford Street, was hot, there were fires in every room they were using. Every answering of the loud bell (they had to wind it up twice to keep it going) was done by Marian herself with a shriek of surprise, as if all these people were unexpected. It was followed by a deep shudder as the freezing air entered the hall, and, 'Come in and close the door—don't let the heat out.'

The front room, hardly ever used except on occasions like these, was decorated with old, tattered paper-chains and paper bells, saved up and used throughout the war because no new ones were available all that time. Marian's dad was always delighted when he took the bells in careful fingers and they yet again opened almost perfectly after so much use. There was a small table brought into the front room for glasses and bottles, of tizer and cream soda. Out in the kitchen was a much larger round table fully extended by its two leaves, so that there was not much room for larger children to move round it. It was set for a sitdown tea.

When Sylvia arrived, last of all the guests, she said 'Hi!' to Marian with her present, a nicely wrapped up new hair slide, to Marian's twelve-year-old sister Alma, and to Ginger and Anne. She saw that Donald, Owen and John were big boys, but not yet grown up (she thought) when Marian's auntie recited their names.

The half hour before the tea was not organised, the grown-ups were busy arranging the table in the kitchen, and it was passed in chatting and laughing and drinking what Marian poured out from the bottles on the table. Also in fooling around. This consisted of good-natured verbal teasing, and then some romping among the younger children and the older girls; except for Sylvia, who did not know Marian's younger brothers and sister as well as the others did. Anne had always been a spirited girl in junior school, and this afternoon her special new party dress was torn in a scuffle on the carpet with Ginger and Marian and Marian's two small brothers.

The older boy guests took no part in this, it seemed to hush and embarrass them. Anne was not angry for herself, but knew how upset her mother would be after all the time and money spent on finding and buying the material and the pattern, and running it through the sewing machine as she pedalled and pedalled for ages. Anne in fact did not mind that the tear exposed a length of her leg above the knee.

It had become easier than during the war to find the ingredients for Marian's cake, and there was icing into which the fifteen candles could be stuck. Tinned fruit was now available again, so opening the pineapple or the peaches stored at the back of the cupboard didn't feel like an audacious sacrifice of part of a precious store.

But before all that came the rationed bread, and the jam, or the ryvita and jam, with cream; and if you were preferring the ryvita, Marian's mum announced, you had to spread the rationed butter on the flat side, 'not the side with the bumps', in order to make it last. Afterwards there were sausage rolls and tinned sardines, which were not very popular. Then the light switch was suddenly operated, and those candles were lighted; and Marian pushed her chair back to stand up and blow them out.

Sylvia watched this short plump girl, who was suddenly wearing a brassiere under her new party blouse, and wondered whether Marian felt the same as she herself did: that she was beginning to be not simply an older child among the youngest ones here—the ages ranged from twelve down to eight—but an adult without any proper access to the adult world. A song said, 'I'm just an in-between...' And yet at parties like this she would play the games and cling on to childhood, as something she resented having to leave because she knew it would never return.

Marian's dad was the perennial master of ceremonies (as he always announced) for the games after tea, which would last until they were all thoroughly tired and naturally wanted to go home. When the games involved music he played the piano for them, not that badly, having learnt in the army. There would be find the sixpence, with everyone in blindfold and the successful seeker obviously allowed to keep the coin. Hide and seek would mean using any and every corner in the small house, with people creating an upheaval and a mess in every room last time, so perhaps that wouldn't be chosen today. There might be the competition to make 'fashionable' hats out of crepe paper and pins, which kept people either busy competing or sitting and watching. Sylvia had won last year, again for a prize of sixpence. And musical chairs, greatly enjoyed while you still circled, but hated when you fell victim to its merciless dismissal of the unlucky, or of the slow and gentle people. There was sometimes the threat of postman's knock, which somehow Sylvia invariably managed to get out of playing. This was dreaded more than anything by anyone over the age of twelve. Surely it was for children, and would not be proposed for people of fourteen—and fifteen?

Now they were suddenly through all the earlier games, including grandmother's footsteps and pass the parcel, without any problems, and Mr Richardson was moving towards the musical chairs. This party was going to be much like all the others; the youngest children wanted that and expected it. They would play musical chairs with speed and passion, and perhaps a suitable one of their number (not the cheekiest or the most violent) would be allowed to win? But Sylvia Freeman still had enough of the child in her to want to win.

A count of participants was done, and four chairs were brought in from the tea-table in the kitchen to supplement the three heavy, stately chairs, and the two deep armchairs in this front room or parlour, one of which was placed at each end of the two rows, of four and three seats. That made nine places for the ten people who would be circling at the start of the game. Sylvia believed she would feel what she always felt. As the youngest child of three at home she had often felt left out of things by Frank and Eileen if her parents failed to intervene to ensure fairness. There were all these places and choices at the beginning of a game of musical chairs, and good luck for everybody except one when the music first stopped. But later it became a case of people just pushing you out of the way if you didn't push them, a matter of ruthless exclusion. Sylvia was frightened of the humiliating moment when she would be forced out of the diminishing circle, loser again. It would require all her mystery and dignity not to slump down furious and disappointed in a removed chair if that happened.

There was an ornately framed wall-mirror in this front room. She looked into it when she had a chance to do that quickly, and believed she could win the musical chairs.

'Are we ready?' A fateful question no one in the circle of ten children answered except for Marian's brother Peter, who was very eager to begin. It came from Mr Richardson seated at the piano. Would he be playing 'Deep in the Heart of Texas' yet again? 'That's all he can play,' Ginger had said last time, and Bob Richardson had not forgotten. So it was 'Jealousy', a tango, this time. With its irregular, springy rhythm it would give him the opportunity of seeming to stop when he wasn't, so the smallest boys would be flopping onto chairs too soon, only to be pulled up again by either Marian's mum or her auntie.

He first of all played on and on for quite a time, enjoying this mean, elementary way of keeping everyone in suspense and wearing them down. Had they already done the circuit four times, about, before he stopped? And Sylvia lapsed happily onto a flat-seated heavy parlour chair, the middle one of three? At one end one of the four boys from nowhere, the twelve-year-old John, was seatless and pronounced 'out', and a chair was taken away, leaving only three on that side.

Then the familiar tune was resumed, but much more slowly now, to perplex everyone. The older ones sang it. 'Jeal-oo-see... Boom Boom.' Reaching it the second time the dad lingered on that three-syllable title word with slow, sustained, resonating chords. Then he raised his hands from the keyboard and his daughter was out. Marian scowled, the powerful scowl of a young teenager reverting to a child's bad temper. It was her birthday, and she was out practically at the start of the musical chairs. 'You've got to take it in good part,' her auntie said. 'Right! Off again!' They had hardly taken three or four paces before Mr Richardson stopped suddenly, at the second of the two Boom Boom chords, and the two youngest of Marian's siblings were fighting for a chair, and the boy, the ten-year-old Peter, won it, and Marian's sister Alma was out.

And all too soon only five people were left. The two big armchairs remained where they were, pushed closer to each other, and only two of the smaller chairs were kept, set back to back. These last few were Sylvia, Anne, Marian's two younger brothers Raymond and Peter, and the older unknown boy Owen. Anne, with the tear in her dress held together by two safety pins, bright and sophisticated, wearing just a little lipstick, regularly top in English in 3A in the Girls' Grammar School, strode bouncingly round and round while 'Jealousy' was taken right on almost to its close before it halted in mid-phrase. It was too fast for her to stop and go back to one of the straight-backed chairs, and Raymond leaped forward to occupy it. Sylvia was watching Marian's father very carefully when she was walking in his direction and he seemed to be similarly watching her from the piano. Eight-year-old Raymond, his youngest, went next, grinning with more grace than his sister. 'Sylvia's been very clever,' Auntie said. 'Very lucky,' Marian said.

One armchair was left, and two players, Sylvia and Owen. Sylvia believed that the dad would play a quite lengthy stretch of 'Jealousy' before bringing the game to an end, and she soon realised that a kind of very fast, rapidly swivelling walk was required. These last two players would be kept going in maximum suspense, keeping the envious watchers amused. Sylvia told herself to keep just calmly walking, and really concentrated, after circling about four times. The secret was to take longer steps when you had just passed the armchair. When she looked down at the carpet at that point, Sylvia saw a 'face' in the pattern which she knew she had to pass quickly to be safe again. It was not a real face but an arrangement of patches of shapes and colours which looked a bit like a lion: the fur, the eyes, the heavy jaws, even a mouth with something resembling the grandly miserable look male lions have in pictures or at the zoo. 'Get past the lion, and you might be all right,' she kept saying quietly to herself. 'Get past the lion!' Owen, in front of her, lingered casually by the empty armchair until Sylvia caught up with him, although not long enough for him to be accused of hanging back and cheating.

Was it the tenth or even the twelfth time Sylvia had fled past the lion clockwise with a large stride, and reached the side of the armchair again? She thought she had just counted the twelfth time and was alongside one arm. Across it was laid a round brass ashtray, cleaned out but permanently stained, set in a wide but thin belt of imitation leather, each end fraying into thin straight strips that hung over the side. Between the two arms was, for a seat, a cool rexine-coated slab, square and dark red, and against the rexine back of the chair was a scarlet cushion. Behind the cushion was an antimacassar lapping over the rear of the chair, offering a faded picture of Fowey harbour in Cornwall.

The piano stopped, Owen was doubling back and getting his left side into the seat of the armchair, but Sylvia's right side was there at the same second, so she suddenly found she was sitting more or less in Owen's lap. The auntie had to arbitrate and be just. She was agreed by everyone there to be a fair person and great fun, so when she called out 'I think it's—oh, what is your name?' and Owen said 'Owen' and she said 'Oh that's right, Owen! I think you've won,' no one, least of all Sylvia, contested that decision and Owen received a little prize done up in fancy paper with string which turned out to be a bar of chocolate.

'Now we'll have a rest, and afterwards—postman's knock!' called out the auntie, who would run this game, and who really enjoyed the groan of horror. The children turned away and covered their faces, but they also laughed. No one said 'I'm not going to play postman's knock!' They were shy about playing it themselves, but they relished seeing the discomfort others would have to suffer. The eight- to twelve-year-olds would have fun seeing the embarrassed older ones compelled to play, and the parents joined in the joke in a faintly cruel way. It would serve the older children right for growing up into young adolescents and becoming awkward. A ten-year-old being banished into the chilly hall to kiss an older girl would be hilarious for everyone back in the party, no difficulty for the wise, waiting girl, rather sensational for the boy if he could have admitted it. When the ages were about the same it was fun for everyone back in the room to count the number of minutes the couple took. There were no prizewinners, no prizes. It went on until everyone had suffered their turn and the supervising adult called a halt and started the next game.

It had occurred to Marian's dad that by this age most of the larger children were too old, but her mum had said it was a custom, and it might be the last time. Besides, the younger ones wanted it and any older girl or boy could stay out of it if she or he preferred, though that would be difficult. If Sylvia, Marian, Ginger and Anne joined in, it was because they summed up the situation in this way: more mature than these older boys, they had command, and needn't fear anything from them. They could handle anything the boys might try, and it was unlikely that these boys would be particularly adventurous. Unconsciously they patronised these boys, and felt entirely safe.

There were pieces of coloured paper with numbers on them, two sets of one to five, for four boys and five girls, Marian's youngest brother Raymond having stayed out of the game. Someone, a girl, had a number drawn from a hat and had to go outside—it was Ginger. Ginger, shivering in the darkness of the hall with only the light from a lamppost shining through the wrinkled glass panes of the front door, had to knock. And the auntie had to take her message through a chink in the door of the sitting room. 'The postman has a letter for No 4' she reported. So who was that? It was Marian's ten-year-old brother Peter. His friend Ian hauled him up from his chair and hurried him through the door. He was no problem at all. Ginger smiled in the dark and got it over quickly, an almost motherly kiss on the side of his lips, virtually on his cheek, and then a pat on the back. Peter returned to the party relieved, and yet with a sense of being cheated somehow. He had been rather in awe of Ginger. She reminded him already of grown-up girl cousins he secretly thought rather beautiful, and was half in love with when they treated him as if he was nearly their own age.

Anne was to go out next, and tripped out rather eagerly. The pieces of coloured paper with the numbers on were swapped around. Anne would be in control of any situation of this kind. All this was too young for her, but why should she give up childish things? Only the day before she had sat in her classroom at the grammar school, when 3A had been allowed to stay during lunch hours in this drastic weather, reminiscing maturely with two friends from the same junior school about teachers and pupils and escapades now a full two-and-a-half years in the past. She had known as a child the sadness of leaving particular places and people, and now as an adolescent she was learning to deepen that into a nostalgia for entire irrecoverable eras of her life. Here was her junior school childhood and its party games back again when she knocked and declared to the auntie she had a parcel to deliver at No 3. Donald, fourteen and Anne's age, blushed, and gave what he thought was a tolerant, good-humoured laugh, and the auntie closed the door on the two of them.

It seemed that he was gone a long time. There was speculation and giggling in the room among the girls. Owen looked embarrassed, because Donald was his friend and he worried a little about him with a girl like Anne. In the end, the auntie knocked on the inside of the door, not wishing to open it and interrupt anything. Donald came back with a second blush, and Anne with a laugh, neither of them answering the silly questions thrown at them. Anne found an armchair to sit in and declared, to no one in particular, 'Oh well, it's all experience, I suppose.' She was using a favourite rueful phrase of her twenty-year-old sister's when things had been going badly, although it did not appear that anything had gone badly for Anne. The next number to be drawn was Owen's.

Owen's knock was very tentative when it finally came. No one was sure whether there had been a knock at all, so the auntie had to ask him through the door if he had knocked, and which number he wanted. He requested to deliver a letter to No 1. This time No 1 was Sylvia, and she went over to the door very neutrally, deliberately not catching anyone's eye as she did that, not heeding the cries of all the young children and all the entrenched adults. Marian, Ginger and Anne cried out less because Sylvia, since beauty and mystery had become her object in life, had become a lesser-known quantity to them, she seemed more remote. Always a quiet girl as a junior, she had not opened out as she entered her teens, but drawn into herself more resolutely. Sylvia had already had an older boyfriend after all, which was more than Anne had. Either Sylvia knew everything and was keeping quiet, or her reticence was a cover for knowing nothing at all.

She went out confidently into the dark hall with its smell of cold wet coats, and a slight remaining smell from tea out in the kitchen, and looked at the boy waiting there. But as the sitting-room door closed firmly behind her and shut out some of the squealing and laughing, she had a sudden rush of panic. It was the naked rawness of this foolish situation, the adults' expectation that these young people should play the children's game and amuse them with their embarrassment. She shivered, felt threatened, had to tell herself that she only faced a big child not much older than the boy she last sat next to in a classroom in the juniors. All this was very confusing and silly, and then Owen said, 'Sylvia.' She was astonished. She had taken in his name when he won the musical chairs, but she could not believe he had taken in hers. She did not reply. Out here it was cold from the draught under the front door, the more so because the evening outside had turned windy. It was not snowing yet again, but the wind sent up gusts of snow from the morning's fall, lying inches deep on its bed of ice.

In seconds their darkness turned into the faint, glistening lamplight, entering through the glass panes of the door and falling onto the stand of coats and the little table on casters where a new black bakelite telephone stood with a white writing-pad and a sharpened HB pencil beside it. It was only the second or third house in which Sylvia had ever seen a telephone. She didn't have one, and now she remembered that Jack's family didn't but were in the process of obtaining one, as he had once mentioned to her with an element of pride.

Between the coats hanging in layers on the hooks of the stand was a mirror like the sympathetic hall mirror they had at home. Sylvia saw herself in it just momentarily, over Owen's shoulder, and was pleased with her reflection. Owen's hair was neatly combed, and slicked down with scented cream; it had the air of hair arranged that way by somebody else, his mother probably, so that he would look respectable for the party. Having spoken her name, he looked at Sylvia with an utter neutrality that matched her own. Sylvia permitted herself to give her mysterious half-smile. Both were aware that back in the sitting room everyone else's mind was on them, no one would be speaking or thinking of anything except what the two of them in the hall might be doing. They were all waiting.

In very long seconds, as their images obtained increasing clarity in this dark, they looked at each other in a very straight way, not evading each other's gaze. They could not withdraw from this. They could not agree to refuse to do what they were expected to do. Negotiating that between themselves would be too complicated. It would require them to discuss it. And Owen knew that he had to start to do it. He would back away if Sylvia tried to start it. He moved his face towards hers, lifted his nose, and pushed out his chin so that his dry lips touched the dry warm line of Sylvia's.

They had done it, then, and Owen drew back his head and they looked at each other. He had done it very briefly, hardly touched the girl's lips at all, so he did it again to confirm the first action. The third time they both did it together, impulsively, a common and simultaneous movement. Sylvia put two hands on Owen's shoulders and Owen moved one hand to touch Sylvia's side under her shoulder as she raised her arms, and they kissed several more times, always fast, always a dry brushing of flesh in this most symbolic and intimate of all human gestures. As it was the first really important love gesture in life it was more significant than the things that came later and involved quite extreme and unmentionable body activities resulting in mess and dirt and reproduction. You ate with your mouth, you spoke with your mouth, you kissed with your mouth. Kissing meant saying you loved, although saying it in words would usually follow kissing. But kissing, the lips put together, was a joke to children, a boring conclusion to an adventure film which brought all decent action to a close, a signal for loud booing in the Saturday morning children's cinema shows, the brave detective, the cowboy, the explorer all kissing the big beautiful rescued lady, the excitement over, the wedding on its way, THE END. Daylight outside, dinnertime. But Owen and Sylvia did this film ending again and again, looking at each other with surprised eyes, discovering a liking for it just when they were becoming too old for these children's games.

They did it so rapidly that there was no impatience from the people on the other side of the door; and then they both instinctively agreed to stop it without saying a word. It suddenly felt as icy as it really was out in this hall, so they went back into the warm room with a calm that was almost a disdain for whatever welcome they received, a playing down of any reaction—no more than one or two teasing remarks—and an impression left that they had followed the rules of postman's knock, kissed, and that was that.

At the end of Marian's birthday party they left the house together, unaware of Pierre-Henri Mallinot slowing his steps as he turned the corner on the way to No 78 so as to avoid bumping into a crowd of children. They all walked away in different directions. Sylvia watched Owen rather wistfully as he strolled off in the damp snow, in case he turned round. Which he did once, but giving no sign that he had seen Sylvia still standing there. Pierre-Henri passed Sylvia as she walked away slowly herself.

Owen noticed Sylvia around the district a few times in the next couple of years, and he usually thought to himself that she had become very large, very tall and beautiful and grand, and beyond his reach. Whereas, when they had kissed in Marian Richardson's hall, there was no bending over for Sylvia or reaching up for Owen. They had both been exactly the same height.

6

And then it was early March, with tentative thaws that didn't last for long, and lengthy suspensions of radio services.

In this southeastern district dried eggs were unobtainable. The red and silver tins, with their easy-to-open lids and small print you had to keep turning round and back, round and back, and hold up to the light to read properly, were empty and given over to other purposes. Real eggs were not impossible to find, but difficult. You needed to know someone who kept chickens in their back garden. Roosters continued to crow too early, though not so early as when small hours air raids woke them and their cries joined in with the ululations of the air-raid siren.

Rationed potatoes were available, but green vegetables were scarce. The Empire recovered its electricity supply and reopened. Fresh bills appeared outside, and Maureen crossed the road from the Rio Café to read them. There was to be a visit for a week in the spring by a travelling opera company doing three different operas over six days, nine performances altogether counting the Tuesday, Thursday and Saturday five o'clock shows, three each of *Carmen* (slightly abridged, it said, being honest in case the cognoscenti complained), of *La Bohème* and of *La Traviata*. Famous stars in this company, who had been away during the war, some of them serving in the forces but some entertaining the troops, had now rejoined. Patrons should book early and make use of a ticket offer that comprised a much reduced price if you came to all three proud presentations. On an impulse, Maureen decided she would go, it would be something new.

People from the Empire were coming to the Rio again, where shortages had never really applied because Spillar seemed to have 'connections'; or that was how you described it. The café was closer than Lyons's, in fact bang opposite the stage door, and more informal than its genteel competitor, the Cosy Corner in the High Street. It might be that performers and lighting people were making sure they had a solid simple snack inside them before the two shows on matinée days, or just that they drifted in for a cup of tea between their working sessions. Maureen was to and fro all the time at periods like this, carrying from the hatch the bacon and egg, with or without fried bread and sausage, the baked beans, the tomatoes on toast Spillar believed he was very good at. And all the time she was doing this she was thinking she was eight, nine, ten days late.

Once when Jack's bus from school (with no Sylvia on it) turned out everyone because, as so frequently happened, it had changed its route and was going straight to the garage, Jack started walking the last quarter of a mile home in the freezing twilight and passed the herbalist's shop. He had been inside it once, wrongly believing it might sell sweets. He had found a dark, faintly scented interior with displays quite unlike those in any other shop, not at all resembling an ordinary chemist's, for example. The herbalist's sold trusses for ruptures, and had a small fitting room. It offered asthma cigarettes. It dispensed delicately flavoured pastilles in slightly expensive, secret-looking packets you did not find in confectionery shops (the nearest it got to sweets). They had been no temptation even when sweets were severely rationed during the war. You asked in the herbalist's about rheumatism and arthritis cures and might be sold remedies that had been proven effective over centuries. You bought *Old Moore's Almanack*, which had forecast at the beginning of 1945 that the war would end that year but would immediately convert into a war of the rest of the world against Soviet Russia (crude depictions of Joseph Stalin, hammer and sickle, etc). The herbalist, a white-coated figure never seen waiting in the front room of his premises but brought out from the back by the bell on his door, recommended everything he sold, including what, in the world beyond his shop, would be called frenchies, but in a discreet corner of his window appeared as Ona, and on the counter inside, as in Redford's barber's shop two blocks away, was Durex. Passing this place on his walk home today Jack saw Spillar coming out.

He knew Spillar by sight, but they had never spoken, so there was no question of acknowledging him in the street. In turn, Spillar, if he recognised Jack as well as knowing all about him from his mother, ignored him. Jack had no theory or suspicion about why Spillar could have been visiting the herbalist's shop, where it was traditional to believe that anyone under fifty and not rheumatic would go for only one particular purpose. Jack's grandfather had been there to purchase some sort of electrical device to apply to his face and reactivate his muscles after a stroke. But it was assumed that few people went there for any non-medical reason apart from buying contraceptives.

Maureen wasn't just thinking she was ten, eleven, twelve days late, which might not be a fatal sign for some people. She was thinking it was ominously late for her. The arrival in the Rio of faces she recognised distracted her a little from these thoughts and fears, it was the only interesting feature of the job. You would have imagined Spillar greeting his celebrated clients with a special welcome, it would have been good for business. But he lacked business sense and the Rio remained a seedy place with dirty curtains and poor, though filling, food.

Sometimes Maureen Hollard would be struck by a desire to say, putting down a cup of tea or tomatoes on toast in front of a customer, 'I know who you are!' But she never did. The most she did was to give stars she recognised a wide and generous smile to imply that she was aware of their identity. They were very pleased with that, it did all that was necessary without involving them in tedious chat with a fan.

There was a suave, rather distant negro she was certain was the romantic pianist and singer Leslie Hutchinson, or 'Hutch'. She only doubted her guess that this model of superior sophistication was Hutch because she had never realised he might be a black man. When you heard him on the radio you could not see him, you could not tell. He didn't sing like other black singers, with Paul Robeson's power or Fats Waller's suggestive cheerfulness. On the day he came Hutch only took a pot of tea, and read a book while he poured and drank every cup, patting his forehead with a silk handkerchief. She believed she had served baked beans to Ronald Frankau, a finely dressed, slightly gruff and yet very polite upper-class man, who had crossed the road from the stage door dodging the small group of children who, even through this winter, hung about collecting autographs when the Empire was open. Mr Frankau had looked cold and spoke posh, but he did give her a small tip and left with a gracious smile. She'd heard somewhere that he was a passionate socialist, for all his stage and radio act as the calm English gentleman with naughty jokes you had to think about before you could laugh.

She took the order (not trying to be funny, she always said) of Beryl Orde the impressionist, whose name—like that of anyone else she hoped to see turning up here—featured on the playbills that week, and whose face she recognised from the *Radio Times* and the local paper. Beryl Orde had coffee and a piece of cake from the rectangular slab on the counter, which Maureen cut. She was rarely heard speaking much in her normal voice, so Maureen was quite surprised to hear she had one and did not address her in the tones of Bette Davis or Judy Garland. She had very firmly waved hair, bright eyes and a good complexion for someone who might be almost Maureen's age—perhaps you learned how to preserve your looks if you were a professional and had to? She slipped off a smart but not expensive coat and sat at her table in a grey two-piece in which—so Patsy Partridge, who had been to the show, testified—she had appeared on stage. How well these people dressed, despite all the shortages. It was as if there were a different world of fame in which you could obtain things and do things beyond the reach of ordinary people. No one famous ever went without, did they? That was a question. You heard of some who went bankrupt, or died in poverty or disgrace. But the famous did live in a special way. Maureen wished she knew how to live in a special way.

All one week she had wondered and wondered whether—well, they were on the bill, guaranteeing good houses, though people had been saying they must have fallen on hard times if they had to come and earn their living at the Empire...What she had been wondering was whether Laurel and Hardy, no less, either together or singly, would come into the café. And what they would order if they did. And how they would behave. On the Wednesday she was sure she had seen them strolling up to the stage door in heavy overcoats and scarves that partly hid their faces, a very bulky tallish man and a thinner shorter figure. But at just that moment a crawling bus blocked out all view of them. If it was them they had disappeared into the theatre when it moved on.

No, she told herself, you would never get Laurel and Hardy in the Rio Café off the High Street here, they were legends, and legends lived in other worlds. But on the Friday afternoon of the week in which they were appearing, she heard the bell on the door sound as she was about to leave the kitchen and just go round tidying and wiping the tables a little. There was only one other customer in the place at this moment, and his order was not ready—and, taking a seat facing the window with his back to the hatch and the kitchen, was this very fat man, who kept his coat on but removed a rather ordinary hat and ran a hand over thinning dark hair with grey strands in it. She could not see his face, and that was unbelievably frustrating. There were creases in his bulging neck and he was reading, she thought, an American newspaper—at least, Maureen didn't recognise it as an English one from where she stood. She felt nervous to go and ask him what he wanted in case it was Oliver Hardy. She turned back into the kitchen and told Spillar. He put down the pan of beans in his hand and looked out through the hatch very cautiously.

'I'm sure you're right. I'm sure you *are*,' he whispered.

'There ought to be a visitors' book,' she said. It was not the first time Maureen had put that to Spillar, but he had never done anything about the idea.

'See to that, will you,' he now instructed her, indicating the pan of beans he had lifted from the stove. 'And watch the toast!' Which she had to leap to, because in these few seconds of inattention one side of it was already threatening to burn. Hurriedly she pulled out the waist-level grill tray from under the gas rings and turned the bread over. When she was able to leave it and glance through the open kitchen door for a moment, she saw Spillar standing and speaking to the fat man. The one other customer, a foreigner she had seen here before and who had ordered the baked beans on toast, paid no particular attention, was reading his own newspaper and keeping himself to himself.

Maureen could not hear anything the large customer was asking or saying, only parts of Spillar's deferential responses. She believed she was hearing the man, who was 'the size of a battleship', she said later, addressing Spillar somewhat severely in a soft southern American accent. And Spillar was saying things like, 'Well, sir, if only we could...If it was anything to do with me, sir...' Then there was polite laughter, Spillar's nervous and louder than the client's. There was possibly this huge legend filling the café, and no one was measuring up to what was happening. There ought to be a camera kept somewhere (she believed there was such a thing as hidden cameras). Why had she never thought of bringing Perce's camera from home?

At this minute of wonder, Maureen Hollard was compelled to keep an eye on this toast, to keep pulling out the grill tray to see how it was getting on, and she therefore missed what exactly occurred next. All she knew was that when she managed to snatch a look through the hatch Spillar was obsequiously showing the fat man out again. Spillar was almost fawningly letting him go just like that, stepping out onto the slushy pavement with him, and illustrating with unnecessarily cheery instructions and elaborate signs the way to get somewhere.

'It was *him*, it was *him*,' he said triumphantly when he closed the door (the bell ringing its first and final farewell to Oliver Hardy) and came back. 'He was an absolute gentleman, of the old school.'

'Why didn't he stay?'

Spillar's pride at the thought that Mr Hardy had been on his premises was still too powerful for him to feel any embarrassment that he had not been able to offer him what the filmstar regarded as proper coffee, of American standard. He wondered where on earth in London establishments like his he could have hoped to get ground coffee filtered through a linen bag, and he felt he had behaved with quite extreme honour in directing him to his hated rival, Cosy Corner (though it didn't have it anyway), Mr Hardy having declined the thought of sitting too publicly in Joe Lyons's.

And Maureen profoundly resented the fact that Spillar had denied her the chance of speaking to the famous Olly, the very man, who had come into the café for five minutes just this once. She could not tell the story being able to say she had had a conversation with one half of Laurel and Hardy. Her friends said, 'Well, I would have gone out and spoken to him!' She never, ever, forgave Spillar for that. She wondered whether it was because she was just a woman and his assistant (as well as something else) and she didn't count.

She was twelve, thirteen days, a fortnight late. She had to count up carefully because she and Perce only rarely took 'rests' together these days. In fact she could not remember when the last rest had been. Nowadays Jack often worked at home on his studies on weekend afternoons, and he rarely went out on weeknights. He would either be still downstairs in the kitchen, or up in his own room. If they went up to bed early Maureen and Perce would have to forget he was in the house.

It hurt her to come to two particular conclusions. One was that she and Perce had probably not had relations for about two to three months. The second was not only a conclusion, it was a decision. Maureen decided that there was only one way of avoiding the most terrible crisis in the family. It was to make sure of having a rest or an early bedtime with Perce in the very near future. It was not going to be easy. Perce came home more and more worried. Luddon had in no way changed his superior, ambitious demeanour at work, although he had done a significantly strange thing that few people in the firm, least of all anyone on Luddon's and Perce's modest level of seniority, ever did. He had asked a few colleagues and wives who lived within range of his home round to a social evening.

Perce had not tried hard to persuade Maureen to go. He appreciated that she had a hard day's work every weekday at the Rio and probably would not enjoy it anyway. He himself did not feel in the least sociable towards Luddon. But it would have looked deliberately hostile to refuse. So he went. On his return, quite early, only about nine-twenty—but Jack seemed already well-entrenched with his books at the little card-table in his bedroom—she wondered if he felt at all like an early night? It was her sixteenth day late. But he had not come back in the right mood for the unexpected suggestion. He had a story to tell that might surprise her. Mr and Mrs Luddon had started off by serving coffee and cakes in a perfectly normal and pleasant way. Their four guests from work, the young Alan Carstairs and his wife, Perce, and an older man Perce recognised but did not know, from an office along the corridor, sat with their host and hostess in an uneasy circle in this smart but very plain sitting room in a house heavily warmed by 'Otto' coal-fuelled boilers, and conversation had been hard to make.

Then, in one of the recurring silences of which everyone was aware, Luddon cleared his throat—Perce did an imitation of the sound for Maureen—and chose a completely different topic: William and Margaret wished to tell everyone about their new-found Christian faith. The stranger from the office agreed immediately, and it appeared that he was one of a small Christian circle in the firm. So all three of them wanted to pass on their good news and invite colleagues from work to feel they could participate with them in their happiness.

Margaret Luddon said she and William had been spurred on to a renewal of faith (it was not a conversion) by hearing a South London bishop address a Christian Science gathering in the town hall. Perce and Carstairs, and Veronica Carstairs, had listened courteously, Alan Carstairs with a polite but slightly inscrutable smile that encouraged Luddon to elaborate on his spiritual experience and talk about the current ice age as possibly a divine punishment for the sins of mankind, which it should have the strength to repent and forsake. After about half an hour in which the three listened tolerantly and said that they would certainly consider what they had heard, they made excuses and left. Next morning Alan Carstairs asked Perce softly, 'Enjoy it last night? We did—no end. Anything's worth trying...I mean, if I thought it could really produce a thaw I'd abandon some of my sins. No more wanking when the wife's not looking.'

Perce granted him a smile, but did not include this part in retelling the tale to others. They went to bed early. They had the chance of a rest on the Sunday after this also, as if the first time had really restarted something. Tired the following day, Perce felt simply annoyed with himself, more than curious about why Maureen should have become so ardent again. Jack had started to spend some evenings revising with a friend from school, Clive Garner, so that an empty house had provided his parents with some privacy.

Maureen saw their renewal of relations as a form of loyalty. It overlay her lapses with Spillar. She had never seen those as unfaithfulness, because she was not having relations with Perce at the time and was not leaving him. Now she was having marital relations again, all of that business with Spillar had ceased. She had never had any romantic feelings towards Spillar. She had merely seized with him one of the few chances life presented to her. You could say Spillar was not a bad-looking man but she did not become close to Spillar on any serious level. Neither of them ever spoke about love after these occasions (as distinct from during them). She said all this to Patsy Partridge, an eager listener to anything like this.

One far-off member of Maureen's family had been divorced, and she married the lover who had caused the divorce, who himself had been married. It was a family scandal, enough for some relations to break off visiting Rosie. So they never met 'this new one, Albert'. It continued to be a scandal, even when people said the second husband was an improvement on the first and the couple stayed together. The divorce had been painful and costly, and covered by the local papers because this divorced cousin was a well-known person in local charities where she lived. Most families had no divorces in their family tree.

Perce did not know why, two weeks later, his wife had gone to the doctor, she had not told him about the visit beforehand. When she came back she was smiling, and when he could not guess why she challenged him to try.

'What could be the best possible reason for coming home happy from the doctor's?' she said. Perce was preoccupied and perplexed.

'Did you think you had something—and you hadn't?'

'I thought I might have something—and I have!'

But she stayed on the other side of the room by the scullery door, on her way to the stove to see about their meal. She didn't come near him. Something told her that if the child was not his it would be hypocrisy to go near him at this moment. She might have been a very foolish girl, but she was not a hypocrite.

'Oh—I see...' Perce said. But still uncertainly. This big warm smile on her face. Then she told him outright.

'I'd love to have seen his face,' Patsy Partridge said.

When Jack was three, there had been some hope of a further addition to the family, more than a small hope because Maureen had entered on a course of exercises to prepare herself. But that had all ended, more than abruptly, within minutes one night, ended messily, conclusively. Fourteen, no fifteen years ago. And now there was a renewal of all the old mental attitudes to expecting, in sequence: furtive secret wondering, then surprise and a degree of consternation (after these years can we really change our settled lives to take this in?). Then pleasure, and pride, and preparation—and care. Maureen went with forms from the doctor to the offices in the council building. There would be the orange juice and the ration supplements for an expectant mother. What to tell Jack, or rather when? Let him guess when she began to put on a lot of weight? He might never guess. He did not look at his parents much.

In the second week of March everyone was saying that winter had become a permanent condition of existence. In Perce's office Luddon would enter and discard his heavy coat and old wellingtons with an air of triumph. The punishment of everlasting cold was descending as he had predicted, though he never made this claim out loud at work. Maureen daily walked to the Rio with more than the usual fearful care, in case she slipped and fell in the street. She had not told Spillar yet.

There were frequent mornings on which it clearly seemed there was little hope of any customers at all. On one such freezing day she took up a position deliberately a space away from him, at the door of the kitchen, just as she had done to tell Perce at home.

'I might be having to think whether I can carry on with you here,' she began.

'I thought you *were* carrying on with me here,' Spillar said, with an affected puzzlement, sensing what Maureen might be about to divulge.

'I've had the tests—and I'm expecting,' she said.

'Phew.'

No astonishment. No exclamation mark. Spillar had always believed he could pass the parcel back to Maureen's husband if anything like this should happen.

He made a big point of getting it clear with Maureen that he was taking precautions every time, it would not be his fault or responsibility if anything went wrong.

'Does he know?'

'Yes.'

There was a pause in which he obviously expected Maureen to say more than that.

'I'm not saying it's you, I'd be certain of that if it was,' Maureen assured Spillar. He heard it as an avowal that activity did still go on with Perce, and it sent waves of relief over him at the horrors avoided if Maureen was sincere and stuck to that conclusion (of course you never knew with women).

Spillar fixed with a strong look the tall, blonde, well-shaped woman in her early forties who had been his 'mistress' as he liked to think of it, ever since one hot day after closing last July. And he was possessed by a strange thought that had never occurred to him at any other time than this, when he was naturally interested in shifting the blame onto someone else: could there even be anyone extra, apart from her husband, with whom Maureen had—?

'Well...I've got to congratulate you, haven't I?' he said, with an awkward, limited grin.

'I suppose so, yes.' She did not smile. For these moments all her intrigued happiness about expecting had receded.

'And the café's going to lose you, then.'

'Yes, I'm afraid I can't stay much longer, Bob.'

It was a rarity for Maureen to call her employer 'Bob'. Anything she called out to attract his attention within the hearing of customers would be preceded by 'Mr Spillar'. 'Bob' was for sexual intercourse only; and if anything more than one-dimensional ever occurred to Spillar about these sexual occurrences, it was his wondering why no woman apart from Maureen had ever called him by his name when they were on the job. Bob Spillar would go on from now telling himself to be more than cautious in the future, at the age of fifty-one a lonely man, a bit of a lad who couldn't settle down, who had no property (unless you counted this rented café), who had no prospects, a hand-to-mouth businessman, a rogue who had never loved or valued anything worthwhile in his life, saving some few sentimental memories.

'You're not packing it in right away? What would I do? I'd miss you. I hope you're all right?'

'I'm all right. I'll leave at the end of the month, after Easter, if that suits.'

'That's—that's—' he looked at last year's calendar, which was all he had on the wall, and worked it out from a little box of important dates in the previous and subsequent years—'that's May?'

'I think it is.'

It was still only twenty past ten, but they expected no morning customers on a day like this. It did not snow or rain, but with the wind the cold reached down into your lungs and liver, and froze even your wrapped-up limbs.

And yet here was somebody, Pierre-Henri Mallinot, entering tensely, for the third time in the last seven months. But it was for the last time ever.

Pierre-Henri never took off his outer garment in the café—or any other public place when it was cold enough outside to wear one. On the coldest days, like today, he sat there hunched up in a huge, heavy green coat which did not seem to fit him very well, though Maureen supposed it kept him warm. People who keep their coats on indoors prove they are uncomfortable where they are, and are ready to leave at any necessary moment. Pierre-Henri actually did feel he might need, one day, to make an exit from one of these places at some speed.

7

And then—

In the middle of the week after that, the Hollards' telephone was installed. There were no telephones for four houses to their left and six to their right. Their immediate next-door neighbour, Harry Foster, said he was thinking about one but couldn't afford it yet. His wife Millie was very anxious to have one, and Perce's theory was that a bit of jealousy in Harry about how his wife might use it was convincing Harry that he would deny her the chance.

There was a custom, or perhaps it was a rule, that you were given very little length of flex inside the house. So the receiver had to sit on a table or shelf in one place, usually in the hall near the front door because that was near the telegraph poles out in the street. But Perce Hollard, who obtained an afternoon off in order to supervise the complicated installation, asked the engineer if he might 'buy' an extra length, and offered him five shillings in the shape of two grey half-crowns bearing the round hairless head of Edward VII. The man accepted the offer, and it was therefore possible to pick up the telephone on its rope-like plaited flex and take it into the front room, or the back room with the frail French windows they called the 'dining room', or halfway up the stairs. They might even manoeuvre it, in its separate pieces, cradle and receiver, between the poles supporting the banisters which ran along the short open stretch between the landing at the top of the stairs and either of the two front bedrooms; though it would miss Jack's bedroom because it was situated well back in the house. It could just reach the floor beside Perce and Maureen's double bed, but not the bedside table. 'Another shilling and it would have,' Perce said to himself. Under Perce's staid, honest surface was a realisation that extremely minor deeds of corruption helped to make life easier.

They would obviously not be in the brand-new A–K telephone directory they were issued with. In the meantime friends needed to be given their number by postcard or in a letter, unless they were connected themselves and could be rung. The Hollards sent the number to friends close at hand, or people at long distance if they felt close to them, or relatives who had no telephone themselves but might wish to contact the Hollards from a phone kiosk in case of an emergency, or a pleasant surprise to tell them about. Maureen sent it to Patsy Partridge. She found Patsy fun, a lively spirit who could be a little dangerous—which was why she saw her only at intervals.

Two evenings of silence followed.

'We can't be very popular,' Jack said. But then, almost as soon as he had spoken, 'It's ringing!' Maureen exclaimed with some excitement. 'Who do you think it is?'

'Someone for you,' Perce imagined. 'And remember you don't have to shout.'

He was used to talking quietly into office telephones, whereas at any time he went into a phone kiosk with Maureen she seemed to think you had to bellow to be heard over a distance. Now she ran down the short corridor into the hall, picked up the receiver, and proclaimed their exchange and number so clearly and proudly that Perce and Jack heard it back in the kitchen. They looked at each other and smiled.

'I thought it would be you,' Maureen was calling down the line. 'I was thinking only today that Patsy would be the sort of person to try me as soon as she knew the number. Where are you?' Maureen had not heard the heavy click of Button A being pressed in a call box. 'You're not!…I see…' She laughed. 'You won't want to be long if he's paying, will you!' More laughter. Then her voice softened. 'Patsy…Patsy, listen!' In the kitchen Perce and Jack could hear nothing of what she virtually whispered into the mouthpiece, except for the occasional repeated laugh. They did not hear her say, 'No, he doesn't know…Of course Perce knows.'

Jack was not to be told quite yet that she was expecting a baby, they had agreed. Perce said that it would have to be handled carefully. He had ruled the roost as a bright only child and his nose might be put out of joint, particularly as he was already grown up. He had these big exams soon.

'Patsy. I knew it was her!' Maureen said brightly when she came back from the hall.

'I was nearly telling you not to stand out there too long. You'll catch cold.' Perce said it with a warning look. He was showing an extra solicitude with Jack's mother which the boy thought puzzling. As if she might be an invalid. But Maureen did shiver as she sat down, and pushed herself nearer the fire.

'Patsy was telling me she'd got one of those Otto heaters in her hall,' Maureen explained. This was true, but Patsy had only said it in passing.

'Is she on the phone then?' Perce imagined Patsy standing and chatting about nothing at all in a hall like theirs.

'No.' Maureen did not say anything more than that.

Next day, they were into the third week of March, it felt as if the temperature was just as low as in the very depths of late January. It could have been just that the long, long winter was wearing Perce down, wearing everybody down. People scattered cooking salt on the pavements beyond their doorsteps, but you could still slip and fall on the spaces they didn't bother with, beyond these clearances. Then, if it snowed again the cleared spaces froze once more. Beds of snow on the roofs of cold houses froze, became ice which shifted and loosened slates during brief hours of warming sunshine. Perce went to work carrying nothing but the *Daily Telegraph* (he often perused, as he put it, the job advertisements on the bus). But Luddon had started bringing a smart brown briefcase to the office, so new that for the first few days Perce believed he could smell the leather.

Containing what? One thing it might have contained, it was true, was a stock of the thin, postcard-size, folded Christian leaflets he very occasionally set down on people's desks as they worked. That was if he thought they would be receptive to them. He did it unobtrusively, and only after whispering to them to ask permission. But it left Perce feeling uncomfortable when he and Alan Carstairs were delivered one of them at the end of one day when no one else remained in their office.

This private campaign was not referred to, except in one remark by one of the three juniors who occupied this room with Perce and Luddon—and Carstairs who sat at the side nearest to Jedleigh's inner sanctum, the small separate office where Luddon had taken his alleged proof of Perce Hollard's inefficiency. One day Dora Parsons, a bright-eyed typist given to sharp remarks, said, 'He's on his way to somewhere.' She meant a mental home. In her mind, possibly, was the eerie story of a popular entertainer who had started to introduce the live Christmas instalment of his radio show with a few words about the spirit of the season and was carried away, telling the audience that they should all take the Infant Jesus into their homes. It took a full minute before someone realised this was not in the script, signalled to the control panel to switch off the microphones, and gently escorted the enthusiast from the stage.

This was not going to happen with Luddon, because he had been quiet and discreet, never raising the topic of religion in the office, only privately. There were whole weeks when he did not give any sign at all of his new-found beliefs. Perce began to think that the religion indicated not that he was going mad, but that he was exercising a certain calculated cunning. With a purpose. When Jedleigh—who never showed any open interest in Luddon's leaflets, though he had been quietly handed one—retired in June (and this time, surely, it was definitely 'when' and not 'if') his job would surely pass to someone in this office. Perce had been taking a hopeful correspondence course in 'Shaping Your Ambitions' (breathing from the diaphragm six times daily, training yourself to remember names of people met only once) but he dreaded lest his own ambition to succeed Jedleigh would be frustrated by Luddon's cultivation of his superiors.

The Hollards had *Picture Post* delivered at home. One morning Perce took it with him to read on the bus. It was snowing yet again, fitfully. It would be a slow journey and he could do with some extra reading. He was also tired. He and Maureen had still another early bedtime the night before, because the nurse and receptionist at the doctor's surgery had informed Maureen that it was perfectly all right to continue 'normal husband-and-wife relations' during the first two or three months of pregnancy. This morning Perce, wanting light reading, opened *Picture Post* first.

In the middle there were four of five pages of pictures of a large international conference of businessmen, politicians and trades unionists beside a Swiss lake. There was apparently a move afoot, inspired by an American Christian, to bring industry, business and workers together, meeting each other in a friendly way in agreeable surroundings to sort out all their differences; which at any time these days seemed stark, fierce and beyond solution. Besides, the world was in a poor condition morally and a worldwide movement to improve behaviour on Christian lines could do a power of good. That was what the participants thought, at least, though *Picture Post* did not necessarily agree with them. The article accompanying the photographs, and even the captions under them, were thoroughly critical.

As he started to read these pages Perce Hollard felt an intrinsic sympathy with those who wanted to reduce conflict, whatever they believed. There was an anti-communist element in this movement, and he approved of that. What Winston Churchill had said about an 'Iron Curtain' threatening the world was a very true warning. What was wrong with bringing people together and getting them to talk to one another? In these photographs the trades union leaders were as immaculately dressed as the powerful industrialists they sat with at dinner; and besides, there were no wine bottles or glasses on the table, another very good thing.

Then he saw one large photograph of a group of bosses and trade unionists chatting in a circle of hotel armchairs round a huge fire in a sumptuous hall. The white flames roared wildly in the centre of this black-and-white picture. And (but the bus was shuddering and shaking, so he couldn't be sure at first) wasn't that Sir Rigby Armstrong sitting there? His own boss? It was. Sir Rigby was leaning forward listening to the conversation in the group exactly as he had leaned forward to scrutinise Perce in his top-floor office some weeks ago. With a fire of the same dimensions.

'From l. to r.,' the caption said. 'In the Grand Lounge after dinner, an affluent shipping magnate Sir Rigby Armstrong listens to Jock Froggitt of the Scottish TUC, Stan Parsons of the TNLU and former mineowner Lord Mountacre…' Perce didn't bother with the other names. The confirmation that there was this familiar face in this circle told him something fascinating and troubling, even sinister: Luddon's Christian convictions might not present any problem when it came to Sir Rigby chairing any interviews of applicants for Jedleigh's post as chief of this department.

Now Perce wished he carried a briefcase like Luddon's. He did not wish to be seen carrying this edition of *Picture Post* into the office. Colleagues might try to borrow it for a look-through, and spot the picture. If Luddon got hold of it he might—if he didn't know all about this already—see an opportunity for himself in this pictorial information. Perce pushed the magazine down as far as he could into his deep overcoat pocket, but it was going to stick out, and anyone might express interest and ask to flick through it in the lunch break.

When he entered the room Luddon was already in his seat, the first you saw as you came in. As usual he was the earliest to arrive.

'The radiator's on again,' he observed.

The radiator had been off for three days, and someone had only yesterday produced a single-bar electric fire from somewhere. Perce went over to the dark-green sharp-edged vertical panels of the radiator and proved it; he had detected the restored warmth in the office without Luddon's information.

'I've told Miss Clissold not to stand with her back against it for too long,' Luddon added. 'It's not going to help with her complaint.'

Perce turned round and looked at Luddon hard for any sign on his face that he was intending to be funny. Luddon had not been present to hear Carstairs's latest office fantasies. Had he somehow heard about them and taken them seriously, assumed they were correct, that Miss Clissold deserved sympathy for a genuine affliction?

She was plump, about forty-five, and enjoyed moving round on any given day from office to office on any excuse, 'meeting other people'. It might be that she had documents or messages for Perce, or Luddon, or something important to put straight into Alan Carstairs's hands for Mr Jedleigh's scrutiny. Whatever she brought, Miss Clissold found an opportunity to stop for a few moments, chat, and interrupt any work going on. It was her habit while talking to stand with her bottom against the radiator, especially when it was functioning, taking all the heat for herself for several minutes. Carstairs told everyone, out of her hearing, that Miss Clissold had haemorrhoids. Not only that, but that unlike most sufferers she was actively cultivating them and they needed the warmth to grow.

Perce hung his coat on the stand in the corner, making sure the pocket from which *Picture Post* stuck out was facing the wall. A routine morning began, with the electric lights full on all the time against the freezing dullness of a day which didn't want to emerge from darkness. Luddon at his own desk indulged in characteristic noises and gestures which annoyed Perce these days, although he had not particularly noticed them until he began to see him as a rival. When he had completed an individual item of work to his satisfaction Luddon would open his lips at their left corner and issue a clicking sound, made by flapping his tongue against his upper teeth on that side—'Tck. Tck,'—when he had shuffled a set of papers together and squared them up to fit a corner of his desk surface. It was a quiet version of the sound emitted by a milk or bread delivery man to urge a bored or tired horse forward, but Luddon emitted it just once each time, congratulating himself on some trivial job well done.

Or there was the habit he started of humming, tunelessly but with a rhythm that suggested the melodies of hymns were passing through his head. Once or twice Perce nearly had to say, 'Mr Luddon, would you mind not doing that?' But he stopped himself in time. It would have shown Luddon that he was succeeding if he actually did want to get on Perce's nerves.

The tone of Luddon's greetings from his vantage point near the entrance, to anyone entering the room from another office, hinted that it was he who was the more senior occupant, not Mr Hollard—certainly not the much younger Mr Carstairs—who required the courtesy of being acknowledged. All of this, taken with Luddon's patent commendation of himself to Jedleigh, especially in that forty-five minutes spent presumptuously last month picking holes in Perce's work, left Perce feeling outplayed. Come June and Jedleigh's retirement, Luddon might have manoeuvred himself into a position where not to appoint him would seem like passing over the obvious candidate.

It was the kind of morning on which the only decent light in the universe seemed to be the electric light in their plain working office. The greyness out in the yard and in the skies above seemed to be deepening all the time. People occupied themselves in a numbed silence. At about eleven-thirty the door opened without a knock and Miss Clissold came round it carrying a thin file. From his own position Perce could not immediately see who it was had entered, only notice Carstairs giving a curious smile and hear Luddon say, 'Good morning, Miss Clissold!'

'Mr Jedleigh has been after me for something,' she said.

Behind her back Carstairs, on the other side of the room, murmured, 'Oh has he, indeed!' But Miss Clissold faced Luddon and blocked his view of Carstairs. 'He wanted it as soon as possible. This morning.' 'Lucky you,' Carstairs mouthed silently, smiling. Perce could not help reflecting that people like Miss Clissold gave people like Alan Carstairs every opportunity.

'That's all right, Miss Clissold, leave it with me and I'll see that he gets it,' Luddon suddenly affirmed. But, interestingly, Carstairs's broad smile stopped there and he raised his eyebrows, a favourite habit. To take anything in to Jedleigh's inner office was normally his own small duty as the assistant nearest to Jedleigh's door. Luddon appeared to be muscling in on it.

'If it's something he wants as urgently as that, I'm your man,' he called out, affably but with some emphasis. Miss Clissold made a funny little humorous gesture with the file, waving it around between the two men, suggesting that she had an embarrassment of offers and didn't quite know what to do. Carstairs extended a hand to receive the file with eager little beckoning movements, but she still hesitated. 'And besides, I'm nearest,' he insisted. Which he was not. Miss Clissold handed it over to him, stopped by the radiator, turned, and pressed her rear end against it.

'Things going well back there?' Carstairs asked.

'Back where?'

'Along in Mr Prodwell's department? Down at the far end?'

Dora Parsons giggled. There was in fact a Mr Prodwell, a gift to Carstairs.

'Oh well—yes. Suppose so. It's not really my affair. I've got a lot of things to see to, but—'

'Keep them flourishing.' Carstairs said quickly.

'What?'

'Nothing.'

Carstairs's face went back to the materials on his desk, on the top of which lay the file Miss Clissold had handed him. He had not been discourteous, he never was, but his humorous abruptness dislodged her from her radiator position. She looked expectantly round the others at work, took the hint, and left.

Quiet minutes later Carstairs said, 'Poor radiator.'

Two or three faces looked up. Not including Luddon's. 'Having to endure the fumes while Miss Clissold nurtures her plant life.'

Dora and Doreen looked up with wide grins. Perce Hollard and William Luddon, very properly, said nothing by way of response. You ransomed your dignity if you laughed at Carstairs at moments like this. What if Jedleigh or some other senior person were to enter the room while you were all laughing at some impropriety in office time?

At lunchtime Luddon fumbled for his own overcoat among the garments on the stand, and the *Picture Post* fell out of Perce's pocket. Perce, still at his desk, did not move. He watched Luddon with half an eye, pretending hard to be concentrating on a quarto sheet of paper in front of him. Luddon had to pick up what he had caused to drop onto the floor. There were at least three other coats on the stand from which it might have fallen. He tried to prop it against the wall at the front of the stand, but it refused to stand up.

'Perce, do you know whose this is?' he asked.

'What? Oh—'

'It's fallen out of somebody's pocket.'

'It's mine.'

'I'm sorry. I'll put it back if—'

'Please don't go to the trouble.'

Luddon was mystified by Perce's abruptness in denying him that duty, and holding out his hand for the magazine; or he pretended to be mystified.

'You might know about something in there,' Perce ventured.

'Do I? Something in this?' He looked down at the *Picture Post* which Perce was pointing at him almost accusingly. He thought Perce's attitude strange.

'Yes. Sir Rigby's on page twenty-nine.'

'Is he? I didn't—should I have seen it?'

'No. Well, I thought people would have seen it.' Perce was backtracking in embarrassment.

A pause. Luddon was still uncertain of Perce's attitude.

'May I take a look?'

'Page twenty-nine.'

Luddon found the page, opened the magazine out to a full spread on the table.

'"Left to right",' he read. 'So it is!' Quite clearly surprised. Now his interest effaced for him the oddity of Hollard's behaviour. 'Yes, I see...Well...Spending the shareholders' money in Switzerland, then. Would you mind if I borrowed this?'

'No. Go ahead.'

'Have it back after lunch?'

'No hurry.'

'Fraternising with Jock Froggitt! Beside a lake in the Alps. Ho, ho!' A deliberately hollow laugh. 'This is a funny old world!'

And it was very odd that the phrase should have stuck in Perce Hollard's mind, and come to his lips two weeks later in the odd conversation he had walking up the road one day with Harry Foster from next door. They were on very friendly, joking terms, but had not formed a friendship. Nevertheless, Perce had to tell someone about Maureen's expecting. He swore Harry to silence about it for the moment, and told him very quietly, smiling. Harry did not respond for several seconds; but then said, looking down at the pavement, 'My wife and I never do anything any more...She doesn't seem to want to—so I've lost the wish.'

Do you say 'I'm sorry to hear that'? Or 'Never mind'? Or what?

'It's a funny old world,' Perce affirmed.

8

But on the day after his father's unreported conversation with Harry Foster—

On the way to school Jack was reflecting on the difficulty of mapping the relative territories of love and sexual attraction. His love for Sylvia had been a pure and obsessed dedication. Physical passion had little part in it, and most of his peers would have understood that, even if someone like Ronnie Walston would not. Or profess not to. Some of them would have tried hard, after such a rejection, to make opportunities with other females. They might have advised Jack to transfer the kind of feelings he had for Sylvia to someone else. That would have been impossible for Jack. Later, he understood that 'love' could involve infatuated sexual obsession. But at this time he did not understand where love and sex went together, and where they existed separately.

He felt ridiculously urgent sexual ardour, without ever trying to speak to her, about a Girls' Grammar School girl seen regularly between the bus stop and Crofton County. It was the sheaf of blonde hair gathered up with a ribbon below the back of the round school hat, and it was the full blouse; but overwhelmingly it was the length and volume of her walking legs, their exposed handsomeness in the shortish blue-and-white school skirt under the navy-blue school coat. It was also the way the long substantial thighs advanced determinedly towards him along the pavement with an odd slight bandiness, and the way she set down her feet at each step. All of these features occurred in his dreams, in a long chain of strenuous night-time excitements in which 'Henrietta', as he had nicknamed her, joyfully participated. He had heard 'Henrietta' laugh once or twice, and this laughter pealed and pealed in his sleeping fantasies, higher and higher and more breathless until Jack woke up with a shuddering laugh of his own that left him satisfied but ashamed of its coarse, broken-voiced timbre.

He remembered after one of these wet dreams a frivolous theory of Ronnie Walston's from a year ago: that when girls 'did it to themselves' (Jack had not realised they did) the better-looking the girl the more amazing was the result for her. Filmstars gave it away. You could see it in some of their expressions in love scenes; they were remembering their climaxes and acting them. Or even furtively doing it on the set while the cameras were running.

Had it really thawed for good now, in the last week of March, with the practice exams for Highers over, telling them nothing except that they needed to keep working, the days of judgement were on their way? It appeared to have thawed, but that had happened before. Still, when the black water filled the gutters these days it was not suddenly halted again by a fierce overnight frost. The pipes were bursting. There would be a spring after all. And here, one Saturday in the High Street, was Walston himself in the uniform of a rating, home from an early spell of compulsory punishment as a conscript in the Royal Navy, which he had somehow contrived to start early, to get it over with. He had been out in the snows on basic training during the worst of the winter, handling ship's gear early on frosty mornings, sleeping with nineteen other conscripts in draughty naval barracks on land, putting up with disgusting services food. Jack had expressed the opinion that His Majesty's Royal Navy would have an interesting time trying to absorb Walston's extraordinary personality. But Elmborough in Jack's Sixth Arts group, who had never liked

Walston while Ronnie was at school, dismissed this as naivety. 'The Navy,' he said, 'will wring out little Walston like some wretched leather glove and hang him out to dry on the rigging.'

And yet that seemed unlikely, given Walston's conversation when Jack met him today, on pavements dry again after the snow had cleared and the sun come out. The Royal Navy appeared to have passed Walston by. From his hearty manner and exuberant opening sallies Jack imagined that he would be full of stories about called-up recruits flooding into ports and finding every girl down to about the age of eleven willing and slavering. But when he voiced this theory to Walston, Ronnie shrugged and seemed to take all that as read. He went straight on, as they stood by the entrance to the Co-op in the sunshine, to suggest that he knew of a level of sexual behaviour on which the idea of such elementary and brutish satisfactions were treated with a condescending smile. For a start, young girls who knew very little but were happy to provide a lot—they grew on trees, they were out. In the second place, easily-obtained lower-class girls were emphatically out.

What Walston knew about, and preferred, was to do with delicacy and 'class' of another kind. It involved practices you only learned about from experienced and expert older women who used a developed subtlety which few boys of eighteen—or nineteen, or twenty—could possibly be acquainted with. Techniques. Instruments. Substances. Atmospheres. He gave no concrete examples. He was not explicit, even if he was insidiously convincing. Walston's activity was, to Jack Hollard anyway, a vision of unearthly sophistication, vouchsafed through purple clouds constantly parting and closing again. In its decadent style it waited in the scented recesses behind the ultimate herbalists' shops. It was an illicit alternative to the coarse world of clumsy hands rooting in the school underwear, or the safe rubber to be extracted from inside the girl before it slipped.

Walston's pleasure realm had a refined and corrupt elegance which existed outside the range of day-to-day existence. This mode of living surely never culminated in the trusses, potions and ointments in the bedside cabinets of the aged, served by this herbalist's premises; or, for that matter, the bedroom drawers of the conventionally married. Walston's sex had its own special quality and dignity, a conception of what it was worth being alive for that virtually amounted to an aesthetic. It was an appreciation of varieties of scented exquisiteness that Jack could not begin to imagine.

'I'm heading for the library,' Ronnie added, as they realised they were not going in the same direction. 'I'm onto the 1890s and what the French writers and artists were doing around then.' Whatever the Royal Navy was doing to, or for, Ronnie Walston had so far left little impression. 'I don't suppose for a moment they'll have the best material on the public shelves. But I can give it a try.'

That side of Walston was unexpected, but so was the development of some other people who had left school before Jack, and Clive Garner, and Terry Arkley, and Tim Elmborough and the others. On Monday morning in the school library they compared items of knowledge on this subject. There was Peters, always well-dressed in school and openly fastidious about his white collar and the creases in his trousers, who had been rejected for military service and was now a rising young trainee in clothes design; hardly 'fashion' or 'haute couture' in his case yet, but he was on his way to it. Or Fulworth, a proud and declared scoundrel, in his early teens a smoker and drinker at home, and not merely on the far side of the trees in the games field. Fulworth already dressed like a man of the world, in a pork-pie hat and tweed jacket, a barfly with gambling companions who seemed to know exactly where and at what price the best totty was to be had in an altogether cruder world than Walston's. Terry Arkley even wondered whether Fulworth hadn't already been a visitor to the VD clinic in the hospital. Visiting with his sick mother, Arkley believed he had seen Fulworth enter a small unlabelled door that gave discreet access to the department where some unmentionable afflictions were treated.

There was a general studies period twice a week, taken by the history master, Dr Proctor. It generally meant that general studies turned into diluted history. Term would end soon, so today Proctor produced one of his 'intellectual diversions'. He had the six members of Sixth Arts attempting prophecies of the future, the next half century, say, basing them on their historical knowledge and their sense of the drift of current events. Each of them had to speak on a wide topic drawn on a slip of paper from Dr Proctor's trilby hat.

Today 'The future of the great powers' had been drawn by Garner, Edwards received 'Sport,' and Clissold made some bright guesses about 'Medicine'. Arkley was fourth, and written on his slip of paper—pulled out of the hat and laboriously unfolded after he had made a show of rummaging around in it unable to find anything—was 'The future of Europe'.

'Geographically, Europe will still be here in fifty years' time,' Arkley predicted.

'I think we might assume that, Arkley,' Proctor said when the boy paused and laughed. Jack wondered whether it could be assumed in an atomic age. 'But in what form?'

'Sir, European civilisation began south of the Mediterranean in Egypt, then it crossed the sea to become the great ancient empires of Greece and Rome, north of that. Rome lasted quite a while, expanding in different directions, but it finally foundered under the assaults from tribes invading it from the north.' Again he stopped.

'Carry on,' Proctor urged, rather pleased with the way this was going. But there were smiles and groans round the table because Sixth Arts had heard this theory of Arkley's before. He was pretending to be reaching extempore conclusions at Proctor's prompting, but he had rehearsed these ideas months ago.

'What we ended up with after centuries of darkness was a belt of civilisation in countries stretching from Britain in the west through France and Germany to Eastern Europe and the Soviet Union. But the communist and capitalist blocs facing each other through the Iron Curtain—if Churchill allows us to look through a curtain made of iron—will in twenty years destroy each other in a nuclear war. So civilisation will move north again to more northerly countries. Cooler climates encourage more rational behaviour, as witness the social system in place in Sweden. So the civilisation of the north will survive longer than all the others put together.'

'That's not bad at all, Arkley,' Proctor said. 'Comments, Elmborough? Let's assume that we have agreed on what this term "civilisation" introduced by Arkley actually means—because that is another subject which deserves several hours to itself. We won't try to explore it now because we might get bogged down in the past, when we are hoping to fathom the future.'

Elmborough wondered whether the entire study of history wasn't bogging them down in the past, but he could not say that. He muttered something about things moving faster in the present than in previous times, communications, etc, and that war would come much faster than Arkley imagined.

Proctor shook his head. 'I fear that there will be no such war,' he said slowly.

'Fear, sir? Fear there won't be a war?' Jack asked.

'Yes, fear it,' Proctor repeated. 'Because what could come is even more frightening than war. Winston Churchill and Franklin Roosevelt underestimated Stalin at Yalta. They gave him a vast beachhead in Europe from which communism can infiltrate all the institutions of all the countries to the west. Perhaps it's already happening. In this country there are communist cells not just in political parties like the Labour Party, and throughout the trades unions, but in shops and offices of all kinds, and universities—and even schools. What could happen would be something worse than war because it would be irreversible.'

'Worse than atomic war, sir?' Jack ventured.

'Worse than atomic war.'

It was a topic on which there was no gainsaying Dr Proctor; they had sometimes tried. He passed his hat to Elmborough, who unfolded his slip and said, 'I've got "Broadcasting", sir,' with a look of consternation.

'So—tell us what will happen to broadcasting,' Proctor challenged.

'Well, sir, it's going to get worse.'

'In what way get worse? Last week you were saying what a marvellous innovation the Third Programme was. Surely that's broadcasting getting better?'

'Yes, sir, but there's talk of finding frequencies on which all sorts of dicey outfits could set up stations, and you'd get more and more Radio Luxembourgs.'

'In the first place anything of that kind done in this country would be illegal. Radio Luxembourg is recorded in London, but it has to be broadcast from Luxembourg, which limits things rather.'

'They could pass laws to make it legal to do it, sir. They've done it in America,' said Garner. 'If anything makes money, it's legalised in the end.'

'Cynic!' said Clissold.

'Go on, the two of you,' suggested Proctor to Clissold and Garner. But neither wanted to say anything more than he already had. Without answers, Proctor took up the thread himself. 'If you were right, Garner, it would mean that the BBC would have to face legalised competitors like Luxembourg, and that might be no bad thing.'

'How, sir?' said Jack, wanting to defend his friend Clive Garner's argument.

'Competition would be good for radio stations—they would be on their mettle to produce better programmes.'

'They might compete to produce worse ones to please the multitude,' Jack came back.

'So you don't have confidence in the public being able to reject rubbish?'

Jack considered that. 'It depends on whether the people producing the programmes want to give them rubbish and persuade them to like it. Appealing to the lowest common denominator. Or challenge them with something worthwhile.'

'You've not mentioned television,' Clissold said suddenly.

'Oh that's a very minor matter,' Proctor exclaimed. He relished these discussions he devised, because they gave him an opportunity which he had nowhere else of expounding his own convictions. No one contradicted him about the importance of television, which few of them had seen, except for Garner. His uncle had a television set and Garner had seen some rather good classic drama on it. 'Well,' Proctor resumed after listening to Garner explaining that television had recently given him some Shakespeare, Eugene O'Neill and *The Insect Play*, 'if we are going to extrapolate—'

'Do you recommend that, sir?' asked Arkley. 'They say it can be harmful.'

The quickness of the quiet-voiced response started laughter around the table. Dr Proctor did not see (or pretended not to see) his joke, and assumed that this was some kind of private humour he failed to appreciate. 'If we look into the future,' he continued, 'and imagine television—which I have not yet seen—on the air for six hours every day, say, instead of just ninety minutes, which I gather is what we have at the moment, there are bound to be those who argue that it should not all be left to the BBC, and there just might be people who believe television should be paid for by advertisements. That exists to some extent in the United States of America already, I believe. And that might even turn out to be a beneficial thing, in this country, if television stations are competing to produce high-quality material. In fact, shouldn't we favour increasing competition as a way of improving standards?'

Most faces round the table looked uncertain, but no one spoke before Proctor concluded his argument.

'Yet I regret to say that I think that that kind of competition is extremely unlikely to come in this country. Labour would be against it for "socialist" reasons'—that word spoken with Proctor's usual contemptuous inflection—'and one can't imagine the old squires and landowners who run the Conservative Party letting it happen. Hollard, your turn.' It was time to pass on to the next subject.

The trilby hat, the last remaining folded scrap of paper... Jack Hollard supposed this exercise, sprung on them by Dr Proctor, who was lazy without any brilliance and had not bothered to prepare anything else, forced them to think on their feet and would be helpful training for university scholarship interviews. But mostly these sessions ended in an embarrassingly, even shamingly, inconclusive way, with Proctor laying down the law in an unconvincing right-wing style and not giving Sixth Arts individuals time to develop their own arguments. 'Proctor has the special gift,' Terry Arkley said after one lesson, 'of making the most fascinating subjects as boring as buggery.'

Jack unfolded the final piece of paper and read out 'The future of the family'. Faces dropped, but Proctor smiled. He had been wondering who would draw this one. It was close to home, and would have to be treated with a degree of tact.

'Good,' he said. 'Now—I assume none of you are family men yet?' His humorous sallies were fairly rare, and always came over heavily unless Arkley thought of some suitable riposte. Now Arkley did indeed say, 'I'm waiting to find out, sir,' and Elmborough volunteered, 'You should ask Edwards, sir,' Edwards being the only one who had a regular girlfriend. Edwards did not take the suggestion particularly well. 'Well, Hollard, the future of the family. What is it?'

All of them thought first of their own families, their parents, their siblings if they had them. Each family seemed fixed and unchangeable: Jack the only child, with his two parents; Arkley with an older brother who had left home, a harassed father and crippled mother unable to leave the house without assistance; Clissold, the school's best bat, another only child, but this time with a mother hard at work in an office in town to hold their household together; Elmborough the last and only boy in a family of four where both parents had, and needed, somewhat lowly jobs; Garner and his brother driven on by a cricketing civil-servant father, captain of the parents' side while his son was at the school, who felt estranged from his whist-playing mother.

Jack began to answer falteringly, but talking sense. 'We have to start with our own families, which we can't see changing in the future in most cases. I mean, no one here is going to see their parents divorce, or for that matter have new brothers or sisters now. Also, we can't possibly say what will happen to us as individuals. We can only look at what's going on around us and make predictions from that.'

'And so?' Proctor was looking at his watch.

'I predict—that the family will have the same number of children as now, or perhaps more, as the state provides the money to keep them—'

'As the taxpayer provides it—'

'—as they are enabled to feel secure and have larger families. But larger families will produce more rebels and black sheep, because no one can get enough attention from their parents. Also, I think the family could break down a bit as the modern world develops and communications get speedier and people want to free themselves from it.'

'Ah, you think so? You don't think the taxpayer will refuse to cough up the cash to support the large families? What do others think?'

Proctor and his wife Penelope ran a two-child household. He was content to settle for this when he saw larger, more chaotic families which his own income was helping to supply with school milk.

The others thought about Hollard's prediction.

'If they've got large families themselves they won't vote against supporting them,' Garner believed.

'Who says they'll always have the chance to vote on it?' Proctor cut in, suddenly. 'Isn't there a trend against democracy and voting? The Soviet Union and its satellites in the east aren't democratic. In those countries the state will decide on the number of children people will have—the state may oblige them to have big families to outnumber us.'

'So if we become a communist country—' Arkley began.

This took Dr Proctor aback, because he was developing an argument to the effect that increasing state power fostered by the Labour government in Britain would lead to a decree forbidding large families because the money to support them would not be available. Arkley had spotted that Proctor was about to contradict himself. But the master dealt with this quite adroitly.

'If—or when—we become a communist country,' he went on, 'our geographical position, as the island on the edge of a red continent with only the Atlantic between us and America—'

'—except for Ireland,' Arkley interjected.

'Well Ireland, honestly!' Proctor was dismissive. Ireland hardly counted, on any reckoning. 'Our island geography could mean that we became the prison camp for the Union of European Socialist Republics.'

'Where forty-eight million people here would all be in prison?' Arkley proposed.

'Yes! We'd all be in prison because the country itself would be a prison. They might run down our population by forbidding us to have more than one child a family.'

As almost always with Proctor, they felt shouted down by doubtful arguments, blustered into a corner by implausible propositions which he advanced not because he believed in them but because he thought his pupils should depart challenged by what they had heard. Garner described Proctor's thinking, years later, as 'a brand of unanswerable nonsense that deadened discussion'.

The bell went, loudly.

'A convenient breaking-off point,' Proctor declared.

It was the end of the day. After a further, listless hour reading alone in the library, Jack made his way home. The house was dark, but he called out a greeting as he entered, just in case either of his parents was already home. There was no answer, and no sound of the wireless, or of activity in the kitchen, or anything else. He was glad. He liked to arrive home and be left alone, able to listen to whatever he wanted to on their radio or on his own portable, a birthday present. Proctor's discussion period had been futile, but he continued to think about his own family. He felt a kind of dispirited discomfort about his mother and father. A school-leaver at fourteen, Perce now took correspondence courses in subjects like 'Giving Your Life a Purpose' and 'Giving Energy a Direction'. Jack sometimes opened the little books in the bureau drawer and recoiled from the dinginess of their recommended disciplines: early rising, regular cold baths, smart but unpretentious clothes, clear and dignified spoken and written English.

His mother he knew to be indulgent, a useful word that was not too unkind. She had indulged him when he was a child, spent the little money she had on such small treats as were still available in wartime, and he felt grateful for her kindness, unaware of the patronage and arrogance it involved to have feelings like this about her—as about his father, to whom he felt grateful for his more severe and purposeful attitudes. She also indulged herself, she was a spendthrift when she had the opportunity, he supposed this was why she took the job in the café.

An only child, positioned, as he was, rather oddly between these two people with whom he had grown up to have few or no affinities, impatient with them and with himself, victim of a love (for Sylvia) he could not conceivably reveal to them, Jack's very different life was one of regular unease and awkwardness. All he knew was that when serious conflicts occurred he had to stand between the two. He knew he would never forget the dreadful winter teatime when his father had let snap and for some reason mocked his mother with a peculiar gesture that had once passed between Maureen and a boyfriend she had had before marrying Perce. He mentioned this much later to an older cousin who had met the young man in question, and she recognised it. Perce had raised his right forearm and the fingers of his right hand to a stiff vertical position, then performed a small slow wave by bending the four fingers of that hand a few times. 'Charlie Happleford used to wave her good-bye like that, and your mother used to wave back to him. But your dad probably did it like he was saying good-bye to her for good—because that's what Charlie did. He ditched her, in other words.'

It was still not quite dark. He would go out to the kitchen and turn on the big mains wireless on the sewing machine and find Hilversum or something, a foreign station with music at this time of day. He left his coat on the stand opposite the new telephone, also his bag of school books. When he opened the door into the kitchen, which faced east and had some of its light blocked by the garden shed and the greenhouse next door, it was dark enough to switch the light on.

Maureen, deeply asleep in her usual chair, groaned, 'Oh no!'

'Oh Christ,' he exclaimed, jumping violently. The shock of finding his mother here when he had assumed he was alone upset him, but so did realising he would not have the house to himself for an hour or two to do whatever he liked.

'You're home early,' he said, well aware of a note of resentment in his voice which he could not prevent.

'Shouldn't I be? There was nothing to do at the café. No one was coming in.'

'Spillar didn't mind?'

'He didn't have to mind. I wasn't feeling very well.'

Jack was still disappointed at losing his time alone, so his words of consolation came out falsely.

'Oh—I'm sorry to hear that.'

In the right sort of understating middle-class tone he had heard used in genteel radio plays, it was intended to show genuine sympathy.

'"I'm sorry to hear that"?' she returned, mimicking him. 'Is that all you've got to say?'

He was wounded to hear his words thrown back at him. He turned round to leave the room, switching off the light again. But he did linger at the door in the restored darkness, which gave Maureen time to be sorry about her remark.

'You can leave it on if you want to.'

There was an indifference to her own wishes in that, even though she could easily have fallen asleep again; and a selflessness about Jack's feelings. He was not to have known that she had come home to rest. Maureen didn't rise from her propped-up resting position in the armchair by a dead fire. She did undoubtedly look exhausted, he could see that, and he sat down. Arkley's sudden revelation of his own mother's illness recently came to mind.

'What's the trouble then, Mum?' He had not used the affectionate word for a long time.

'Nothing really. Just tired.'

She smiled, and he leant over and put an arm round her, another action not attempted for a long, long time. But no, she would not tell him yet. She would not reveal this secret now and surprise him too violently. She would keep to their plan of telling him when she left the café after Easter, in roughly three weeks' time.

'I ought to stir myself and get us some tea,' she said now, rearranging the disarranged hair which Jack thought exposed the lines on her face. But she did not move for another ten minutes, or longer. They both went on sitting in silence in the quickly falling darkness, in this shabby kitchen with the chairs she and Perce had had since they were married.

He rose to put the light on when he eventually heard his father's key in the front door. Perce, when he entered, was plainly anxious about something, he had a displeased and harassed look. What does it take to bring fear and trembling into ordinary lives?

'There's going to be a complete upheaval in the office,' he said. 'I don't know where it's going to leave me.'

He could see a hole opening in the ground.

9

There was no hole opening yet for Pierre-Henri Mallinot at 78 Benford Street, even when an unexpected letter arrived.

'Mr Mollie-Knot—letter for you!'

The post, which usually came before or during his English breakfast, was late one morning at Mrs Lettie Orlop's, and Pierre-Henri Mallinot had gone back upstairs to wait for the arrival of his first Saturday pupil. It was Easter Saturday, but he had three pupils to see because their parents were most determined to secure the best possible School Certificate results for them.

He had steady correspondence from his pupils' parents, but the white envelope was the first official-looking letter he had received since he had made a home for himself in Mrs Orlop's house. Though widowed and lonely, and earning the greater part of her income from her lettings to respectable gentlemen or ladies, Lettie Orlop was thankfully no great chatterer, asked few questions, and gave little away on her own side. She had lost her husband in the First World War, but never wished to speak about it and receive sympathies. She kept herself to herself, as did her rather secretive current resident, so that a letter for him was quite an event. She could not stop herself saying, 'It looks official.'

'I may have some work with the university,' he said, when he had opened the envelope. He felt he had to tell her that much, in case it worried her or caused suspicion.

The letter was an invitation to go and see Mr Hooper at the Examinations Board, in its bleak, ill-furnished office in Bloomsbury. What did Pierre-Henri expect from an English academic official like Hooper? A neat, punctilious, unsmiling coldness, he thought. In the event he was reassured and favourably impressed by the man's manner. Hooper invited him to sit down and gave him a warm and genuine smile across his cluttered desk. Any well-qualified native speaker deserved a welcome at a time when travel and exchanges were still comparatively rare, and money was short, in the long aftermath of war.

Hooper had a series of questions prepared about Pierre-Henri's education, his degree at Poitiers, his subsequent life as a local bureaucrat with minor responsibility for schools. He did not press his visitor for documents to prove his qualifications because he could easily appreciate, from the hints he dropped about constantly changing homes during the war, that personal papers could have been destroyed or lost. Yet he did ask if his visitor had a student photograph—of his graduation perhaps?—which Pierre-Henri later supplied. M. Mallinot had no acquaintance with the examining process in England, or the mainly routine meetings of examiners' panels. But he left no doubt in Hooper's mind that he could handle these matters.

Of course Pierre-Henri Mallinot was not at ease inside himself. But the small gestures of nervousness Hooper noticed were entirely understandable in a man who had endured so much. As it became clear that Hooper was interested in providing him with examining work, he relaxed a little and even impressed him with his admiration for the French spoken by British army officers with whom he had been in contact; this being a complete invention. 'It relieved me of any false assumption that the insular English were bad at languages,' he said. 'That was not our experience at all.'

He emphasised 'our' without specifying who his comrades were, and where or how this particular impression had been gained.

It crossed Hooper's mind that M. Mallinot's reticence about his resistance experience might suggest secret service connections which he was required to keep confidential to this day, perhaps even for a lifetime. And was it conceivable that Mallinot's very residence in the United Kingdom suggested an espionage mission? Not aimed at the British, he supposed, but perhaps at dubious French residents who had not entirely rejected the Vichy regime and had hung on here at the end of hostilities—too frightened and guilt-ridden to return?

In view of these small doubts he pressed Pierre-Henri to meet an examiner who had been working for the Examinations Board for some years now, to 'hear what the work involves'. In fact he was interested in having Mme Duparquet's judgement on him.

'You'll have your set of printed rules and instructions,' he told him with a smile. 'But Mme Duparquet can tell you exactly what it's all like so that you can decide. Not that you'll need any instruction, I'm sure.'

'What region of France does Madame come from?' he wondered.

'Oh, she's lived in England for over twenty years. But I think she came from somewhere rather close—Boulogne, or somewhere like that.'

That was a double reassurance; and one day Pierre-Henri came up to this same dull, ordinary little office to meet Mme Duparquet. He went with more than a little apprehension, which became fear as he walked along the corridor to Mr Hooper's room and knocked. He knew that if he was, by a one-in-a-million chance, recognised, everything was finished. His cover, his livelihood, his residence in London would become known. There was no reason at all why Mme Duparquet should know him, but he did believe in the malice of coincidence.

She turned out to be loquacious, exuberantly conscientious in telling him what was involved in being an examiner, utterly harmless, and to some extent helpful. She was also full of herself and her other work, and did not ask him questions. When Hooper casually asked her later what she thought of M. Mallinot she had next to nothing to say but seemed to have found him acceptable; so Pierre-Henri was appointed as an examiner.

Those train journeys before he crossed the Straits of Dover had been the most unnerving stages of his flight from the Charente, especially with the changes he had to make at Périgueux and Paris. He needed to be circumspect and careful, moment by moment, in each train, hoping for crowds in which he would be lost, hoping also that the little hotel he had stayed in near the Montparnasse Cemetery—a place he had spent several nights in before this—would not regard his present journey as suspicious.

Reliving these stages of his journey in his mind at Mrs Orlop's he thought he might be able to exorcise them, as it were, by jotting down in sequence what had happened. He might be able to get a better grip on everything by moving gradually from past to present. Initially he would go back to the immediate cause of his decision to leave, the days before he quietly closed the door of his home in La Tignelle and stepped out into the dawn street with his suitcase. Accordingly, 'La Tignelle—the phone calls' was what he wrote on a spare page at the back of his pocket diary.

Pierre-Henri had not expected to receive any private threats or warnings, because in post-war France people and organisations sought out their victims very publicly. Anonymous phone calls were not the style when your name might be listed prominently in a column on a front page. Therefore Pierre-Henri was surprised to have the four calls on consecutive Saturday mornings, each at the same time.

The first call was silent, an eerie silence without even any sound of breathing, and it went on despite repeated requests to the caller to identify himself. Then he rang off, abruptly, the phone slammed down as if with anger, and the call was not repeated. That could have been a error on someone's part—though they might have had the grace to speak to him—and he thought nothing more of it. But the second call came with his name and a curt greeting, though nothing more. 'Claude Derrichet?' (The full name was spelt out very slowly, as if someone official was ponderously making sure of getting it right.) 'Yes?' 'Hullo, Claude!' Then the same thing occurred, there was the sound of the phone going down emphatically and the dialling tone resuming. The third call, at the same time to the minute on a Saturday morning, added just one phrase. 'Claude Derrichet?' 'Yes?' 'Claude, we know everything about you.' Cut.

He had been regularly reading the journals which, over a year since the war ended, were still keeping up the vendetta. He read for the names of people cited as those still to be brought to justice. He read for place names. A few days after the second phone call he was reading the Parisian correspondent who pseudonymously and patriotically called himself 'François', and spotted a reference that seemed more, and worse, than a disquieting coincidence.

> Charente is one of the departments in which French patriots are currently active in bringing to light the names of those disguising with peacetime mendacity their record of wartime betrayal.
>
> They include men and women who now wear the innocent masks of humble officials and petty bureaucrats in the mayoral offices of larger towns like Angoulême or Périgueux and the neighbouring smaller communities. Patriots are at work in La Rochefoucauld, in La Tignelle, in Montbron. Traitors, we know everything about you. You are marked down for punishment.

The voice in the third phone call Pierre-Henri received had used that same phrase, 'We know everything about you'. If that was the case, Pierre-Henri said to himself, why was he not named outright in one of these publications? *Les Vérités de la Paix*, for example? Did they not have enough evidence to incriminate him? Were these perhaps just idle threats?

On the fourth Saturday the message was the same and the intention was now unmistakable. 'Claude, we know everything about you—and you will be meeting us in a few days' time.'

These calls, he learned much later, were the work of one rash member of the group pursuing his case. They were made with the simple purpose of scaring him, severely, as a first punishment. They had the effect of scaring him away. Had he stayed where he was he would have been in no less danger; but his flight emphasised his guilt and merely reinforced their determination to see the processes of justice applied. Besides, he used on the fourth occasion a phrase he immediately regretted.

'Well, who are you? And what do you want?' he shouted down the phone. 'This is the fourth time you've phoned me and—'

The caller did not put down the phone this time. He was still audibly there, though he did not say anything for a full minute. His breathing could be heard. Perhaps he was disconcerted by the strength of Pierre-Henri's response, expecting this to be a man who would tremble and be afraid. But his reply was not that of an amateur hoaxer.

'You will find out exactly who we are in a few days' time when we call for a talk with you. We are friends of someone you used to know, and we have a lot of information about your past.'

Pierre-Henri Mallinot was silenced by that. He only managed to say, 'But you have no evidence—' This was his worst mistake. It was an admission that in respect of some unnamed person there was a case to answer. So he stopped, and cursed himself for offering that degree of admission. At that point the caller did ring off.

'"Your past"?' How much would anyone know? Since moving to La Tignelle, in a region of safety, in July 1940, with his mother long dead and his father recently also departed, he had been carefully uncommunicative about his past. He had inherited from his father enough money to set up with a modest villa in this small, unknown town in the Vichy zone of France. His education had been wider and deeper than you would expect in a small-town bureaucrat. He had excellent English, for example, from his travels with his parents as a child and adolescent, and then there was the Spanish learnt in order to go to Spain in the late 1930s and make useful contacts with minor Falangist notables. It occurred to him too late in London after the war that he could have gone to General Franco's Spain instead, except that his English was superior to his Spanish and provided a better chance of earning an unobtrusive living. Then he also had a little German from his trips to that country in the same period. But that was of small use now.

After inscribing in his diary 'La Tignelle—the calls' he had written 'Trains and boat'. But before those came the planning in anticipation of his flight. And in none of his preparations until the very last moment had he allowed for the coat. On the night before leaving he remembered it, opened his wardrobe, pulled it out from under the three blankets which covered it on the wardrobe floor. He did that because as soon as he remembered it he realised that in no circumstances could he leave it there. It would incriminate him beyond any doubt if someone found the garment René had been known to wear. It had to be taken with him.

It had to be folded tightly and pressed down and covered up in his suitcase, which would make the burden heavier and leave no space for other necessities. It was possible that he could wear it in London if it became cold, because there both the wearer and the significance of the coat would be unknown. With little time before leaving he did not go to the risky trouble of disposing of it somewhere in France. He took it with him. 'The famous coats of the Green Foresters' were a known and popular symbol of the resistance in the region, but he would not dare to wear it because he would be noticed in the garment which had been the property of a taller and larger owner.

So he packed everything he needed to take, including the coat, in this one heavy case, which would need to be shifted constantly from hand to hand. The earlier he was away and up to the station in the morning, the better. He set his alarm clock and sat in his wide armchair fully dressed to sleep if he possibly could. In fact he did sleep, though for much of the time he dreamed that he was awake.

On waking at four a.m. he drank just a little coffee, spread some jam on a piece of bread and made that his breakfast, then cleared everything away tidily so as to leave no impression that he might have left in haste. After that he went upstairs and opened the shutters at his bedroom windows. None of the other upstairs shutters had been closed; Pierre-Henri lived here alone and they were never closed. When he reached out and engaged the small hooks that fastened these dark-brown wooden boards to the stone front walls of the house his care was not only due to immediate caution but out of the knowledge that he might be doing this for the last time for years. Closing the shutters in this or any house, anywhere. He assumed that if he found a place to live in hiding in London he would be opening and closing English curtains.

A very dull morning light entered, exactly the light Pierre-Henri Mallinot was glad to leave in if he had to leave at all. His home was a small detached residence which faced empty ground. It stood apart from a long terrace that turned into a street with houses on both sides a few doors up. There his footsteps began to echo, but every house he passed had its shutters closed, including the one with the lamp clamped to the wall at first-storey level, still shining. He passed the letterbox where yesterday, after a day at the office, he had posted a letter to the mairie to tell them that he would not be there today, that an aunt in a village up the line towards Paris from Périgueux had died, leaving an invalid husband whom no one would look after unless Pierre-Henri departed at once to make arrangements.

He had not underestimated the weight of this case; but he had to hurry, and with no one in the streets to see him he slung it repeatedly from left hand to right hand and back again, glad of the relief afforded by every change. He met no one at all until he walked awkwardly in through a swing door at the station and saw the ticket clerk already there.

This ticket was for a village on the far side of Paris with a name similar to that of a small township near Bordeaux. All this he had devised to conceal his real destination, which was Paris to start with; there was just a chance that later someone who asked the clerk might believe he had travelled to the village only an hour or so away. He recognised the older ticket-office man and the young uniformed porter covertly smoking a small cigar at the end of the platform in the dampish morning, but he did not know either by name, and did not think they knew his.

The short 6.12 train was on time, and occupied by as few people as he expected. He had done a test run of this route as far as Paris a few months ago in case he ever needed to do it for real. He sat in a compartment with a grandmother, or a woman of grandmotherly age, in charge of an obviously delicate child—who had no energy for misbehaviour—and smelt the buttoned upholstery and looked at the faded sepia photographs of Parisian scenes. When they did speak, very briefly, he learned that the woman was taking the boy to Périgueux on an early-in-the-day hospital visit.

He did not feel any sense of his safety increasing as he sat in the train from Périgueux to Paris. True, the people who sat with him were clearly not country or small-town persons from the Charente who might recognise his face. But if one of the well-dressed strangers soon to fill this compartment identified him, it would be somebody significant—an officer from another mayoral office, or a local politician or businessman making a longer journey. Such a figure might casually speak to him, ask him where he was going (with more luggage than usual), and remember. He might provide someone else with the information later, after Pierre-Henri had disappeared. Or—the worst of all possibilities—tell someone else, deliberately or accidentally, that they had seen him, in time to impede his departure from France. No, that was unlikely! He told himself not to be paranoid.

This landscape he gazed at from his window seat he knew fairly well from many journeys. But he looked at it today with the eyes of someone condemned to see it for the last time and focus its detail with alarmed vividness. The train rattled first through an undulating semi-industrial countryside. Then they were out of that and crossing a region of almost wild green heathland. There were numerous small stations at which they did not stop, and then a long narrow open road of tarmac; alongside which the train unaccountably slowed down without ever stopping. A cyclist in labourer's clothes and hat pedalled beside them at no great speed at all, all the time striving painfully to keep his machine upright. He was staring up all the time at the train windows. The man was in no hurry whatsoever at eight-twenty on this cloudy, empty morning, and scrutinised the faces looking out at him. Pierre-Henri turned his head away.

They increased speed again. Telegraph wires next to the track were dipping and rising, the smoke from the engine blowing in front of the windows and blocking the view, dispersing, covering it again. And here the outskirts of a familiar place, preceded by a tunnel and ramparts of sooted stone walls on which old, dusty ivy made an outdated effort to grow. Next was a park with weeping willows, and tall correct town houses, four storeys high, larger and more prosperous than anything in La Tignelle. It was Poitiers, his university city. Where even yet someone might know him. He covered his face with his hand, sank his head into an uncomfortable corner, pretended to sleep.

It was such a long, slow journey. They were passing through endless lush cattle country with frequent villages of small, low, gabled houses. A river. Plains with recurring water-towers. Pierre-Henri began to think those were like stationary gendarmes, stern reminders of something in this richly green countryside of post-war summer in a poor, afflicted land of shaken, nervous poverty, of rancour and revenges.

One particular water-tower looked up at Pierre-Henri from over the horizon of low green hills in the middle distance, its head appearing like a small tee on which a golf ball would rest. This tract was the prelude to a flatter, even greener stretch of country, stretching on and on for nearly an hour without change, a kind of steppe. He had seen it before, from this same chugging train, with its sturdy old engine and sedate, fading carriages, in the years of the great Marshal Pétain's firm-hearted France. But he had never looked at it with such attention, or with such a blend of concentration and nostalgia. Then the view began to take in villages with red-roofed cottages and square-towered churches that caught the mid-, no, the late-morning sunshine lighting small clumps or thicker circles of trees and even forests.

Until, with a sudden succession of longer and shorter tunnels, it was Paris.

Pierre-Henri had even practised, before this, getting from the Gare de Montparnasse to the little hotel near the cemetery, and on from there by Métro to the Gare du Nord; though in his practice run he had, of course, finished at the Gare du Nord, not rehearsed the entire journey on to Calais. Now, for real, he spent his night at the hotel, where he was unavoidably recognised. He made sure that its *patron* knew that he was on his way to his poor uncle's house, a relation he had deliberately mentioned before. All these few night hours he passed in Paris he felt—as always—truly swallowed up by the sheer size of the metropolis, its crowds of grey-faced, secretive-looking shabby Parisians crossing the city both ways on their way to work or on their errands on this particular day, or simply tugged by their destinies. Every one of them was reassuringly unknown to him, except—

There was this one real scare, a sudden and utterly convincing fright in the early morning on his Métro trip to the Gare du

Nord. The man seated at the far end of this not-very-full carriage could easily have been a brother of René Picquart. He was almost a double: tall, with broad, heavy shoulders, a serious but offhand air, an identical way of smoothing his hair back. When the Métro train halted for several minutes between stations, and the carriage was uncomfortably, sullenly silent, the individual coughed and cleared his throat in the way René did that. Here, at Pierre-Henri's feet in this Métro train very early in the Paris morning was René Picquart's green coat, hidden under other clothes in a large old suitcase. The throat of this Picquart was defying its owner's attempts to unblock it, he coughed again, a baritone cough from his wide chest aimed at dislodging something thick and irritating down there. And scared by this sound which had the timbre of René's voice, Pierre-Henri Mallinot felt for the handle of his suitcase, considered for a minute how he would pick it up, make for the door, operate the heavy handles.

In his diary he wrote 'Paris to Calais', but in his memory he jumped that tense morning journey. Each train had been the same sort of uneasy, wary experience. He resumed his memories with the dismal ferry from Calais to Dover, remembering the odd mixture of relief and renewed fear as he stepped aboard this little vessel. It lurched and swayed and threatened nausea even as it floated in the harbour.

Where to go on it? Where to go on board in the illogicality of this, a fine day for his frightened escape from his homeland, with this all-embracing, all-mantling space of blue above and around, a clarity exact enough to keep the disappearing coast visible and the approaching island growing, minute by minute? Under this canopy the ship rolled more emphatically in the darker, richer surrounding blue of water, a swell that sent people staggering along the deck laughing without happiness; then caused some to surrender and sit down with a bump, or descend into the interior to scan their faces converting from white to green in tilting mirrors screwed to rust-riven metal walls while a dull throbbing melody of engines droned hard behind them.

Pierre-Henri was never seasick. Not that he had known more than two or three occasions on which to test this infallibility. But at those times he just knew he had no proneness to that strange malady, which he found difficult to understand because people did not realise you had to be sensible and go the way you were tilted, then you could stay upright. You had only to relax your muscles and comply with the movement of the boat, let the sea lurch you where it wanted to. How else would the boat itself survive but by complying a little with the sea?

At first he sat on a too-narrow green-painted seat by the dipping and rising rail and watched the sea in this hazardous Channel. He watched until he felt another need, and presumed himself safe enough to risk the bar. This was a mistake, but not for any reason more important than that it propelled him into the orbit of a bore, an individual in converse with the dour barman when he arrived.

Returning holidaymakers did not go to this small and dingy corner of the lower deck; only determined drinkers patronised it on the short crossing. The bore had had it to himself until now. He was spreading his legs on a stool at the bar with his double whisky gripped in his hand. The bar appeared to be very close to the engines, and Pierre-Henri took up a place at the only table, close to a shuddering wall, painted white but steadily rusting.

'Sir!' called out the barman to Pierre-Henri, asking his order in a tone of relief at having someone else to address. But the bore cut across him with a brisk greeting.

'Going home? Or going abroad?'

'I go abroad, and hope it might be home for a while,' Pierre-Henri replied. It was an evasion, but more candid than he would have dared with almost any other interlocutor. This person, obviously English and unimportant, was the only kind he was not going to fear on this journey from presumed danger to assumed safety. Their conversation had been started by him in French, and they continued in that language.

'So you are planning to remain in England when you get there?'

This enquiry sounded too acute for Pierre-Henri's comfort.

'If I am happy I may remain for a little while.'

'Happy...'

His questioner repeated the word as if he was pondering it very deeply. Suddenly he felt safer. The man looked a thorough, determined bore, and confirmed it with that one-word reaction. But no bore is diverted from his or her concerns for long. Pierre-Henri found he had turned out of courtesy to face this man, who now got down very unsteadily from the barstool and came over to the table where he had seated himself. The barman smiled in sympathy as he received his request for a French beer.

The stranger's leisure clothes had once been expensive and, at time of purchase before the war, fresh, smart and stylish. They consisted of heavy tweed trousers, surely hot in summer, a thick jacket, a shirt for outdoors. The impression of healthy country wear was completed by the knotted silk scarf worn instead of a tie. Above the scarf came a once-handsome, now worse-for-wear though good-humoured, face belonging to someone perhaps in his late forties or early fifties. The features signalled entrenched middle-age, a liking for drink, a consciousness at heart of its owner's profound inadequacy. Yet there was something sensitive and kind in the eyes. Above the eyes was a lined forehead, and, above that, fair wavy hair with a ginger tint, quite a lot of it, with few grey hairs so far. So the customers in this bar on a British ferry, laid up and refurbished after its service at Dunkirk in 1940 and now carrying peacetime passengers, came to this: a French patriot of the extreme right escaping from retribution, and a near alcoholic from a good family with a goodish grammar school education to which he had not lived up. Cyril Baxton had settled into a menial job in a men's out-fitting department.

'Ah...Happy..."Happiness"...A crucial, and an utterly elusive, condition.'

Pierre-Henri made no reply except to give a slow repeated nod and murmur 'Yes.'

'You're French? I'm Cyril Baxton.'

'Yes, I'm French.' Pierre-Henri Mallinot did not add his name and Cyril did not ask him.

'From where in France?'

'From a little place near Paris.'

'What little place?'

'It doesn't matter. You won't have heard of it.'

He was prepared to see Cyril Baxton as harmless, but not eager to give him even fabricated details of his background. It might encourage him to ask more, and become interested, and seek acquaintance.

'All I tell myself is that "happiness" is like the crock of gold at the end of the rainbow', Cyril asserted. You walk towards it'—a deep sip of his generous inch of whisky—'and then you start to run towards it...And you are nearly there and it has completely vanished. Despite D.H. Lawrence's girl getting there.'

He said that because he somehow intuited that he was speaking to an educated man, who would understand the reference. Pierre-Henri knew enough about Ursula in *The Rainbow* to explore and qualify Baxton's interpretation. But he held back on the same principle as before.

'But that bloody lighthouse of Virginia Woolf's,' he added. 'The buggers never get there. I shall buy you a drink.' Because he was wanting one himself, he hoped that the Frenchman would offer him one instead, but there was no sign of that so he decided to be the English gentleman. Pierre-Henri could have given the Virginia Woolf assertion an outright denial—he knew that in *To the Lighthouse* the eponymous premises is reached—but merely provided a complaisant nod. Cyril Baxton took it as double agreement, to his thesis and his offer.

'A beer again. That's good of you.' He did not specify which sort.

Cyril gave the barman Pierre-Henri's order and turned back to him. 'Been thinking: do you have a personal rainbow? Or your very own lighthouse?'

The beer was a pint of English ale this time, strong, bitter and tepid.

He did not give an immediate answer, and for a minute or two they talked about the boat and the crossing as if they had strayed too near some difficult territory.

'I had my own rainbow,' Pierre-Henri was suddenly saying five minutes later, halfway down the heavy glass. 'But for the moment at least—' he gave a mournful shrug, 'it has utterly vanished.'

Baxton looked at him with surprise. Referring to the rainbow he had not used the masculine pronoun applying to arc-en-ciel but had said 'elle'. It was a risk with a reasonably good French speaker like Baxton, who caught the nuance.

'So your rainbow is a "she"? There has been a rainbow in the shape of a beautiful woman in your life?'

It was the first time in his life that Pierre-Henri had ever delivered confidences to a stranger, and he was glad to do it when it didn't matter; after all, there was no one in France to whom he could have confessed this much. The chance of confessing to a drinking companion he thought he would never see again after Victoria Station in London, or perhaps even after Dover, was one he felt some relief in taking. Not fully and properly confess, of course. Only up to a point. He replied, 'Yes. But like all rainbows she was a false phenomenon, an illusion. A "celestial illusion"—Verlaine!' Baxton nodded; perhaps spotting the reference, perhaps just pretending to.

Pierre-Henri began to set the sequence of events in order in his mind. It occurred to him that when you can speak a foreign language rather well, and are proud of that, you are liable to talk more frankly and openly in it to a native speaker than when you are using your own tongue to speak to a countryman. He had to be careful. He had fallen in love with Marcelle the moment he met her at the desk in his doctor's surgery in La Tignelle three years ago, in 1943. This attraction to her, which he believed turned into an entirely unselfish love, preceded any knowledge of her origins, her earlier life, her being a Jew. She had arrived here because she had been enabled, by influential friends, to live in an obscure town in the Marshal's France as somewhere temporarily safer for her than German-occupied Paris.

They quickly became lovers—and soon he was to find out that investigations into the Jewish population of Vichy France would require his mairie to supply names. The owners of some names would be marked down for imprisonment, or deportation. He protected her. All of that time, a good part of 1943, they met regularly, almost always in his own house unless they took risks and dined out. Because he loved her he had made a plan for Marcelle to escape if or when matters became too dangerous—it might not succeed in getting her out of the country, but whether it succeeded or not it would put him into jeopardy.

Then he discovered she had been unfaithful to him. But the protective plan, with all its hazards, had had to be put into effect. Marcelle, whose name was on a list of deportees, had been able to escape to a neutral country. But never, never had she taken any step at all to contact him since the day she left. She had vanished, a rainbow, a celestial illusion. It was heartless. And the ruthless, impenetrable silence of women was far worse than the hatred of men. Men accorded you dignity with their hatred, they made you feel worth their violence, worth attacking with fists or knouts or guns, you were the better for not being ignored, despised, written off. Left alone, your resentment of the cruel silence of a woman was no more than drops of water running off a greased surface.

'Sometimes I think that Marcelle only pretended to love me. She was several women with several sets of feelings and attitudes,' he said to himself. 'I was "cultivated" by the woman I thought loved me, cultivated for her own purposes. She told me nothing about another lover.'

But Pierre-Henri Mallinot had not said a word of this to Cyril Baxton, he had only thought it while he failed to listen to Baxton's development of his own themes, of obstinacy, of ignorant and insensitive cruelty on the part of women. As the man rambled on, through the new double whisky Pierre-Henri bought him, he gradually became completely certain that he had been right to choose care and stay silent, although nothing divulged to Baxton would necessarily have been remembered, let alone used against him. And yet, who knows? To have made himself more conspicuous in Baxton's memory might have helped him later.

The ship docked in Dover, and before saying good-bye they confirmed the validity of their original analogy: women were like beautiful rainbows tempting you with false gold. Pierre-Henri did not see Cyril Baxton in the customs shed, and wrongly believed he had left his life for ever.

10

But the first day after the Bank Holiday, back at work in the spring wind and rain—

Perce Hollard slid his soaking umbrella unhappily into the slot provided for umbrellas on the office coatstand. It would wet the hems of the coats on the pegs above, but they were wet already and it would not matter.

There would be renovations in the department starting any day now, though no one knew which day and what they would entail. Perce was still upset this morning about the way in which the information about the impending upheaval had reached him—from Luddon, as they were about to leave the office the night before. Why had Luddon been told about it first?

'How did you hear this?' Perce had asked him lamely. He could hear the vulnerable note in his voice, and feared he was giving Luddon a chance to be superior.

'Had it from Alan Carstairs.'

Carstairs had left the office by then.

'From Carstairs? Can we rely on Carstairs?' He had nothing against Carstairs, quite the contrary. But Carstairs was a somewhat junior source.

'Carstairs had it from Jedleigh. Apparently Sir Rigby wants to make it a general face-lift. To keep up with the times.' And then it did occur to Perce that Carstairs, as an informal assistant and general dogsbody to Jedleigh, would have been quite likely to know.

Not much paint had been applied to anything except government and armed forces premises during the war. In the first post-war year there had been newspaper series with pictures about offices, shops and homes that had been smartly refurbished, with an exemplary application of the will to do it. Raising morale was as important in peace as it was in wartime, the papers said. Anti-Labour newspapers insisted that it was patriotism, not socialism, that attached them to the cause of brightening up Britain.

Last autumn Fitch & Armstrong had begun its own refurbishments. The sumptuousness of Sir Rigby Armstrong's own top-floor office was the result of an extensive revamping; and then expensive work had been done on the next floor down, where colleagues appointed from Sir Rigby's extended family enjoyed big airy rooms. It had not been assumed that this process would move on down to the ground floor. But that seemed to be the plan, and there would be a deal of disruption. It would include a subtle reordering of hierarchies in certain departments, because people would be occupying different kinds of office space. Some would be promoted to better rooms, larger and more prominent desks. Others would lose out.

'Some of it will still be on War Damage,' Luddon believed.

'Not a lot, surely?' Perce suggested.

'You'd be surprised at what the firm can get out of the government. Not just rebuilding bombed premises. Window-frames on buildings that survived—like this. Doors. Renewing plaster on the ceilings.'

How did Luddon know all this? Was he guessing? Had Carstairs told him? 'Do we know anything about when?' Perce was painfully conscious of questioning a well-informed Luddon about the facts.

'There's a notice coming round.'

Merchant shipping prospects were picking up, as they needed to. Work was becoming more intense, requiring more speed and more care. The form-filling done to satisfy the Board of Trade was never-ending. The red tape! Was it really believable that in the middle of all this Sir Rigby Armstrong was declaring a total redesign of their offices, a shifting of desks and cupboards and files, a herding of people together in smaller temporary quarters, a two-week closure of the canteen for 'improvements'? It was believable. It was going to happen.

All day today it was quiet. 'The constipation before the shits,' Carstairs commented.

This slim, jaunty young fellow with the thick fair hair brushed back puzzled Perce Hollard. Carstairs looked not much older than his son Jack, but he was married, and Perce had met his thoroughly acceptable young wife Veronica that night at Luddon's. Carstairs appeared to work hard, but his attitude to the work and to personalities in the company was one of flippant disrespect. Nevertheless he appeared to be trusted by Jedleigh, and he had always been pleasant and cheerful towards Perce. Even deferential, seeking advice when he needed it.

In these wet dog days Luddon would sometimes lean back in his chair and pick up a small rubber band. He would stretch it between the thumb and the first two fingers of his right hand, and gaze out into space, and think. Occasionally he would click his teeth in the usual way as if he had come to some secret conclusion.

One lunchtime, at the end of one of these thinking sessions, when the office was completely empty of everyone except for himself and Perce, he said, 'You know, I reckon I'll try for Mr Jedleigh's post when he retires in June.'

There could not have been a more bitter moment in Perce's entire working life at Fitch & Armstrong. It was as if the job had already been offered to Luddon on a plate and no one else would even be considered. Perce thought: is he setting out to browbeat me into thinking I am too old and not eligible?

'You will?' was all Perce said.

'It'll be five years in May that I've been here,' Luddon went on, as if to himself. 'It all lies in the hands of God, of course. But I'm thinking it's time to move up or move on.'

There was absolutely no response Perce Hollard could have made to these musings that would not signal either plain hostility or an abandonment of the fight. Fight it was, Perce believed. For his own dignity, his own reassurance, for the protection of a security, of a life, threatened by Luddon's designs. The man had been so clever to outmanoeuvre him in this style…

'Wouldn't you think so?' Luddon persisted.

'Up to you,' Perce replied in a very low mutter, words he could hardly bring himself to speak.

They were interrupted by the entry, without knocking, of a uniformed messenger delivering notice of the decorations beginning on Tuesday of the following week. Luddon put out his hand for them first. He read them through and whistled before he handed the two foolscap sheets to Perce. There was to be assistance in shifting the heavier items, but staff had to move their own lighter furniture themselves. The four rooms at the front of this second-storey floor (that included Jedleigh's department) would be redecorated first, and their inhabitants temporarily accommodated in only three smaller rooms, at the back, looking down into enclosed yards, 'getting no sun all day,' Carstairs thought.

Jedleigh himself was considered too elevated to be crushed into the same space as the six people from his department and three from next door; so a cubby-hole room had been found for him in this accommodation, a little space two steps up from their level, with a glass panel in the door so that he would be able to look out and watch them. When the moving of offices began they realised how tiring it was going to be. Hollard, Luddon, Carstairs, the young junior Terry and the two girls Dora and Doreen were obliged to cart a lot of the stuff along the narrow corridor without any help from the builders, Jedleigh simply telling where they should position it at their destination. Struggling at opposite ends of unwieldy tables or desks, or on the other side of emptied cupboards, they warned each other not to go too fast, or to look out for their fingers in case they were jammed against walls or door-frames. Perce found some of Luddon's advice patronising—as if he had never carried furniture before.

Next it was going back for the drawers from inside the desks, and it was faster to carry them full than to find spaces to empty them and carry the contents separately. Of course they were crammed with years of rubbish. Perce hurt a wrist in the process, strained it under the weight of a full drawer of documents. And these seven people, plus three exiles from another office, would have to suffer cramped and farcical discomfort for at least three weeks.

Jedleigh stood with his carefully drawn personal plan on a piece of paper, telling everybody precisely where things were to go, a still point at the centre of a maelstrom of confused activity. He was at his most dapper, as if wanting to stress his dissociation from the dust and muddle and cynical laughter and frayed tempers. He wore, as always, one of his two or three almost identical suits, a red-to-russet tie with a gold pin stuck in it, a smart white shirt with cufflinks at his wrists, and a spry waistcoat, naturally. He seemed to take pleasure in informing Hollard and Luddon with a smile that they would have to share one small desk between them because a lot of furniture was going to be stowed for the moment in a storeroom along the corridor. 'Mr Carstairs over here,' he said, suggesting he work from a tiny individual table next to the steps to what Carstairs soon called 'Jedleigh's overground bunker'. The three other staff forced to join them from a different office were to sit at a small trestle table along a wall. When all the places were ready for occupation Jedleigh asked everyone to assemble and test the convenience of the arrangement.

'Now. Let us all sit down and see how it works,' he commanded merrily. And everyone sat while he surveyed them. 'You happy there, Mr Carstairs?' Carstairs closed his lips, smiled with them closed, raised his eyebrows as if he was thinking about it, then nodded rapidly and silently three or four times. 'You, Mr Hollard?' 'I'm fine, Mr Jedleigh,' Perce replied. He was not fine; he would be near enough to Luddon to smell him. 'You've done well, sir,' Luddon complimented him. After the appraisal of those three (but why ask Carstairs first?) it would have to be all right for the others. 'I've never been able to get so close to Miss Parsons before,' Carstairs now suggested; riskily, Perce thought. Looking across at Dora Parsons at the large typewriter he had just carried in for her (which weighed heavily on his tender wrist) he saw that she was in fact about one foot away from Carstairs and was wearing a thin tightly-fitting pullover. In this smaller office he was even more conscious than before of her attractiveness, conscious of her perfume, of the way she shifted her legs under the desk.

Jedleigh ignored Carstairs's remark except to renew the merry smile of moments before. He went up to his own diminished territory and closed the glass-panelled door on his resettled staff. Miss Clissold came in without knocking (as usual) and carrying a whole sheaf of papers.

This culminating event seemed too good to be true. Dora Parsons gave a laugh and covered her mouth, too obviously. Miss Clissold gave no sign of noticing, and dropped her material on Carstairs's desk as if it had been the old spacious office and not this crowded waiting room where Jedleigh, like a teacher, Perce thought, had just allocated everyone a classroom place. Carstairs looked airily at the documents, smiled, and produced from a drawer in his temporary desk a paper Miss Clissold needed in return; a piece of unexpected efficiency that surprised Perce Hollard.

'I think Mr Prodwell will require this,' he said. Miss Clissold had already taken up a traditional position against the one very narrow dark green radiator near the door, which had to warm the entire space—not that it was as cold as it had been. She ran her two empty hands down it for whatever warmth they could derive, then bounced forward to take the document he was handing her, and went out again closing the door. Carstairs's cheerful courtesy covered up for the subdued irreverence of the three juniors. The suppressed giggles turned into noisy laughter the moment she had gone. Miss Clissold must have been able to hear it.

'Please!' Luddon demanded. He did not smile or laugh at all. He gave the juniors a fierce look, and seemed to want their three new, temporary colleagues to be aware of it, and aware of his authority. Perce looked at him with a questioning expression which Alan Carstairs appeared to notice—he glanced over at Perce with raised eyebrows again, not smiling but with a trace of faint humour in the look, as if agreeing with Hollard's summing up of the situation: Luddon appeared to be trying to establish himself as the boss of the office, natural delegate of Jedleigh on earth. It could be, Perce told Maureen in the evening, that everyone would later look back on this as the day when Luddon took command.

These people were trapped shoulder-to-shoulder where they sat, hardly able to move from their seats without asking others if they might. Conversation, let alone sallies of humour with Jedleigh so near, had to be in low tones—though Perce had noticed that Jedleigh always turned a deaf ear to laughter in the normal office. Had Jedleigh objected to Carstairs, the usual cause of the laughter, he could have shifted him to another department without difficulty. Outside, the corridor was already noisy with banging and whistling from the decorators. It was virtually blocked by their ladders, planks and paint-pots. Carstairs now broke the few minutes of awkward silence after Miss Clissold's departure and Luddon's reproof. He did it with no more than a murmur, as if talking aloud to himself, not looking up from his table.

'Miss Clissold's looking a bit strained this afternoon,' he observed. 'She helped move all the stuff from Mr Prodwell's office this morning.' This was a fact; but Carstairs was not expressing any sympathy. 'All that lugging of furniture…' he continued. 'No fun with her complaint.'

'I didn't think it was a complaint,' Dora said, just as quietly. 'I thought she was *growing* them.'

'So she is. So she is!' Carstairs said grimly. 'But she's been a victim of her own success. They're far too developed for her to cope with.'

One of the three staff temporarily housed with them asked Dora what they were talking about, and Dora laughed. Luddon looked even more disapproving. 'We think that lady's got haemorrhoids,' Dora explained. 'From warming her—warming herself on the radiators in all the offices she goes to.'

Carstairs looked so concerned and serious that the new people still wondered whether this was a joke at all.

'Haemorrhoids can drop at any moment,' he said. Everyone in the room was listening, because they couldn't do otherwise. 'She was helping Mr Prodwell to move his huge desk a few doors along the corridor, and all the time they were teetering on the brink!' Luddon was trying to send a look of deep displeasure in Carstairs's direction, and failing to catch his eye. 'When she went back to shift something else they suddenly dropped and unrolled—right down the corridor. Like a Turkish stair carpet. Some people thought they *were* a carpet. She had to retrace her steps winding them in again. The end had got tangled up with a stepladder. The builder complained to Jedleigh—' who at this point appeared at the door of his tiny inner room, seemed to forget why he had come out, and retreated again. 'The boss learned that this particular builder was shop steward for the Amalgamated Union of Builders and Allied Trades. Apparently there's the prospect of a walk-out, because rounding up escaped piles doesn't qualify as an "allied trade". Jedleigh didn't know that but he took his word for it, and referred the matter upstairs. The lift was out of order—' a fact; it had been out of commission for three hours on this difficult day, 'and the staircase was blocked with furniture. The shop steward had to get out through a window and climb down one of Miss Clissold's branches.'

None of this went back with Perce to Maureen. What he did tell her about was his horrid proximity to Luddon, and Luddon's attempt to tell off Carstairs for not concentrating on his work and for being frivolous (he did not explain further)—and how all of that made his own situation even worse. They went to bed late this night, and at three a.m. he woke up aghast at an appallingly clear and peculiar nightmare.

Perce Hollard rarely had nightmares, but when he did have one it gathered in everything from his slightest apprehensions to his profoundest fears. It would shock him with what it told him about himself, and about the thoughts that could get into his head. It usually needed some alarming event to produce what he called 'one of my bad dreams'; but this time it was just the displeasing, claustrophobic prospect of work crushed together in the crammed temporary office where Jedleigh had sat them like good children. This one was a variation on the dream he had had about Dora Parsons the week before.

Ten-thirty on a cold morning at Fitch & Armstrong, and Perce had been pitched out with other five-year-olds into a sunny yard for playtime. He had been told to remember that at twelve-fifteen (and he had learnt how to tell the time now), his mother always came and collected him at the gate in the redbrick wall which screened the yard from the road. There was a metal bar on the playground side of the gate, to control the rush of children out of the building at dinnertime or at half-past three; and another barrier on the pavement outside. It stopped you running out into the road and being trampled down by a horse pulling a cart—or even, sometimes, there might these days be one of these new motor vehicles, because Perce was five years old in 1905.

Perce walked round the first bar and found the gate open. If it was open, it must be dinnertime. He waited a minute for his mother and other mothers to arrive, but they were all strangely late. Therefore he thought he would walk part of the way home and meet her on her way to school. He passed one street corner after another but still she and the others did not appear, and when he turned up into his own street it was as empty as the rest. When he walked up to his own doorstep he was able to reach the heavy brass knocker on the door, and hammer it against its base a couple of times. He must have grown a good bit while at school that morning.

There was no answer, so he knocked again. This time the door opened, but instead of his mother there was Mr Clarkson, the doorman at Fitch & Armstrong. He was really at the firm's big front door, downstairs. He apologised to 'Nobby' Clarkson for making such a ridiculous mistake, and the doorman admitted him to the building. 'Thinking I was still in the infants' class at school, I ask you!' he observed. But Nobby only grunted. Reaching his office, he found it was now an enormous room in which everyone sat so far apart that they could not hear what each other was saying unless they used microphones or signals. It seemed years that Perce, on a small obscure desk, and Luddon far away at a much larger one, went on working, but eventually lunchtime arrived, and he found he was joining an eager crowd making for the sandwich bars and light lunch cafés of the area, walking immediately behind Dora Parsons in a very attractive long skirt of the kind beginning to be in favour with foreign fashion houses.

But on a further, closer look Dora was not wearing a long skirt, she was wearing nothing at all. It attracted no special attention from the people in the street, or his office colleagues, or from Perce himself for that matter, but Dora was completely naked. Then his son Jack was suddenly running up beside him on the pavement, eager to tell him something. 'I'm sorry,' he said to Jack, 'I've got to catch up with Miss Parsons and tell her something before you go to university.' Dimly he was believing that Dora was his newborn daughter, but he did realise that Jack had not gained his scholarship to university yet, that would be next year. 'Will you be able to keep me while I'm at university?' Jack was demanding to know, quite fiercely. Perce could give no answer except to indicate the naked, fully grown Dora in front of him, who was somehow simultaneously a naked female child. He was struggling to suggest to his son that the new baby would be expensive too. But with his inability to understand so many things turning rapidly into a panic, Perce Hollard was doing some intensive mental arithmetic, basing it on the salary he might receive if he were appointed in Jedleigh's place when the boss left in June.

There was suddenly an indefinable tension among the crowds on the pavement and Perce understood that it threatened him in particular. He had broken through into the centre of a ring of people, many of whom were strangers, but those nearest to him were close colleagues at Fitch & Armstrong. The ring encircled Perce, and the naked Dora, and Jack. The impression he received was that they had arranged themselves like this to watch some kind of contest. 'You owe it to me to keep me at university,' Jack shouted, his face red with fury. Everyone around the enclosing circle laughed, and applauded this challenge. 'But you're forgetting,' Dora Parsons called out, stepping up to Perce. She was absolutely and touchably naked, breasts, loins and all, except for a silky drape round her shoulders, as in *The Judgement of Paris*. And she was his daughter as well, which frightened him to think about when he was awake again. 'You haven't given me anything yet.' 'Yes I have,' Perce was declaring. 'I've given you all the love I have left.'

He took out a folded piece of paper from his pocket to prove it. What it showed was Jedleigh's plan for the temporary office seating. Dora looked at it when he showed it to her, and lifted her eyes to heaven. The crowd laughed loudly and coarsely and clapped hands. 'Well, I haven't given it to you yet,' he admitted. 'Because you are not even born.'

Dora Parsons covered her mouth to hold back a derisive snort of laughter at his words, and pointed a finger of accusation at him. He turned to appeal to the others, but in the front row of spectators Jedleigh was openly laughing, and next to him so was Miss Clissold, and there was Carstairs, smiling and shaking his head wisely. Then, for the first time since the dream began, he saw Luddon, in the second row of the crowd. Winking.

11

Sylvia had been in hospital for a tonsil operation when she was five, but she had never visited someone in a hospital before.

Her walk, following the signs down the long disinfected corridors and into the ward past the fearsome Sister's room, strengthened her; she was from an outside world of health and vigour. Passing the pale faces in the beds along the wall you felt you were almost a nurse or a doctor. Visiting times were short two-only-at-a-bed sessions. You waited outside for your turn, went in and said Hullo, and were greeted as if you were a surprise, her mum struggling to be bright.

It was her heart with Mum. She had always had some kind of trouble with her heart. Grandma had been the same, though she did live until she was sixty-seven. Sylvia's father and her sister always said about Mum that 'it would be her heart'. You could not say that they had not warned her, after what the doctor said, but what else was Mrs Freeman to do with a family of three all living at home to look after, until Frank, her brother, was conscripted?

With only a little money coming in from Frank in the army, and a bit from Eileen when she wasn't squandering it hopelessly on clothes ('You've got the squander bug, Eileen,' Mum sometimes told her), what Tom Freeman provided from his job at the bench in that factory simply did not add up to enough. So Rebecca Freeman had to go out cleaning, up to town by tram on a workman's fare early in the morning.

That tonsil operation, at five. Almost the earliest memory of Sylvia's life. Before it, all the coughing and the colds, practically every fortnight a new bout of something or other, and no remedies from the doctor. That is, until Dr MacCullen came into the district with a bright new waiting room in what had been the flower shop at the end of the terrace. The display windows had been painted green so that patients waiting to be seen by the doctor were not visible from the street. When you went in, as Sylvia did with her mum all those years ago, you looked round the room, counted the faces, and said, 'We're next!' when the last face there at your arrival had gone into the consulting room.

'I would advise having her tonsils out,' Dr MacCullen had said to Mrs Freeman after her umpteenth visit with her youngest child. While he was persuading her that it should be got over before she started school, and assuring her that it was not hazardous and would cost nothing the way he arranged it, Sylvia played with the tortoise on the floor. From a bowl on his table he would take an orange wrapped in tissue paper. Unwrapping the fruit he would set it on the polished floor, spread the half-opened tissue over it, and give it a light push. With a whisper of paper the orange rolled, and the legless, headless tortoise moved under it. Until it rolled out from under its shell and was an orange again.

The trams roared past the room in the Royal Hospital overlooking the main road; every tram braked hard for the stop opposite, and it would be bringing back her mother and father, or her grandma, to take her away again, wouldn't it? But no one came back that afternoon and evening, or the next morning either, and then she was watching ceilings spread out and change along a rattling rubber-wheeled corridor and through a shushing door where there was a flat brown table onto which she was lifted and laid down by people in white masks.

During this lifting and laying she saw what looked like a saucepan with boiling water seething out from under its square lid. She thought she saw a scissor-like instrument being taken out of it, and when a voice said, 'Keep very still, Sylvia,' she asked its mask, 'Is this having my tonsils out?' and the mask truthfully said, 'Yes, Sylvia,' with a surprised little laugh at this precocity, and fitted something soft and cool over her face. But she was suddenly very frightened, and struggled. The word 'Sylvia' went screaming round and round in her head and she was frantic in a void of coloured light that slowly steadied into the light over her head in the bed in the room with the trams again. Outside one was braking with a descending roar at the stop, and perhaps this was bringing her mum again.

'Hullo, Mum, feeling better?' she said to her mother, the one in bed this time.

'I never felt bad really. I don't know what I'm doing here. I'm a fraud if you ask me.'

'We're not asking you, Rebecca,' Dad said. 'And you're not a fraud. You had a nasty turn and you've got to rest,' he repeated, in an exchange made every day in this situation between people at a certain stage of life.

She gave a thin, doubting smile. Sylvia could see its weakness when it was turned to her to convey reassurance. For the first time ever, Sylvia experienced the desperation of having nothing to talk about when you needed to.

'Is there anyone else you know in here?' she asked: which she thought might be a clever way of encouraging Mum to cheer herself up by talking to a neighbour. Rebecca Freeman frowned disapproval.

'There's a woman I've sometimes seen on the bus,' she told Sylvia. 'Who likes to think she's twenty years younger than she is.' She did not know she was referring to Maureen Hollard's friend Patsy Partridge. Tom Freeman and Sylvia smiled at this. Mum liked to have strong opinions about people.

'Where is she?' they both asked her at the same time.

'In the last bed at the far end.'

They looked and saw a bright-faced woman, slim-looking, highly made up, inclining forward in her bed and talking vigorously to two visitors; or just to the woman, because the man sat quietly with a bored or embarrassed look and was not joining in.

The three were too far away for the Freemans to hear any of their conversation. Perce Hollard was quiet beside Patsy's bed because he did not like her, and thought she was a bad influence on Maureen. He was unhappy about being dragged along on this visit to see Patsy, who was in hospital for some woman's ailment Maureen would not disclose, a gynaecological matter, he understood, but went because he and Maureen had not been out together for many weeks, perhaps visiting the Empire in the winter had been the last time, and it would be good to go out more together with Maureen's 'event' coming. He feared the subjects Patsy might tempt Maureen to discuss.

'What do you want?'

'Oh a girl. Perce wants a girl, he's been dreaming about having a girl.' Perce had, and a week on from this he would have the dream again in a different form.

'Have you thought of a name yet?'

'Give me time! I've only just started.' They laughed. And it still did seem unbelievable. They chatted on, more loudly, with more laughter. Perce could not endure it. He made a genuine excuse of finding a lavatory and left them. The moment he had gone—

'And you honestly can't be certain who the—? Who the "you know what" is?' Even Patsy was tactful enough to lower her voice and shape her lips for this question.

Maureen shook her head.

'In the best of circles'—a joke she had with Patsy over many years—this sort of thing didn't happen. But it flattered Maureen to have Patsy's extreme interest, even if Patsy could sound flippant about it. She could forgive her because she was lively, she was fun, she always cheered her up, even now she was in hospital herself. Perce's astonishment at finding out she was expecting had given way to a quiet, supportive pleasure. That made it easier for Maureen to put out of her mind the grim knowledge that this could not be his child. But she had given up making calculations, she just allowed herself to believe that it was Perce's. Spillar was entirely content to assume that as well, and did not ask her about her progress because parental concern was definitely not in his plans.

'What if you had twins?' Patsy now said with a shriek. Patsy herself had them, Jeffrey and John, both fourteen, how time flashed by.

'Oh, my God,' Maureen said.

Then Patsy repeated something Maureen remembered having heard from her when the two of them worked in the grocer's shop together, back in 1940. 'You can have double conceptions, you know. If there's a second lot within twenty-four hours. I think I may have, with the boys.'

Maureen shook her head, she did not want to listen to all this again, it assumed she herself was capable of the sort of behaviour Patsy regarded as natural in her own life. But Patsy could not be stopped, she loved talking scandal about herself.

'It can mix with the first lot. Jeffrey's the image of Wilf in the nose and chin, but his eyes are blue and his hair is red like Ian's. And some days when he's not behaving he gives me a mischievous look that's Ian all over. On the other hand, John's been the double of Ian from the start. It's one of the reasons why twins aren't always identical. Mine certainly aren't.'

'I don't see mine being twins,' Maureen said firmly to stop all this as she saw Perce returning. She realised he was in a mood to put the visit at an end. When they walked down the ward to the door and out into the corridor they passed Sylvia Freeman sitting alone beside Rebecca, lying back tiredly in her bed, Tom Freeman having been called out to see the Sister about his wife's condition. All Maureen took in was that a strikingly mature-looking older girl was receiving some pointed remarks about her appearance from the patient, presumably her mother.

'Well, I just think you're still very young to be using lipstick, Sylvia,' she heard.

As they left the building Maureen was thinking there is not the slightest chance Jack is not Perce's, thank God. Any relations with Charlie Happleford had stopped with her engagement to the reliable Perce, who had obtained her 'on the rebound' after Charlie waved her good-bye, except there was one later occasion after she was actually married, and that must have been (how long?) at least fifteen months before Jack came into the world. Patsy had another theory about 'delayed action' which she did not believe in the very least. She'd told Perce all about Charlie and his courtship charm (except for the sexual things) and even spoken of that way he liked to 'wave' good-bye. He even did it when bidding good-bye to her for the last time, which made Maureen think he wasn't serious, but he was. This was what Perce had done during the row resulting in that conciliatory visit to see the show with the nude girls at the Empire; as if to say, 'Any more of that from you, and it's farewell for good.'

Maureen had not come to Perce on their honeymoon as a virgin, but she did not think he realised. He did come to it as a 'virgin' himself, he told her that as a precaution in case he was incompetent or ineffective, and she had to believe him. All he had done about that side of marriage was read a book which he still kept in a bedroom drawer under his socks.

When the Sister closed her door behind Tom Freeman, she began, 'I asked Nurse to send you here because there are things I feel bound to tell you—in confidence. Please sit down.'

The seat was a shabby chair borrowed from a patients' dining room somewhere in the building, the sort that fitted a heavy leather-covered square slab into a square space. If you had to carry it other than in a horizontal position anywhere, you removed this item, or it fell out and hit your knee or your foot. The entire structure seemed unsteady. The hard seat wobbled in its frame, and Tom Freeman wondered for a moment, as an overweight man, whether he might be in danger of falling through it.

'Mr Freeman!' Sister was Irish, severe in feature, with bright eyes that did not twinkle. She was grey, fiftyish. She kept her hands clasped as she spoke, resting them on a hospital folder in front of her which she had just opened. 'It's about Mrs Freeman.'

Would it be about anything else? Tom Freeman was thinking. Sister drew in breath slowly and audibly through her mouth, as if she was going to breathe it all out again with a stethoscope applied to her back. She exhaled somewhat before continuing, and it was almost a sigh of impatience. A crucifix rested on the standard cloth of her sloping bosom.

'I am very sorry to have to say,' she said, 'that the news is not a good thing at all. You have a daughter, Mr Freeman?'

'I have two daughters. And a son in the forces. One of my daughters is with me this evening.'

'A young daughter?'

'The other one is older—twenty-one.'

'Your wife badly needs to be taken care of when she goes home. She should recover quite well if she's allowed to rest, and that's where daughters can help.'

'The young one's at school, Eileen's at work.'

'No one who can stay at home for a while?'

At this point the chair cracked and collapsed under Tom Freeman, the top of its right front leg remaining in its aperture but a jagged fracture halfway down detaching it from the wooden bar that supported it. There was no space on that side of the office for him to fall onto the floor, so he hit a cupboard door and sat down, and when he shifted himself it swung open to show a display of completely empty medical bottles. Sister was on her feet and out from behind her desk, full of anxiety, full of strength as well, bending down unnecessarily to help Tom to his feet with hard hands searching for his overcoated armpits and not finding them because this big, passive man felt as irritated, angry and frightened as he had ever felt in his fifty-six years of life, and got up by himself.

'Ah, I'll fetch you a better chair, Mr Freeman.'

'No, you won't,' Tom said. With pained and scared indignation he piled up the bits of the shattered chair in a corner of Sister's office and faced her standing up for the rest of her dismal information.

On their way home Tom was upset and bad-tempered, and finally did explain about the accident with the chair, and his daughter Sylvia laughed, which hurt him. Sylvia took the news about her mother's health very casually, he thought. Her feelings for her mother resolved themselves into something closer to pity than to love, though there was a scared love for Mum when she considered it a little more. When they reached home Tom switched on the radio and sat staring at the small, dull fire while comedy shows coasted along on their familiar jokes and voices. Sylvia went immediately to their bedroom, because Eileen was still out and she would not be disturbed.

There had been a row at her mother's bedside in the hospital while her dad had been with the Sister. Wearing lipstick had been an assertion of her right to do that, she was nearly sixteen now.

'Eileen's not been encouraging you, I hope,' Mum had said, displeased that Eileen had not visited her more than the once before this, when she had been in the Royal for a week.

'No, she hasn't.' Eileen had been using lipstick for three or four years and, if anything, she had discouraged Sylvia. Eileen came in early one afternoon and found her sister applying some at the mirror in the hall. 'Whose is that?' she asked. 'Mine.' The word was uttered resentfully only when she had finished applying some to her upper lip and rubbing her lips together. 'You didn't buy it yourself?' 'I did!' (Who else would have bought it?) 'What with?' 'I saved up for it.' And Eileen supposed Sylvia could have done that. She didn't spend on anything else, and the war had persuaded people to be careful and save. Sylvia wore her school clothes out of school, they virtually had to at the Technical College because nothing else could be afforded. She still had the blue coat that she was wearing in the winter on the long walks with Jack, though it looked shorter now than when it was passed down to her. The lipstick was a small something extra.

'I think you're after the boys,' Mum said from her hospital bed. 'You don't want to get like that Vicky Medhurst. I don't know why they want her to look like that. Got up like a little dog's dinner. She'll be going the way of Sally Jennitt.'

Vicky, twelve only, lived two doors along in their row of upstairs flats above the shops, the other side of the cork factory. Sally Jennitt, who was about Eileen's age, lived farther away, on the opposite side of this increasingly busy road, but Mrs Freeman knew her mother from meeting her at the shops. Mrs Jennitt was deliberately quiet about Sally, an only daughter. Sally went to and fro between home, where she lived with her widowed mother, and some work somewhere at irregular hours, lavishly made-up, a conspicuous peroxide blonde whose gaze came wildly at you out of eyes shining behind mascara and fixing you with a look you felt you couldn't get away from but had to. One story said she was a dancer. Sylvia was horrified to think she was being compared in her sick mother's mind—as a warning—with either Vicky (younger and sillier) or Sally (several years older and mixed up in some undisclosed sinister world). Thus she said to her mum from her bedside, suddenly and nearly shouting, and she regretted it later, 'You can think what you like, I'm not being compared with Sally Jennitt!'

'I didn't compare you with Sally Jennitt, I said Vicky Medhurst was—' But there her mum broke down from exhaustion and shame at her blunder because Sylvia had been a lovely girl. Before this lipstick business. Heads turned round in the ward.

Sylvia was upset about it too, and cried in the bedroom. But she was not going to become like Sally Jennitt. She opened the mirror set in the wardrobe door for a long thoughtful stare at herself fully clothed (not like Sally Jennitt), so she ended up only looking at her face and hair. She saw beauty as a matter of face and personality, not something required of the whole body, as with a bathing-costume beauty. In a scrapbook given to her by her dad at Christmas she kept cuttings of beautiful women she would have been proud to resemble. These were black-and-white images from magazines and newspapers, but hardly any were famous. There was hardly one filmstar, for example. Some were from knitting-pattern books and very ordinary journals for women at home, nameless beauties modelling clothes or demonstrating the implementation of recipes. Straying into the servants' quarters one day the prince might spot the knitting book and demand that the young woman on the cover be summoned immediately to the court. The picture would have to be one of a model with flowing black hair because Sylvia had decided to have that, not have it cut, or set—though a girl at school with a hairdresser mother had her hair set, to everyone's admiration except for one or two teachers.

Sylvia was growing taller, much taller than her sister and her sad, sick mother. Outstripping her friends in height: Marian, who had filled out rather than grown up, Ginger who had stood still, fresh-faced and tomboyish; and Maria, the lucky Spanish beauty with the startling bright eyes, who had stayed small. Their past seemed to have been receding faster and faster after Marian's fifteenth birthday party no more than a couple of months before, when they had all privately realised they were not children any more, childhood would be left now to the twelves, elevens and tens. Besides, people were saying that the young were growing up faster these days and (they dropped their voices) maturing faster. It was the orange juice supplied to expectant mothers and the milk given out in those third-pint bottles at school.

On the Saturday after the hospital visit Sylvia began a Saturday job at the local Mandelston's, in the Ladies' Department.

It had been Eileen's idea, now that their mother was unable—for the moment at least—to get up to town for her cleaning job; the family needed the money so badly…Sylvia had not particularly enjoyed the day, mostly spent watching other young, but permanent, assistants to learn what she should be doing. The older women who worked there seemed too busy to help her very much, and the only person who was at all kind chanced to be one of the older men.

At five-thirty she left the shop and boarded a bus for home in the High Street just as Pierre-Henri Mallinot was alighting from it; and happened to sit down on the upper deck behind two boys of her own age who would have recognised her had they turned round; which they did not, being absorbed in loud and exuberant talk. Sylvia didn't recognise them at first, they were now so much bigger and noisier and more confident; but gradually she realised they were two members of her junior-school class from four long years ago. And she could easily hear that they were swapping news about girls they had known at that time, and what had happened to them; including some astonishing transformations and revelations.

'Remember what Judy Penerley was like?'

'Yes—I know what you're going to say—enormous!—right out here!' Two hands sagging under invisible breasts in front of his raincoat.

'And Mavis Tarrington—' an exhaled 'Aah!' of pleasure and comical passion, one hand outlining downwards the shape of Mavis's bosom and hips.

'Anne Loughton is much the same as she used to be…'

'She was always flirty though, she'd be worth a try. She goes to the Grammar School, doesn't she?'

'Have you seen Hazel Pointon? She's left school already. Do you remember when she used to look after the school rabbit?'

'Ronnie Walston used to say it spent most of the time under her pullover.'

'She's been seen around with Maurice Tapley.'

'Maurice Tapley? The miserable little sod who told on Derek Mann?'

Derek Mann used to hide in the high classroom converted into an improvised air-raid shelter by the building of a brick wall inside the windows; it doubled as a cloakroom. Derek and his cronies put on their gas masks, switched off the lights, and hid there to scare girls collecting their coats at the end of the day. Girls reported the problem and Maurice Tapley, who did not like Derek Mann, disclosed that people were 'saying it was Derek Mann', which he thought let him off the crime of actually telling on Derek to the fearsome Miss Merridale. And now Maurice was going round with the wonderful Hazel Pointon.

'And he's still about six inches shorter than Hazel.'

They laughed, and the subject of height awakened other observations.

'Reggie Jones is over six foot.'

'But!—But!—have you seen Sylvia Freeman lately?' the other boy offered. He dwelt on the surname to emphasise the change that had taken place in the inconspicuous Sylvia. 'You wouldn't recognise her. Remember a quiet, mousy little thing with a hair-slide? She's right up here—' raising a hand to the highest level it would reach, almost the roof of the bus, 'and higher, and she's fantastic. Not that she's got it that much in the figure. She's just fantastically tall, and beautiful with it. As if you wouldn't be allowed to speak to her. Like a bird coming out of a chrysalis.' They laughed and punched each other at this, which referred to someone's mistake answering a question in their class in the middle of the war.

Sylvia had not recognised the new voices, any more than she had the changed features, of the two boys. The voices had deepened and roughened and become quite unlike those of the small boys she now realised she had known well. But when she did recall who they were, she was astonished and overwhelmed by the praise she had overheard, even if they had thought her 'mousy' to start with. People who had turned from mischievous classmates into grown-up strangers had judged her as a stranger herself and acclaimed her beauty. She was stepping into a new existence. She had only a short journey home, and left the bus before the two boys could realise she had been sitting two rows behind them.

12

It was humid spring without any question now, which it naturally should have been at the end of April, and—

Across the road from the Rio Café the Empire was advertising the imminent operas. This was for the following week, and Maureen would have to hurry to book. She would never get Perce to go, and Jack was studying. Jack liked classical things and listened to them in his bedroom on his portable, but he would never come with his mother to an opera at the Empire. She had hinted at it in a joking way weeks before, and he had smiled and said nothing at all. So she would go alone. But why not? Her evenings were her own, weren't they?

She had no activity to stop her going. She would try the first opera, on the Monday night, and if she liked it she would go again. She liked popular things from opera on the wireless. Richard Tauber had been an opera singer, an announcer said once. 'You are my heart's delight.' Was that out of an opera?

The Monday and Tuesday nights it was *Carmen*, the Wednesday and Thursday *La Bohème*, the Friday and Saturday *La Traviata*, with matinées of all of them, school parties warmly welcome. Three big operas in one week from this touring company of 'famous singers…' She had heard of all of these operas and looked at the performers' names on the posters. She could not put a face or a voice to them if their pictures were not on the playbills; but if they were, she did not think she recognised them.

Someone standing behind her reading the names remarked to her companion, 'Who's he when he's at home' about one singer. But Maureen was respectful. The singers were famous in too high a world for her to have heard of them.

'Well, I'm off then,' she said to Perce on the night. 'What will you do?'

'I don't know.'

It was not dark yet, but he might take his usual walk when it was, as this was, a dry, mild evening.

The Empire was only respectably half full; but people were spread out so it seemed a lot. It was the first time she had been here since they had been to see the variety show with the nudes posing as famous paintings, on the night she and Perce had had the awful row and he'd done Charlie Happleford's little wave of good-bye in mockery of her as if to say 'You lost him, and you'll be losing me if you go on like this'. Looking round at this smaller audience she thought they were definitely a different sort, a posher lot and very serious about everything. The orchestra tuning up looked larger, although she couldn't see from where she was whether it was the same band with the usual Empire conductor. There was an air of extra bustle and smartness about all the proceedings. Then came the hush when the lights went down.

Why was everyone starting to clap? Nothing had happened. The curtain hadn't gone up. It was applause for the conductor, that was it. It undoubtedly was a special conductor for the opera, not the regular conductor of the Empire orchestra, Leonard Canthorpe. This was a stern, suave man in evening dress who only smiled slightly into his spotlight as he bowed, and sent his eyes up to look everywhere into the recesses of the dark, even where nobody was sitting. A roll on the drums brought the national anthem, for which everyone stood, and then sat down and resettled.

After a moment of very deep silence the orchestra struck up such a thrilling, such a familiar tune. Maureen Hollard began to love this, feeling she was not on completely strange and frightening ground. She knew *Carmen* had a beautiful Spanish heroine with a colourful temperament, and a bullfighter who fell in love with her. She did not like the idea of bullfighting, but she retained a respect for handsome men in almost any capacity. There was, as the curtain rose, a large door in a factory wall with a poster of a good-looking couple smoking cigarettes stuck onto it. And a spiral staircase up from it to a sort of bridge which did not look steady, and disappeared behind another building, possibly a barracks because there was a black-and-white picture of a cannon on its wall and a bunch of soldiers was hanging round its door.

'Is there a young corporal here?'

'That is me, my dear!'

'But I am looking for one called Don José—do you know him, please?'

'Don José? Him? We all know him.'

'You do? So will I find him here today?'

This young woman singer with plaits seemed hardly out of school. She had a piercingly clear voice, though rather shrill. A sensible young girl, she preferred not to go inside the barracks but wait for her young man to emerge—with a commanding stride and moustachioed handsomeness! He sang about his honour and his contempt for the hussies streaming out of the cigarette factory located so conveniently next to the barracks.

Maureen thought she would be able to follow everything going on from the singing, but she couldn't. It didn't really matter, though; she was content to watch, listen and dream, an expectant mother in her forties yielding to the pull of romance. Half of her knew that the scenery was shabby from being carted round from place to place, and it was too small for the famous large expanse of the Empire stage; and the costumes looked well worn. The other half of her forgot that knowledge. Here were soldiers recruited from the poor, and factory girls from the slums, and you did not have to be rich to have a romantic life.

She knew the sort Carmen was, despite her lovely voice, and didn't understand why men fell for that. It made it worse to see that this Carmen tonight was probably her own age, dressing to draw the men and obviously succeeding—because Don José was passionate at first sight. Her flower meant more than his dear mother's kiss. There was a trace of the Carmen in Patsy Partridge, and vice versa, though she should never say that of her friend.

Had she herself done anything to captivate Spillar? She drove the thought from her mind. Was Don José as honourable as he said and looked? Desert an honest country girl with plaits the moment a gypsy flings a flower at him? The fat bellowing bull-fighter had the best tunes but Carmen was right to reject him for the humble, handsome corporal, who brought out that flower and sang to it. Spillar had not been handsome, or young, or in the army. If only you had time in life to consider your alternatives and sing about them. Perhaps that was why she was so much enjoying herself. In opera there was time (you did not have it in life) to live in grand romantic ways.

The interval was for twenty minutes, so she stretched her legs and walked up the gangway among people loudly showing their knowledge and enthusiasm. No one knew her and greeted her. Jack liked his own music, his symphonies on his portable radio in his room, but perhaps the child inside her would be the really musical one? The moment she had this thought, she worried. Dangerous things were happening to the characters on the stage. It was the sort of story from which you did not expect anyone to come out happy. Opera and Shakespeare were about tragedies happening to people. Back in the luxury of the darkness she sat down with a new fear of how it would end; but an enjoyed fear.

Sure enough death turned up—or was turned up—in the cards with which the gypsy smugglers were playing after the interval. Maureen always thought the cards malicious. If you didn't try them you never learned anything, but if you did try them they would repay your faith by doing the dirty on you; like God, her cousin said. And it's no good collecting them all up and trying again. The cards don't work like that. Carmen sings it out: 'You can't avoid the things the cards are saying by shuffling them again…'

It had been in Maureen's mind to consult the cards, when she could do it alone one day, about her forthcoming baby. Here and now she decided not to. She stopped trying to follow the words now, not because it was difficult to catch them all but because she just wanted to go with the flow of the music. And suddenly, fifteen minutes into this scene, Don José has to choose between his dying mother and Carmen. Is he really going to leave her with that leering bully of a bullfighter? He is.

There was a long wait in the dark, no lights going up, heavy things shifted behind the curtain after Don José has decided that his mother comes before his gypsy love. He will return to Carmen, he swears he will. But in this last scene we are back in Seville, someone in the row behind Maureen says that. It is dazzlingly bright and bursting with people. How often can they manage to wash those costumes? Some of the ones worn by extras look both in need of a wash and as if they wouldn't survive one. The soldiers have become young bloods of the town, the gypsy girls have turned into singing orange-sellers. There is the roar of a crowd produced by half a dozen voices behind the walls of an arena. And Carmen has deserted the good-looking and finally honourable corporal for the middle-aged matador.

When Maureen opened the front door at home and entered the house (some other music was playing on Jack's radio upstairs) her mind still could not leave the last tragedy. She was not convinced that Carmen was worth it, but Don José's love when he returned—and she renounced him for that pompous man and threw back his ring—was wonderful to witness. The passion in every gesture, every nerve, every note. Surrounded by the huge crowd, and the police, and the victorious matador who looks bemused at what is happening, Carmen dies. Carmen dies. Maureen knows Jack is in, and Perce is reading the newspaper, and she can't, she won't be able to try to, convey to them anything of what she feels.

'Did you enjoy it?' Perce asked her.

'Yes.' She could barely speak.

She put the programme down on the arm of his chair for him to look at, and he even picked it up and turned the pages. Then he said, ten o'clock though it was, 'I'm going out for a walk.' Which he had not yet done.

This was a regular and agreed habit and Maureen never joined him. It was as if they had a dog he had to walk. They had never had a dog, but it was a night walk alone, for exercise, kept up from the war. Some men went out to smoke unpopular pipes, but no one in the Hollard household smoked, except for Maureen occasionally. Perce liked to take late walks because he would not be stopped in his meditations by people he knew. He sometimes met dog-walkers, but did not know any of them. One weird dog-walker he never met now because the police had become wise to him.

The man had repeatedly walked his dog, a sad and cowering whippet on a short lead, never speaking to anyone, not even giving a curt greeting to people regularly seen. Ten-thirty was his favourite hour for exercising his dog, and he wore a smart newish raincoat. Other dog-walkers gave their animals a little more freedom in these still, traffic-free night streets. This walker didn't, the whippet was always mincing along feebly at the end of the lead. The pair were never seen to return to a house in the area, but always paced away briskly in another direction after about half an hour. But before that the man would be constantly stopping to let his thin hound attend to its meagre functions, sniff a lamp-post, even savour a low garden wall. On occasions he seemed to be obliging the dog to halt and sniff even when it desired to pull away. Why? Didn't a whippet want to run? It was not even an old and frail whippet, it had a wiry, resilient look.

The activity was explained when two people in different streets complained independently to the police that this man would hold the obedient dog hard on its lead for minutes at a time and gaze through the chinks in curtains drawn in lighted rooms. Plain-clothes officers in similar smart raincoats went out with or without their own dogs (though there was one heavy police poodle involved) and watched. Despite striving to make the dog an excuse, the man was prosecuted for a peeping tom offence. There was a hole cut in his raincoat pocket and the fly-buttons had been cut from his trousers.

Perce would be reminded of this bizarre, vanished stranger when he noticed houses where the curtains were not quite closed, or did not reach the middle of the window. He would be reminded of something else, too, and feel the weight of his tin hat on his head again. A serious duty when he walked these streets as an air-raid warden during the war was to draw the attention of householders to the least chink of illumination escaping from their premises.

To allow any light to be seen could bring down prosecutions on their heads, though Perce only had the power to warn, and report if necessary. Those patrols had become thinking walks, as well as tours of inspection; the process continued tonight.

He had been taken on at Fitch & Armstrong in 1939, and it was a step up from his lowly clerical tasks in the old job. He had worked with Fitch & Armstrong 'non-stop throughout the war', as people liked to describe devoted service in an employment which gave no pain but little pleasure either. He had gone up every day on the bus through the phoney war, the blitz, the flying bombs and the V2s. The call-up age had not caught up with him, though he told himself, as a fit, cricketing and patriotic male, that he would have gone willingly if it had. Then, after the war, there had been an influx of ex-service people who were younger than Perce, like Luddon in his thirties and Carstairs at no more than twenty-two. It was Luddon with his short spell of war service who came in to block Perce's prospects of promotion. And now Maureen was expecting a baby eighteen years after Jack's birth. Perhaps a daughter on the way, or so his dreams had told him; he had told no one else in the office so far.

His future progress seemed a matter of tangled threads and dead ends. For Luddon, Perce would become a subordinate after Jedleigh had gone, assuming that Luddon was automatically in line for Jedleigh's position. To Alan Carstairs everything would seem simply funny, no use talking with Carstairs (who got on well with Jedleigh) and hinting that the young man convey Perce's hopes and fears to the chief. No use at all talking to Jedleigh, who might take against him if he put him under any pressure.

It was all much easier when he walked these streets with his head weighed down by the air-raid warden's hat, now kept upstairs at the bottom of their wardrobe. Nowadays he nearly always followed his wartime patrol route as he was doing now, turning left outside the house, right at the end of the street, right again up the parallel street, left at the top, left again down a second street, this going on to pass four blocks of terraced houses not including his own terrace. It took, at his slow pace, fourteen minutes by his watch.

He hoped that the wonder of a blacked-out real ghost city under the light of a full moon had gone for ever; but it had indeed been a wonder when you could see it. On cloudless wartime nights every detail of streets and houses was there, static as if absolutely frozen. You could read by the moon. The weird pallid, silver strangeness of it had hypnotised him, and went on to haunt Jack's imagination long after. On such nights everything had been iced with this all-pervading grey luminosity, lining every gable, entering every crevice between blocks, reaching into gardens to pick out bushes and give midnight shadows to sheds and trees. In the country you would still see landscapes under such extraordinary moonlight, but a city struck still by it was never to be seen again, and never to be forgotten.

At the end of the war it had taken Perce Hollard some time to go on this walk without slowing up, under the restored lamp-light, to look with a torch for unexploded firebombs or odd inexplicable objects lying in the middle of the road. He used to expect all back gates at the ends of these terraced blocks to be left open, to provide access to back gardens where holes were cut in fences or hedges or broken into walls so that wardens or firemen or rescue teams could pass through. The holes were repaired now, all the gates closed again, people shut off in their privacy. No short cut home. When he entered the kitchen tonight Maureen was still deep in the skimpy threepenny programme from the Empire.

She almost ran out of the Rio at a slack moment next morning to book for *La Bohème* and *La Traviata*. But not before a very curious conversation with Spillar. She had to tell someone about *Carmen*, so she revealed all her feelings about the evening before, did it the moment she arrived. Spillar listened, and nodded with a patience she was too talkative to notice; but his interest when he had a chance to speak intrigued her.

'My old mother,' was what he suddenly said, 'used to sit at the piano when I was a boy, and play some of these old opera melodies—and sing them...She had no voice. But she used to have a go.' He looked at Maureen with a strong and sad expression, asking her to take in what he had just come out with. Never had Bob Spillar said anything at all to Maureen about himself, his parents, his vanished wife—nothing, that is, except that his wife had vanished and left him to run the previous café by himself, which was why he had set up in this smaller one. 'My mother wasn't much of a pianist either, but she'd taken lessons to have something to do while she was carrying me and she got a lot of pleasure out of trying.' He said this oblivious of any effect it might have on the thoughts of the expectant mother he was addressing. It was the sort of quiet time on other days when he would propose they close the café for a while, have a coffee break, and go upstairs. But he knew that she would forbid that today. 'I can almost hear my mother now,' he said after a pause, with water visible in his eyes.

At this moment Maureen felt a peculiar rush of pity for Bob Spillar which she had never known before, and asked him one or two other things about his life. Few people ask others about their lives unless they are emotionally intimate with them, and she had only been physically intimate with Spillar, so had never bothered until now. His had apparently been an educated family, his father had been to college somewhere, and he himself was one of six, second from last, with three others who had been scholars and had done well for themselves, one even being as high as twenty-seventh in a firm of fifty-one solicitors. There had been books in the house when he was a boy, but his brothers and sisters were always grabbing the best ones. Two of them learned musical instruments, but he was never encouraged. He said he was sometimes in trouble but he did not elaborate. He had set up his businesses with his small share of his parents' money, not that he had ever been much of a success.

This being the mid-morning after the day of a matinée, the cleaners in the Empire had more to do to get it spick and span for the evening, and were coming to the Rio after turning up for a spell of earlier and longer-than-usual work. They were a noisy crowd, usually blustering in and flopping down in fours or fives, but today a group of them was followed by a solitary small, smiling, grey-haired woman who was instantly protected by the others and asked what she would like.

Sylvia Freeman's mother, called Becky by the others when she was always Rebecca at home, had been two weeks at home before she ignored the ward Sister's advice. As if she could 'take it easy at home for a while'! She was the mother of a hard-up family, she had to have a job. If it could be nearer home it would save the travelling, such a strain in the winter. On warmer days this spring she had strolled this neighbourhood wondering about offices and small industrial firms—then, on an impulse, walked into the Empire. There was a job for her there because they were changing cleaners all the time, they paid so little, they were not unionised.

This work was not much harder than cleaning at home, except that she cleaned at home on top of her hours at the Empire. All you had to do was tip up seats and poke a broom underneath them, manoeuvring sweet wrappers or discarded programmes into your dustpan. There was no vacuuming to do, that was done by others and mostly in the gangways. There was no scrubbing involved in the Royal Circle where they asked her to sweep, it was all carpeted, only the gods and the outer staircases had stone surfaces that required a periodic go with bucket and water. Nevertheless it was tiring for Rebecca Freeman, who attracted pity and friendliness for her stay in hospital and her awkward, uncomplaining smile. Maureen had begun to talk to this sociable woman who worked in the Rio and to mention her family.

'I've got the three. My boy's in the army, he's nineteen. My eldest daughter is twenty-one, no boyfriend yet, she doesn't seem to find them. The youngest is the one with the looks, she's nearly sixteen. She's had a boyfriend but nothing serious.'

There was no reason why these two woman should hit on the connection between their children. 'She's about five foot ten already, she's outgrown all of us.'

'I've only the one—so far,' Maureen said. That was all she thought she could safely say. 'A boy. He's much brighter than his parents.'

When Maureen sat down in her seat the next night she wondered whether the old cleaner could have swept under it earlier that day. She thought of Rebecca as old, but in fact they were about the same age. Maureen was as excited as she had been after the Monday night experience of *Carmen*. She saw that the woman who had been Carmen had a part in this opera. What was it like to be these people, night after night before different audiences? Surely you began to feel you led a different, romantic life yourself? The chores and routines, the scrubbing of clothes until your fingertips were scarlet and softened by the soap powder and scalding water, the mangling of garments fed and pushed and scooped up into the space between the rollers, the shaking of them, the pegging of them to the line in the back yard with pegs from the row gripped in your teeth, all of that would have disappeared or been forgotten in the continual romance of your existence. Perhaps you could, even if you were an ordinary person, find a means of charming all that away or ignoring it (like the characters on the stage)? But no, only riches could do that.

Tonight she sat in the Stalls. That was expensive of her but she wanted to be nearer everything. When she had first been brought here as a child, it was to the gods. Up endless scrubbed stone steps, round and round, the windows smaller and smaller until there were no windows and only cream-painted cold brick walls. And out into the shabby stone seats of the gods, hard on the back. The first thing you saw was the plaster ceiling opposite, from which wires with lights hung down and cherubs blew trumpets. Then you realised, at six or seven, that you were seeing the ceiling and the cherubs as if it was the floor and normal. It was not the floor. Because the floor was right down there and dreadfully distant. Where the conductor of the orchestra came out and stood was tiny. The places where the orchestra sat and played fiddles or drums were not big enough for living people. The stage far away down there was only the size of a dolls' house.

Worst of all was the horrible space at the level of your eyes in the middle of all this, the empty air in which a few thinning and flattening strands of smoke were already rising from the audience below. During the evening that became a cloud, a bed, a plateau of smoke you could almost walk on and Maureen, seven years old, started to tremble. From this came her lifelong dread of heights, anywhere, outdoors or in: the gaps between steps, the sea visible through the planks on a pier at the seaside.

To pay for her seat, both times, she had dipped into a private flower-decorated tin box in the muddled and messy food cupboard, behind the square bread bin. Her savings were hidden under the pad of cotton wool in this tin, on the top of which her housekeeping money rested; and she had taken out a pound, much more than enough to book a Stalls seat for these two performances. So she was just eight rows from the stage where the curtain going up for *La Bohème* showed a bare room where young men were shivering in a cold winter, most appropriate. There was no fuel for the stove at the back, resting against the wall of the arena brought in from the last scene of *Carmen*.

'And we'll die if we can't eat,' sang the more vigorous but less handsome of the two persons on the stage, who was the army officer from *Carmen* on Monday night. And the corporal, Don José, was the young author scribbling at the table and rubbing his hands to keep warm, except that tonight he was pale and thin—or thin-looking, because he was a good actor as well as handsome. Maureen hoped he would have more luck tonight. So as not to know the ending she had not read the second half of the programme. When you looked at the end of a library book you couldn't always tell if you were going to like it from that, because there wasn't enough information. But the end of an opera synopsis told you too much. She would wait to the end and see.

A third young man joins the first two—Maureen seemed to remember a gypsy from *Carmen*. The three warm themselves by the brief fire created when they burn the manuscript of the author's play, which is very funny and Maureen laughs while most of the people around her only smile. Now there is a fourth young man, and she can't recall what he was in *Carmen*, only that he was doing something very different. The audience behind her gasped at the delicious food that now arrives on the stage because, apparently, this young musician has poisoned an Englishman's parrot. This is quite unlike the world of soldiers, factory girls, gypsies and bullfighters in *Carmen*, but again it is a real world and very romantic at the same time. People live in it. It is not happening, as they say, on another planet. How and where would you find such a world? Only the poisoned parrot and the murderous musician strike an odder, less believable, less pleasant note.

What does ring true, though, is the knock on the door and the sick girl's plea for help. How and where would you find such a world to fall in love in? And to feel the overpowering emotion that won't have *No* or *Wait* said to it? Does this only happen to the young, and if so why didn't it happen to her when young? I am expecting a baby, which can happen to romantic lovers in books and plays, but not very often because it ends the romance side. I didn't have a romance, I just gave in to Spillar's idea. His precautions didn't work, or I must have read what Patsy Partridge called my 'moons' wrongly.

This young woman knows what she's doing. It counterbalances the forwardness of the young corporal—she means the young poet—who has not sensed how cunning a sick woman aware of her beauty can be. She came down those cigarette factory stairs and knocked on an imaginary door, and the singing, starving young poet, accidentally left alone, falls in love with the beauty dying of consumption and embroidery. She is the petite, plaited girl from the country in *Carmen*, now with rather lovely loose hair.

It was going to be love and death, Maureen felt certain. But there had to be a third thing always—love and death and youth. That was it. Your chances passed when you were too young to realise you had them. If she could only go back. There was no way to go on…But it was dreadful to think about that for more than a moment, because it would cancel out Perce and Jack and all her life after the age of twenty-three—and give her only Charlie Happleford. Was this impossibility of going back the reason why women friends and relatives of her own age mocked (a bit enviously?) the romantic ardour of the young and all its stupidities? Unless they were genuinely glad it was over? Patsy Partridge, of course, would have denied that it was over. She wondered what Patsy was really in hospital for. Not one of the ailments of advancing years, she was certain. Maureen's cousin said, 'Mother's got kidney trouble. You always get something for your last years, I wonder what mine's going to be?' Patsy never talked like that. But now her thoughts were drifting, and she wasn't paying attention to the performance.

While the Empire remained dark there was now an even-longer-than-before shifting and dropping of objects behind the curtain. And then they were in a street outside the café to which all the young men had gone. The singing stallholders were in the clothes of the citizens of Seville, slightly adjusted and supplemented to make them look like inhabitants of old Paris on Christmas Eve. That brassy Carmen was now named Musetta, and had a lovely song Maureen recognised, about people admiring her beauty as she strolled the streets. Wasn't she well on the way to being a street girl? The simple-hearted (but clever) little Mimi with the voice that reached out and up to the gods was almost lost in the colourful hubbub about the passion of the poet's friend for this noisy, overdressed woman who was just a nuisance to all her men. It was awful for Maureen to feel more like her than like Mimi for a moment…

At the end of tonight's first interval a short man wearing a ceremonial chain and accompanied by a smart, tall woman arrived conspicuously in one of the boxes, and there was muttering among the audience as the lights went down: the Mayor and Mayoress of the borough were here! Maureen had to hold up her programme in the dim light from the orchestra pit to see that it was 'outside an inn on the outskirts of Paris'. There was a door, and voices, and singing, and in a spotlight Mimi singing and pausing to cough silently. This must be some time further on, not Christmas Day. There were stories of life in that cold room, and of jealousy: 'I think he tries to see inside my dreams.'

A certain amount of jealousy is all right. In fact it's good to have it so you know there is some feeling for you left in him. But jealousy can be so exhausting. You can never be reassuring enough, and it goes on and on and gets to be about smaller and smaller things. Thank God Perce never met Spillar (but would Perce have been as jealous as he could be in the past?). The poet Rodolfo is saying goodnight to Mimi, and she to him. They are parting. But his painter friend emerges from the inn quarrelling with his loud lover, and they interrupt them. Musetta is decisive: 'I can't stand the kind of lover who behaves as if we're married.'

Meanwhile Rodolfo and Mimi seem to have agreed that their love must end: 'When the flowers come out we'll part.'

All at once, with barely any scene-changing, they are back in the freezing room at the beginning, the painter and the poet together; and they are still in love with their respective women, Mimi and Musetta. So far in these operas every woman starts with an 'M', Maureen thought: Michaela, Mimi, Musetta—oh, with the exception of Carmen. The men are apparently all upright, not always the case in life; but if love were more romantic, like this, they would be. They love the women, for all their faults and their unfaithfulness—even Mimi is unfaithful, it turns out, despite living with Rodolfo and keeping the bouquet he bought her under her pillow.

Now the four young men are finally all together in this room again, there is a lot of humour and horseplay. But suddenly Carmen—no, Musetta—is back again, and she has brought Mimi with her, and Mimi is dying. It seems it was true she went off with a rich aristocrat, and the poet was jealous. She rode with him in a grand carriage, but now she is dying she comes back to Rodolfo. What Maureen is doing this week is living with these young (or not so young) people in all the passion and glamour and dignity of their love—and seeing that the finest love has to be destroyed because, if it goes on, it is no longer particularly fine. She almost wants to leave before the end tonight, but she doesn't. She realises her thoughts are pitifully confused. She watches and listens without trying to work it all out a little more clearly. She cannot speak at all when she gets home. Jack comes in behind her and she does not ask him where he has been.

He had been tempted out early, while the evening was still light, by Clive Garner, who was also on the telephone at home. The two friends met like this when the sense of crisis about the exams now only just over two months away threatened to render them weak and dispirited. Weekends were good working times because parents were often out and revision could be done in comparative silence. Weekdays produced more tensions. Clive's parents had recently bought a television set which, for two hours every evening, jabbered without pity in the room below his bedroom study.

They walked past the Empire and Jack knew his mother would be watching the opera going on inside, *La Bohème*, but he did not mention it. They drifted along the High Street without money to spend on the one or two coffee places that stayed open in the evening. They had only some small change, and against their better natures, as Clive put it, they crossed the boundary of his long, open frontage and entered Joe's.

Joe's Arcade was For Amusement Only. Or Frustration Only, as Terry Arkley revised it. They passed the first glass cases, inside which for a penny you could briefly activate and manoeuvre a long metal arm with a closing claw to pick up a tiny toy dog or a half-a-crown from a deep bed of coloured beans. They went on past Joe himself, instinctively not catching his eye. He sat always at a raised counter dispensing change and overseeing his premises, descending to sort things out if there should be trouble. He had a habit of giving a hard, unwelcoming stare to anyone entering his arcade. In the meantime, his assumed wife circulated among the machines, or occasionally welcomed customers to her circular roll-a-penny table. She was standing hopefully by it tonight, but Jack and Clive showed little interest. They talked about her table as if she were not there, or would not hear or mind what they were saying.

'Statistically you have about the same chance of your penny coming to rest on a "12"'—thus winning a whole shilling—'as a meteorite has of landing on the Centre Court at Wimbledon,' Clive maintained.

Joe's wife understood, but a deaf ear and patience was something she applied in worse cases than this. All the same, the remark was irritating and her gaze followed Clive and Jack around the arcade. She saw and heard them both burst into laughter about another game, but she could not see which. She looked at her husband and shrugged; he went on watching them himself.

Down at the end was a game usually manned by someone they took to be Joe's daughter, a thin, tall, fierce girl of about twenty whom they had nicknamed 'Goneril' some months before. If enough players were available, and you needed about five for it to be worthwhile, everyone paid twopence and was provided with a small net on a stick, something like a shrimp net. You stood behind a circular counter, held the net out in front of you, and Goneril pressed a switch. Out of a kind of broad funnel in the centre sprayed a good number of ping pong balls. You could not move your net to try to catch them, you had to keep it still, clustered with other people's, and hope balls fell into it. More often they missed it, dropped back into the hole, and were ejected again. But when you had six you won, told Goneril, and collected sixpence.

It was entirely and absolutely a matter of chance. A rueful phrase spread around among a few school patrons of Joe's: 'It's the way the balls happen to fall'. There were variations on it. Clive Garner once said, 'My balls don't quite fall for Miss Stapleton,' the haughty headmaster's secretary, who was at first sight twenty-five and attractive but lost the love of the sixth form by complaining if they laughed too loudly near her office next to the library, their form room. But the phrase was most valuable as the expression of a stoical reaction to some reverse or misfortune—dates with girls going wrong, cricket rained off, examination failures.

There was one utterly and touchingly serious use, when Chadwick in Sixth Science reported his father's long-feared yet nevertheless sudden and shocking death by saying, 'It was all about the way the balls were fated to descend.' After that the phrase was largely discarded. It was the end of Joe's contribution to the life of Crofton County Grammar School.

Jack and Clive moved to the next gaming device, the one which they did believe offered them a small chance of winning. You had six ball bearings lined up under glass, in a channel at the side of the frame. You pulled on a worn black knob available to your right hand, and let it go, telling yourself you could vary the speed at which you caused a ball to move. The first one shot up to the top of the downward sloping deck, wavered with almost human indecision, started to wander down towards its farewell at the foot of the frame. On its arbitrary course—but the odds were against it—it hit, if you were lucky, certain electric coils, and a score registered in lights in a panel above the top of the slope. Not only that, but luck spawned luck. Hitting one coil often bounced the ball onto another. Twenty, forty, sixty. From coil to coil to coil, perhaps as much as a hundred and twenty with a single ball bearing. Three hundred would gain you a prize, five shillings, a sum which showed how rarely you could expect that amount of luck.

There was no way of diverting or influencing the ball once it was on the slope. On the wall, prominently, above every device, was the supreme law of the arcade, described by Ronnie Walston long ago as the eleventh commandment: DO NOT [THOU SHALT NOT] TILT THE MACHINE.

Clive Garner and Jack Hollard took turns when they had combined their resources to put sixpence in the slot. Clive managed eighty with his opening shot, a promising start. Jack's first ball advanced the score to only a hundred and twenty, no fault of his. Clive raised it to a hundred and eighty with the third ball. They were in with a good chance. Jack thought that an energetic shot—shooting the ball up as fast as the mechanism would permit—was the right tactic. Instead, the ball careered right round the circular top of the frame and down the left hand side hitting no coil whatsoever. Still a hundred and eighty. Clive tried a less energetic shot. The ball was desultory, indifferent. It wandered down between coils as if it didn't care. Towards the bottom it did cannon off two coils adding forty: two hundred and twenty, with one shot remaining. Jack had only to equal Clive's opening score of eighty for them to win. Why should they be denied victory?

'Up to you, Jack!' Clive said, standing aside. Jack stared at this last ball, which had to give them eighty points by hitting four coils. In these moments it was actually more deeply serious than anything in life, Sylvia Freeman, the exams, his parents, the Sixth Symphony of Gustav Mahler, soon to be broadcast on the Third Programme. Jack took the worn knob in his fingers. He felt it indecisively; then went for a strong shot. He pictured a ball that hit the top of the frame with some force, ricocheted from it, zigzagged from coil to coil crazily right down the deck casually achieving four hits and more, calculation and fortune combining and smiling on them.

It did strike the top of the frame hard. But it did not start on that zigzag course. For a second or two, due to a spin put on it accidentally in its despatch, it actually stopped. Or paused. Forsook gravity, anyway. For several long seconds. No, it was less than one second, because a second in these games is very long, a ball can do a lot in a second. However long it was, it was long enough for Jack to see that if left to its own trajectory it would roll straight down the deck encountering no coils at all. It needed assistance. Jack Hollard did what he believed he would never do in life. He put out two hands and slightly tilted the machine.

'Can you read what that says?' bellowed Joe just behind them. 'It says DO NOT TILT THE MACHINE.' It was not the cheating which enraged him; if merely assisting the ball to perform its function was to be called cheating. He was scared of damage, scared of someone separating a machine from its legs, even overturning it, smashing it. 'I'm telling you here and now I've had enough of you wandering in here and pleasing yourselves. You can bloody well get out and not come back, thank you very much.'

While this was happening, the influenced ball bearing had struck nine coils in its downward progress, nine buzzes and a final score of 400 showing in lights.

'But we've won,' Clive said very boldly.

'Hurry up!' Joe said in a loud growl, without touching them but pushing himself ominously close. They were simultaneously aware of a group of lads not really like themselves, not County Grammar School pupils, hanging around out on the pavement. There was something contemptuous in their stance. It portended trouble they were anxious to avoid. Jack was ashamed to feel the tears of a child starting in his eyes at this unfamiliar, outside-world aggression in a place they had assumed to be friendly. Did Joe really prefer these characters lurking on his forecourt to their own mild and harmless behaviour on his territory? Well, that was Joe's loss then, because they were certainly not coming back. 'And I don't want to see you here again,' Joe loudly repeated just as Jack thought of that; which somewhat spoilt the finality and dignity of their departure. As did the gesture of one of the young spivs out on the pavement, who had seen and overheard everything and now strode forward to ruffle Jack's hair while his pals laughed.

'Hard luck, Lord Snooty,' he said. Clive seemed disposed to take up the issue, but Jack pulled him away. Back home he let himself in quietly, and went rather quickly up to his room.

For *La Traviata* on Friday night Maureen had booked a seat in the front row because the more she saw the nearer she wanted to get. It fascinated her to be so near this very smart, stern conductor with his low bow as he guided the orchestra through another opening melody she recognised. She could see some of his many players in their cramped pit, all in evening dress, all looking as if they felt a sense of occasion. When they were tuning up they were smiling, but when they were playing they were not. Producing these touching melodies was, she saw now, a job like any other. One week it would be in the Empire here, next week in the Palace in Manchester, then the Lewisham Hippodrome, and on to the Alhambra in Fieldenhurst—a very posh audience you would get there.

Then she had a rush of horrifying thoughts as the curtains parted on this rich scene, so mixed up she nearly fainted and held on to the arm of her seat as if she was at the dentist's. She displaced the elbow of a well-dressed man next to her who gave her a look that instantaneously 'put her in her place' as someone he didn't expect to find in one of the best seats in the house. Maureen wasn't dressed for it, was she? He was, evening dress, no less, like the musicians, though his jacket, shirt and tie were not as well worn as theirs.

It was thinking of Spillar remembering his musical mother that started the flood of mixed ideas in Maureen's head. She was coming to see these operas with a baby inside her from a man not her husband, as likely as not. The child might be the musical one, it could miss a generation, there was Spillar's mother, and the first scene was the home of a courtesan, which was a prostitute who had made it in the world, not the five-shilling girls waiting in the dark shop entrances down Deptford High Street. By going upstairs with Spillar she had become something not much superior to them. Not something like Carmen. But Musetta, perhaps—and now Violetta, sung by the same large and vigorous woman of about her own age, who was so colourful and shameless and rich in her sins. Maureen was the 'mistress' of the proprietor of a dingy café where she served the things he cooked on several low gas rings at once with toast from the gas grills underneath and passed through the hatch to her. She put them down in front of workers from nearby sites, and cleaners from this theatre. And sometimes famous people who appeared there, and needed a break before rehearsing—and he hadn't even called her out to meet Olly Hardy!

She and Jack and Perce were not the inseparable trio they had been in Jack's childhood, in holidays before the war, when they hoped as Perce rose in the world at work that they might one day move to a better house in a better neighbourhood, maybe a house given a name instead of a number, something like MAUPERACK, combining their own three names. They used to live in a world of hope. Now they did well to stave off despair. Girls in her own district like Sally Jennitt did well by destroying themselves. It was the class you were born into, Maureen was in the class where the best you got was a mauling from Spillar on days she felt willing to let him do it. Though maybe Violetta began in Maureen's class and worked her way upwards. Starting when she was young…

But suddenly she was jerked out of this frightening, muddled train of thought by realising that Carmen and Musetta were not this Violetta at all. And vice versa. Violetta had taken some of Musetta's, and even Carmen's, brighter garments from the other operas, ironed them, and padded herself out. Violetta had the clear soprano of Mimi, and Carmen was not to be seen in the action, unless she was one of those singing extras at the back? This Michaela and Mimi had expanded!—the plaited girl who did embroidery was singing the courtesan's part, although it was clear that Violetta was ill and there was no recovery from illness in opera, and Violetta would die.

All three of these operas were turning out to be about colourful, free women in love and dying tragic deaths. For a moment it felt to Maureen like bad luck to realise that. But for another moment she took in the lavishness of this tableau of the rich and the immoral, its same staircase, not outside a cigarette factory or in artistic lodgings, but in a mansion inhabited by high society. Here was the same good-looking young man, now a suitor with more wealth than he could have dreamt of on the other evenings, and far better clothes, in fact the best men's tailoring Maureen had seen all week. This Alfredo could send notes of sympathy to a notorious fallen woman when she was ill, visit to ask after her every day, because he had the money and the time to back up the cheek. No one would have paid any attention to a poor man doing that. But this one had a headstrong streak about him, Maureen could see that. He was a young man who could declare love for a famous sick beauty of dubious reputation who numbered barons and marquises among her friends...That was different from the other lovers, but what they all had was this wild romantic temperament that put love first as if there was no other way to live life.

Maureen sat in the front row close to it all. She could see all the repetitions of clothes and scenery and makeup and gesture from night to night; but the nearer she got the more enthralled and overwhelmed and convinced she became. If they acted them and sang about them, these things must happen in life, to some people. They were not impossible. It was just that in her own life she had missed the moment, missed the turning, that would have given it a romantic meaning.

A young man could fall in love with this woman who was some years older than him. The power of love could persuade her to go and live with him in the country (after the first of the two intervals) where he appeared to have a beautiful house even if he made do with some of the furniture shared by Rodolfo and his friends in a Paris garret in *La Bohème* (but the stove looked more dignified here). Maureen could not fully believe in the father pleading with the woman to drop his son because it was giving the family a bad name.

She could not see Perce going to a dicey girlfriend of Jack's in the future and begging her to give him up because he hoped his daughter (his daughter!) would pick up a lot of money in a very respectable marriage.

Here as well a lot depends on the cards. They turn out well for Alfredo, but he behaves badly with his winnings—did gaming ever bring you anything good?—and is challenged to a duel. After a long darkness of scene-shifting and an atmosphere of impatience in the theatre, a lot of fidgeting, the curtain rises on Violetta's original room. Maureen notices that these people can afford a doctor to be there in long attendance. He was there, though he had nothing to sing, at the beginning. Now he does sing a few lines it is an over-hopeful medical verdict he delivers. Does he want to make Violetta happy with reassurances that she will soon be well again? Is he preparing the audience for a greater shock when she finally dies? Because she is bound to die, Maureen knows that, though not without a declaration of undying love.

In opera you die passionately loved. With dignity, and everyone notices and mourns. That is not going to happen to her, Maureen feels. The fear pursues her all the way home. Again she says next to nothing about her evening, and this time doesn't put the programme down on the kitchen table because she does not believe Perce—or Jack—will want to look at it. In bed she says she is very tired indeed tonight, she doesn't know why, and turns away from Perce to lie with her eyes open for an hour and then dream and dream and dream that she is still lying with her eyes open.

13

And then there was Mrs Lettie Orlop, who had grown a soft spot for 'the young Frenchman', as she thought of him, and as she called him when talking to neighbours. His name was still proving difficult to pronounce properly, so that description of him had to do. 'Keeps himself to himself,' she would say to persons in the street who enquired. And she would silently add to herself, 'and that's no bad thing.' She had had lodgers who didn't. Pierre-Henri Mallinot was respectable. Mrs Orlop was not a gossip, but with him there was nothing to prattle about. Anyone you could seriously prattle about could be a burden as a lodger.

In this May as the evenings lengthened Pierre-Henri continued to work at home for much of the time, his only visitors being the children he tutored and their mothers and fathers. He himself would open the door to almost everyone because they all came punctually at appointed times. So he was going down and up the stairs repeatedly, and escorting them to his upstairs front room. There they would sit beside him on hard chairs at the dining table where he never dined. This pattern, which developed quite quickly as a result of the success of his newsagents' adverts after he had been with Mrs Orlop for three weeks, was, his landlady assumed, followed on all the days she was out at her part-time work at the Ladies' in the recreation ground. If the lessons were still going on after she came home at dusk (and in the winter they were) she could hear the comings and goings on the stairs, the drone of his voice repeating French phrases, the higher tones of the children responding if they were not shy and mumbling; and it was pleasant, it brought life to the house. When her lodger had no pupils he was very quiet. Later in the evenings he had the wireless on in moderation and softly, because the French programmes he found on the dial did not give out a loud signal. In the daytimes when she was at home he was often out.

He never talked about where he went, or for that matter about anything much at all. 'Yes he keeps himself to himself—all the time,' she reassured inquisitive people, none of whom had any complaints. Privately she felt, 'He's not very forthcoming,' that was how you could describe him. And eventually, because she rather liked him in his reticent way, and was relieved that he turned out busy and clean and a good tenant (he paid his weekly rent on time), she added to that thought the idea that 'perhaps he's a bit lonely. He never says anything about France and home, and perhaps he doesn't have a home there to go to?' She would never ask him, oh no, she herself was not the inquisitive type.

Through the winter she had started later at the Ladies', well, she opened up at nine-thirty. So she was able to lie in a little longer and make her lodger's breakfast at a more reasonable hour. In his first months here in the summer he had had to take it at seven because she started work at eight, and soon it would be back to that kind of routine. One Saturday when she was not going to work (she only worked one Saturday in two) she had time to linger after she had put Pierre-Henri's breakfast down in front of him, and ask him about something on which she had never uttered so much as one word of opinion.

'Are my breakfasts to your liking?' was what she enquired.

Pierre-Henri Mallinot's smiles were infrequent, but after a few seconds passed with a look of surprise at her suddenly wishing to know what he thought, and an attempt to hurry some of her toast down his throat, he did smile. While he was swallowing and preparing an answer, she added, 'You don't leave anything much.'

She continued to stand by the table, and for a few moments he was dreading (it was almost as strong as that) that she might sit down on the chair opposite and commence a conversation involving questions. Having put down the teapot and the china jug of milk on her first trip, and the cornflakes, boiled egg and buttered toast on her second, Lettie Orlop had nothing to do with her hands. She fingered her apron at her neck. She became conscious that she was doing it, and that it might make her look nervous, so she ran the palm of one hand over the back of the other, aware that both hands hurt rather. Was that because the Council had changed the cleansing fluid she was issued with in the convenience, and the new fluid was crueller to the skin?

'I eat everything because your breakfast is always very good,' he said, with enough charm to make it sound sincere. It was not altogether insincere.

'I try to ring the changes,' Mrs Orlop explained. In the embarrassing inertia that gripped the two of them in this chilly front room on a late March morning when there was no sunlight available to fall into it, she suddenly thought it was a funny thing for her to say. Something to do with bells, she reckoned, the way you rang out the old year and rang in the new.

'You do it very well,' Pierre-Henri went on.

There was a pause. He did not like to take a bite at more toast in case he needed to respond to further remarks. Lettie Orlop stood there watching him lift her teapot with its spout poking out of its knitted cosy, and tilt it to pour out strong tea into the cup. Why didn't he pour out the milk first?

'Do you like a boiled egg harder than I make it—or softer?'

'But it is nice every time. It does not matter to me very much.'

This conversation was going to falter into absolute embarrassed silence. He gave a second smile and a polite shrug, reassuring her that he was happy even if her enquiry about the egg had not been clearly answered. And now, to his relief, they were interrupted by the abrupt clatter of the letterbox out in the hall.

'It's for you,' she said, coming back. And because letters were a private matter and it was nosy to stand and look while someone opened one, she left him alone when she had put it down beside the empty eggshell in its cup. She had seen its French stamp when she picked it up from the mat.

The fact was, Pierre-Henri had resisted Mrs Orlop's initial kind attempts to provide English breakfasts for him out of her own rations. The idea of such breakfasts had been alien to him, but he was now coming to find them acceptable through habit. Still he didn't understand why cornflakes allured the English. Why did they want to go on eating them even when milk and sugar were in short supply? Mrs Orlop had told him that in the days of the bombing she regularly had them for breakfast with water. The porridge she had been serving up for him on desolate winter mornings in February was an inexplicable dull sludge. He had read somewhere that a tradition of historical friendship between the French and the Scots did not necessitate a French affection for either porridge or bagpipes. Mrs Orlop began to set a tiny tin of golden syrup with a sleeping lion on it beside his porridge bowl, with a teaspoon. A teaspoonful of syrup, allowed to fall in a slow thin thread onto the moon surface of the porridge did enable him to eat quite a lot of it and not offend his landlady.

Once he tried to write in syrup the first letters of Marcelle's name, then stopped because it was childish and he was not a child...But the fried breakfasts, much more filling and offered as a weekend treat, rang too much of a change. Mrs Orlop realised his reluctance, and if she had an egg for the young Frenchman she usually boiled it. She told herself she ought to try other ways with an egg and see if he liked them. Now, beside the cracked remains of today's prim boiled egg, was the letter with the French stamp.

Pierre-Henri had only ever had English letters, from London: communications from parents about the lessons he was giving their children, and the business letters from the university. There were more slices of toast, cut into halves, which he had intended to spread with marmalade, but he forgot them at the sight of the French stamp and Paris postmark. No one was supposed to know he was in England, let alone at this address in an unknown corner of southeast London. Fear and horror halted him at nine a.m. on this morning just before Easter, the rain now falling. He hardly wanted even to pick the letter up, let alone open it.

But wait a moment. This letter, although addressed to him by his assumed name, had not originally been sent to this address. Someone had crossed out its original typed destination, and added 78 Benford Street. It had first of all been sent to the examinations office in the University of London. Someone there had received it and scribbled a forwarding address. This reduced the power of the missive to hold and horrify him. He opened it.

Someone in Paris had—it was a good-hearted notion, but it had scared Pierre-Henri Mallinot—someone in Paris had considered it a good idea to publish a kind of bulletin linking all the French teachers working in universities and schools abroad, country by country, so that they could meet and socialise and exchange thoughts about spreading the word 'for France and French civilisation' in these bleak post-war times. To contact such persons they had communicated with various central educational organisations. These were asked to supply names and addresses, or sometimes just names if addresses were uncertain or changing, or if people preferred to keep their addresses to themselves. Pierre-Henri had asked the university of London not to give out his address. But his name must have gone, without it, onto some list of the university's French contacts in London, and been provided for this eager—tenacious—Paris office. It was quite an admirable patriotic venture; but their communication had worried him.

All the same, a letter in his own language inviting him to be in touch with French citizens abroad could not fail to remind him of how much he was missing France. What spirit was there in his life in London? After the initial relief at feeling out of reach, anonymous and safe, it had turned into a kind of apprehensive tedium. How much longer could he go on living here without regularly speaking his own language, except for the banal repetitions of the textbooks he used with pupils: 'Julian is happy in Paris. He goes to the theatre and sees the great French dramas'? Recently, Pierre-Henri had only been to the Empire and seen the nudes posing and shivering as Cézanne's bathers, reminding him of Marcelle. He kept clear of any place in town where he might run into compatriots who recognised him; which certainly meant he forbade himself the great gallery where the Cézanne was, or the concert halls when French music was on the programme. Or the cinemas showing French films, though they were at least dark.

But he would certainly not reply to this letter from harmless strangers who had been put on his scent for their benign purpose. He should put up with what he had chosen, surrender himself to fearful obscurity, allow these people to infer from his silence that he did not wish to know about their activities. Eventually he would be deleted from their list as a non-respondent. France could surely not remain a vengeful, vindictive nation for more than a year or two longer. When he could no longer detect any rabid zeal for pursuit from the radio, or from the few extremist publications that were still persecuting his like (he did need to make rapid visits to town for those), he would return unobtrusively to La Tignelle, re-open his shuttered house and live in it until he could sell it and move, fade into another background in another place. He did not do what he could have done: write NOT KNOWN AT THIS ADDRESS on the letter and post it back again.

Three weeks after Easter, for the very first time, Lettie Orlop tried Pierre-Henri Mallinot with Shredded Wheat. When he had cut it and scooped it up on the spoon and trundled his way through it, she brought a treat, as she thought of it: a firmly poached egg on a piece of buttered toast, and more of the usual toast to follow it. The marmalade was already on the table, in a glass pot with a silver lid, with an aperture for a little silver spoon (a wedding present). And then, the breakfast being complete in front of her lodger, she returned with two letters for him.

'You *are* popular,' Mrs Orlop said, a painful compliment for a friendless and lonely man.

The one with the French postmark was on the top because she had the kind thought that he would want to open that first. Again it had been re-addressed by someone at the university. He did not recognise the handwriting of the French sender, but he knew immediately it was not the same as that on the re-addressed letter of two weeks before. Upstairs later, he checked on that.

He forgot the poached egg for some time. He did eat it, but only when it was cold. The envelope had seemed very light, and he first thought there might be nothing inside it. He was correct in that. When he slit it open with the table knife he discovered it was empty. Simply posting an envelope without the letter inside it, that sort of thing could happen, he had done it himself. But to Pierre-Henri an empty letter with a French postmark was too much like a silent phone call.

The second letter was no problem at all—a schedule of the examining duties he would be undertaking for the university in under two months' time. Each individual would arrive for his oral ready to conduct intelligent social conversation to break the ice, then read aloud a prepared passage of French prose or poetry or other material. This could be followed by some dialogue about the piece the candidate had chosen, which the examiner would not know in advance. Marks would be awarded for accent and for general command of the spoken language. It was not well paid, but it did not look burdensome and it would provide just a little intellectual interest and stimulation.

The ordinary empty letter had the effect of starting dreams which blended nostalgia for the France he missed with renewed fears about his safety. He could dismiss those in daylight in this corner of a foreign city, but at night…Worst of all was a nightmare in which he imagined he had woken up not in Mrs Orlop's back room but in the small hotel bedroom overlooking the yard in Périgueux, and gone to the window. The strongest feeling in this dream was disgust, and a sick hatred of Marcelle, with which he then actually woke up, in bed, in southeast London—and had to ask himself the question, Did he still love her? When the dream faded he knew that he did.

If next day Mrs Orlop came up the stairs after an unexpected knock at the front door and said (unbelievable, but if this were to happen!) 'Mr Mollie-knot, there's a young lady here to see you'—would he embrace Marcelle? Welcome her in? Ask her to sit down, talk with her, then actually enact the fantasy—the one that came of the reality in his home in La Tignelle during Marcelle's visits? Get her to undress slowly in front of him, stand wholly naked for a moment or two while his desire became overpowering, then stand and move across the room to her?

The window in the hotel bedroom, through which he had seen the man in the coat in life—not just his dream about that night—the window through which he had seen René Picquart, as his name turned out to be, in the darkness of the yard wearing the coat Pierre-Henri Mallinot had brought with him from France; which hung now in this wardrobe at 78 Benford Street…

It had been a Tuesday, one of those two nights of the week, then or Friday, when Marcelle could not be with him. She went regularly by train to Périgueux to see a friend she had made there, a woman who had collapsed with a nervous breakdown and also had an ailing mother, so that Marcelle would sometimes stay overnight. When she did that she caught the earliest train back in the morning and went straight to her reception desk at the doctor's—where Pierre-Henri had first met her.

That Tuesday night Pierre-Henri was on the mid-evening train back to La Tignelle from Périgueux, where he had spent the afternoon on some local government business. A mere two hundred metres outside the station it broke down, at eight o'clock, under a full, embracingly brilliant moon. It was half an hour before a railway official came down the corridor repeating and repeating to the few passengers that they had no alternative but to get out as best they could and walk back along the line to the station. No, there would be no prospect of another train tonight, this was the only available train and it had a locomotive problem. There was no bus to La Tignelle either. There was a waiting room in Périgueux station (as if the locals in the train did not know that) and perhaps this train would be able to make its normal first trip to La Tignelle, and stops beyond La Tignelle, starting at five twenty-seven a.m.; though that was unlikely because they would probably have to wait until daylight. Pierre-Henri knew of a small hotel in Périgueux where he had never stayed, but which he believed to be inexpensive and decent; an official from Vichy visiting different mairies had been put up there by arrangement with the mayor of the town, and had no complaints.

He managed to jump down onto the track himself without difficulty, but then had to offer more or less to catch, and convey safely to the ground, an elderly man who begged him to assist him with his wife. The old woman was too scared to launch herself into the arms of the two men, and there was confusion as to which of them should try to seize which part of her. Finally she dropped, heavily but without injury, onto the heads and shoulders of both of them, with an aggrieved howl as if everything happening was their fault. What they would do about getting home to a village two stops before La Tignelle (a pricy taxi-ride no doubt) he did not ask. He did not want to take further responsibility for them. He picked his own way along the gravel between separate tracks, led on by the low platform lighting ahead of him. Once through the station he made for the Hotel Moulin Blanc.

Which in fact provided him with a presentable dinner, a cheap but very acceptable wine, coffee somehow, even cigarettes when he asked. The *patron*, no doubt short of business, was too effusively welcoming, though; and he was glad to go upstairs to his room at about ten. He asked if he could take the newspapers with him; he had nothing to read, and the room was not fitted with a radio.

The voices which suddenly began in the next room—but who were their owners, no one had appeared at dinner or in the lounge where Pierre-Henri drank coffee and smoked?—were low, as if they were being kept down deliberately. The man's voice talked tensely, in solemn tones, and the woman's voice, interposing remarks in what was almost a monologue, was almost as deep and serious as his. Not one word could be made out. It sounded as if the two were pursuing some topic intently, but without animation, resignedly. Pierre-Henri doubted whether it was worth applying an inquisitive ear to the wall, and why should he even have thought of that? A spy's instincts, an official's? It was an ordinary couple having an ordinary conversation; except that a husband and wife in a small hotel on a January night did not usually talk so persistently, on and on like this. Ten-thirty, eleven—long after he had gutted the newspapers and dropped them on the floor. If this colloquy didn't stop soon it would be ruining his chances of a good sleep.

But just after eleven it did stop. It stopped without any sounds of washbasin or bidet taps running, or chairs shifted, or someone opening a door to pass along the corridor to the bathroom. Something else started: different, active and eager, sounds now, the wordless articulations of people suddenly engaged in an act of physical love. Engaged in it, moreover, as if there had been, at a given moment, instinctive agreement that it should happen, that no verbal or physical preliminaries were needed. And as if the participants expected that it would be over fast, a rush to get there each for his or her own sake, no lingering in affection, no solicitude of one for the other, just the ejection of breaths and cries through open mouths from the back of two throats simultaneously as the effort went on. Almost a resentful, virtually a brutal, snatch at the ultimate pleasure which went indescribably beyond any other sensation of skin, or palate, or of heat or cold or pleasure or pain on a human body. It was as if it was far from the first time this had happened between these two people within these few hours of this cold night. The silence on the other side of the wall when he had entered his own room two hours earlier would have been the exhausted calm after the first time.

These noises, which he had never in his life before heard emitted by other people, only by himself with—well, with others, true, but with Marcelle was the only experience he wished to remember—such noises heard behind this wall repelled Pierre-Henri. He had no wish to listen more closely and hear more of what might be happening in the next room. Was this how he might himself sound in these ecstasies? After he and Marcelle had played their game of her standing naked in front of him so that he could contemplate her and she could, as they described it, 'watch his desire for her grow'? The noise also began to horrify him now, because this woman's abruptly deep, regular gasps of surprise and pain, given as if this act was entirely new and surprising in the almost unbearable pleasure it gave, were like Marcelle's own cries.

And then, after a few more seconds, it became much worse than any of that for him because he became convinced—soon he knew beyond any question—that they literally *were* Marcelle's cries he was hearing. It was Marcelle's, his mistress's, own voice he was hearing, rising to a climax he recognised; hearing it through the wall here, in the shabby Hotel Moulin Blanc in Périgueux on a freezing January night.

Now he did press his ear to the wall. But as he did that the sounds stopped. There was only a subdued, tired murmuring going on; then a silence. Then, briefly, there were long breaths drawn in profound sleep, the man's breathing; they became a snore, broken and restarting. Pierre-Henri let the sounds continue unheard by him and fell back on his own bed, a double bed as it happened, so that he splayed out arms and legs, and shivered; and wept.

He must have been extremely tired because he suddenly decided that this was ridiculous, a delusion. Paranoia. If he was so certain it was Marcelle giving out those deep gasps behind the wall he could go and hammer on the door and confront her. And what if it turned out not to be Marcelle? He would be embarrassed—but reassured. Could he do such a thing for his own peace of mind? Everything was very quiet now. It was twelve-thirty a.m., no hotel clatter going on, probably the rooms downstairs were as silent and dark as death, the *patron* himself snoring gratefully somewhere. Pierre-Henri knew that he himself could have been asleep and dreaming that he was awake, he had had that experience from very early in life, the long time when he had gone to bed early.

But no, he had not imagined it, guilty and jealous though he might be. He had not imagined the unmistakable voice in the next room, descending from the soft, light tones of normal conversation on a scale of repeated, forced breathings, down to the painful notes of ecstasy he had so often heard. He had not dreamed it, because suddenly the voice was raised in a burst of loud talking, louder and clearer than any they had done earlier, which the man halted by exclaiming, 'Marcelle, please—quieter!'

He did not hear their door open. But he heard it close again, very softly. Then feet passed along the narrow corridor, a man's feet, lighter footsteps following. He waited, then turned out the light in his own bedroom when it was clear that no one was returning, because he had heard sounds below his window and wished not to be seen looking out to see who had made them. He stepped out of bed in the dark with a rustle of the newspaper he had cast onto the carpet. What did this room overlook?

The moonlight was bright beyond the curtains; if he pulled one of them aside very carefully he would be able to watch any activity down below in the yard. It was only a small space between walls, but the high moon vividly illuminated all of it. The light enabled him to discern with absolute unquestionable accuracy what he most dreaded seeing: a woman, Marcelle, wrapped up well against the cold in a familiar coat, saying good-bye to a man she was kissing, who was wheeling a bicycle into view from somewhere out of sight, an outhouse perhaps, and then hoisting himself into its saddle.

Mounted, this unknown individual kissed Marcelle again, rode away round a corner with a wave of the hand, and pedalled out into the street with a clicking of wheels in the silence. He wore nothing on his head, so a tangle of dark hair was showing. He wore, this was quite visible in the bright grey light, a heavy green coat.

14

'Mind you, I shan't be here to enjoy it,' Jedleigh took to saying very softly each time he vouchsafed a remark about the improved office to which they would soon be moving back from these uncomfortable quarters. Alan Carstairs's reaction (out of the chief's hearing) was, 'Mind you, it will all happen by around 1970—with luck.' There would be new furniture—more metal filing cabinets to replace the space-wasting free-standing cupboards, new telephone extensions apparently, more convenient desks and brand-new, much-needed curtains. 'It's going to mean a bit of staff reshuffling,' Jedleigh let drop ominously another time, 'but I'm afraid I shan't be around to see how that works out.'

The telephone extension system was being brought up to date everywhere on this floor. It was happening, illogically and inconveniently, long before the redecorated offices were ready for occupation. One Monday morning there was a knock on the door and an entry without waiting of two men in dungarees identifying themselves as 'engineers from the GPO'. There was already one telephone apart from Jedleigh's personal line, up in his alcove—it was on Carstairs's table—but the engineers had instructions to instal a further one in this tiny space. The plan was to instal it on the opposite side of the room.

The only sensible place for it was the shared desk of the two most senior clerks, Messrs Luddon and Hollard; there wasn't sufficient flex to take it any farther. This was carried in with reverence by the younger of the two engineers. He set it down on the end of the temporary desk occupied (with Luddon) by Perce, who worked on, shifting it without thinking to the middle of the table to make room for papers. The connection was made to a junction box on the wainscot behind him, and the thick flex neatly nailed down along its upper edge. Then the older foreman engineer went out, came back, went out again, came back again, all the time surveying the work they had done. At last, 'That's it, gentlemen—and *ladies*. Pardon me!'

They both left. The phone, black and shining, looking too new to be useable, stayed in the centre of this shared table, irrelevant for now but a symbol of status in its future use when this tiny office was refurbished in turn and became someone else's sanctum. And yet it all at once rang, the same double ring as any telephone but with a fresh, commanding timbre. And Luddon, not Hollard, reached out a rapid hand and picked it up.

'Hullo?...Well I only know it's Mr Jedleigh's outer office... Room number?...Oh...Well, er...I see, you're just testing...Well yes, it did ring in this room...As you can hear...Yes...Yes... Thank you, of course I will.'

Luddon replaced the receiver, dialled a single number and waited. On making contact he called loudly down the line, 'Are you hearing me? Yes...Fine! Thank you.' And Perce realised that Luddon had automatically claimed the right to answer calls to their desk.

On the Friday week after this, Jedleigh decided he would 'make everything formal', as Carstairs put it two hours in advance of the moment. There had been a sunny lunch hour to enjoy. Nobody knew where Jedleigh went for lunch. It was hardly ever the office canteen. It was not Lyons's, or any local Victoria establishment like the Polonia, or the modest but excellent Magnet, some way down towards the bridge but quite reachable. Yet Jedleigh always took lunch, and left his staff to itself. Today, though, he was back early and lingering in the outer office chatting to the three juniors. Perce noticed that he was especially cordial with the comely Dora Parsons and felt something very like jealousy of the old man. Smart as ever, with what looked like a brand-new tie of an unconventionally redder tint, with colour in his cheeks as if he had just taken a vigorous walk in the park (but then he had), and a generally optimistic air, Jedleigh was waiting until absolutely everybody was present.

Perce was the first to take in this scene, and was surprised to see it happening today, although everyone had been expecting it soon. Carstairs entered behind him and took it in his stride, making his way to his desk next to Miss Parsons with jocular apologies for pushing past people; and sitting down. Luddon was last, a minute or two after Carstairs, and looked taken aback—Perce recalled that he had not been there when Carstairs was hinting that this occasion was going to happen that day. It was mid-May, and hot. It would be a relief to get out of this cramped space—but into what?

'Everyone here at last? Good!' Jedleigh called. Then he paused, not because he was designing a little drama and stopping for effect, but—or so Perce thought—because he was moved, and needed to control his emotions. Everyone knew he was about to utter something serious and final about himself. An end to the best part of his life.

'I thought you should be the first people—with the exception of Sir Rigby and the directors, naturally—to know my intention,' he began. 'I'm told there'll be a party of some sort or other later on, when the company as a whole will have the opportunity to raise three cheers for my departure. But I wanted to say something well before that, to the people who have been closest to me.'

No one truly feared that Jedleigh would spoil his announcement with a protracted oration, it would not be his style. But now they were tense on his behalf, wanting him to come to the point without letting himself down. There was, they realised, a kind of odd affection for Jedleigh in his department.

‘I want to say how great a pleasure it has been to know all of you here—some much longer than others—’ with a look in Perce Hollard’s direction, ‘and some more recently—but I appreciate what they have contributed, just as much. What a—what a privilege it has been to have you here. To know you. To work with you. To have your comradeship.’ Was Jedleigh wandering? And that word ‘comradeship’ was a curious one to use. ‘These have been difficult times. If this is peace’—they sensed that a prepared witticism was on its way—‘perhaps wartime was not so bad after all. No, I shall miss you all. I shall miss you a lot. I wanted to say that I shall be retiring finally on Friday 13th June. Procedures for finding my successor are already in hand—’ (are they indeed!), ‘and he, whoever it is, will be working alongside me from the beginning of June, which is two to three weeks’ time, isn’t it! Isn’t it... Well—well, thank you.’

He stopped; but he seemed uncertain whether he had finished. And if he had finished, how he would turn and mount the two steps to his personal alcove? Everyone looked at him in these seconds. All of them smiling, some nodding approval. But there was no time to wonder whether they should applaud or anything, as Dora put it afterwards; because there now came a sudden, unexpected intervention. Alan Carstairs rose from his place near the window, his features completely straight and sincere, his voice calm, his manner uncharacteristically solemn. He spoke the words with no preliminary throat-clearing, no hesitation. He said, ‘On behalf of us all, Mr Jedleigh, I would simply say that we all greatly appreciated what you have just said about us. We have come to see you as a friend as much as a boss, sir. I want to say—for all of us—how sad we shall be when it comes to your leaving.’

People nodded again, and there were general murmurs of agreement. Any frustrations, grudges or small resentments were forgotten, or at least overlooked. In everyone’s mind was the thought that they could have done worse; that, all in all, Jedleigh was Not a Bad Old Stick. But catching sight of Luddon's features in profile Perce thought he caught a twitch of surprise and annoyance, as if he believed he should have been the man to make the apparently impromptu gesture Carstairs had made. Too late now. Jedleigh had disappeared rapidly up the steps and shut the door of his fastness.

Two days on from that Luddon began to call Perce Hollard 'Holly'. 'Holly'—though Luddon could not have guessed this—inflicted a humiliation. It leapt back over forty years and returned Perce to his childhood. It took him back to the infants' department at school. To Miss Wolfenden, his teacher at the age of five. When it was 'Pay attention, class!' or 'Now let's spell our names, shall we?' Perce had to be 'Percival', because in 1906 Miss Wolfenden believed children should learn quickly how to spell their full names. Spell them out for themselves and the rest of the class to appreciate. 'P-E-R is Per. C-I is ci. That's Perci. V-A-L is val, that's Per-ci-val,' he would pronounce. 'Well done, Percival,' she would cry, and proceed to take the surname. Perce managed everything rather well. Constance Tillinghurst had a harder task, as did Archibald Harsoldon—but they both succeeded in the end. In relaxed moments, though, unusual for the period and for the teacher, it could be 'Holly' for Percival, because it distinguished him from the ill-behaved Percival Dibdin, Perce being both brighter and better mannered.

For Perce to be 'Holly' to an office rival sent him back to his infancy at the age of forty-seven. He felt unspeakably patronised. He thought Luddon was seeking to proclaim his inferiority. It might not have been so offensive to him if it had been affectionate and informal, and if it had not started now. And if the others had ever used 'Holly' in a relaxed and friendly fashion. They had not. For Arthur Jedleigh (behind his back sometimes called 'King' Arthur), for Alan Carstairs, and for the juniors, it was invariably 'Mr Hollard'. But, as with so much else, to protest about it would have been out of proportion. It would have revealed to Luddon that he was sensitive about it.

One Friday Perce felt like getting out of all this. He would go out for lunch to a café because he knew Maureen was going to the hospital for tests in the afternoon and had excused herself from providing a big tea. He walked quickly down to the Magnet in Regency Street, where they served generous, well-cooked, inexpensive meals fast and cheerfully. Sitting there alone when he arrived was Dora Parsons, who may have had the same end-of-week feeling. It would have been grossly unsociable not to join her. Wouldn't it?

And—'I notice you're "Holly" now?' was one of the first things she said. Out of the office, as short a time and distance away as this, it was surprising how you began to think you could be frank.

'Yes, I've noticed,' Perce said, delighted by this perception.

'Are you called "Holly" by anyone else?'

Perce shocked himself by thinking that if Dora did it now—though not back in the office—he might not mind.

'No one ever has—since I was in the infants'.'

'Do you mind it?'

He tried to shrug, but the gesture wouldn't come. He did mind it.

'I do mind it.'

Dora smiled.

'I thought you did.'

'You did?'

'Yes.'

He did not know exactly what to say.

'Don't let it get you down,' she advised; and he was astonished. In the claustrophobic office atmosphere, everyone either talked work or just joked to pass the time. No one spoke seriously, about anything. And here was the very attractive Dora—whom he had to confess to himself he desired, and it was a shameful instinct, what was happening to him?—the usual kind of office junior, the typical typist, saying something sympathetic and humorous, and even somewhat intimate.

Then there was the Tuesday morning ten days later, a genuine early summer day. The sun came radiantly through into their shaded office, it was higher in the sky now. By noon it was finding its way even down into the deep, damp well between the offices of Fitch & Armstrong and the coal office and the civil service block on its other two sides. Some rays of warming light fell on Carstairs's desk and Dora Parsons's typewriter, showing up the dust on the legs of its keys. Dora rolled up small strips of blotting paper and tried to springclean them, an effort which Perce found pleasing; but Luddon gave her disapproving glances. Dora persisted, despite—or perhaps because of—the looks she was getting from him, and smiled at Perce conspiratorially.

Sometimes Perce travelled down in the lift with Dora, and wondered whether he could ever begin to confide in her in more detail about his opinion of Luddon's behaviour and his worries about it from his own point of view. No, he could never do that, he decided. It would appear that he was making some kind of invidious approach.

'Do you know?' Carstairs exclaimed in a silence at about three-thirty. 'I could learn to love this office. Just when we're about to move back into the old one, I could learn to love it. You see what the spring has done already? It's curled up the corner of my diary.' And it had. The trim, thin leather binding of something lying on the desk in front of Carstairs had truly wrinkled in the unaccustomed sunshine. But was that thick book really a diary? It was not a personal pocket diary. It did look like a work diary of some kind, come to think of it, the sort of diary you kept on your desk to inscribe appointments in. Carstairs would be joking. He only ever joked (except when he made that little speech for Jedleigh). Work diaries began at a higher level. Jedleigh obviously had one. Luddon would have liked to justify having one. As for

Perce, he sensed that he would only ever be a name written down in other people's.

'Aaah!—to be sure, to be sure—as the Irishman said to explain why he put on two Durexes—' Carstairs called out in his Irish accent, ''twill be a week tomorrow we'll be moving back.'

They looked at him. No one asked him to elaborate. But he did, reverting to his curiously, purposefully, posh London tones. 'You'll see transformations. On the side where the sun comes in they've given Miss Clissold a special room.' The juniors, and even Luddon, looked up at this, but they ignored what he then went on to say. 'It's to be a conservatory. She's going to take saplings from her piles and plant them out in pots. Everyone in that department will have the responsibility of watering them...The best ones will go on sale in aid of charity.'

Carstairs's prediction proved correct in some respects. They did move, unexpectedly, without a preparatory announcement, after precisely eight days. On that morning Perce's bus had broken down. He waited an angry twenty-five minutes for the next one and passed Nobby Clarkson at the front door downstairs ten minutes late. When the lift door on his floor opened, he was immediately into a chaos of activity. Here was Carstairs, with Luddon at the other end, painfully shouldering the burden of a familiar desk on its way back to their usual office from the temporary quarters. And Dora, following with an office chair, greeting Perce with an appealing smile.

Naturally Perce took off his coat and jacket as fast as possible, draped them over a banister, and joined in, before he could be accused, even jokingly, of arriving late to avoid hard work. Their temporary room was almost empty by the time he reached it, with only drawers full of documents left to bring along to their redecorated original office. He was too late to help with much of the lifting and carrying, but in humping one huge desk with Luddon—and he believed the mishap to be Luddon's fault—he hurt his right wrist again. He hurt it badly enough to apply a hot water bottle to it at night for a week. Then it felt completely better, and he forgot about it before he seriously considered the doctor. Which was well; because he was also considering something else: the thought that he should try a little cricket again before he became too old to bowl a ball.

The office had been absolutely drastically altered and Perce was dumbstruck at the changes. The wooden partition which once separated them from a small adjacent office had been removed, adding perhaps fifty per cent to the square footage in which they would work. Or that was what he thought at first, not realising that space had been created by the simple removal of a number of hefty cupboards and cabinets. It had also been reduced by the introduction—where the partition had been—of a new dividing wall of light wood, in which one half was mainly a large glass panel.

Behind it, Jedleigh (or one day soon Luddon, he thought?) would have more room, and also a means of overseeing work going on in this redesigned outer office. Carstairs would have to mind his behaviour. Jedleigh himself was already installed, to enjoy a brief glory behind the shining new glass screen. A second desk was visible in his new sanctum, and it had a new telephone of its own—no, two new telephones.

Noticeable in their transformed room was a distinct echo, apparent when they had finished the lugging in of furniture and had come together in this brightly painted space. It was evident when Carstairs began to speak, with Jedleigh sitting in his new sanctum behind the glass and paying no attention. So now it was Carstairs officiating for his retiring chief, standing with the sheet of paper in his hand and describing arrangements, very briskly indeed. Places in the room, with their advantages and drawbacks—proximity to a door, a window, a radiator—were allocated (presumably on Jedleigh's instructions) without asking their recipients for any opinion. 'Miss Parsons—Dora—you will be here. Miss Drew—Doreen—next to you—here. Mr Langley, this is your position. Mr Hollard here. Mr Luddon here.' It was organised so that the three youngest members of staff were seated with their faces visible to Jedleigh—or the new boss; Luddon surely.

And why had Jedleigh gone to so much trouble when he would no longer be here with them? Why should he have specified, for example, that the two seniors, Perce Hollard and William Luddon, should have individual new desks, but not close together? One desk was to the right and one to the left of the central door that opened from his inner room. Perce's chair was positioned unfortunately, behind that door as it opened; but Luddon's was in full view, on a spot where Luddon would be seen and consulted first by anyone opening the door and coming out. Unless it was Luddon himself who would be coming out in future. The one, still the only one, outer office telephone was on Luddon's desk.

It was as if all this was happening to demonstrate Perce's disadvantage, closing him in, dumping him in a corner. He talked to Maureen at length about this that evening, hardly troubling to conceal from her his fear that there might well not be the money to raise the new child and see Jack off to college.

But now Carstairs came out of Jedleigh's new haven again, closed the door behind him, stood at the foot of the steps, and made a curious announcement.

'Mr Jedleigh has asked me to inform you of something.'

Coolly uttered, with a light expression on his face that just stopped short of starting a mocking smile. There was something bright about his eyes for a moment, even though his lips and his cheeks and his tone of voice gave away nothing. 'I'm to pass on the fact that there is going to be a vacancy in this department next month, which will be advertised in due course in the normal internal way, in information posted on the relevant notice boards and included in the quarterly magazine of the company.'

Insofar as they could, now that they were not facing each other, people exchanged expressions, sent out sideways glances of puzzlement. Of course there was going to be a vacancy—Jedleigh's own senior post. Everybody knew that. Why announce it like this? It gave the impression that this important appointment might come to be made after competition inside the company only. Not with advertisements in the *Daily Telegraph*, for example. Jedleigh could not have been flattered if that was the case—was it so unimportant that they were not seeking the best talent from rival concerns? But at this moment he sat benignly contemplating them all through his new screen. No one could yet tell whether voices, conversation could penetrate this glass barrier.

'Mr Jedleigh also hopes that everyone likes the new floral curtains when they arrive.' As yet, the windows were bare; the room was far lighter than usual. The sun was making the room uncomfortably warm. The radiators were thankfully off. 'And he says we should all be grateful to Miss Clissold for the generous donation of discarded knickers that made it possible to create them.'

15

Pierre-Henri supposed he slept two hours, perhaps as much as three, before he was woken up by the ringing and rattling of the alarm clock the *patron* had been able to provide.

He was used to short nights, capable of working next day despite lack of sleep as long as he could make up for it the following night, or at most the night after. But this was brutally different from any past experience that had deprived him of sleep. He felt confused, exhausted, horrified, humiliated, frightened, vengeful. He knew in the morning, knew it with the cold calculation of his own kind of paranoid jealousy, that he would be preparing himself very carefully for an appalling confrontation with Marcelle.

'You're not busy at this time of year?' he said to the *patron* when he received his breakfast roll and coffee; said it as casually as he could manage.

'Oh—just a few. The commercial travellers, of course. Sometimes there'll be people booking in for weekends. We can still depend on the couples, you understand?' A confiding smile, as if it was ridiculous to think that the war not long ended for France, but still going on in the rest of Europe, would interrupt romantic liaisons in Marshal Pétain's honourable Republic.

Pierre-Henri smiled back, and said, 'I think there was a couple here last night? They had the room next to mine.'

'They didn't disturb you?' The man seemed prepared to answer a complaint; but he spoke with a smile.

'Not in the least.'

The *patron* paused for just one revealing moment, looking Pierre-Henri in the eye firmly, judging him. Then, 'They're regulars,' he said, as if assuring his questioner that there was nothing wrong or suspicious going on. But this disclosure was the opposite of assurance for Pierre-Henri Mallinot.

'They are?'

'Yes. Mr and Mrs Picquart.'

'A married couple?' Pierre-Henri's briefly incredulous expression was interpreted as a smile, and the man gave an uneasy chuckle.

'Yes—apparently. This is the only chance they have to spend time together, for the moment at least. They live—and she works—in one of the little towns half an hour up the line, Montbron, or your La Tignelle or somewhere like that. That's too far for him to get home, so she…' He dropped his voice to continue, quite sure he could safely convey this much to a man who had said last night that he was a local government official in La Tignelle stranded by the train breakdown; it might help to be this far open and candid about what little he knew, not appear to be concealing anything when there was nothing to hide. 'I believe he's in some kind of defence installation work, out in the forest…I gather he only gets home about once a month.'

'There's a family? Children?'

'I think not. Newly-weds, if you ask me.' Then he at once regretted going so far, even with harmlessly indiscreet information, and went off at a tangent to strengthen his credentials as an honest, patriotic man. 'I suppose we've all got to be prepared for whatever could happen, even though we're no longer at war. Marshal Pétain and Mr Laval are very aware of the need for that, wouldn't you say, sir?'

'I didn't see Mr and Mrs Picquart at dinner.'

'No—they don't take meals, sir. Young love!'

'They've left already?'

No, Pierre-Henri didn't say that, he stopped himself just in time. He knew perfectly well that they had left, and the manager would have wondered what his purpose was in asking so many questions.

It was two nights later, as arranged, that Marcelle came to Pierre-Henri's house, at the usual time she could get away, about seven. She always came for a meal, it had been a regular custom. On this occasion he had cooked something relatively light and simple, nothing out of the ordinary. He had had lunch at the mairie himself and Marcelle had taken a snack in the one small bar and restaurant in the modest town centre of La Tignelle.

It was an understood preliminary to the love they would make later. Pierre-Henri took particular care with the detail of timing tonight, because he had planned exactly when he was going to speak to Marcelle, and had repeatedly rehearsed the exact words he was going to use. He would ask direct questions to which he must have frank answers; and he had prepared his own response to any of her responses, whether they involved feigned innocence and denial, or brazen admission, or tearfulness and pleas for pity. Nothing would happen unplanned; right up to Marcelle's leaving the country.

He was proposing to begin it all with fierce abruptness, and not give her any time or opportunity to devise strategies of deception. But he would talk about other topics before they sat down to his meal, and while they ate; and keep off the subject of Périgueux and her visits there unless she referred to Tuesday night for any reason; which he hazarded she would not. And then—at the moment he had poured the coffee after this modest wartime (no, Vichy peacetime) meal, and set it down in front of her, he would suddenly begin.

He knew the likelihood was that everything between them had to finish. But he loved Marcelle. When he greeted her at the door, warmly, hurrying her in out of the cold, he was aware of that as if nothing at all had occurred. He also found he was no less obsessed than before with the prospect of making love to her; though that was unthinkable tonight. Everything moved in the direction of one purpose. He intended to dispatch the unfaithful Marcelle Levine into another place and into the future—and, so to speak, preserve her there. As for 'Picquart', if that was his real name...That was a subject they would not discuss.

So after they had eaten, and she had settled into the usual one of the deep old armchairs he had inherited from his parents, he went round the small table to give her her coffee, and she thanked him. Then he sat down in his own chair and picked up his own cup, all of this being a detailed ritual set by many months of meeting. He would always look over the top of his cup at this moment, as he took a first sip, and he would smile. By custom he would know, if Marcelle smiled back and nodded, that love would be made very soon after, perhaps beginning when both had finished the coffee and returned their cups to the table.

Tonight, though, he looked up at her over the coffee cup in his hand and did not smile. He simply said, 'You went to see Delphine on Tuesday night?'

He tried to say it altogether neutrally, but he heard an edginess in his voice and feared that it would alert Marcelle to what he was about to reveal.

'Oh...Yes, I did.'

'You didn't get asked to stay and help overnight?'

'Not this time. I caught the train back.'

She would have to say that because there were no buses from Périgueux to La Tignelle after about nine in the evening until early in the morning. There was a final train at about ten-thirty, which of course had not run. 'I'm glad I did. There are getting to be so many things I have to catch up with once I've taken a night away. And Dr Villeneuve notices if I'm looking tired.' And Marcelle proceeded to list the reasons why she preferred not to stay the night in Périgueux. She was chatting hard to try to cover up the lie, Pierre-Henri thought. He knew there had been no late train back, no early morning train either. He had checked all this thoroughly when he went through Périgueux station himself at just after ten—and had to wait thirty-five minutes for the very first train that ran following the breakdown of the one he had caught the evening before.

Marcelle must have discovered there was no dawn train and taken a bus. If she had waited for his own train he would have seen her, met her, there were very few passengers on it. Marcelle did not want Pierre-Henri to believe that she could have stayed overnight. Wouldn't it have been easier to let him believe that that was the case? He never did fully understand her determination to convince him that she had returned. Was it because she did not wish him to suspect that she had had any reason for staying in Périgueux? If he had the least remaining doubt about the voice crying out beyond the wall, if he told himself he merely imagined that he heard a man in the next room actually addressing her by name, these thoughts were banished by her plain falsehood about her journey back.

'I was in Périgueux myself on Tuesday night,' he observed quietly.

This unsettled her, her face showed it. He went straight on, not wanting to give her time by leading up too gradually to the point.

'I was staying in the Rue Moulin Blanc on Tuesday night, and so were you. In a small hotel also called the Moulin Blanc. Marcelle, you were getting your orgasm with another man in the room next to the one I stayed in, in the Hotel Moulin Blanc, at about eleven o'clock on Tuesday night. I heard everything. What is his name?'

He thought this shocking, coldly direct question might work. And how sound the strategy proved, cancelling any possible protestations or fabrications before Marcelle Levine could even begin to think of them. She sat there with her fingers still holding the handle of the cup, pale and still and defeated. And she was immediately terrified, he was sure, for many more reasons than his discovery of her infidelity to him. She was utterly unable to say anything at all.

He would let her take her time, and not yet say anything more himself. He decided on that policy because the very first thing she said or did after being caught out might be revealing. What would follow after whatever she found to say first? To his list of possibilities he added regret, repentance, a promise, an assurance that it would not happen again. A few of these, even any one of them, would help her. Defiance in any form would not help her. That would be very hard for him to take, probably impossible. It would destroy his love for her, negate their entire relationship, shatter her security. But it was unlikely that Marcelle could contrive to be defiant, even if she wanted to.

She went through an age, as it seemed to both of them, of silence and trembling before she said something. Then what she told him was contained in one plain and amazing sentence, in a soft deep whisper, looking away from Pierre-Henri and down at the floor.

'He is called René Picquart.'

So the *patron* of the Hotel Moulin Blanc had been given the real, or at least the same, name.

'Where does he come from?' A rapid second question; and there would be more.

'He does not have one address at the moment.'

'So not La Tignelle?'

She shook her head.

Pierre-Henri Mallinot was still riding on Marcelle Levine's waves of shock, and getting truthful answers. He wondered when, and how, she would make some attempt to defend herself, cover up something for her own protection. His response to that was well prepared.

'And he wears a green coat?'

A pause. She shook her head again, as if to dismiss the relevance of the question.

'I don't know what colour coat he wears.'

'Yes you do. You've been seeing it every time you go to Périgueux "to visit Delphine". It's a green coat, isn't it?'

Another pause. Silent unwillingness to agree at first. Then, agreement.

'It's a green coat, yes,' she said.

'And your name is Marcelle Levine?'

She gave a snarl of hurt and humiliation and disgust at his implication. How could he! How could he possibly presume and dare and…

'You know what my name is,' she growled helplessly.

'It's Marcelle Levine? It's not Marcelle Grenier?' he persisted.

Now she shook her head in impotent fury and disgust, from side to side several times, as if she was trying to deny that any of this was happening to her.

'It isn't Grenier.'

She was crying desperately now, deeply shaken by what he was doing.

'And I've helped you by making sure your name is enrolled in all the essential records here as "Grenier"?' he asked.

'Yes.'

And of course he was still in love with her. Because he suddenly realised that her immediate confession did concede some degree of loyalty to him, the lover she had visited (and would surely have been seen visiting, and even dining out with in the town once or twice?) instead of the illicit lover she had met in a winter hotel room. Also there was nothing in what she said or how she reacted to his questions that suggested defiance.

'And in the time that I've been helping you I might have been in some danger myself? If I had been discovered to be protecting a Jew who later turned out to be having an affair also with a man wearing the green coat of a local branch of the maquis?'

But this produced in Marcelle a sudden, furious need to answer him back.

'Claude—you really say *your* danger is equal to *mine*?'

And he could not reply to that, because it was true that there was no equality between the degrees of danger they might suffer.

'There are scores of people in green coats who have no connection with the maquis,' she went on.

It was an answer which gave him a means of escape from the moral thicket into which his invocation of danger had cast him. It was much easier to say something in reply to that.

'Listen to me. Please,' he said. 'We have spoken about this, and you have even recognised that officials in my situation are in some sort of danger from both sides. From the government side, if I am not doing what it thinks is my duty—and from the enemies of the government who would punish me if I carried out the government's orders. If they had the power or the opportunity to do that. Listen. There may be, or there may not be, a detachment of the maquis concealed in the forests not very far from here, moving around on foot—or by bicycle. They may have assembled a cache of arms in an area which the militia would be very cautious about entering; or they may not. But it is widely known that the local resistance, in whichever forest they may be, wear green coats—any kind of green coat—to camouflage their movements. And as a symbol of their opposition to the government at Vichy. Other people have taken to wearing green coats as a token of solidarity.' He hated that last word and gave it a contemptuous emphasis. 'Your "friend" wears a green coat, I saw him leaving that hotel with you, and he was wearing a green coat. To my mind that makes him only one thing. You do not wear a green coat in this region of France unless you belong to the opposition or are making a gesture.'

She was astonished at his knowledge of her movements on Tuesday night. Perhaps after all he was no more than a government agent, a spy, an informer? Some of his interpretation she could have attempted to reject, because René had never gone beyond hinting strongly that his work in the forest might involve maquis connections, and Pierre-Henri was indulging in pure conjecture about the resistance and its symbolic forest coats—perhaps to see if she would provide him with more information? He had taken his theories too far. The idea of parts of the forest being out of bounds to the militia because detachments of maquis outcasts were living a life of exile in them was no more than his contrived fantasy, she was reasonably sure.

Her resistance friends in Paris had never suggested she would find contacts of that kind in La Tignelle. They had simply urged her as a Jew to leave that city at the first opportunity if she valued her life, and had given her the name of a doctor, a trustworthy former communist in a little remote town in the Charente called La Tignelle, who would give her lodgings above his surgery and employ her as a kind of receptionist-cum-housekeeper.

At the doctor's reception desk she had been unavoidably noticeable. There had been a flu outbreak in the area, a rush of people seeking attention and remedies, fit people who worked out of doors as well as more sedentary persons who had picked up the germs in their shops or offices. She had even wondered whether René Picquart's flu, when he arrived to see the doctor and engaged her in earnest conversation, had been a pretence, an excuse to visit Dr Villeneuve's surgery simply because he had noticed that she worked there.

On the other hand, Pierre-Henri Mallinot's flu had been perfectly genuine, it developed into a touch of pneumonia; and he had not given any sign of interest in her until his third and final visit. It was on that occasion that he knew he would miss seeing her now that he was better. In those long periods sitting in the doctor's waiting room and watching her at work, he had fallen in love with her not only, he thought, because of her outstanding loveliness but because of a kind of charm and urban sophistication you did not often find in La Tignelle. He himself was an educated man, a graduate of Poitiers University, no less. But he had not so far done as much with his life as he would have wished.

He told her all of this early in their affair, and in her own loneliness and her sense of her own life having come to a halt she had returned the love of this not unattractive yet withdrawn, enigmatic, apparently friendless man; who had responsibilities in the mairie he never said very much about. This was before she knew anything about Pierre-Henri's political background, and before she told him that she was Jewish; though not before she imagined that to know a local official might be helpful in the future.

That turned out to be the case. He swore to keep her secret when she told him, and also to ensure that she was unalterably enrolled as 'Grenier' in the records of the mairie. And Picquart? His own flu infection had been very mild. He was manifestly healthy from his daily work in the forest and from all the cycling he did. Moreover, René was a kind of man she had never met before, a countryman with an impressive native intelligence and—given the contacts he hinted at—some admirable revolutionary instincts. For a few days Marcelle was intrigued to think that not one but two men were declaring love for her. Something like it had happened to her in the past, when she was very young, in Paris before the war. But there these matters could be handled differently, in the atmosphere of a great city and according to the codes accepted in the intellectual circles in which she moved. How had she been so foolish as to think that two love affairs, about each of which she had strong doubts, could be conducted without the fact being noticed in so small a place as La Tignelle?

Her answer, as she now freely confessed to Pierre-Henri, was that she was able to sustain the delusion by keeping her lovers well apart. René fortuitously helped her in that. She gladly accepted his proposal that they meet only in Périgueux (where she had already made a convenient friend, Delphine, who would cover for her) and conduct themselves with infinite care and discretion.

He listened to her without interrupting the flow with further recrimination or accusation. Everything was propelling him towards a stratagem he had long been working out in case it was needed, a scheme that would separate Marcelle and René completely. For other reasons also, its time had come.

One of his recent duties had been to check over the official register of the small Jewish population of La Tignelle in case of—or was it in readiness for?—any instructions as to...But he was never, never going to betray Marcelle, even if she had betrayed the profoundest love he had ever bestowed on anyone in his life. He believed that at some time very soon instructions would come to collect together in one place at a certain time, with the minimum of luggage and belongings, all Jews and suspect strangers for transport to a holding centre somewhere else in France. He believed that higher officials than him would some time soon be arriving from Périgueux, or Bordeaux, or even Paris to scrutinise every name the mairie had on its lists.

Therefore what he proposed to Marcelle tonight represented a timely and altogether sincere concern for her care and protection. There would be a risk for him in implementing his plan, but it would be taken in her interests. He did not confess (but she could easily guess) that it would be taken in his own interests as well. He himself would not find it difficult to cross the border 'on business' on a visit to Switzerland occasionally, and there the two of them could seek to restore what Marcelle's 'lapse'—he was so grateful for the word—had threatened to destroy.

To consider all this she got up from the armchair and went over to the window, which was overlooked by no other window. It faced onto Pierre-Henri's back garden, and Marcelle tried to see the short lawn, and the bushes, and the far wall that ended the garden, through and beyond the lighted room reflected on the glass; as if there might be a route to freedom out there. But their chairs and the table and the pictures on the walls were painted brightly on the garden and everything else outside. Suddenly she knew that she would accept his proposal. And that she would employ it to seek a world remote from Claude Derrichet, René Picquart, La Tignelle, Périgueux, all of this confusion and emotional pain. Perhaps even remote from France itself. She would be forcing her way through the images on the glass to a free darkness beyond them, dangerous in itself but the only possibility of escape to another world; and perhaps another self.

He would arrange and pay for her to go across the border to neutral Switzerland, on a purely private visit to fictitious relations. He hoped and believed, having been shown it by her in the past, that she could travel safely on the passport in the name of 'Marcelle Grenier' that had been produced for her in Paris. Pierre-Henri knew a family in Geneva, the husband and wife were old political friends, who would gladly take her in and conceal her identity. She should absolutely not disclose that she was Jewish any more than she did in La Tignelle, because they were, how should he put it, right-wing people. It would be advisable to suggest that she required to be protected from the consequences of any possible invasion of France by the Americans and the British; and the vendettas of certain French people.

He told her that she should make this move as soon as possible, and tell no one in advance that she was going. Otherwise there was a real danger of her being asked to answer questions locally, as a recent incomer to a small provincial township from Paris; then of being interrogated by the department police and transported prematurely to one of the camps where Jews were held before being sent on to Germany.

'Who apart from you in La Tignelle might know my background?' she asked him. 'Who would have found out—or been told? Is it really just now that I'm not safe here? Or has that always been so?' She wondered whether she could take his word for it that the danger had suddenly increased, or whether the whole plan was dreamed up to get her out of René's hands, and there was no imminent threat to her safety.

'No one in La Tignelle has told anybody anything,' he said. 'You will just have to believe me when I say that you have less than two weeks to think about this—and go.'

He was wrong in that assertion. Had Marcelle stayed she would have had up to a month; but only that.

A month was what René Picquart had.

16

But then there was Maureen.

She was having these 'fears and frights', as she named them to herself. She seemed to remember this sort of thing when she was expecting Jack at the age of twenty-six. But these feelings are buried by time, you can't really remember the pains and strains you worried about when you experienced it nineteen years before, and whether it was the same as what you were getting now. Maureen had passed the stage of feeling sick while she was getting breakfast, and thought she had settled down. Then some strange shiverings started, and stopped again, and did that three or four times daily. She thought these may have been imaginary, and nothing to go back to the doctor about. She did phone Patsy Partridge about them, and Patsy, both of whose children had grown up and married, was reassuring, and said all sorts of feelings were quite normal, you told yourself there might be something happening but there was not. But in fact Patsy couldn't remember, either, whether it was normal. She was two years older than Maureen, had married early, and borne her children at twenty-two and twenty-four.

The actual tremors began shortly after her trips to the Empire for the operas, in the week after that when she was spending all her evenings at home. She only once or twice felt them while working at the Rio, mainly when she was home and felt an urge to rest or sleep before silently telling herself, 'I have to start thinking about tea.' She thought they might be due to standing up a lot during the day in the café, but also wondered if the three operas last month hadn't proved too exciting for her. So it might be psychological. She should find ways of taking her mind off her pregnancy. But she had few friends, only Patsy really, and Perce couldn't stand Patsy.

One hot Monday afternoon on her ten minutes' walk back home from from the Rio the tremors could not have been the result of imagination because they turned, as she said later, into definite real pains. And yet after half an hour of rest in the kitchen chair they were gone. It was the next day that she could hardly get home after a day of 'peculiar twinges' in the café. Not that it had been a particularly strenuous day. Beyond the hatch Spillar had been moving around in his stained apron in the grim kitchen at no more than a leisurely speed, shifting from stove to stove and humming tonelessly. From the café tables you could not see through the hatch to the other side, and you were not supposed to. It was only Tuesday, but Maureen already looked forward to the weekend, when she did not work and could rest. The Rio Café never opened on Sundays, and on Saturdays Spillar managed by himself. The pubs pulled people in on Saturdays, and besides, he didn't offer the kind of fare that the posher shoppers liked to rest with: tea in pots, scones with margarine and jam, the slice of cake people could get at the Cosy Corner. Or the portion of tart on a plate from the cafeteria displays at Lyons's, where the days of the nippy serving you at your table with a small complete tea for sixpence had vanished with the war. Funny to think of it, Maureen said to herself, that nowadays you were actually *served* by me, at the Rio, when you had to queue along the racks and take your food away on a tray to your seat (sometimes gone when you reached it) at Lyons's.

She was taking the walk up from the corner of their road much more slowly than usual. When she was indoors she closed the front door firmly and as usual called out 'Hullo!' quite loudly in case Jack was already back; which he rarely was, because he was a sixth former and a prefect and school kept him busy. Most days he would stroll home slowly with his friend Clive Garner (just 'Garner' as he referred to him) discussing school matters. Today there was no answer to her 'Hullo!' She dropped her coat onto its usual hook and turned and felt light-headed. Her hand went to the telephone to ring Patsy and have a word when a definite pain made her draw it back again. When she looked in the hallstand mirror to straighten her hair, 'I am pale,' she thought. The definite pain was not passing. She told herself that she must close her eyes and rest and not worry. Slowly she reached the kitchen.

Is it my bowels, she said aloud as she sat down carefully in her chair? It was not quite a bowels pain, it was closer to the griping, drawing pain that you connected with a period. This time it was two-and-a-half months, or more, into the nine. No one, not the doctor or Patsy, had ever told her whether you could have a small ordinary period while you were expecting and not lose the baby. She tried to comfort herself with that peculiar possibility. But the pains were worse than period pains would be, and they were sudden, without any of the tensions coming a day or two before a period. She had an increasing sureness, as she sat there, in pain when she moved her hips, that the worst thing of all was going to happen.

Where to go? What to do? The bedroom? The bathroom? Back to the telephone, to ring the doctor? Ring 999 for the ambulance? No one would be pleased if this was a false alarm. The pain was now almost too violent and cramping for her to move at all. She had to do something because she had a dreadful certainty that something was going to happen, and she could not just let it happen without help. She had to move out of this chair before Jack came in. He had not been told anything yet about her expecting, he was only due to be told at the end of the month, when she left the Rio.

Yes, she would ring the doctor, but could he come and see her at such short notice? She reached the telephone going dreadful pace by pace back up the hall almost crying because it hurt so much and she was so frightened. Dr MacCullen's nurse was there earlier than usual for the opening of today's evening surgery, and she said she would cycle round herself. Maureen was to tell herself to be calm, go and lie down upstairs at once, leave the front door on the latch and wait until she arrived. A woman would be better than her man doctor, charming and sensitive as he was, good with Sylvia Freeman about her tonsils ten years before, though Maureen knew nothing at all about that. She opened the front door cautiously in case anyone saw her, she did not wish to speak to anyone. There was no breeze today, so it would not blow wide open but just lodge on the doormat if she managed to bend down and pull it up a fraction.

She did that, and now knew that she certainly wanted to go to the lavatory, whatever else was wrong. Maybe that would explain everything, get it over and see, she would laugh at herself if it was only that. But could it be blood that was coming now? In front of the lavatory seat she lifted this navy-blue skirt, released the studs on her suspender belt and saw the red in the 'thick ones' she still wore although it was May and practically summer. It was watery liquid, and not deep blood-red, so it looked the same as her monthly period blood, didn't it? She lowered her thighs onto the cold black wooden seat and there was a terrible heave in her lower parts as something warm passed through them.

'I have done a number two,' was her immediate thought. That was what she told Patsy later. 'I let it happen, and strained a bit, and thought it was a number two after all. But my insides were dropping out—that was what I thought was happening. When I wiped it myself, though, it wasn't the usual, it wasn't your bowel motion, it was blood and slime. And when I got up and looked down in the pan it was a—a lump of something that had like a vein in it.'

She heard the doorbell ring, and a voice calling out, and it was the doctor's nurse, who came in and closed the door behind her.

'Where are you, Mrs Hollard?'

'The bathroom.'

Maureen felt too weak to do more than stand half-clothed over the pan and whimper as she looked down. The whole of her future had torn itself away and she had done nothing to prevent it; as if you could do anything to prevent it. The future was completely changed, all the routines and schemes and plans and hopes were gone in a moment. The coupons at the back of the cupboard were never going to be used. 'I just stood there,' she told Patsy, 'and the nurse came round the door and we both stood there and we both looked, and I said, "I've lost it, haven't I?" and she said, "I'm afraid you have, love." I said to her, "It's all gone, has it?" "Yes," she said, "it's all gone. Where's your bedroom, love? I'm going to put you to bed and get you a nice cup of tea."'

The nurse went to the bedroom and came back with Maureen's dressing-gown, and took her along to the bedroom with towels and a bowl filled from the hot-water geyser. When she had done that and before she returned to wash Maureen she pulled the lavatory chain. Maureen was ashamed to think that the nurse could probably see that the bedclothes needed changing and that the counterpane was old and so drab. The hot sweet tea was welcome, and Maureen started telling the nurse that she needed no more looking after now, she would be able to rest, it was all right. She had wanted to cry, but did not—how strange, because she had been terrified, and in deep distress as well as pain. Nearly an hour later she had not wept. The nurse left with cheery instructions that she was to get on the phone at once if anything else happened. And the doctor would come round as soon as he could.

She heard a key in the front door and it was Perce, because he always closed the door faster and with more of a slam than his son. He slammed it more and more often these days, with the thought that he was putting an end to another unpleasant and frustrating day. Luddon had called him 'Holly' three times. He was aware that when Jedleigh came out of his brand-new inner office, or for that matter Carstairs came out (because Carstairs now had a desk in that same new room), the opened door blocked Perce's view. But he forgot all of this when he found Maureen was in bed, and when she told him why.

Perce Hollard had grown used in this last ten weeks or so to the idea of a renewal of his fatherhood. For this very evening, as it happened, he had been preparing a speech to make to Jack; not to tell him, yet, that he would be having a new sister, or brother, but to prepare the ground for telling him that, by stressing that he was very important to his father and mother and that they were as keen to see him do well in the exams as he was himself. Nothing would be allowed to stand in his way if he wanted to go to university, though the money side of things was not going to be easy or simple.

Should he change his plan and not now make this speech? He decided not to change it, being so long prepared to do it; besides, it still applied even if now—even if now there would not be...But he was too shocked and distressed to find Maureen in her present state to take this thinking any further. He had not done any preparation in case this thing should happen to Maureen. But he had prepared himself for talking to Jack and he would go ahead. Sitting on the bed beside Maureen he wondered if he should have felt like weeping, but it remained that he did not weep. Straightforward birth or death had its proper phrases; but for the end of a being that had neither been born nor died there were no accepted words. They sat there wordlessly for over half an hour.

There was, though, something else to do soon, because Maureen was declaring that she was not going to be able to go to the Rio next day and she was not in a state to talk on the telephone to Spillar herself. (As she was telling Perce this they heard Jack, mercifully later than usual, coming into the house and closing the front door in his usual quiet fashion.) Spillar needed to be told the reason why she was not going to be there next day. With Jack now home it was not going to be possible for the call to be made in his hearing from their own telephone; even stretching the flex to carry the phone into the bedroom would not take it out of earshot.

It was after six-thirty. The Rio would be closed because Spillar hardly ever stayed more than half an hour clearing up after Maureen left at five. In any case the café was not on the phone. But Spillar had once given Maureen a 'home number' in case of emergencies, and she gave it now to Perce, who would take a walk to a call box. He left the house without saying anything to Jack except that he wouldn't be long and they might have to fend for themselves because his mother was not feeling very well and was sleeping.

Get this over and done with. But in the phone cubicle he first, from habit, pressed Button B. He owed the custom to his son, who told him once that he and another ten-year-old would sometimes be rewarded with two pennies someone had failed to retrieve when he had failed to get his call through. But how unpredictable machines were! Today just a single heavy penny fell out, and Perce placed it on the ledge above the telephone directories while he fished in his pocket for another.

How was he going to convey this information? Maureen had forbidden him merely to say that she would not be going to work for a day or two, she wanted the nature of her illness to be made completely clear to Spillar right away. That was curious. As he dialled the number she had written on this piece of paper, he realised he did not know himself whether Maureen had ever got round to telling her boss that she was expecting, which was why she was leaving at the end of the month—and so he probably had the task of telling Spillar that, divulging that she had been going to have a baby but now was not.

She was sending her husband to convey that to the man whom he could not guess had been her lover. For Spillar, the information that Maureen had been pregnant could come as a surprise, a shock perhaps, as it had to Perce. But Perce had become used to it and pleased with it, whereas Spillar would not have had to because he had never known about it. This was a very odd task Perce now faced. He might be receiving a stranger's shock at the news that she had been expecting as well as his sympathies on hearing that she was not expecting any longer.

The brisk double rings of the phone at the other end sounded softened, almost muffled, as if they could be affected by the acoustic of the space in which they sounded. But when, after several rings, a voice answered, it echoed as if its owner was picking up the receiver in a somewhat hollow space, possibly a corridor. Perce pressed Button A, the pennies dropped, and tentatively he asked, 'Please, is it possible to speak to Mr Spillar from the Rio Café, please?'

'Speaking.'

This was a quieter voice than Perce (he did not know why) had imagined.

'We haven't met, I believe…' (Of course they hadn't met, but this was polite to say.) 'This is Hollard. Percival Hollard. My wife is Mrs Maureen Hollard who works for you in the café.'

At the other end these spelt-out formalities were received with silence. Then—'Yes?' Spillar answered, with an uncertain, interrogative note in the voice. 'Oh, yes…Good evening, Mr Hollard,' might have been a more expected reaction, Perce thought later. But then the way people answered telephones depended a lot on what they were doing when you rang and interrupted them, didn't it?

'My wife has asked me to ring you because she isn't well. She isn't well at all, and she can't be at work tomorrow.'

'I see.' Why, Perce wondered, was the man being so quiet and reserved?

'Mr Spillar. I don't know whether she told you this. Mrs Hollard was in the early stages of expecting an addition to the family.'

The silence following that was different from the initial silence, because Spillar easily intuited that he needed no information of this kind if Maureen's illness were not something to do with being pregnant.

'Yes, I did know, Mr Hollard…I did know,' he said. He was waiting.

'Well, I'm very sorry to have to give you the news that—that she's lost it.'

Someone tells you that they are sorry because they have bad news to break. And usually the recipient does not have to be openly grieved rather than just sorry, unless they are a relative. If they are not genuinely upset, excessive profession of grief is unnecessary, it easily sounds false. Knowing that he was more than likely to have been the father of Maureen's child, Spillar could not remotely think what it was appropriate to say to Maureen's husband. I am talking to a man whose wife I have got in the family way, he thought. He doesn't know I have. And it might not be the case that I have anyway. But the odds are that I *was* the father. He is saying that he is sorry she can't turn up for work because she's lost the baby. Honestly, I am relieved if she's had a miscarriage, aren't I? But all Spillar said after thinking that, after drawing what sounded like a breath of shock—or he hoped it did—was, 'Oh, I am very sorry indeed to hear that, Mr Hollard. I did know, as I said…It must be a terrible shock to her.'

'Yes, it is a shock. A bad shock.'

There was now a longish silence. Longer on the telephone than face to face. It was impossible for either man, husband or lover (which the husband was not aware of), persons who did not know each other, to imagine what could be said to follow this.

'She must get herself well again,' was what Spillar eventually came out with. There was really a very odd echo in the place where he was speaking, it was inexplicable. Was it a shared phone in some kind of passageway? There was nothing relaxed and normal about Spillar's telephone manner. The voice was peculiarly quiet. But there was a hardness in it. In the circumstances it sounded too down-to-earth, though not exactly abrupt.

'It was when she got home this afternoon...She's in bed, resting. It hasn't been good at all. She hopes you will understand.'

'Will I?' Spillar asked himself silently. 'I suppose I will.'

'She promises to be in touch with you as soon as she can.'

Silence for a bit, the silence of all the listening air out there on the line between these two quiet men finding it impossible to conclude this desperately uneasy dialogue; which it would have been so much easier for two women to have done.

'Thank you,' Spillar said weakly.

And again no warmth, no sympathy for Maureen. Or for me, Perce thought. It might have been easier if we had ever met. But, all the same...Spillar depended on Maureen and might have shown more concern.

He put down the receiver and pushed against the door of the phone box to enter the evening air, which felt much cooler than when he entered it. A woman waiting to use the phone called out 'Thank you!' as if he had caused her a long wait. Had he? He could not believe that. When he reached home Jack had not been up to the bedroom to see his mother, assuming that she was still resting and asleep; when that was the case she preferred to be left to herself. He was in the kitchen sitting at the empty table as if wondering when their tea would be ready.

'We might have to fend for ourselves and let your mother rest,' Perce repeated, worrying him about her because he was being so reticent. This was exactly the kind of moment he saw as suitable to make his speech—Jack not studying, doing very little, not looking gloomy or irritated or tired. Though probably hungry, as he was himself. 'She's not very well,' he continued.

'It's not something we need worry about, but she'll need looking after for a while.' He did think for just a second that he should make Jack completely aware of the seriousness of this situation for Maureen by coming out with the truth. But he did not. He had no permission from Maureen to do such a thing. It would also be too sudden for him to produce the right words. So he went on with his original intention.

'Jack!' he said, with a long-unused stress on the name to make the boy realise he was about to say something very important. In the past, Jack had been able to tell whether good or bad news, praise or reproach, was to follow entirely from the tone with which his father pronounced his name. But today he couldn't, the sound was completely neutral. The fact that he had used this startling form of address did make Jack aware that something momentous would be said.

'I realise—I hope you realise—that you mean a great deal to your mother and me,' he began, immediately leaving Jack altogether at a loss to see why his father had chosen this particular time for some momentous utterance. Had something significant happened—something to do with his mother's feeling unwell—to make this speech urgent and necessary? 'I know you've always been a boy for your mother rather than your father.' ('Have I been?' Jack silently speculated. He could not interrupt the tentative flow of Perce's words.) 'But we've always been both behind you in whatever you want to do. I've made a dreary life for myself, lad. I want you to make a better fist of it than I have, and I'm telling you we support you. You've been grown up for a long time, it takes parents a lot of getting used to—and I've never told you what I've just told you, and I thought I ought to.'

Jack had heard, and only half taken in, all the tales about Luddon, and Jedleigh's impending departure, and his father's fear that he was being worsted and even insulted in his office. He admired his father, he quoted his jokes and his stories at school. But now he knew more than ever that affinity, closeness, intimacy was more than he could feel, and transmit to his father, whatever he said in this low, intent voice before they went out to the scullery and set about finding their own tea. Therefore Perce believed, not incorrectly, that Jack had grown far away from him and needed the reassurance given today not because it related to anything else that had happened but because he had prepared himself to give it around now anyway.

'If you decide you want to carry on with your education after your exams in the summer, go to university and so on—we will do our best for you.' Then his father seemed to be hesitating before he said the next thing, which was, 'We don't have anyone else to do it for, after all.'

Dr MacCullen came next morning and told Maureen, after examining her and asking just a few questions, to be sure to rest completely for at least three days. During the daytime, with Jack at school, she could have the telephone at the end of its long flex on the bedroom floor and talk to anyone as much as she liked—except that Patsy Partridge was the only person she felt able to trust with her confidences. Not that Patsy was the ideal listener to her complicated sorrows. Patsy could be too brisk. 'We must think of some way of cheering you up,' Patsy actually said; not the right note at all. It was as if she could not understand the grieving that Maureen felt even more than the physical pain, the pathetic loss of hopes and assumptions and plans. Patsy seemed to have excitements of her own which took most of her attention, though she was not disclosing them yet.

On the fourth day, Saturday, she was fully up, dressed, and about the house. The official explanation for Jack and the neighbours was that she had had 'a nasty stomach upset'. It was still chilly in the morning and at night, but the midday weather was very warm or even hot, and she felt she could not keep Spillar waiting any longer for the decision she had made while lying in bed and resting.

First of all she made a short expedition to the shops to test her legs, and came back smiling. The sun shone, she only encountered people she did not need to stop and talk to. Jack was up, but back in his bedroom working by eleven. Perce sat and read the *Daily Telegraph* in clear enjoyment of the idleness of the weekend. At eleven-thirty Maureen told Perce that she was going down to the Rio to tell Spillar that she was giving up the job altogether, having already told him of her intention of doing this if the weather was fine and she felt capable of the walk and the task. 'You are sure?' Perce asked her; again. 'Yes, I'm sure.' 'Do you want me to walk down with you?' Not to accompany her into the Rio Café, but to be certain she was well enough to walk there and back. 'No. I'll only be ten minutes.' But he noticed that she had put on a best blouse and skirt for this ten-minute mission.

'I might be out when you get back—if I go and see Garner about this cricket idea.'

'You really think you might play *cricket* again?'

'I don't know. I don't know at all. I might.' But really he was flattered that Garner should have come up with the idea, and one brief test of his abilities was not going to do him any harm, was it? Reg Garner was the father of Clive Garner, Jack's sixth-form friend. For two years during the war Reg and Perce had been air-raid wardens together in the wardens' post in which they both did duty. The shared duties never resulted in anything more than continued acquaintanceship, greeting each other when—fairly rarely, because the Garners lived in a slightly more elevated street—they met at the shops. The consequence of one recent meeting was that Perce had, half in joke, offered himself for a Saturday match arranged for the mainly middle-aged cricket team Reg organised and captained in the park. The visit to Reg this morning would result in his being given, in effect, a trial as a bowler for this side.

Maureen stepped into the empty Rio Café with her words well prepared, at around twelve noon. The moment the rough bell rang and she was inside the door she already saw it as a place of the past. Here were the cheap chairs and the oilcloth surfaces of the tables which she used to wipe down, the salt and pepper in their chipped glass pots, the bottles encrusted with darkened deposits of sauce where the caps were screwed back on them after use. And the heavy cups and saucers, from one of which Oliver Hardy had not deigned to drink Spillar's coffee.

And there was Spillar peering through the hatch to see who had opened his door, the first time anyone had done that on this bright Saturday. All of this had once been and no longer was, she saw that as she looked at it. Spillar would just have to realise that her miscarriage had been like going into a tunnel and emerging in a different place altogether. Her world had relaxed into another kind of light, a newness after the year with him, a regained freedom.

He greeted her with no idea at all of what to say, but he had an intuition from her manner and her smart clothes that she was not going to return to work—otherwise she would have phoned beforehand to tell him when she was coming back. He had spent the last few days with no more decent a feeling than a sense of guilty relief. He had always had an eye for the women, had sometimes laid plans and made preparations as to when and where things could happen, and it hardly ever worked out. With Maureen it had worked out only too well. He had never before given a woman a child, let alone a child that miscarried—that left him in pride, then confusion, then despondency and then relief, in a most singular succession. Better to have had relations with a married woman who was still having relations with her husband than to have all this happen with a young unmarried girl of the alluring sort he hadn't the faintest chance of attracting. On the other hand he did not rule out marriage, even now, though he was going to rule out the landlady of the cold house of linoleum corridors where was he was lodging these days until his fortunes changed and he could once again find somewhere of his own.

Still, could Maureen have changed her mind and told her husband whose child it could easily be that she had lost? Surely not, he concluded; and he found he was correct in that regard. But Bob Spillar could not think straight about the whole issue.

'Hullo, Maureen.'

She had not forewarned him that she was coming. Using her name, something he hardly ever did, was an automatic means of acknowledging that a lot of things had changed since she was last here; it sounded to her almost like a reproach. Because what had happened was a physical event more than likely connected with what had passed between them, they looked at each other with the candour of people whose bodies had been joined in sexual intimacy.

'I'm going to give up work,' she said. Not 'working for you', but 'work'. To say it like that was both true and less negative about the job Spillar had provided.

'You are?' Only a small questioning in that. He could already see that there would be no changing her mind.

'Yes.'

'You feeling all right now?'

'Yes. I feel all right. It's all right with you if I don't come back? Isn't it?'

'Yes.'

'Will you get someone?'

'Don't know. It's not been that good lately. I'll have to give it a think...Summer's never so good...' It had been partly lack of custom that had started their affair in his rest room, out of the window of which she had leaned on that summer afternoon last year. 'I've got to think...I might get some part-time assistance...' And so on.

Why didn't she say something else? She was letting him go on and on.

'Was it very bad for you?' he suddenly wondered. It sounded like no more than curiosity, being said without a tone of even false sympathy.

'It was bad. It took a few days—but I've got over it.'

It all seemed a long time ago, although it had only been Tuesday.

'Will you find something else to do?'

'I told you—I'm giving up working.'

There was a pause in this dreadful exchange, in which he could only say out of kindness (he thought), 'If you're short of money and you do change your mind…'

'I shan't be changing my mind, Bob.' The use of his name echoed his use of hers at the beginning. 'Good-bye then.'

Maureen was already halfway out of the door with its bell still ringing when she remembered something and turned, and spoke again. 'Since you mention the money…There was the two days this week.'

Spillar paid her on Friday afternoons. She had only been here on Monday and Tuesday this week. He shook his head, as if to blame himself for forgetting, and went to the till Maureen usually managed. That rang; and he lifted the lid to fumble among the greasy contents of one of its compartments. Eventually he produced a green pound note which he pressed into her hand, closing her fingers over it to affirm that he was being generous.

'Oh this is far too much!' she exclaimed. He knew it was.

'No it isn't. You take it.'

She looked down at the dirty grey and green token in her hand, and back up at Spillar's face. She raised her eyebrows as he took his hand away from hers, and opened her shut fingers. She folded it into four and tucked it into one of the silk pockets inside her handbag, which she snapped shut in a businesslike way. Then she turned back to the door and left without repeating her farewell.

After a few yards' walk in the direction of the High Street with the idea of taking a look at the shops, only a minute away—'Well look who it is, if my eyes don't deceive me!' The woman speaking to her came up from behind, and Maureen turned to see that it was exactly who she thought it would be: Patsy Partridge.

Patsy had always looked—the word used by the flirty manager of the large corner grocer's where they had both worked for two years was 'vivacious'. 'You're looking most vivacious today, if I could say so, Mrs Partridge,' he would say. 'But then you always do look vivacious.' In the war it was the makeup she seemed still able to obtain, and the clothes, also the little earrings and the bright eyes; although her required white coat in the grocer's toned things down rather. Today Patsy had the same look, the identical manner—the shrill greeting was typical—as she had a few years before; though not surprisingly after all they had had to endure, she did look older and there was a kind of desperation in her abandon, her flushed cheerfulness, at the age of—forty-eight was she? 'Life is not going to be very long whether or not there is a war on,' was one of the sayings she lived by. And, 'To me it's a short life and a gay one.' Sometimes she turned up at her counter position in the morning looking as if she had had no sleep at all the night before; there having been no air raids to keep her awake.

'It's you!' Maureen exclaimed gladly.

'Maureen! What are you doing this minute?'

'What do you mean? When? Now?'

'Now.'

'I was going to the shops. I've just been—'

'But you're not in a hurry, are you?'

'Why?'

An inspiration, that was what she was having. And a peal of loud, bright laughter at the thought of something to cheer Maureen up after what had happened to her.

'I've got a date. Fancy coming in on it? Come on!'

'Where?'

'The Cosy Corner.'

The Cosy Corner, only two minutes away up the High Street, was a pet hate of Spillar's, a focus of his general contempt for empty respectability. 'Flowers?' was his aghast reaction when Maureen suggested buying some for the tables in his establishment. 'I'm not running the Cosy Corner,' he told her. For Maureen to go straight from ending her employment with Spillar to the Cosy Corner would feel like a blatant betrayal. Then she realised she owed no loyalty to the Rio any more, would not be seen by Spillar, and went.

'Why are we really going here?' she asked at the door. Patsy laughed. Even the bell at the Cosy Corner (which was not on a corner) rang more sedately than the one she had just rung leaving the Rio Café. But surely they would be unlucky? Every one of the eight or so tables was occupied.

'There's no room,' she suggested.

'Yes there is. Oh ye-e-es there is!' And, in the same sentence, 'This is my old girlfriend and workmate Maureen Hollard. We've just run into each other for the first time for several weeks. Maureen, this is Cedric—and this is Raymond—Ray.'

Patsy was speaking to two middle-aged men sitting at a table laid for four in the middle of the room. There was a pullover apparently belonging to one of them laid over the seat of one of the two free chairs to reserve it. Patsy had been expected, and was not late because the two men had not been served with anything. She was laughing gaily about all this, vivaciously, what fun it was! But sitting down opposite Patsy, Maureen thought she saw something strained—and rather drawn-in, or sunken—about her eyes that contradicted the cheerfulness. She was now going on to the two men about Whitlake's, the grocer's, in the early days of the war, the owner and his special allocation of petrol as a 'businessman', how he employed this tall blonde-haired lady as a secretary—but no one believed he had a typewriter—

who would go out with him in the beautiful Armstrong Siddeley ('you could smell the leather of the seats half a mile away when anyone opened a door') and one night, when the two had got into this car to go off somewhere after the shop had closed, his wife had come out with a spanner and smashed his windscreen as they sat there.

Maureen was thinking, 'What have I let myself in for?' Here she was, five minutes after using a lot of courage to go and tell Spillar that she wouldn't be coming back to the Rio, listening to Patsy Partridge put these two strangers in the picture about who she, Maureen, was, with these exaggerated tales about Whitlake's and these three dead people, the husband owner, his mistress blonde and his wife. All of them had been killed and never found after the direct hit by the V2 in February 1945 on the parade where Whitlake's was, in broad daylight, luckily long after she and Maureen had ceased to work there.

When a man came to take their order, peculiarly trim and eager and deferential with his precise little notepad, they decided on coffee, which he was seen to go away and measure out behind a counter in dessertspoonfuls from a tall bottle on the shelf—so that was not very different from the Rio Café. Oliver Hardy's disappointment would have continued at the Cosy.

'Ray's a bookmaker,' Patsy said suddenly. 'Any tips for the Derby?'

'Pearl Diver,' said the other man, Cedric; an accurate prediction.

'No!' Raymond came in emphatically. 'Don't waste your bet. Realise the favourite doesn't never win in the Derby. But apart from that you'd be better off with—' he mouthed the name of another horse silently, as if he wanted to keep it dark from the people around him. He needed to open his mouth quite wide, and show gold teeth at the side, and nicotine-stained front teeth, but even Patsy and Maureen could not hear him.

'Say that again.'

The same action, but this time the name was just audible: he named a mount which was scratched about ten days later.

It was as if all the two men needed to know about Maureen was that she once worked in a grocer's with Patsy, because neither of them politely asked her anything else; although she could feel them looking at her and making rapid male estimates of her physical features. They knew Patsy already, but this new Maureen was an object of natural curiosity. She did not feel displeased about this. She appreciated some attention after what she had been through; she had wondered whether she would ever feel wanted in that way again. Someone had once said to her, 'New friends are what you want to get you on your feet again after a tragedy—not just old friends, because they may be very nice but they'll *remind* you of it.'

Raymond had a moustache and the sort of faintly greying brown hair that may have been firmly waved or perhaps had just grown like that naturally, hard to say. He had warm and pleasant, yet wary brown-to-black eyes which looked at you carefully, possibly judging you as a punter. His brown suit was well-pressed and still smart, but it shone in places and it did smell slightly of tobacco. Cedric—but what was the connection?—was the more reserved, the duller of the two, but Maureen at this moment would have trusted him more. He had a full, rather pale face and wore grey flannels and a sports jacket, and some kind of club tie with a sparkling imitation gold tiepin.

The man, hardly to be given the status of a 'waiter' in the Cosy Corner—he seemed more of a stand-in helper for busy periods—set down the coffees with precise care. 'This is yours, then. Without sugar. And this one's yours, madam. *With* sugar. And these are the black coffees.'

'Ooh, you don't *say*!' said Raymond, quite loudly. But the man did not appear to mind, even smiled as if accepting a compliment.

There was a spurious energy about Raymond, a would-be 'dashing' quality, Maureen thought. Put on for the women maybe, but it amused her. Perce was steady and good, reliable, never dashing, not even when courting her. The very moment she came to this conclusion about Ray, looking at him and laughing at his response to the 'waiter' when the man had gone, she happened to turn her head to get Patsy's reaction and Patsy had rested her hand for a second or two on Cedric's hand, which turned over and clutched Patsy's momentarily, and released it as if to say, 'Yes, but not here—and not now.' People were peculiar. Cedric looked very dull. Once again there was that drained look under the glow of cosmetics on Patsy's high cheeks. The light on her from the bright sunshine today did her no favours where she sat.

Somebody said, in a murmur, 'They're open!' Maureen looked very doubtful and worried, but consulted her watch as if that would decide it. What exactly would she be doing going to a pub in this company? If she was late, she could quite truthfully say that she had run into Patsy, but—

'Oh just a quick one, come on,' Patsy said.

Outside again in the High Street, on the way to the Black Horse and Harrow, Patsy unexpectedly returned to Maureen's subject as they walked together behind the men, who couldn't hear them. And returned to her conclusion about it.

'There's one way of looking at it—and it might sound hard but it isn't really—it's that you've got your liberty, if you see what I mean.'

'What?'

'You've got your liberty to please yourself again.'

Maureen was shocked and did not reply. Being pregnant had confirmed her romantic sense of herself, even if Spillar had been no kind of opera hero. But to have her terrible, agonising loss of that creature she shed in the bathroom seen as a renewal of freedom…

Patsy was already onto another subject.

'What do you think of Ray?' she asked her quietly.

17

Meanwhile Jack had been reflecting on something else altogether.

That phrase his father used at one point in their odd, uncomfortable conversation on the day his mother had been taken ill—'You've been grown-up for a long time'—reminded Jack of a famous occasion in his school life some four years back. It had involved what seemed to be a ludicrous underestimate of the knowledge possessed by most boys in 4A in that wartime winter when the school was in evacuation in Herefordshire and living in three large houses converted into hostels.

One Friday afternoon they were due to spend the final period of the day crowded with 4B into what had been made into the music room for the weekly session of well-known and popular, sometimes patriotic, French songs—encouraging the use of French, encouraging these sheepish, broken-voiced adolescents to sing. There would be the 'Marseillaise', of course, and 'Madelon', and the cleaned-up version of 'Auprès de ma blonde':

> Auprès de ma blonde,
> Qu'il fait bon, fait bon, fait bon,
> Auprès de ma blonde
> Je passerai toute ma vie.

But on this particular Friday they were directed to remain in their usual classrooms because both the French master, who coached the boys in the words, and the music master, who played the piano, were indisposed and absent.

To supervise them in this lost period, and presumably to ensure that they spent the time in profitable private study, came the senior history master, Mr Alderstoke. He was a bachelor, a disciplinarian, a humourless leonine figure in his fifties who comported himself as if he was born to be a headmaster—but had unaccountably failed to achieve that status.

4A, fourteen and fifteen-year-olds, were not just severely instructed to 'Go on with private study, and I'll come round to see what you are engaged on,' as they expected. They were asked to put away their books, sit still, 'and listen very quietly.' Accordingly they arranged themselves as told, with nothing on their desktops except clasped hands. They wondered what was going to happen.

'I want you all to mark every word I am going to say to you,' Alderstoke began, with even-greater-than-usual gravity. What on earth was this? It could not be anything about the war because nothing momentous was imminently expected and, besides, any 'stop press' news spread around the school population like a forest fire. 4A soon appreciated that Mr Alderstoke intended to speak about a much more personal and private topic.

After a few more preliminaries, 'Your voice, if this has not partly happened already, will soon—as they say—be "breaking",' he said. 'That is to say, losing its high tone and becoming deeper. Most of you are still—I notice—singing the hymns in morning assembly with your high-pitched boy soprano voices.' ('Are we?' Jack wondered.) 'But already some of you have had to try to adjust your singing to a deeper level. You may have been a little surprised—embarrassed—to hear your voice drop down to a lower pitch in the middle of talking. You may have felt your faces and realised that a kind of soft down has been growing on them in patches, and that in places it has become rather rough and bristly. If you look at your chests'—'If you look?' Jack thought—'you may have observed that there are hairs on them which were not there before. And you may also have noticed that you are growing hairs on other parts of your body.' ('If you look?')

Ronnie Walston's face was now a picture of incredulity, not at what Alderstoke was describing but at the fact that he was venturing to instruct them in this way at all. His regular companion and fellow-sophisticate Bradburn, who sat next to him, bore a similar expression on his thin, fierce features. Immediately after this extraordinary lesson he said he wondered just how far Alderstoke was proposing to go. For the moment, Alderstoke only went as far as to put to 4A a simple question, to check whether they were following his meaning. Perhaps he himself needed a respite from the nervous effort required to carry his venture even as far as this.

'All this indicates that you are experiencing a process in your life which everyone goes through, for which there is a general name. Is anyone able to tell me what this stage of life is called?'

Jack Hollard could no more have raised a hand and offered 'puberty' than he could have grown wings and flown out of the door; which he certainly wanted to do. He doubted whether anyone else in 4A could have said that word either, in the presence of the fearsome Alderstoke, and surely no one was going to propose the wider, more neutral term available, were they? It would be too simple. Did Alderstoke realise the kind of conversation that went on in the dormitories of this evacuated school, the yard outside, the publications that were passed round, the sight of photographs alleged to have been found in parents' drawers when back at home for the weekend? Because of wartime staff shortages they had a few women teachers in this boys' grammar school. Miss Ingrew, who taught them geography and religious instruction, was much admired by certain boys. Bradburn said she was 'very slinky'. She was unable to turn her back on 4A to write anything on the board without a low voice somewhere at the back of the form slowly and solemnly enunciating the word 'con-cu-bine'. But no one was going to gratify Alderstoke with the word 'puberty', although it was clear that it was the answer he sought.

In the embarrassed silence, with many boys anxious to get Alderstoke out of this fix and hear what he would say next, Rickford's hand went up from the front desk.

'Yes, Rickford?' Alderstoke sent a strangely eager look in his direction.

'A-*dol*-escence, sir?'

There was a mild but audible groan, hardly more than a cynical exhalation of breath around the room at Rickford's toadying to Alderstoke with this inoffensive word.

'Adol*es*cence, yes, excellent, Rickford. Adolescence. That is the general term for the period of life, but the particular term for the changes themselves is "puberty".'

This was promising, and Jack saw Ronnie Walston lean forward receptively with the faint beginnings of a merry smile on his face which Alderstoke, a master quick to register dumb insolence, fortunately did not see. He shifted somewhat in his chair in front of the form, and looked round at the blackboard. This caused 4A to wonder whether he might be about to write up these terms, even offer diagrams. If so, he thought better of it and resumed his discourse.

'And,' he went on slowly, 'we can also speak of *sexual* changes. Important *sexual* changes. You will also be noticing various things happening in the behaviour of certain organs of your body. You may find them puzzling, even a little alarming. A boy may believe he has a kind of illness, or think these things are only happening to him. He may even think there is something wrong with him. But I want to assure you that that is not the case, and that you are not alone in experiencing these things. It is the common experience of everybody at the time of puberty. It is normal. Does anyone have a question?'

4A, with its wide range of sexual awareness from the awesome worldliness of a Ronnie Walston or a Geoff Bradburn to the comparative innocence of a Rickford, was collectively on the edge of its seat, though the predominant feeling was of intense curiosity about Alderstoke's purpose in giving this lecture—and whether he had been asked, or had decided to do it for himself.

Next to Walston, Bradburn slowly put his hand up. Alderstoke frowned a little, quite aware that Bradburn, while never in trouble for anything you could name, was regarded as a subversive influence in the school. People sitting at this moment in a position to see Bradburn's face, on which he had deliberately fixed a pale and serious expression, congratulated him later on pretending that he genuinely needed to be enlightened by Alderstoke. The master looked at Bradburn as if he would have preferred almost anyone else to come up with an innocent enquiry at this stage.

'Is it all right to ask this question, sir?'

'What question, Bradburn? Go ahead.'

'Do girls get the same thing as boys, sir?'

If Alderstoke registered the subdued wave of hilarity that spread through 4A at this enquiry, he ignored it; or chose to treat it as a demonstration of simple ignorance. Could he have heard it for what it was, a mocking challenge, and decided against a reproof which would have ruined the atmosphere when he was setting out to be sympathetic and helpful? He chose to do the only thing possible, treat it as if it was a serious enquiry rather badly expressed. But a curious expression of suppressed irritation appeared on his face; as if girls were emphatically out of bounds on this occasion.

'Well yes—yes. You are perfectly right to ask. They do. But in a different way, and that is another subject.'

At this point those sitting near to Bradburn later said that he was about to ask a supplementary question, but Walston put a hand on his arm to restrain him, correctly judging that he had gone far enough and that anything more would awaken Alderstoke's deepest suspicions.

'Are there any more questions? No? Well, then. I think I may probably have said enough for now for you to go away and think about it. And in particular I want you to have no fears about anything. What you are going through is, as I say, absolutely normal, and I want you to know this: if there is anything, anything at all, that you are finding strange or perturbing, please know that you are welcome to come and see me and ask about it. At any time. You do not need to tell or ask anyone else that you are coming, or mention that you have been to see me. It would be a private, confidential chat between ourselves, and I shall be very pleased to help you about any problem that is perplexing or worrying you. Is that understood?'

Jack could see Walston nodding, it seemed too enthusiastically. But he never heard of anyone taking up Alderstoke's offer. No one in any other form had ever heard of Alderstoke giving a talk of this kind before, and the enterprise was, as far as anyone knew, not repeated. Alderstoke left the school staff and returned to London at the end of the year, but perhaps that was absolutely normal retirement, or a preference for the city despite the hazards of the war.

A week after his father's quiet words to him about the future, the cricket season had begun, and Jack was batting. It was already very late May but the weather had turned hostile again. His hands, on this chilly, windy afternoon were cold in his gloves because it was proving a long and freezing spring, not yet summer at all. Later there was a story that this year's Commonwealth visitors, the Indian side captained by the Nawab of Pataudi, had taken the field in their first county match with frost on the grass...It was always the same, the summer sport beginning with the air frigid—then the winter rugby getting under way in cricket weather, serene and cloudless heatwaves arriving as September established itself. The grass on the field was green and long, even though the groundsman had been regularly out with his motor mower. He had also recently acquired a personal horse. But there was nothing of that magical mown smell that could make summer matches so pleasant to play.

Today's was the first on the list of significant games, a trial match on a Wednesday, which would decide who would be selected for the 1st XI. House matches would follow that, and later would come the annual Parents v. School fixture, which the School almost always won. Saturdays (and just the occasional Wednesday) were given to matches with other schools, and on the very last Saturday of term the School would play the old boys and almost always lose.

Jack Hollard was playing for the 1st XI as one of seven surviving members of last year's side. The other four were selected as the best people remaining from last year's 2nd XI. They faced an implausible collection of aspirants traditionally called 'the Others', the tail of that second side and one or two from the old 3rd XI.

School umpires at this early stage of the season were still inexperienced, and though staff umpires brought more confidence to the task they were not irreproachable. Kenrick of Sixth Science stood at this moment in his umpire's position at square leg, but rather too far away (his desire to stay at a safe distance?), looking timid and apparently too absorbed in his own thoughts to show close interest in his duties. The umpire currently at the bowler's end was Mr Medhurst, an elderly mathematics master who was known to lose count of the number of balls delivered in an over. Jack attributed the disaster of his own innings to some mental uncertainty about whether the delivery he was about to face was the sixth in this over, or the seventh, or even the eighth.

It came at him with complete accuracy, but very slowly; and Jack was convinced that the bowler's feet had trespassed over the line before it left his hand. But 'No-ball' was not called by Medhurst, and the delivery looked set to be a very full toss. Jack reacted to it with a combination of contempt and a conviction that by now his eye was well in and he could do what he liked. He believed he had time to advance down the wicket, take this harmless effort on the volley, and help it over the heads of the offside field for a couple of runs or maybe even a boundary. A mistake. When this cleverly disguised slower delivery pitched in front of him, he connected with an edge of the bat only, and the ball rose higher and a lot nearer than intended. Someone who had very happily allowed himself to be set at a deepish mid-off position, where you might usually avoid hard or risky work, saw the ball illogically and rather gently dropping towards him. He caught it, not having to run any distance, with humiliating ease.

Even for the first scrappy game of the season it was a shameful lapse. It was not excused. The sports staff were quick to reprove Jack. 'Pretty poor badminton stroke, Hollard?' said Ferguson, a French master with a special passion for cricket, as he returned to the pavilion. A worse humiliation followed. The 1st XI were actually beaten by the combined forces of the two lower sides. It was a bad omen for school cricket this summer.

Perce would invariably raise his eyebrows in a silent question when Jack came home after a match. If, or when, he did that today, Jack thought, he would simply shrug and declare bluntly, 'I got a duck,' and go straight to his bedroom to read. But instead of doing that Perce looked at his son and said, 'Harry Foster didn't come home last night...He was found dead in Sussex this afternoon.'

Harry was their next-door neighbour, a cheery, boisterous man, Jack thought. This was a shock that disturbed Jack more profoundly than he ever said.

'Marriage is a funny thing,' his mother murmured, inscrutably. What was the connection? Jack had a sense of something dark and beyond his understanding going on, the more so when a neighbour later said that Harry felt he 'had failed his wife'. Had it been on the warmer Sunday, or even the Monday, this week that he had wandered into the back garden for air? And found his father chatting with Harry over the fence? Harry had asked him how he was getting on at school, the least answerable of questions; and he had told him that things were all right.

Probably fifteen years younger than Perce, Harry always seemed normal and healthy despite some bad war experience. He had been in the army in North Africa and Italy, had been injured and brought back to recover in England; after which he had been available to be involved in the Normandy landings, and had seen the battle in the Falaise gap. Somewhere, somehow in that campaign Harry had fallen ill without being wounded, took no further part in the fighting, came home to England and his wife a second time, was fully discharged from the army just before the last crucial battles of the war began.

'But what happened?' Jack was too shocked, too frightened by death of any kind, to ask anything else.

'I was only talking to him in the garden on Sunday night,' Perce said. But that was no answer.

'I know. I talked to him too.'

Something apparently fixed and permanent had gone out of Jack's life, but neither war nor accident nor any expected illness had been to blame for it.

'Apparently he went off to work as usual yesterday—but he didn't turn up there and he hadn't rung them. No one thought this was anything peculiar. Harry and Millie don't have a phone—perhaps the people at work thought he must be at home sick and couldn't contact them. Millie works, and she gets home before Harry does. She got his tea—but he didn't come home to eat it. At eight o'clock she went out to a phone box and rang Harry's brother in Greenwich, but he had no idea about what could have happened. She didn't tell the police at once because he'd done similar things in the past, when they'd had rows—but he'd always come home very late the same night, or very early next morning. He'd stayed with friends on those occasions, but she went out and phoned one or two likely people and they hadn't seen anything of him. So she finally got in touch with the police.'

The police had nothing to tell Millie Foster. They just took her name and address and promised to let her know if they received any information. She then rang Harry's firm but they were just as puzzled as Millie herself. She then tried to think of anyone else she could ring if they were on the phone, even quite remote friends and acquaintances in case Harry had recently been in touch with them. She came up with a mere two telephone numbers and there was no answer from either. Then the police arrived, in the middle of the afternoon.

Nobody ever discovered where Harry Foster had been between Tuesday morning when he left for work and midday on Wednesday when he was found. It was thought he might have been wandering somewhere all night, and then bought a ticket for a train at Victoria.

Before finishing the story in the present Perce began to tell Jack about a conversation he had had with Harry over the garden fence some time last summer. Jack did not understand why his father was digressing, but he did not interrupt him. Whatever Harry wanted to talk about, and he was a talkative man, it was almost never his wartime experience. It was as if he wished to put it out of his mind entirely. But one night they had been discussing the terrible overcrowding in the London rush-hour trains, one reason why Perce made the journey to town by bus. Harry told a story on that occasion that could have been a sign of something. He told Perce that he remembered being on a troop train on the way to the coast. Although no one officially knew, Harry could make a fair guess that they were to be shipped out for the landings in Normandy (in his case after he had seen all that service in Tripolitania and Italy…). It had been intimated that wherever they were going they would not be back very soon.

On this troop train there had been standing room only for his unit. Harry was in a space between two carriages of crowded compartments, jammed up against a lavatory door. The train was stopped on a main line somewhere down in Sussex and they were held there waiting for about half an hour. As they stuck there, every couple of minutes came a loud whistle and an express would go hurtling past on the next line, shaking them to bits. Harry told Perce he was nearly flattened by the draught from the passing train because the window was open on this muggy morning, to get some relief from the atmosphere of men and sweat and smoke. Harry stood uncomfortably between the lavatory door and this open window of the exit door with nowhere to move his feet—because of all the kit and so on taking up the floor space.

He told Perce that he could have put his hand out of that window next time there was that hooting from an oncoming train, and pressed down the outside handle and opened the door and fallen into the path of an express. That way he would have got out of joining in the invasion of France, and he wouldn't have seen all the horrors he had. When he told Perce Hollard all this he was laughing. But—

Harry had caught a train with a corridor that was fast from Victoria to Foxstead Woods, then went on down to the coast. Somewhere along that line after the latter stop there was a pause between stations for an express train to pass through. Harry must have gone along the corridor, yanked up the heavy leather strap on a door between carriages, released the outside handle and fallen out—thrown himself out—in the path of another train. The policeman who came to tell Millie had been told by the Sussex police that this had happened before in the same place. Apparently Harry had been killed at once, and his body badly mangled. The police had recovered his wallet and contacted the headquarters in his locality as soon as they could, which was actually not long after Millie's visit to them. There was no doubting the body was

Harry Foster's, but Millie had to go next day to identify what was left in the mortuary down in Sussex somewhere.

The words his father used—'what was left'—were what terrified Jack most of all. They were worse to him, as he had known Harry Foster so closely, than anything experienced or read about in the war, worse to him than the sight of bombed places in London, more shocking than Coventry, Hamburg, Dresden, Belsen, Hiroshima, Nagasaki. Those words were about someone who had until yesterday lived next door. Jack's father had been an air-raid warden. Someone in their road had once coldly told Jack that, along with the rescue men, Perce had once been called out to collect bits of bodies after a V2 bomb had hit the market in the High Street. They had just put a sack in his hand and said, Go and pick up whatever you can find. If you're not certain it's part of a body, if it's got blood on it shove it in the sack, we'll sort everything out later. His dad had never told him about this episode, or anything similar. Or his mum, he supposed. 'What was left.' His father had walked around smoking ruins looking for what was left, and two years later had come out with the phrase in his shock about the news of Harry Foster's, their next-door neighbour's, death. The war remained in Perce in the hard words he used. It had stayed in Harry Foster's mind as well. Harry did not throw himself from the train the first time, and escape Normandy, Falaise, the rest. He went on the train journey the second time and did that. He cancelled out his experiences the second time.

What was the stricken Millie to do with Harry killing himself? At the end of Perce's account of what had happened, a scream of grief came through the wall from next door, where Maureen was sitting with Millie, trying to offer her more sweet tea (which she refused). Disbelieving son and father sat in silence, unable to say anything about the sound. Then, after a silent full minute, 'Marriage is a very funny thing,' Perce affirmed.

18

On the very first day, a Saturday, of June—

'You are not doing it properly,' Sylvia's sister Eileen was telling her.

Much later in her life Sylvia did come to forgive Eileen for so many well-remembered instances of bullying and bossiness, more of those than moments of friendship and fun. 'I leave one single thing to you and you mess it all up,' Eileen was saying.

Tom Freeman did not really seem to know what he could do here at home before they left. If there was anything. Well, he had done a bit of cleaning of the place under Eileen's instructions, and with his oldest child Frank in his national service uniform helping them out, or getting in the way. The girls, or Eileen really, had put out the plates and cups and saucers and spoons on the table, with room provided by pulling out the one extra leaf. There was not much space left now, here in their front room. There would not be enough chairs for people to sit down, not that they expected many. Writing those letters to them, going out with small collections of pennies to the telephone box along by the shops, had been sufficient. Not nearly everyone had replied. Tom supposed that some who had not answered would nevertheless turn up; if they had not already died themselves, he said ruefully. Life was getting to be like that.

Sylvia had been arranging flowers in the vases because Eileen had thought they should have some to brighten up the place and they had gone out early to buy them. Eileen had supervised Sylvia when she was pressing hard on the scissors from the sewing drawer to cut through the stiff stalks, but Sylvia had appeared completely incapable of arranging them in the two receptacles she had, one vase far too large, the other too small and narrow.

'Let me do it.' And she pushed her aside, so that Sylvia stood nearly crying as Eileen fussed with the positioning of these expensive early summer blooms. Sylvia connected flowers with beauty and happiness, she loved flowers from remembering they once lived in a house with a garden where she watched them growing and knew the sequence of flowers from the back door along the fence to the end wall: first the alyssum, then the tulips, then the peonies, all this on the sunny side and nothing much in the shady parts of the garden. Now she had to see the flowers in these vases on a day like this, she almost hated them for changing their character.

Saturday, then. The day was mostly given to cricket matches against other schools but this week there had been a cancellation. Rain looked likely, although so far it hadn't started. The way friendships worked at the senior end of Jack's school, most of all in this year leading up to Highers, and particularly in these last few weeks before the exams started, was that no one met out of the school during the week, and not very much at the weekends; only in the holidays when time seemed relatively plentiful. It was a serious life. Neither Jack nor Clive belonged to the youth clubs that produced girlfriends for some of the others, bending the unofficial rule that whilst studying for Highers you did not have friendships that distracted you from work—though not *breaking* the rule.

On this Saturday, though, Clive Garner and Jack Hollard were walking to the station at around one-thirty. One of the set plays, *Antony and Cleopatra* was showing in town, and they had tickets. They were early, and crossed the park, and made a short cut along various sidestreets or less busy thoroughfares. It was not a coincidence that one was the road where Sylvia Freeman lived, though Jack did not say so to Clive. He had never told Clive about Sylvia. What had happened still felt bad and humiliating at times, but at this moment, all of three months later, the worst feeling he had was an aching nostalgia which led him to guide Clive towards the station past Sylvia's home.

The cork factory two doors away from the printing shop above which Sylvia and her family lived seemed to be at work even on a Saturday afternoon, judging by the tapping and hammering and ringing they could hear; or which Jack heard clearly because of associating it with Sylvia, and Clive barely heard at all. Turning his head to glance at the small factory premises, then instinctively up at Sylvia's window, Jack missed for a second the two solid black and shining vehicles leaving the light flow of traffic along this road and drawing up at the kerbside in front of two other, smaller cars already parked there.

Clive was aware of them first. "'Boys and girls are level now with men,'" he said, "'And there is nothing left remarkable beneath the visiting moon.'" This was not a completely appropriate quotation, and the remark sounded gratuitous to Jack, who was suddenly standing there open-mouthed and frightened in case this could be something to do with Sylvia. Immediately came the most drastic thought of all—perhaps even Sylvia herself could be in that coffin in the first of the two big black cars. Jack knew that was unbelievable; but for a moment he could almost think it was true. Could it be? After Harry Foster…

Knowing they were not pressed for time, the two young men stopped and turned to watch respectfully what was going on, instead of just walking past. A lingering horror and incomprehension at the thought of Harry Foster's suicide joined in Jack's mind with the thought of Antony's end in the play, commemorated with words about death the leveller, to give him the worst surge of fear and trembling he had ever known. Sylvia? He found himself shaking now, muttering to Clive something about 'I know the people who live at that number,' and Clive not registering the dread in his friend's voice.

Out of the hearse stepped its young driver and his front-seat companion. The two of them walked solemnly across the pavement to the outer door giving access to the passage from which a house back door opened onto a dark hallway and stairs to the flats above the printer's premises. Sylvia and her family lived on the first floor and there was a second-floor flat too, so it was not necessarily a funeral involving them, was it? The driver stood back to let his older colleague, tall and pale and clearly the senior undertaker, open the door and pass through first. As he did that, he looked back neutrally at the coffin in the hearse, which had only two sprays of flowers and a green wreath resting on it. Jack followed his gaze and saw that it was not very large, possibly it contained a young person, a large child, or a small older man or woman. No one as tall as Sylvia.

It seemed to Jack that the undertaker and his driver had been an age on that other side of the outer door, which was somewhere he had never been himself. But eventually the door opened again and out came a drably suited older man about the age of Jack's own father but more bent and less healthy-looking. He was followed by the undertaker, who took up a position on the wide pavement midway between the door and the hearse and nodded the minimum of grim-faced greetings to a group of mourners emerging to be escorted by the driver either to the passenger car or to one or other of the two private vehicles. Next after the older man was a plump young woman in grey with a black scarf over her head, who immediately linked arms with a young man coming after her, a soldier in khaki with a cap on his head. When she appeared to say something to him he took the cap off, but he did look uncertain as to whether he should have done that already. There was no sign of Sylvia.

These three went to the funeral service car behind the hearse. Then a further couple, elderly persons, emerged, the woman crying, the man guiding her to the first private car, a small Morris, with his arm round her shoulder. Following these two was a somewhat defiant-looking older woman walking by herself in a dark crimson two-piece costume and a navy blue blouse which did not suit it. She looked up and down the street as if she expected to see someone, or just see more people than were there. But the only figures attending on this small event were Jack and Clive. This person then went on to the Morris, and sat in the back.

After her came a younger pair, dressed up in dark coats covering clothes similarly not quite suited to a funeral. These were probably relations of the dead person who were not close to the family. They opened the doors of the second parked private car, a grey-green Jowett Javelin. They were the last. There was nobody else at all. Not Sylvia, Jack could see.

But why was the back door of the passenger limousine still open, and why was the plump young woman in grey about to alight from it again? And then drawing back because someone else, apparently expected to join them but late in coming out, was suddenly on her way to the cars?

It took Jack several moments to realise that this *was* Sylvia and feel infinitely relieved at the sight. This delay was partly because Sylvia seemed for a moment what in truth she now was: taller than when he had last set eyes on her, probably now taller than Jack himself because she was wearing high-heeled shoes. And partly because she was wearing black entirely, everything she had on was black. The coat, the blouse and skirt under it, the stockings and the shoes were so starkly black, so dark and elegant and brightly clean, that in these same long seconds Jack wondered whether this was not Sylvia at all but someone resembling her. A sister? A cousin? But the walk, and the way she moved her head and her arms, were unmistakable as she crossed the pavement in a half-run and entered the open door of the limousine and hurriedly pulled it shut behind her. She looked so changed from the shy girl Jack had walked with, was dressed with such daunting maturity, moving so beautifully in just these few steps that he felt she was now beyond him, that he could never hope that such a transformed creature would accept his friendship, his love.

Sylvia Freeman gave no sign of having seen Jack Hollard standing about ten yards away watching. As the small procession of cars moved away very slowly, with the senior undertaker from the hearse pacing in practised dignity beside it, Jack saw Sylvia in profile through the rear window of the limousine. Her head was bowed and her face white, icily and distantly lovely, and resembling the older girl or young woman wearing grey next to her, as well as the young soldier in uniform; and he realised that it must be the mother of the family in the coffin. He and Clive now resumed their stroll towards the station, but did not want to overtake the four cars, which covered the hundred and fifty yards to the corner in reverential slowness. Would it go at that speed all the way to the cemetery, Jack wondered? It would not. He saw it halt at the corner, as it had to, and collect the walking undertaker at that point. When it was free to do so, it turned the corner and was rapidly out of sight.

Sitting back in an ample corner of the car, Sylvia felt in the pocket of her coat for the keys to the downstairs front door, and also those to their own flat on the landing. Eileen had told her that when Mum arrived in the hearse in the road downstairs everybody else should leave first. Sylvia would be the best person to wait until they had all gone, then lock both doors and bring the keys out with her. But once out in the passage she was stopped by a fear that she had not properly locked their own door. So she let herself in again and made sure, then had to re-lock the downstairs outer door and was late emerging, to Eileen's tense irritation.

The coat Sylvia wore was not familiar to her any more than her other funeral garments were familiar. They had all been borrowed from Mandelston's, where she had been doing the Saturday job for seven weeks now. She had taken them away at twelve o'clock today because she had asked for the afternoon off for the funeral, and this borrowing had been done at Mr Baxton's suggestion and with his permission. Eileen had been utterly horrified. 'Who is this Mr Baxton? Has he got the authority to let you bring these home? How is anyone to know you haven't swiped them?' She had not been in the least reassured by her young sister's saying that Mr Baxton had made her absolutely swear to drop in and return the clothes the same day after the funeral, and put them back into his hands in a bag, and he would make sure they went back to the appropriate drawers and coat-hooks. It perturbed her even more to hear that this Mr Baxton was an older assistant in the Gentlemen's Department who had been very kind and friendly to her.

Sylvia had in fact noticed and recognised Jack. She assumed that he must have heard about her mother's death and had turned up to see the funeral cars leaving the house. She was impressed by this. But she did not think for a moment she could show she had seen him. It would be impossible, with a boy she had given up—the boy her sister had told her to give up—to reveal that she knew him (with the cars waiting) and she certainly could not make any sign to him. You could not wave to somebody from a funeral car. Besides, she felt very odd in funeral garments which Mr Baxton had persuaded her to try on in the shop when the boss of the Ladies' Department was not there to see her. Sylvia could appreciate that Mr Baxton himself might be liable to be questioned about it if Mrs Laidlaw found out. For that reason she was going to have to return the blouse and skirt and coat and scarf very quickly to him, with no one else in the shop seeing her. The black silk stockings she had bought for herself.

The speech of the vicar at the funeral in the cemetery chapel was unbelievable. How could he be talking about her own mother?

He said nothing very much about her personally, but then he had not known her and they had not known him. He offered some words of comfort to her father, whom he named. And then to her brother and her sister. And finally some to Sylvia herself as the youngest, which was kind and nice of him. He said the family should hold itself together as one after this tragic loss of a beloved mother, and think of each other in their grief, and the older ones should all think especially of Sylvia, who was so young to have to face such sorrows. Yet all of this was unreal. Mum would surely be back at home in her apron handing out sandwiches when they returned, wouldn't she? Asking them, what had her funeral been like? And what had made them rather late coming back? Her dad, never a noisy or vigorous man, seemed even quieter and slower now than he usually was. All of his small stock of humour and resilience seemed to have been exhausted.

It was Eileen who put the kettle on when they were back at home, and brought out the dry sandwiches and cakes from the larder. To her surprise and relief everybody could find a seat in their living room because it turned out they had exactly the right number of chairs, nine: for Dad, and next to him Uncle Bill and Auntie Daisie, and talking to Daisie Mrs Whirnell from upstairs, in her crimson clothes, who had lived alone in that third-floor flat after Mr Whirnell, or Corporal Whirnell, went. She had the habit of saying, 'I lost my husband during the war,' and when people said they were so sorry she added, 'Oh, he wasn't killed or anything, he just decided not to come back to me.' Mrs Whirnell liked to give advice, and was giving some to Auntie Daisie at the moment. Bill and Daisie's son Barry found something to talk about with Frank because he had begun his own military service right at the end of the war, thus had finished it last October, six months before Frank was called up. He and his young wife, the somewhat prissy Lucy, sitting silently next to him and enjoying the sandwiches—if she always ate as hungrily as this why was she so thin?—had married two months after Barry came out of the army. They lived with Barry's parents, so all of that household was present and no other relations. Not that there were any others living near enough to think of attending the farewell for this small, unnoticed life. Death happened, didn't it? Tom Freeman sorrowed passively, hardly ever spoke about his wife Rebecca later on.

Mrs Whirnell knew the cost of living, the rent, the gas, the electricity, working to provide just for herself. Tom would be on a low wage at the cigarette factory. A boy doing his military service was not bringing home much money, if any, for the family. Eileen wouldn't be earning much from the dodgy proprietor of that little clothes place, and like Frank she hadn't passed any exams. That left Sylvia. Sylvia was the brightest of the three. She was the youngest, but of the three children she was the one who had made sure she looked really smart for her mother's funeral. Neither Sylvia nor Eileen told Mrs Whirnell how she had come by the clothes that had so caught her eye.

There were a few memories to exchange, but not very many. Nothing surprising, let alone remarkable. There were silences during which everybody drank more gulps of tea. Mrs Whirnell's voice rang out clearest and longest across the subdued room. She was always like this about illness and death. Perhaps she had been pitched into this philosophy of unfeeling, almost cruel, practicality by her husband's desertion? Unless that streak in her personality had helped to cause his departure…She saw the plain needs that followed on every tragedy, the heavier despair echoing on in dull, everyday ways after the shrieks of anguish. How were the Freemans going to live without their little mother and her regular job? Every family needed its mother. She, Beattie Whirnell, couldn't be mother to these two young ladies and the older boy. But she could help to get them onto the right path.

'You're fifteen, aren't you Sylvia?'

'Fifteen and three quarters.'

'You could leave school then?'

'Yes.'

'Seems to me you will have to leave school now?'

'Don't know.'

Mrs Freeman was no longer there to intercede and protect Sylvia, leaving Sylvia the more vulnerable to Beattie's pressures. Thus Mrs Whirnell's loud advice came to alter Sylvia's life considerably, because she found herself suddenly wondering whether a permanent job in Mandelston's Ladies' Department might not be an attractive thought.

19

Thus, eventually—

One day Jedleigh came out, closed the door of his inner office behind him carefully as if he had a special purpose in doing that, and stepped down into the main room with the increasing smile of a man willingly letting responsibility drop from his shoulders. It was a smile several people in the office had recently noticed.

'Mr Jedleigh looks happy these days,' Dora Parsons had said, and it was true.

Jedleigh looked around him and, instead of making straight across the room as he usually did, swung round to the right and stopped in front of Perce Hollard's desk. This was lunchtime. Luddon had gone out, so had the other two juniors, Doreen and Terry, leaving only Perce and Dora in the room. Today Dora had brought sandwiches cut for her by her mother, so would not be going out to seek a lunch elsewhere. Neither would Perce Hollard, who liked a quiet lunchtime chat with Dora when that was possible. Carstairs was nowhere to be seen.

'I see we are neighbours,' Jedleigh said to Perce.

Perce looked up with some surprise. He was being spoken to informally in a way he rarely was by the boss of the department, and it was not a matter of business, to be discussed while he remained seated. So obviously he pushed back his chair and made to stand up.

'No—sit down Mr Hollard—please...' Jedleigh smiled in a very warm and relaxed fashion now. 'I didn't realise until I saw your application last week how close we lived to one another.'

Perce had completed his application for Jedleigh's post with endless care, in pencil first, with a rubber beside him, read it and re-read it under his breath, inked it in, read it again, posted it assuming despondently that Luddon would not have to write one. He would just be asked to fill Jedleigh's shoes, the job going to him without even any formalities. It was time wasted for Perce; but he had to try.

'Where do you live, sir?'

'I live in Witham Grove.'

Witham Grove was on the other side of a class boundary, in a region where detached 1930s houses stood at the end of little gravel drives, some of which were beginning to be inhabited or re-inhabited this spring by small cars proudly polished on warmer weekend mornings. On one side these homes were built on a higher level, you went up a short, steep, concreted slope past the car to get to the front door. The Grove was certainly quite close, no more than fifteen minutes' walk away. How come he and Jedleigh had never met at the shops, or on the way to the office in the mornings? It was easily explained. Witham Grove and the shops serving it were rigorously divided from Perce's district by the railway line. It was simpler for Jedleigh to come to work by train than to walk an extra ten minutes or so and catch Perce's direct bus. Besides, Jedleigh's shops were more select and expensive. Witham Grove looked in a different social direction. One of Pierre-Henri Mallinot's pupils, the one brought by her mother to Benford Street in a Lea Francis, came from Witham Grove.

'I have a suggestion,' Jedleigh went on, staring straight into Perce's eyes; a penetrating look, but friendly all the same. 'It is: That you come round for a cup of coffee, or maybe something a little stronger, on Sunday evening, say. Anyway, this next weekend if you possibly can. Just yourself this time, as it's short notice. Iris and I will invite both of you properly another time perhaps.'

'Er—yes, sir.' Perce knew that there was nothing to stop him accepting the idea. But the speed of his acceptance was because of his astonishment that Jedleigh should have come up with it. For some reason he could not remotely guess, Perce Hollard was being favoured. Letting him down gently was what he concluded.

'Not because you feel you have to, you understand—but if you would like to. There's something we should discuss. Would Sunday suit you?'

'Well—yes—Sunday evening as you say, sir.'

Perce rarely, if ever, walked in the direction of Witham Grove. It was well outside his patrol as an air-raid warden. He checked the route he would take on a map of south London spread out on the kitchen table, remembered the subway under the station, and decided it needed as much as twenty minutes to be sure he was there on time.

It rained on the night, so hard that Perce wondered whether he should not seek to put off the appointment. But there was a problem about that: he did not have a phone number for Jedleigh and if Jedleigh had one (which he surely did) it did not appear to be listed in the directory.

Under the railway tracks, reached in about ten minutes, was this dim, tiled pedestrian tunnel Perce passed through to find that the rain had lessened when he emerged at the other end, in the light of a summer evening, in a cleaner, smarter district. The contrast was noticeable, the chilly rain sparing the more affluent neighbourhood. But suddenly a tall girl, Sylvia Freeman, whom Perce did not know, came running through the tunnel after visiting Cyril Baxton in his tiny flat, virtually a bedsit, at the top of one of the older, larger houses in the Grove. This figure was drenched, so it must have been raining there just as much. He looked at his wristwatch, with its face blurred by rainspots, and mistook the second hand for the minute hand.

Although Perce knew no one in Witham Grove and had never visited a house in it, he knew where it was and the map had only confirmed it. The Grove was characterised by some people in his road as 'the part where the posh houses begin'. As he entered this region he felt constrained to be, and to look, well-behaved and polite. Why? He was already a polite and well-behaved man, he considered. He worked for a fairly impressive shipping company in the Victoria area, rumoured by some to be destined for a move to the docks in the future. Perce would mark a cross against the name of the Conservative candidate at general elections, he always had, because it gave him a glow of pride to feel himself one of a class of Conservative voters. But his home and his life were not on the same level as those of the people in Witham Grove.

The first ten or so houses were built on that higher ground, and Jedleigh's, he saw from the numbers he was passing, would be one of them. It did not have a car, but it did have glossy ivy, the brighter for the rain fallen on it, which covered the side where a porch light already on illuminated a fairly grand suburban front door. But as Perce covered the last twenty yards it suddenly began to rain harder again, in fact very hard.

How curious and uncomfortable it felt to be meeting his boss at his home. Work and leisure never mixed easily. They should be kept apart. Luddon had made a mistake (never repeated in the office, so far as Perce knew) in asking people round for a religious evening. Only the knowledge that Jedleigh would soon no longer be his chief reassured him. After a few more weeks he would no longer have to arrive at work aware that he had seen something—however little it might turn out to be—of Jedleigh's home life in Witham Grove, and therefore behave differently towards the boss because of a privilege accorded to him. It was all a mystery. But—had Luddon already been here?

He rang the bell. There was no immediate answer, no sound at all inside the house. A faint light in the hall, seen through the wrinkled glass panes of the door, told him nothing. Yet eventually, as Perce was about to ring again, it was strengthened by another light being switched on. The shadow of a figure, not a large figure, advanced. The door was opened. Jedleigh was there in grey flannel trousers and a knitted pullover.

'Mr Hollard. Splendid! You're early. You're first!'

Perce looked disbelievingly at his watch, almost prepared to deny he was early; and saw that he had misread it the last time he had consulted it in the rain, and was here almost twenty minutes too soon.

'Oh dear—I'm sorry, sir. My watch must be fast, unless—'

But what was this about his being 'first'?

'No need whatsoever for anything resembling an apology. I'm delighted to see you found me without too much trouble. Now let me have that umbrella and that coat. Typical summer appears to be with us all too soon.'

Perce knew that he would be taking in everything about Jedleigh's home so as to tell Maureen about it later; she had been most intrigued to know he was going there and was rather relieved not to be invited herself. As he relinquished umbrella and mackintosh to his host's charge he saw a picture on the wall to his right, a strong, square, firmly moustached face with tinted cheeks, Joseph Stalin. Farther along the wall was a framed photograph, coloured in a similar fashion, of what appeared to be a Russian revolutionary scene. Unusual this was, except that patriotic pictures of allies had not been uncommon on the walls of homes, schools and places of work during the war.

There were domestic sounds in a kitchen nearby, but no one else appeared, and when Jedleigh guided Perce into a large back room facing the garden the two of them were alone. On a low table, on a runner, Perce saw three china mugs, three very small glasses, and a plain glass bottle with an unidentifiable label, half-full of a colourless liquid. Were the words on this bottle in Russian? He thought so, the script was different. As he took his seat he could not help seeing that the bookshelf under which his armchair was placed was packed with volumes about the Soviet Union, communism and communists, and the war on the Russian front.

But Jedleigh of course noticed the not altogether accidental interest Perce was taking in all this, smiled, reached up, prised a book out of a top row, opened it at the title page, showed it to him with pride.

'Signed for me by Mr Litvinov himself,' he said. Perce could only nod in bewildered acknowledgement. 'Willie Gallacher signed the photograph,' he went on, pointing to a framed face his guest hadn't yet noticed, a balding man in spectacles with the smallest of smiles on severe lips.

'So *that's* Willie Gallacher is it,' was all Perce could manage to offer in his amazement. With every few seconds passing in this house, every remark made by the man, Perce Hollard was watching the old Jedleigh with whom he had worked for years—never knowing, or guessing, or trying to guess what his politics were—vanishing in front of his eyes. Perce obviously disapproved (he was conscious of the uncomfortable tone of voice with which he accidentally reacted) of Gallacher, Communist MP for West Fife.

If he looked disapproving, that was regrettable in view of Jedleigh's pride in these possessions, and he would have to take extra care. He had, after all, been specially invited here for some purpose, and despite the shock of seeing these exhibits in a house in Witham Grove he should be polite and well-behaved in Jedleigh's home. Dropping his eyes he took in the hammer-and-sickle on the mugs set out on the table.

'I've been a member of the party since it was founded,' he said. 'Can't claim to be a founder member but I was recruited by one. I suppose it's in my blood.' He did not explain that remark. 'We have a good and very lively—very effective—branch in the borough. We might put up a candidate next time round.'

'Have you visited the USSR?'

It seemed obvious and courteous to enquire, what else could he say? And it sounded to him like a neutral, an easy question.

'Not as a delegate!' Jedleigh laughed. Laying claim to a decent, humble status? 'But three times as a holidaymaker. Now I'm going to have the time, we intend to make a few more trips and a few more contacts...Would you prefer coffee? Or a touch of vodka?'

Perce had never tried vodka. The offer presented him with a quandary. In truth he did not fancy the experiment of a 'touch' of vodka, which might in these peculiar circumstances (Jedleigh looking very frank, relaxed and cordial) turn out to be a generous glassful. It might be too much for a first venture, and he might have to drink it all, out of politeness. You could not refuse or abuse the hospitality of your seniors by leaving most of what they provided you with...And then, he thought that if he took some it would increase the sense of being part of a conspiracy, of suddenly moving in an alien, dangerous world. In Jedleigh's home, of all places. By Jedleigh's invitation. It was all extremely puzzling. Why should Jedleigh suddenly single him out for an evening of sociability when he was about to leave the company?

'A very little vodka,' he heard himself saying. 'But with some coffee, perhaps?' Respect, deference and moderation died hard with Perce Hollard, in fact never died in him at all throughout his lifetime.

'To be altogether honest with you,' Jedleigh went on as he poured the drink, 'I have not enjoyed much of the time I have expended in the service of Fitch & Armstrong. All I can say is that it has provided me with some useful insights into the inner workings of a bit of late capitalism. You don't have to agree with me, but when something is rotten the character and progress of the decay is worth studying, isn't it!'

Perce was so deeply astonished by this extraordinary confession from such a loyal bastion of the firm that he forgot to prevent Jedleigh filling the glass with vodka to the top. When he pushed it across the little table to Perce he had to do it with extreme care. Then the doorbell rang, and he straightened himself up to go and answer it.

When Alan Carstairs entered the room he did not appear to experience any of the surprise Perce Hollard felt (and must have shown at discovering who the other visitor was). Carstairs did not react in any particular way to Perce's presence, other than to greet him with a nod and a silent half-smile in his direction. It was not so much a greeting as an acknowledgement, as if he had been fully expecting to see him.

All he said as he sat down without being asked and saw the table of mugs and glasses, was, 'The usual, Arthur. Thanks.'

'Iris!' Arthur Jedleigh now exclaimed with a kind of eager bark of welcome to his wife, who suddenly appeared with two jugs, the coffee and the milk, then went back to the kitchen for sugar and spoons. 'Not to be confused with the Industrial Research and Information Society.'

'What is that?' Carstairs asked, and received no answer. Iris, in an apron, had heard the joke before. She quickly received a perfunctory introduction to Perce from her husband (but not to Carstairs, whom she appeared to know already), then retreated again. Arthur Jedleigh himself—Perce realised he had never heard the known Christian name actually used before—did the honours, giving Carstairs as big a vodka as Perce's, then seeing to his own glass. What on earth was going on?

'Our futures!' he said enigmatically as he raised it. Carstairs grinned now, and raised his glass vigorously. He and Jedleigh looked at Perce together as they did that. He felt scrutinised, obliged to lift his own glass similarly, which he did with an uneasy grunt of 'Your health.' He did manage not to choke on the first draught of this colourless fire ever to surge across his tongue and down his throat; but it took all his concentration. He was very glad not to have to say anything until Jedleigh had finished what he now began to explain.

'Mr Hollard—will you be happy with "Percival"?'

'Of course—fine.' Still in utter bewilderment, fire burning in his throat and oesophagus. He could not say, 'Call me Perce,' obviously.

'Percival. You won't have known, but you will know now, that Mr Carstairs—Alan—has been interviewed and offered my post when I leave. Naturally he has accepted the offer.'

The glass of vodka, still virtually full, threatened to tremble and spill in Perce's hand. He could not dare a further sip already, so he turned and put it down on two available inches of bookshelf behind his left elbow. Next to *Soviet Communism: A New Civilisation* by Beatrice and Sidney Webb. He looked at Carstairs, whose mouth was open so that he might have been taken to be smiling. But a closer look at his eyes revealed that he was not, and when he closed his mouth his face had one of the most serious expressions Perce had ever seen on it. A different Jedleigh, a different Carstairs.

'Oh...Congratulations, Mr Carstairs,' he found he was able to say. 'I'm very pleased to hear it.' As much as a rival applicant for the job (except that he had not realised he was) could be sincere, he was sincere in saying that. He was the more sincere for registering that the appointment had not gone, as he had assumed and dreaded for months, to Luddon.

'Now the point is, Percival,' Jedleigh resumed, 'that in years of service you are much the most senior person remaining in the department.' Perce was still so surprised at Carstairs's appointment that he had not not started to wonder why he himself should have been passed over for a man so much younger. Especially one who had cast himself so persistently as the office clown. He did reflect, though, that Carstairs's function as Jedleigh's chief younger clerk, unofficial assistant, and willing runner on errands to higher persons in the firm must have given him an advantageous position which he had silently cultivated. And, interestingly, very little of the humour, and none that Perce could actually remember, had ever mocked his immediate boss.

'You are seven years senior to Mr Luddon in service, I believe? And a bit more senior in years?'

'Yes.' Perce confirmed both statements. He was beginning to feel his years if Carstairs, at no more than twenty-seven, was leapfrogging older men. But to have Luddon put in his more junior place in comparison with Perce cheered him, and was surely a good sign, or something? On the other hand, what difference would Carstairs's promotion make to either him or Luddon anyway? The answer to that unasked question was provided quickly, and was completely unexpected. To give it, Jedleigh took a good gulp of his own vodka and went on.

'I spoke to the director who has charge of appointments, and suggested that with the department expanding into its larger office, and business looking up somewhat, it deserved to be allocated another fairly senior post. For once, somebody actually listened to an opinion of mine. So would you feel able to move into Alan's—Mr Carstairs's—office when he's in harness? And share his responsibilities—as a deputy head of the department? Next in line to him? In a new post? There will be a rise in salary, of course.'

There had been that unexplained second table in the new office...With two new telephones on it, the same as Jedleigh's own table—or Carstairs's table, as it was going to be. Perce noticed at once that Jedleigh was not using words like 'senior', 'superior' or 'chief' about Carstairs's relation to him in this new arrangement. He was talking about shared duties, being sensitive of the effect on an older person of working with the younger rising man. There would be more equality about it than existed between Jedleigh and Carstairs at the moment. It was unbelievable, impossible to take in. For weeks. But at this moment Carstairs nodded, smiled, looked very happy with the idea; as he continued to be throughout the conversation.

'Alan would like you to accept, if you are happy to work alongside him. It would be an internal arrangement—no advertising outside the firm.'

'I should very much like you to agree, Percival.' When Carstairs said this he pronounced the words in what amounted to stern, almost reproving tones, and an almost threatening glance—which he softened into a wide smile as if to indicate that he was joking, the old Carstairs of the office fantasies. But in that second, given the context of all this, Carstairs became formidable, a figure of unexpected and disconcerting power.

'"Perce" usually,' he said, for want of anything else to say, now rendered mildly informal by the vodka, and capable of that correction. He knew that whatever he said he could not afford to hesitate. He reached behind him for that vodka glass, took it into his hand, and drank more. 'Well—of course I accept.'

'Miss Clissold is coming into our office, by the way,' Carstairs said now. At that, Perce nearly did choke, because Carstairs's expression was wholly serious, very solemn in fact. 'No one can provide a better link between departments—she's made it her business for a long time, as I think we all know.' And Jedleigh was looking serious about this, and nodding a lot.

There was only one other possible thing for Perce to say, knowing that if a new post—as Carstairs had announced that day—had been approved at executive level, there could have been only one other possible candidate. He could have asked, 'What will Mr Luddon's position be?' But he stopped himself saying that, and in any case Jedleigh pre-empted him.

'We considered Mr Luddon's position,' he said, 'in case you are wondering. Frankly we believed you would make a much better fist of the new job. You are an older servant of the company, and you deserve it more. If Mr Luddon wants to prove himself, he has plenty of time in which to do it. And elsewhere, if he prefers to.'

There was a very short but noticeable silence in which Perce and Jedleigh both fortuitously looked at Carstairs as if expecting him to say something.

'Not in *my* office, at any rate,' was what he said.

20

Something different and unrelated—

On the following Wednesday a sturdy figure in nautical cap and dark blue bellbottom trousers was walking determinedly towards Jack Hollard along the pavement. Jack was on his way to school and was late. There was plenty of room for two people to pass each other, but this large young sailor was likely to collide with Jack unless one of them took a step aside to avoid the other. Yet when Jack tried to do that the sailor advanced squarely in front of him. And stopped him short in a disconcerting, aggressive fashion.

'Look out where you're going, Hollard!' Ronnie Walston said.

The challenging briskness of Walston's manoeuvre underlined the difference of their experience in the nineteen months since Ronnie had left school at the end of his fifth year. First he had gone into the head office of a retail concern in town, then he changed that job for something similar that paid better. Then he was conscripted into the navy (his own preference) for his military service, and sent to a naval barracks on land while Jack was still carrying a small old leather briefcase, his mother's birthday present, to and from school. Jack was aware that if he passed Highers with any ease he would be launched into an attempt to scoop an Oxford or Cambridge scholarship in the autumn of this year.

He told Walston that much when he asked, and put a sardonic edge on what he was both proud and apprehensive to be thinking about.

'Tell me. Is it true,' Walston asked him very seriously, 'that at either Cambridge or Oxford—one or the other, I forget which—one of the colleges has a life-size painting of God?'

Caught out (and he cursed himself later for being so easily taken in by Walston), Jack replied, 'Oh, I don't know. I'll have a look round and see, if I go to one of them for the exam.'

Walston only smiled, sparing Jack any mockery for his innocent answer; and went on to an even larger subject.

'In the end, what do you reckon you'll do for a living? When you've gone through college and come out the other side?' He asked because he had his own answer ready and it would put Hollard in his place—though Walston was not unfriendly, or even faintly arrogant on this point, just pleased with his idea.

'I'm waiting and seeing,' Jack said. Which he was. 'Maybe not my father's kind of work.'

'Nor me, neither!' Jack had no idea what Ronnie Walston's father did, though he assumed it was something worldly, because Walston gave a worldly impression. Perhaps it was even an underworld, of black marketing or small-scale straightforward crime. Or it could be that it was nothing of that sort at all and Walston's view of life was an original rebellion against respectability. 'I reckon there's a pretty good living to be made out of shady books and magazines—and all sorts of weird products—as long as you keep within the law.'

He was already late for school, it was nine-fifteen. What was Walston talking about? Making a living out of obscene or banned books or something? Did he mean it? Walston was smiling at his evident bewilderment.

'Do you ever go up to the Charing Cross Road, or Soho?'

'Yes—'

'I bet you just go to the highbrow bookshops, don't you!'

There was no denying this, though Jack would have denied that adjective, used by his father when he was in a bad mood and impatient about what Jack tuned into on the radio.

'Well, even in some of *them* there's a back room where they've got all the hot stuff. But. You go to any smaller shop in that area, particularly down the sidestreets, that's got ordinary popular books out in the front on shelves, or in the window—and you go into the back room or basement—or upstairs—and it's *Berlin Ladies of Pleasure*, or *Diary of a Young Girl*, or *A Schoolboy's Confession*. They're not shit hot because they've got to keep within the law. But they're on the way. If you get on good terms with the proprietor he'll find you something imported—under the counter.'

'For a price?' Jack suggested, feeling sophisticated.

'You've said it. But—you go and ask why he stocks this sort of thing—' here Walston turned up the palms of his two hands to denote the Jewishness of any interlocutor in such a shop, recalling to Jack the antisemitism in some of his fifth-form humour—and he says, "*But it sells*!"'

Jack was about to say that because something sold it did not automatically mean that it was good, it could mean exactly the opposite. But he gauged that Walston would not appreciate that argument; and besides, he was already onto something more.

'I've read loads of that stuff. Loads of it. And I reckon I could write it better myself. In fact, I knocked off something and sent it to one of the magazines, a publication I bought in a shop in Old Compton Street. They didn't print it, but they wrote back and said it was definitely on the right lines, and I was welcome to try them again if I wrote anything else.'

Jack listened to this with incredulity. Yes, Walston had done well in his General School Certificate exams (wasn't there even a rumour that he had gained an unlikely distinction mark in English Language?). But he had never had any notion of entering the sixth form and aiming for a college or a university.

Was he saying now that he genuinely wondered about making a career in writing—there was no other word for it—pornography?

'You can't get away with bare-bollocked filth at the moment,' he was going on while Jack looked at his watch. 'But just wait. I reckon it's all going to ease up—maybe very slowly, but eventually they'll get away with describing a little more of this and a little more of that. Showing a little bit more of the naked truth in magazines and films. I'm going to get in on all of that if I can.'

'Is there a living in that?' Jack could not begin to believe it. Or not believe that there was a living for a grammar-school boy with General School Certificate and Matric. The world of the squalid book and the lewd magazine was surely inhabited by dirtier, more furtive persons who had barely any proper education at all, just enough crude intelligence for that debased level? Jack recoiled from that world, despised it, feared it—and was amazed that Walston should even joke about taking it up. Because he was joking, wasn't he? Everyone talked in public about stamping out that sort of activity, and whenever Jack had to skirt Soho (he never went *through* Soho) he realised how much he applauded that necessary process—which wasn't proving very successful, all the same. As for the women around Piccadilly Circus, of any age but to him looking mostly rather old—the women who walked past slowly and stared frankly in his direction...Walston was destined for trouble if he took up with all that, wasn't he?

And where was the Walston he had met not more than a month or two before this? Who had been on his way to the library to look up some French literature from the nineties, if they had anything worthwhile? Today he appeared to have plunged straight into the world described by French decadent poets without showing any talent or desire to write about it, as they had done...Had a few months of naval service had this effect on Walston?

'There's a whole bloody packet of money to be made from sex publications,' he was insisting. He seemed to be happy to betray all the serious education given him by the school in wartime to pursue a life on these suspect fringes of society. That was what Jack was thinking. But perhaps this was a phase through which Walston would pass on his way to a completely ordinary job in insurance?

Yes, he was sure that Walston was spinning a peculiar and typical fantasy that fitted in with all his apparent knowledge of sexual activities. Jack would not have seen Walston to be a prophet of times to come and opportunities for what Jack called 'betrayal' far beyond anything he was capable of imagining. And yet the chance meeting and what it told him about human aspiration stuck in his memory and left him uncomfortable; just as the two deaths this spring, Harry Foster and Sylvia's mother, had hurt and scared him and probably induced the kind of dream he had finally woken up from, oversleeping and late for school (now very late), ninety minutes before.

Harry Foster had taken his own life, horribly, and Sylvia's mother was dead in that ordinary and pathetic, and yet strange and bizarre way, and the world was breaking violently into his own uncertain peace of mind. The *Borough Mercury* carried the story of Mrs Freeman's death. She had been found in a seat at the back of the Royal Circle in the Empire, where she worked as a cleaner. On a matinée day she had been cleaning under the seats in preparation for the evening, when she sat down for a moment's rest, presumably, or because she felt groggy. The other cleaners believed she had already gone home when they themselves left.

Someone coming in early for the evening show found her. He was shortsighted, and when he consulted his ticket and went to claim his seat from her in the dim upstairs gaslight he realised he was disputing his reserved place with a corpse. Perce read out the item from the *Mercury* oblivious of any knowledge his son had of the dead woman, and made the sort of grisly joke of which he was sometimes capable—this time at a moment when Jack least wished to be reminded of sickness or death. '"Mrs Rebecca Freeman, 48, was at first mistaken for another member of the arriving audience by people taking their seats for the Sid and Beryl Burgess Show." Apparently,' Perce commented, 'it was heart failure that killed her, not the show.'

'I've got to get to school,' Jack said to Walston, who seemed prepared to go on for even longer expanding on his plans. 'I've got to captain the 1st XI in a match against St Bart's this afternoon.' It was one of the two Wednesdays when they had a match with another school.

'So you're still playing that game?'

Jack had a clear memory of making a lot of runs off Ronnie's bowling in a form match just before Walston left school...

The dream. He thought it the worst of his life; without his realising, his own mind must have been designing to terrify him. It was so bad that he had to confess it among Sixth Arts during morning break in the library, and pretend to be laughing at himself for having it when he was still shaking with fear inside.

Around the table as they waited for Ferguson to arrive for a double period of French were all six members of the form. Someone had said, 'When I closed my book and switched off the kitchen light last night dawn was breaking. I didn't bother to go to bed after that.'

'I did sleep,' Jack said. 'But I had this hell of a horrible nightmare. I was going down the stairs at some place I stayed at with my parents when I was about seven. There wasn't any bathroom on the top floor of this boarding house where we were staying, and I was back there in my dream and having to go down to the floor below in my pyjamas—but it was broad daylight. And I turned right instead of left outside the bedroom door and found the wrong staircase. It was a second, narrow staircase leading to the kitchen or somewhere, I actually did it once for real, which is maybe why I remembered it. I was going down and down and it turned into a kind of spiral staircase, with stone steps. And suddenly I could hear the footsteps of someone coming up towards me.

'"The Man in Black",' said Arkley, naming the radio horror show they had all listened to. Jack laughed with the rest of them, but uneasily.

'It wasn't "The Man in Black",' he continued. 'But last week we had a neighbour in our street, a neighbour who did himself in by jumping out of a train into the path of an express.'

This also had been in the *Borough Mercury*, and Clissold said, 'I read about it.'

'Well, when I got to the next turn in the stairs what was coming up—the footsteps I heard—was not a complete person but only part of a body. It was just from the belt—a kind of army belt—down to the feet. Khaki trousers and big army boots. And the fly-buttons were all undone and just gaping open, but there was nothing left where the genitals should have been.'

'So you said,' Arkley suggested, '"Pardon me, old chap, but your medals are showing."' General nervous laughter at this, with Jack joining in.

'No, I didn't,' he continued. 'I was bloody sweating. But the next moment I'd woken up—and I was in bed at home. But—'

'You mean there's more?'

'—just as I was giving this big sigh of relief that I'd only been dreaming, I had the feeling that the dream was still with me, I couldn't get rid of it. I mean, it was like I was wide awake, and it was morning, and there was someone coming up the stairs, maybe my mother to see if I was awake or not. Then the door opened, and I was still dreaming—and there was the top half of the body of this bloke that had killed himself. Just his head and shoulders and chest, coming into the room and speaking to me, carrying something on his shoulders—a kid, or a large baby or something. And it was dead, with its head falling forward. And then I did wake up.'

Was it because of the obvious seriousness with which Jack had told the story that Clive Garner exclaimed, 'That was some dream!'? At the end of the account they were all silent. They could all have confessed to dreams as frightening as this, and it reminded them of their own nightmares; of which they were afraid. They would have liked to think of further jokes with which to exorcise the conclusion of Jack's. But they couldn't. And then suddenly Ferguson was through the door and sitting down at the end of the table and they were back to their standard Higher School Certificate anthology of French romantic verse.

That afternoon Jack took guard by placing his bat at middle-and-off in the usual way, and tapped a slight dent into the grass as much to look confident and expert as to achieve anything useful. Then he stood up, pushed his shoulders back, looked around him, and actually did take in the fielders' positions before bending over his bat to face the first ball. The opposition this afternoon presented a parody of keenness. St Bart's were conspicuously smart, striving in the field to give an impression of lethal attention to these opening bats. Clive Garner was captain of cricket now. He had just won the toss and obliged the visitors to field. They were the 1st XI of this Catholic academy which prided itself on the number of candidates it produced for the priesthood, or at the very least for the monastic life; a monk who appeared to be one of their games staff had come with them today. Most of their players seemed very large, and it was believed that St Bart's could keep boys until the age of twenty if they decided on a priestly or monastic vocation. Jack's fellow opening bat was Clissold, and on their way out to the wicket he observed, 'God grants indefinite exemption from military service.'

The St Bart's opening bowler was going to be fast, judging from the long walk he was taking before he turned and looked at Jack. Before beginning his run he stood for a moment enigmatically still, ball held in his left hand at waist level. Then he glanced upwards. And crossed himself, with his head dipped slightly forward during the action. Finally he started his forward progress, very slowly.

This run was very odd. It increased in speed with every step on the way to the crease, but at the last it seemed to check itself with a flamboyant stamping of feet and flailing of arms to effect a delivery that arrived at no more than medium pace, with the promise of safely passing Jack's off stump. Jack quickly thought that if he ignored it as beneath his dignity, merely lifting his bat away, it would do no harm. He was right. The wicketkeeper, standing only moderately far back—significant in itself—collected it with no difficulty, as if he knew very well the trajectory and pace of this man's usual deliveries.

Jack believed his eye was already well in after a dozen or so much nippier balls in the school net from one of his team-mates just before this match started, so he thought he would leave the second ball alone in the same way. He kept well away from the third ball also, and was correct again; and this series of innocuous challenges to him, to poke at a delivery and dispatch the ball to one or other of a group of large but agile-looking slips—this was becoming boring. It really should not be allowed to finish as a maiden over, giving St Bart's an undeserved pride in thinking they had the school openers bottled up.

But then, between the fourth and the fifth deliveries, at exactly the moment when the fellow's arm was stretched out to catch the ball which had been lobbed by wicketkeeper to gully, from gully back to bowler, Jack had a sudden and startling vision. It was what Clive Garner later described with a smile as 'an epiphanical revelation'. It was an improvement on Clive's idea in Joe's Arcade a couple of months before: that life was nothing better than gaming, you bet or gamed against impossible odds and you had to lose. Clive's notion was too dramatically, gloomily elementary. Jack agreed with the analogy of a game, but, specifically, cricket itself provided a much more sophisticated metaphor.

You did not simply bet with arbitrary odds of about one hundred to one against you, with one dull, preordained unfairness conquering you, as in the amusement machines. In cricket you were given a variety of chances and rewards; if you failed with the bat then there might be the ball, or even the field. Nothing in the contest was tedious or predetermined because the animosity of the opposition came at you in so many different forms. It varied from bowler to bowler, and often from ball to ball, so there was the possibility of being dismissed by any one of a number of bowler's skills or batsmen's errors. Most of the danger was unexpected, as in life.

Each game of cricket was long, as life could be long. Like life, it required application and endurance. But, as in life, there was in cricket a wide range of chances if you applied yourself with energy and ingenuity, and if you were determined to endure. Jack thought all of this as the St Bart's opening bowler was plodding off again to that distant point at which his long and pointlessly energetic run would commence. Jack recalled the words of a famous philosopher paraphrased by Ferguson and repeated by this cricket-loving French master on many occasions: 'Cricket, far from being slow and boring is the most exciting game of all because there is a potential crisis in every ball.' For the first three balls of this over, Jack decided, I have courted no crisis and taken no risks. Then, as the bowler turned, ran laboriously forward, accelerated as before, Jack also had an incongruous, out-of-character, enlivening thought, possibly spurred on by the conversation with Ronnie Walston in the street that morning. It was that hitting a four and seeing the ball cross the boundary would be like getting into a girl.

This delivery, intentionally or not, was an improvement on the previous three. It was pitched very accurately on middle-and-off, and came faster through the air and off the ground. It had to be dealt with. Jack, as he described it to Clive, stiffened the sinews of his forearms, summoned up his blood, stepped forward, and drove it through the St Bart's covers. The outfield was damp and slow, not mown very regularly because of the recent rain; but the ball was departing with gratifying rapidity. Clissold was shouting 'Yes!' at the other end and leaping forward. He was already halfway down the wicket before Jack had recovered from his surprise. They ran two, the ball was beyond the reach of the nearest St Bart's fielder, it had almost reached the trees under which Sylvia Freeman would be sitting on a Wednesday afternoon in two months' time. Then it did reach the trees, and the boundary. The umpire's arm went round in a horizontal arc. It was not necessary to run any more.

St Bart's lost by forty-six runs, Jack scoring thirty-four of the school's 128 for eight.

At this late time, with the exams starting in days, there was a subdued kind of hysterical humour about Highers around the Sixth Arts table in the library. If they labelled all this effort absurd, it did help to keep them going. Beyond the exams lay the prospect of competing for university scholarships or places, and the name of Vanstone was constantly mentioned by the masters, especially Ferguson, because he had been casually very good at French. Vanstone had been school captain and the most notable academic talent seen in the place for years. He was also extremely adult—and unconventional. He smoked Turkish cigarettes in the prefects' room but let it be known that no one else had the privilege of smoking at all. He brought the *Daily Worker* to school and left it among the other newspapers to which the library subscribed. He had no objection (though he did not play himself) to the prefects' poker games, but he made a condition. The cards would customarily be dealt onto opened copies of *Everybody's*, or *Illustrated*, or *Titbits*, which could be rapidly closed if any unwelcome visitor arrived in the prefects' room—the Headmaster himself had been known to call in. Vanstone insisted that the game be played on copies of the *Economist*, or the *Spectator*, or the *New Statesman and Nation*. When Vanstone won his Cambridge scholarship and left, the unconventionality in the sixth became cruder. The most popular game in the prefects' room became the one someone named 'invisible badminton'.

The prefects' room was small, eight feet by nine at the most, with room only for the table, a few chairs, and an open, free-standing unit with several bookshelves. This was six feet and six inches in height, and few books were ever kept on it. Teams of literally any smallish number—most typically two or three against three or four—selected themselves. The bookshelf was then shifted into the centre of the room so that neither team could see its opponents on the other side; and someone screwed up a sheet of foolscap paper into a tight ball. Each player would take a book in his hand as a 'racquet' and someone would shout 'Coming!' and 'serve' the ball of paper over the top of the book-shelves. The purpose of the game was to prevent it reaching the floor on your own side by despatching it back again.

If a player failed to intercept it and bash it back with a text-book on its arrival, the ball might become lodged between bodies jammed together in the tiny overcrowded space. If you moved, it might drop to the floor and lose your team a point. Extraordinary manoeuvres and contortions were necessary to prevent that: the ball might be stuck between two knees, belonging to one or to two persons, and extreme skill was required to rescue it, convey it to the top of the bookshelf unit, and send it over to the other side—without warning this time, as it was 'in play'. There was no fixed duration for this game, defeat being accepted when either exhaustion or boredom or the school bell halted the action.

How could any of the current Sixth Arts approach the standard set by Vanstone, only one year older than them, in sheer self-possession? In matters of clothing, for example, it was not a question of money. Vanstone's parents were not affluent, nor were they spoiling him. Vanstone simply maintained that when he was due for a new item he would acquire the cost of it from his father and make absolutely his own choice of a garment without parental advice. Jack still, at eighteen, went with both of his parents to the shop, as if he not only had no money but no reliable judgement either.

Two Saturdays before Highers began, Perce, Maureen and Jack Hollard went along the High Street to look for a new sports jacket for him, and ended up at Mandelston's. Jack went into the Gentlemen's Department with them in a mood of reluctance that threatened to turn into plain resentment. He walked along rows of jackets on hangers with indifference, turned and looked away. And through an archway dividing this section of the shop from the Ladies' he saw Sylvia.

It was his first sighting of her anywhere since the day of her mother's funeral. Sylvia was standing in what could only be required staff clothes near a display of jerseys in that Ladies' half of the shop. He had seen her in the distance talking to a middle-aged or perhaps elderly man assistant, who seemed to make his apologies to her and came over into the Gentlemen's to see if he could 'be of any assistance' to the three Hollards. Jack was not sure that he himself had been actually seen and recognised by Sylvia—any more than he had when he saw her enter the funeral limousine—though she had followed Cyril Baxton with her eyes when he left her side.

Now Jack was letting himself be measured by this suave, jocular assistant, whose accent was surely closer to that acquired by Vanstone during his visit to Cambridge to sit the scholarship than to the tone and vocabulary of most people employed in a men's clothes store. The social significance of this was mysterious to Jack Hollard. This person seemed genuinely to be of upper-middle class 'extraction', a term which always reminded Jack of the dentist's but now had him thinking that this man appeared to have been extracted from his own class and unaccountably dropped into this humble occupation.

Looking in a mirror at one of the jackets he was trying on, Jack knew that afterwards he was going to go back to Mandelston's and speak to Sylvia. What had dropped her into this situation, when staying at the Technical College would have prepared her for far better things? He knew about her mother's dying, but he did not manage to think on from that knowledge and work the rest out for himself.

'I don't like him in that,' Maureen said, about the jacket that her son had liked best. Third person, as Jack stood in front of his parents and Cyril Baxton. (At this moment Pierre-Henri Mallinot paused to look in the window displaying men's mackintoshes.) 'It's got a spivvy look,' Maureen insisted.

'What's "spivvy" about it?' Perce wondered aloud.

'The colour. He can't be seen in a colour like that.' The jacket was well short of a navy blue, a little lighter than an Oxford dark blue; but it was bright, and to Maureen it seemed too loud, too jazzy, liable to attract attention. Jack was aware that the only good way of attracting attention was through a special sort of conventional smartness, for example a well-cut dark grey suit.

'I call it quite smart,' he said, arguing with them in the first person. He tried pleading that it was five shillings cheaper than one which his mother had preferred; but it made no difference. He gave in to her wishes, his parents (or rather his father) were paying for it, he would never hear the end of it if he had his own way.

He had to leave with them because he could not immediately say he was going to speak to a girl assistant in the Ladies' Department. But they understood when he declined after another hundred yards to join them for more shopping, or window-shopping. On this cloudy, mild early summer afternoon he doubled back to Mandelston's and made for where he had spotted Sylvia. And was immediately face-to-face with her. She was undoubtedly taller and much more the fully grown woman than when they had walked out together in winter snow. It daunted him to see that, and have his reaction to her appearance on that Saturday of the funeral fully confirmed. His heart and his breathing reminded him how daring this was.

He had not prepared anything to say to her apart from a greeting. He noticed that her face was fraught-looking and pale, as well as made up, and he suddenly came out with what he was noticing without even saying 'Hullo'.

'You look as if something's worrying you.'

She was surprised, not at seeing him (she had noticed him ten minutes earlier) but because he knew she was upset.

'They're accusing me of something.'

He did not know what on earth to say to this.

'Me or Mr Baxton.' As if he knew who Mr Baxton was. It was so clear and painful in her mind that she almost assumed he would know.

'Accusing you of what?' he mumbled back at her.

'Some money's gone they were collecting for someone leaving. Gone from the teapot.' As if he would naturally appreciate that collection cash would be stored in an unused silver teapot on a low cupboard shelf.

'That's awful...How much?'

'Nearly nine pounds.'

It was several times the cost of the sports jacket in the parcel under his arm.

'What will you do?' It was not a sufficient answer.

'Wait till they find out it wasn't me. Nor Cyril neither.'

'That's who? That's Mr—?'

'Mr Baxton...Cyril. We'd been seen near where they kept it.'

'But there's lots of people work here. And there's customers.' Accusations of this kind would be much more serious at work than at school, but Jack was finding little to say to help Sylvia.

'It's bound to turn up,' he assured her.

An older woman assistant pushed past the two of them and gave Sylvia an unfriendly, hinting look. Jack knew he had to go, staying would bring Sylvia more trouble.

'Can I see you some time? You can tell me all about it?'

'Sylvia!' the woman said, passing them again; a sharp reminder of duty in the business of the shop.

'I've got to go now,' Sylvia said; only that, so nothing was arranged.

The new jacket was intended for general use, school and home. School uniform was not compulsory in the sixth form, except for the tie and the hated cap. No one's parents had much money. Clothes would habitually descend from older to younger brother with the post-war shortage of clothing as an excuse. It was not the custom anywhere in the school to notice a different garment because it would usually be unnoticeable, even familiar. So Jack's Saturday sports jacket was very prominent, though not quite in the same category as Vanstone's new suit. In the sixth the standard term for recognising conspicuous new clothing was not 'Spiv!' as used in the lower forms, but the one used by Ferguson to praise homework that did not deserve a high mark but at least showed sincere effort: 'Quite commendable!' As Jack entered the library on Monday morning Clive Garner turned from his locker and called out, 'Quite commendable, Hollard!' Someone else said, 'I say!' When Clissold entered the room he asked, 'To what do we owe the honour? Is this *de rigeur* for Highers?'

But only three days before the fateful beginning of the exams Elmborough produced a notable surprise. Into the usual gathering at the lockers and around the table before the beginning of morning lessons in Sixth Arts he came in wearing an altogether extraordinary black suit.

The jacket was a very smart, double-breasted affair, but so different from anything on show in post-war tailors' windows that it was obvious it had not been bought or manufactured very recently. It was tight-fitting, with wide lapels. The trousers were similarly stylish, but more 'normal' in shape, not claiming attention, as the jacket did, for its dandyish, if respectable, features. Overall, the suit was one you might expect to see worn in a posed photograph of forty years before, the garb of someone standing with dignity in a studio while the photographer required him to be absolutely still and buried his head under a black cloth to focus him in the viewfinder of a large square camera set on a tripod. It would not have been wearable as an office suit in a firm demanding unostentatious decorum in its servants, because it did not appear to go with solemn business weekdays. It was a party garment, suitable for weddings or possibly as a Sunday-best suit for walking out. It was a suit made with an indefinably debonair pre-First World War cut; designed to be dashing and conspicuous.

'What on earth, Elmborough?' Jack exclaimed.

Elmborough laughed as well. He had expected this kind of response and anticipated a lot of vigorous comment, possibly also disapproval from the staff. The Elmboroughs were a family of one girl and four boys, but this suit could not have descended from one of Elmborough's two elder brothers. A bright, virtually new yet utterly antiquarian phenomenon, it had a different, poignant origin.

It had been the property of Elmborough's grandfather, who had died during the snow in February, just before his sixty-ninth birthday. He had bought it in an ordinary tailor's in around 1906 as a mildly rebellious gesture not long after he was married and his wife was already expecting Elmborough's dad. 'There's not going to be much cash around when the little one arrives,' he had reasoned with himself. 'I might as well splash out on something I can wear with the chaps while I can afford it.' It cost Charlie Elmborough as much as seventeen shillings and sixpence.

But it remained a suit worn only on special occasions, because marriage, home-furnishing and the first child left little time for going out on the town or even down to the local public house after work; or even going out with his wife, who developed surprisingly into a home person and disapproved of his men friends.

'I put a stop to a lot of that!' she would announce triumphantly in later years. By the time Charlie Elmborough realised he was not likely to use it very often, the fashion had changed. He would not have raised more than five shillings for it by selling it second-hand. When he died it was almost as good as new. And though comically outdated, it was sufficiently formal for a sixth former to try it out in school as an alternative to a blazer or a sports jacket.

'Extremely commendable,' was Clissold's remark. 'School Sartorial Shield.' But it was Proctor, their history master, enthusiast for specific prophecies and general theories about the future, who was persuaded to make the most intriguing comment.

'What is your verdict on Elmborough's suit, sir?' Arkley asked him.

'I'd noticed it.'

'Yes, but what is your verdict on it, sir?'

None of this was unkind to Elmborough because Arkley put a tone of implicit admiration of Elmborough's daring into the question.

'It's very smart, Elmborough,' Proctor suggested, playing this carefully. 'Yes. I like it.'

'It's a suit my grandfather had, sir, and hardly ever wore. He died, sir in the cold, in the winter...And well...'

'It's perfectly fine,' Proctor assured him, to check any delayed possibility of hurtful humour around the table. 'Who knows, you may have started a fashion.' Elmborough grinned, so it was all right. 'In fact, there must be a lot of extremely stylish suits hidden among the ancestral mothballs all over the country—waiting for the chance to be worn.' To be quite sure, he looked at Elmborough's face and saw that he was actually pleasing him. So he went on. 'Everything comes full circle in fashion, doesn't it! If you want to know what will be fashionable in seven years' time, take a look at what was all the rage forty years ago: your Edwardian grandfather's Sunday best, still in the wardrobe.'

21

At Mandelston's Sylvia had all the mirrors she could have wanted, except that they were really for the use of customers. When Mrs Laidlaw remarked on Sylvia's lingering and turning in front of one body-length mirror on the second day of her full-time employment, her words were, 'That's supposed to be for the customers.'

She said it without smiling, as a check to any incipient slackness. And the rebuke cancelled out nearly all of Sylvia's pride in going from a Saturday job in Mandelston's to a proper permanent job, with responsibility for persuading people to buy things and a small commission on every item she managed to sell.

Early in her first full week she realised that Mr Baxton, who had been so nice to her on her Saturdays, dropping in from the Gentlemen's Department to chat with her and keep her cheerful whenever he had the chance, inviting her round to tea that Sunday—above all helping her to borrow, quite without Mrs Laidlaw knowing, some beautiful black things for her mum's funeral (which she smuggled back wrapped in some brown paper in a shopping basket)—she realised that Mr Baxton was not a senior staff member at all; which was what she thought he must be.

He walked up and down importantly in the Gentlemen's Department, but he had no position higher than that of 'assistant'. It came to Sylvia slowly and indistinctly—because hierarchy among her elders was something she did not grasp—that Cyril

Baxton was an older man in a junior position. Therefore it was a daring escapade for him to fit her up with those mourning clothes on that Saturday, and send her off in them to her mother's funeral. He had probably been risking his own job to do that, which was much more serious than risking Sylvia's Saturday job. Cyril did not make a meal of all this, he only hinted; but Sylvia saw the point quite quickly and felt all the more grateful.

Leaving school had been sorrowful for her. She was past school-leaving age, and had every right to leave school at any time. But the Technical College rather expected everyone to stay the full term and fulfil all their talents. And it was a good school, which prided itself on giving Shakespeare and Brahms (via Miss McIntosh and the fierce little Mr Osric Evans) to pupils studying dressmaking or elementary plumbing. Sylvia had studied *Macbeth*, and found every animal referred to in the play after Miss McIntosh just happened to say, one day, 'There are lots of animals, wild and vicious animals, mentioned in this drama, and that reflects the fact that *Macbeth* is a play about wild and vicious people.' In her list Sylvia even included 'the cat in the adage', which she thought of as a poor little furry thing in some sort of cage or box.

Saying good-bye to her closest friends was the worst, even though most of them lived in the neighbourhood and she was sure she would go on seeing them. They were sad that Sylvia had to leave with her mother dying, and they kept saying so—which caused her to cry even more. The last day was a horrible day. The class had held a collection to give her something. What they gave her was not valuable, not useful, not money, not even cashable, like a book token. They gave Sylvia a framed picture of a young girl in beautiful clothes, by a French artist. It was what came to the mind of their form teacher, Miss Bennett, as something that would enable Sylvia, who was very talented in dressmaking, especially in the needlework side of it, to go away with good memories of a school in which girls learnt to make lovely dresses and perhaps take up the trade. And in which Sylvia had made so many friends. True. But a gift of money would have helped her a lot more.

The friends. Marian she would unquestionably go on seeing. And Ginger. They both lived nearby. But their worlds would separate because Sylvia's working life and the people she would meet in it were so different from school. Not as different as Ronnie Walston's naval life was from Jack Hollard's sixth-form routines, but different all the same. Strangely, Sylvia would find the worldly Anne from another, posher secondary school, easier to talk to in the street, as if she had belatedly caught up with Anne's sophistication. Maria, the girl of Spanish origin, who seemed to have the world of love and romance at her fingertips, Sylvia had recently seen working one day at half-term in a dreadful little café at the bottom of Greenstead Road near the High Street, and the miserable thought of the colourful Maria coming down to that disappointed her. It deterred her a bit from making any attempt to renew acquaintance with her.

When the rattling alarm clock went off in the morning, with the usual grumble from sister Eileen, who had another twenty minutes before she needed to surface, Sylvia went on lying there as usual for as long as she could afford to. Eileen might growl and kick out, but she fell asleep again immediately, whereas Sylvia lay there half-awake waiting for Mum to come and get her up. She waited for her to give that comic rapping on the door, and open it, and shout, 'Rise and shine, young ladies.' There would be breakfast, for both of them, when they finally appeared: the hot porridge, cooled by milk and decorated with dessertspoonfuls of golden syrup and eaten from the circumference of the plate because it was cooler there, and possibly bread and an egg to follow, but that was a treat. The clock had always to be watched, the girls had to be chivvied, and hurried away.

But Mum was dead. And that breakfast had been the custom for only—how long, a couple of months at the most? Because, in the time she was employed as a cleaner in the city office, Rebecca Freeman had to be out much earlier than Sylvia or Eileen. That was an era of morning chaos, and hunger, and rows; whereas the recent routine, when her mother had only to get as far as the Empire by mid-morning, were pleasant to remember. Sylvia loved to recall her mum being there at breakfast and not having to think of catching a tram at around seven and paying the workman's fare of twopence. Some mornings these days the tears would begin as soon as the alarm went off, she would turn her sobs into the pillow and clench her fists and try to will her mother to come back out of her grave in the cemetery and knock on the door of their bedroom again and have the porridge, and the bread and marmalade, and even the egg, waiting.

You went through this faked brick archway from one department to the other in Mandelston's. The staff in these two halves mistrusted each other, there was mutual contempt, almost a sort of quiet war between the older ones. Just beyond the archway on the Ladies' side was a door marked 'Staff', which meant the women's washroom at the far end of a passageway, but before that on the right was a small kitchen area, not regularly used, with a sink, a work surface, and a tiny gas stove on which a large, iron kettle could be set to boil water for tea made in a striped china teapot or coffee-and-chicory made in cups from a liquid poured out of a bottle. A bit of a fuss. There was also a low wall cupboard containing a small extra silver teapot pushed to the back of a shelf full of junk and still kept inside an original cladding of brown paper. It was never used. This small kitchen space, its cupboard and stove and teapots, were important in the next fortnight of Sylvia's life.

Mrs Laidlaw, head assistant of the Ladies', had no regard for her Gentlemen's opposite number, Mr Dindswell, and thought the men staff under him were vulgar and lazy. Dindswell had lips raised a little at the corners even when he wasn't smiling, which gave him an artful look. He couldn't help this, but on the other hand it went with a sly character. Mrs Laidlaw's resentment was aggravated by the fact that Dindswell, on the edge of retirement, was also the overall manager of the branch, whereas the superior sales record of the Ladies' was what kept the store prospering. Mrs Laidlaw believed she had every right to be the boss of the shop herself, if there were any justice in this world. She made that clear, with strong hints, whenever anybody came down from head office to inspect the branch and examine figures. The Ladies' side was where the profits were made, and the Gentlemen's displays were not always well organised and tidy. The visitor might nod, and jot things down, and nothing would happen; but then it was always a man who came, wasn't it! The Gentlemen's staff had jokes about Mrs Laidlaw among themselves, exchanged during moments after those frequent occasions when she had been to see Mr Dindswell with some complaint, or a demand about the way displays needed to be set out, or report on the inadequacy of the heating in the Ladies' section of the store. Some of the jokes were sexual jokes. They had no foundation in reality. They were untrue, and unfair.

Mrs Laidlaw noticed a tendency among the younger male staff to hang about near the archway between the two departments and engage the younger women assistants in her charge in aimless conversation. 'Phyllis, there is a customer waiting,' she would say pointedly. Or, 'Barbara, I do need some help with these new blouses that have arrived.' What upset her most of all was the interest shown by Mr Baxton from the Gentlemen's (who really should have known better at his age) in attracting the attention of any new young member of her staff.

She found Baxton revolting. When Barbara was new he latched on to her within a day, trying to charm her with advice about how to talk to customers, how to guess what they could afford to spend, how to choose the right clothes to show them by having a good 'dekko' at what they were wearing when they walked into the shop. The sight of Baxton hovering in the archway became nauseously familiar. Once or twice she practically had to drag Barbara away from him. Why were these girls so impressed? 'I don't know what they see in him,' was one obvious comment. 'I wouldn't pass the time of day with him if you paid me' was another. The truth was that Baxton contrived to present himself to them as 'a character', and in dull, routine work a character can be a relief. Mrs Laidlaw became annoyed with Barbara and began to make her feel that day-to-day life in the store was tiresome, if you had someone nagging and carping all the time. Barbara left for Marks and Spencer's before long.

But now it was Sylvia, who had not looked the sort of girl who would be taken in by Baxton. Sylvia's mother had died, Mrs Laidlaw knew that. She had a good appearance and a good manner, but there was this very sad, almost forlorn look on some days. Baxton made a beeline for her, darted in on the pretext of helping her with something when really none of the men from that part of the shop should have crossed the boundary with the Ladies'—there was no absolute rule, but that was the custom. The senior women assistants noticed what went on between Baxton and Sylvia, and though they sympathised with Sylvia's loss of her mother, they did not think it right for Sylvia to permit his approaches. When they were by themselves they were contemptuous of the junior women. In Sylvia's case this turned within a fortnight into mild ostracism. If she asked them things and they were even slightly busy she received quick, clipped answers from faces that turned away. Sylvia assumed it was because of her newness, or her youth, or because she had fallen among 'huffy' people. On the other hand, the men, particularly Mr Baxton, were friendly, a bit flirty but quite nice.

Dindswell was retiring soon now. Twenty-four years in the shop, can you believe it (some didn't), eight years as its manager, meant that he would receive an official farewell and a decent gift of money from head office. But it was put about by the men, his main assistant Mr Hobhouse in particular, that he deserved some sort of farewell gesture from his own staff, which meant everybody, men and women. As it happened, Mr Hobhouse would be retiring himself in a month or two, after a similar long spell of service. Hobhouse hoped for some mark of gratitude from staff when he himself departed, so he could not honestly go round collecting for Dindswell. People would think he was hinting the same thing could be done for him. Besides, he wanted to get out of the misery of cornering people for cash they did not want to cough up.

The best person to do it would be the next most senior in age, who had been there longer than anyone younger than him, Baxton. Which was why Baxton one day went through the archway with a very serious look and quietly made for Mrs Laidlaw—because he, also, wanted to get out of the task. Here was an opportunity for Baxton to get his own back on Laura Laidlaw for some of the cool, hostile looks and remarks she had delivered to him over the months. He would say he had Mr Hobhouse's authority to enlist her help.

'Mrs Laidlaw,' he said with an attempt at seriousness which for a second almost converted into a grin of pleasure at what he hoped to bring off; though to grin in asking her this would be fatal. 'Do you have time for a very quick word about something?'

'Yes?'

Baxton dropped his voice to produce a significant murmur.

'You'll know that Mr Dindswell leaves on Friday fortnight. Mr Hobhouse would like a little collection to be made for him to present him with something from the staff to mark thirty-two years of service.' Mrs Laidlaw looked surprised at that figure. 'He can't really do it himself as he's leaving in a few months, and he thinks it would be most appropriate for you to do it as very much the most senior and respected member of staff.'

Leaving her no time to interject, Baxton went on to explain the amounts Hobhouse had it in mind that senior and junior staff members might contribute. The thought was that Dindswell should be given something appropriate to his activities as a weekend angler. From the staff, permanent and part-time, of some twenty people, it should be possible to raise around ten pounds. It would be more than enough for quite a handsome folding stool for him to sit on beside a canal or a river on a Sunday, his old seat having been bought with a school prize in his teens. If it proved cheaper, he could no doubt spend the balance on other angling equipment. Baxton would be very happy to go and purchase the gift if Mrs Laidlaw undertook the collection, on both sides of the shop, and presented it to Mr Dindswell with a few suitable words on the day.

Baxton knew that Laura would resent the whole idea, and was delighted by the mute irritation she showed as she listened to him. It was just possible that she would come out with an explosive refusal; possible but not very likely, because she had something to lose by staging an outburst which Baxton would report to Hobhouse. For a few moments she was silent while a pained, impatient look worked its way over her features.

'Am I really going to go round and—? Why hasn't this been thought of before?' was what Mrs Laidlaw said. It made her view clear, but did not expose her to accusations of awkwardness. 'I've really got so much on. I'm seeing about the new summer displays all next week.' She continued in this vein while Baxton nodded in sympathy, even managing to say, 'Well, yes, I can see that' and 'Well, that's a very fair point.' He knew she was putting up a show of resentment before finally making a grudging acceptance of her duty, with a latent suspicion that she had been (which was true) tricked into it. In the end, with an ungracious sigh, she said, 'Oh—very well, then. I'll do it. But—'. Whatever she might have said then she held back.

She found a spare paper cash bag that afternoon and began on a round that turned out even more tiresome than she feared. It involved catching everybody when she could and providing them with a low-voiced explanation: 'Mr Dindswell, as you probably know, is retiring very soon—the end of next week. I thought it would be very nice if we made a little collection for him.' So she gave herself the credit of having had the idea and for showing willing about putting it into effect.

The cash came mainly in small silver, and even in coppers. The bag was not heavy and the sum was not considerable; but having made good progress on her first day of collection, she preferred not to take it home with her. Having decided that, she felt even more reluctant to leave the premises on the second day with additional money. Therefore she left the bag in the place she had decided to store it on the first day, a very unlikely place for anyone to look, the small silver teapot wrapped up in brown paper at the back of the junk-filled cupboard shelf in the small kitchen space on the right behind the door onto the passage leading to the women staff's washroom. She made cautious trips to this hiding place two or three times a day as the collection mounted up. That happened slowly though, because it was difficult to catch the assistants in the Gentlemen's Department without running into Mr Dindswell himself. Besides, the male assistants knew what she was after and were avoiding her.

Sylvia felt proud to receive her wages, plus a small commission for one or two successful selling efforts, at the end of her first week. It was not a full week yet, wages were made up only to the Thursday, which was early-closing day, so she had a complete six days' wages plus commission to look forward to the following week. She was lonely; but after being paid (and she did not find it tiring work) she felt reconciled to working here despite the high-and-mighty dignity of one or two of the senior women staff. For two whole days running she was even something approaching happy—and then one of those small things occurred that can spoil everything in one second.

It was nearly lunchtime. She was turning aside from a display she had been trying to rearrange a little to make it look tidier, and she bumped into Mrs Laidlaw carrying a silk petticoat thrown over the bar of a coathanger. The petticoat slid off, and ended up as a pink pool on the floor.

'Did nobody ever teach you to look where you are going?'

Sylvia bent her head, walked away, made for the half-open staff door, pushed through it with a little run noticed by Cyril Baxton near the archway, closed the door, broke down completely behind it, went into the little kitchen area.

'If Mum hadn't died I wouldn't have to be putting up with all this,' was what she said to herself. It was not what she said aloud when Mr Baxton, having left a moment or two for her to recover, followed her in.

'Now what's happened to upset you?' he said very softly, knowing genuine distress when he saw it. Sylvia was red-eyed, still blowing her nose, on a tiny handkerchief with violets on it; but recovering.

'She's at me all the time,' she said.

'Mrs Laidlaw?'

'Yes.'

He thought inappropriately for a moment of the lyric sung sometimes at the urinals in the men's staff washroom:

If you'd laid Laura
Like I've laid Laura,
Oh—oh—OOH! What a girl!

Since they had conspired together when she was only doing her Saturday job, and he had done that daring thing of helping her to borrow some clothes for her mum's funeral, and he would understand the situation, Sylvia said, 'I keep thinking about my mum,' without bursting into tears again, only patting her eyes with the hanky and sniffing. Cyril (she had started to use his Christian name) was a bit of a fraud, even at an impressionable sixteen Sylvia Freeman could see through him. He reminded her of the sort of character in British films who was smartly dressed and spoke with a 'refeened' accent, but was just a charming, hopeless small-time rogue or cad. They could be funny sometimes; Sylvia enjoyed Cyril's humorous remarks.

But mainly it was that he was the only person in this place who had shown her any kindness.

'You look to me as if a cup of tea would not come amiss. You've got time, Laura's gone to lunch.'

Cyril, she thought, always spoke to her like an equal grown-up, it was in his voice. The upper-class accent flattered her. She had heard or read somewhere that a lot of people who came from upper-class families learned from their education to be nice to everybody, no matter what their class.

'All right,' she said, agreeing to tea.

Baxton turned to the ledge, spooned out some dried milk from a shiny red tin into two cups, left the sugar for Sylvia to choose or not to choose, made tea in the old china pot by the sink. The kettle rattled unsteadily on the stove and the drink was made. Tea made with concentrated dried milk was a horrid experience, but people drank it, and there was nothing else here to offer. Cyril and Sylvia now took a simultaneous sip looking at each other over the cups. Sylvia pulled a face, but altered it into a smile and gave a nervous laugh, and during the laugh Mrs Laidlaw, who had not gone out to lunch, came round the door and looked at them as she went past on her way to the washroom.

Four days later—

'Well, they're the only people I saw in there that day, that's all I can say,' was her opinion.

The bag containing the carefully counted eight pounds fourteen and six had disappeared from the silver teapot kept in the lower cupboard.

22

And yet, at more or less the same time—

'Not if you're me, you don't.'

Maureen Hollard was laughing to protest her innocence of ever wanting to do such a thing.

'I bet you have. Some time,' Ray Naughton imagined, with a funny eager look.

'But I thought you didn't bet. You said that,' she maintained. 'Other people bet with *you*. That's it, isn't it?'

'You have done it, though.'

'No, I've never. I've seen it done—and I thought it was disgraceful.'

'Where've you seen it done, then? Pevensey, or somewhere else they've got a licence to do it?'

'No. On the stage.'

'On the stage? You've been up to the Windmill in Soho? *You*?'

'No!' Maureen's voice was staccato and high-pitched. 'At the *Windmill*?' Scorn. 'Why would a married woman go to the Windmill indeed? At the Empire I've seen it.'

'At the *Empire*? The Empire here?'

'Yes.'

But Ray shook his head.

'Women in the nuddy? On the stage at the Empire?'

'Yes! They were posing as famous paintings.'

Ray laughed loudly, and shook his head again in complete disbelief. People here in the Black Horse and Harrow, where he and Maureen were sitting at lunchtime, looked round at them for a moment.

Earlier, Patsy Partridge and Cedric had been with them for sandwiches, and pieces of pie, and drinks. But the other two had left, on some pretext or other. Maureen had an explanation if she was seen there alone with Ray: she had happened to run into someone she worked with years ago, and they'd decided to have a drink together and remember old times. It was true of Patsy. But it was not true of Ray Naughton, bookmaker and divorced husband.

She wanted to stop this part of the conversation, which had somehow gone on from outer garments—after a compliment on her blouse, and a preference for it to someone else's blouse in this saloon bar—gone from blouses to skirts to underwear; and then, via a bit of flattery of her figure by Ray, to the subject of nudity.

How on earth did she let him get onto the topic of nude bathing and sunbathing, and whether she'd like to do that and would mind being seen in public with nothing on?

'But you asked me about my husband.' She tried, with this, to guide him back to an unfinished subject of five minutes before. 'He's taken up *cricket* again. After twenty-five years. Quite serious about it.'

Ray saw that he could not pursue the other line for the time being.

'Cricket…' He said that as a neutral, toneless echo of the word as Maureen spoke it. You couldn't place bets on cricket with Ray Naughton, so it did not interest him. He was a racecourse bookmaker. Horses, yes. Dogs, yes. Cricket, no.

'He's going to be playing against our son's school. Jack's the opening bat of the 1st XI.'

Ray showed no special interest. The information emphasised that she had an almost-grown-up son.

'What's your husband do to earn an honest copper?'

'He's in a shipping office. Quite high up now.'

Nothing was openly announced in Fitch & Armstrong yet, but Maureen could make the little boast in view of what Perce had told her on coming back from Jedleigh's on that wet night, last Sunday week. Her face now shone with pride, and she went on talking indiscreetly about Perce having a rival in the office trying to do him down and cut him out of promotion, but Perce had stood his ground and done his work conscientiously and in the end they'd rewarded the right man. He would be second in one of the most important departments in the firm, and they'd created an entirely new post just for Perce. He would get a rise, which would help because their son Jack was a clever boy, she didn't know where he got it from, not from her, that was for sure, and he would be going to university next year, or when he'd done his military service.

Ray made out he was listening for about the first third of Maureen's account. But as she went on he glanced away across the bar, out of the window, anywhere, though he kept on murmuring 'Mm?' 'Really?' 'Yes?' in his throat, and nodding. Then Maureen realised that, having changed the subject, she was embarrassed about it. He was not interested by what she was telling him about Perce. She was starting to bore him, and she did not want to do that. Here was a man paying her gentlemanly attentions (unlike Spillar), who had bought her a drink after her friend Patsy and her boyfriend had gone, and she was boring him. It would not do. I'm not after a romance, she told herself, especially after Spillar. But the polite, perfectly decent attentions of a man were rare things for her these days—and she was spoiling it by boring him. So she stopped, and just smiled.

'Would you ever go to the races to see if you liked it?' he asked her after the pause following Maureen's sudden stop. An hour before, she had said she had never really thought it would appeal to her. She raised her eyebrows to show him she was wondering.

'Well…I might.'

'I could always arrange something. The Derby would have been very good. Except it's very crowded. Something less crowded might be better.'

But he knew he could not pull any strings regarding the big races you could easily reach from London. Ray could do no more than treat her to a simple ticket for somewhere or other. Lewes, perhaps. Brighton?

'I don't know. Patsy would have to come.'

It was a vulnerable admission, almost agreeing to the idea as long as she was not expected to go alone. Ray spotted that. Maureen was thinking, 'What am I doing?' I was persuaded into that situation with Spillar and now I could be carrying on with Ray Naughton. All this when I'd never before carried on ever since I was married. Before I married Perce you could say I did carry on a bit, and I told Perce everything. Sometimes one affair was brought up by Perce even now—there was that night we had the row back in the winter and he did the waving good-bye to remind me of Charlie Happleford. Why aren't I shocked by what I'm doing? Because I'm not, and I'm not ashamed either. I'm just muddled. I'm forty-four years old, married with a grown-up son, and I'm letting Ray Naughton, who you can see is a kind of charming older spiv, a divorced man, take liberties. Not real liberties, but what you might say were verbal liberties, turning the conversation in funny directions and dropping hints.

'Why would Patsy have to come?' Ray asked. 'She could come, yes, of course she could. But why does she have to?'

Maureen could not say, 'Because I would feel safer and it would make it respectable, and I could tell Perce I'd just gone with her and no one else.' So she said, 'Because she's my friend, and—' failing to complete the sentence. He smiled, granting Maureen the right to set her own terms at this stage of their acquaintance. If he couldn't get her beyond this stage he would give it up. But it was worth a try.

'All right. Why not you and Patsy, and Cedric as well? Make a party. Go to the races and all have a little dinner somewhere afterwards?'

This was now becoming really tricky. Perce never objected if she wanted to go out alone somewhere in the evenings, for example go to those three operas at the Empire in one week. Or even, for example, go once or twice with a neighbour to a whist drive where she would certainly meet other middle-aged men, though usually with their wives. She had done that. But to take a day at the races without Perce (who would not have had the least interest, and would be very surprised to know she was interested)—and go with two other men even if Perce was not aware of that—that was so blatant it would not be possible. The barriers put up by married life and its deep-rooted habits shut out, for her at any rate, expeditions of this kind. She just didn't see she could.

'I just don't see it's possible for me to get away. I couldn't explain to Perce why I was going. He'd want to know all the details.'

With every excuse she found herself actually regretting the difficulty of taking up Ray's suggestion, which sounded innocent enough, didn't it? (On the other hand, was she encouraging him by discussing it?) To pretend she was just going to Brighton or somewhere with Patsy, it would be possible—but to be seen at the races or in a restaurant there with two strange men...She knew that there were people living nearby who went to the races. There was a popular local bus driver who ran bus outings to Epsom; with the consent of the London Passenger Transport Board he took them in his red double-decker.

Ray looked a little downcast, she thought. The implication had been that it would be his treat, and Maureen was turning up her nose at it. She hated to hurt anyone's feelings, she knew what it was like herself. So when he offered her another drink, which she declined, she did accept his offer of running her some part of the way home. She could be dropped at a discreet distance from her own house, she was sure.

She was thinking, as she sat down next to him in the passenger seat of the black Austin 16, that this was only about the fifth or sixth time she had ever been in a car. Along their road there were, out of one hundred and four houses, only three with cars parked outside. Before the war there had only been one car, the modest Ford owned by the Thompsons. She and Perce had been invited out for one trip in it, what they called romantically a 'moonlight excursion'. Everything in the area seemed different from the dark interior of this vehicle, you could not see as much from the windows of a bus or tram at night because the lights interfered with the view. To watch it all flashing past in the dimly lighted streets—the full moon, the reason why the Thompsons had chosen that night for the drive, was for long stretches the only illumination—was amazing to Maureen, a completely new experience. Apart from that drive, there being no one in their family who owned such a thing, she had only ever been in a car for weddings or funerals.

'You haven't closed it properly,' Ray said. He leaned across her, in a discreet way that nevertheless involved his leaning against her, reopened the half-closed passenger door, slammed it fully shut. The starter button he first twisted so as to activate the choke; but it still needed three or four determined pulls, each time giving out an hysterical whine which refused to convert into ignition. Then finally, with a crisp clunking flip of the right indicator into an horizontal position to signify that they were moving away from this kerb outside the Black Horse and Harrow, the spacious black Austin with its oak dashboard and light leather seats, bags of leg room for the tall people Ray Naughton and Maureen Hollard were, went out into the light lunchtime traffic of the High Street carrying them softly and, she thought, so luxuriously forward on what would only be a few hundred yards to the point where she would ask to be set down and walk the rest. She scanned the pavements for faces she recognised and, to her relief, saw none.

'How do you like Old Faithful?' Ray asked her. 'Old'? The car seemed very new.

'I like it.' Apart from those hired limousines for serious occasions, it was the best she had travelled in.

They covered another thirty yards in slow silence before he said, 'I don't know about you—but I rather fancy a cup of coffee.'

She felt so reluctant to be seen with him again in the Cosy Corner, which they were now passing, that when he said, 'It's only a little detour to my place,' and he told her it was in Witham Grove, she suddenly said, 'All right.' She could hardly believe that she had said it, she actually did know she was crossing a boundary. But she excused herself by thinking that it was the daytime after all, it was not that she was going to his house at night. Then it would have been quite appalling for anyone to see her.

Reaching Ray's place meant driving under the arch to the other side of the railway. It struck Maureen as strange that this was where Perce had come to visit Jedleigh and hear about his forthcoming promotion. She had never set eyes on Mr Jedleigh, so they would not recognise each other if their paths crossed here (which they would not at two-fifteen p.m.). A firm social barrier was descending to seal her off, since few people on Maureen's side of the railway ever had reasons for coming here.

The house had its own drive, a short steep concrete approach, and a very pleasant porch in front of the door; although she noticed that the woodwork needed the repainting received by some of the houses in her own road since the end of the war. In Witham Grove all the houses looked as if they were owned by people who had done very well very recently, or had had them left to them. They must need a lot of money to keep up. Maureen wondered which of these categories Ray belonged to. People said bookmakers always did well…

'There you are!' Inside the front door, closing it behind him, a bark of pride in Ray's voice. 'Go in and take a seat and I'll see to some refreshment.'

Where he motioned her to go was a front room, a parlour with heavy floral curtains, a rather darkly furnished place. The three-piece rexine suite, cold to the touch when you sat down on chair or sofa, was deep brown in colour, the carpet and the wallpaper and the pictures lighter but still not adding much cheerfulness to the room. Who chose it, she wondered? Was it Ray's idea? Or his departed wife's? Like their front room at home it tried for a deliberately posh and formal air, being kept for special guests and occasions. The fire was never lighted except then; when it smoked, and soot fell.

The difference was in the pictures. Perce's and Maureen's three parlour pictures, which they never looked at again once they had bought them, were of dark, obscurely romantic scenes in unidentifiable foreign places, sunsets and dawns in perhaps Italy or Spain, grandly framed and bought in the kind of shop that was selling junk but aspired to trade in antiques. Ray's pictures were all much smaller, photographs mostly, of horses, courses and little groups of interested parties chatting in paddocks: jockey, trainer and owner in ascending order of height. Maureen went round looking at them before she sat down, supposing she ought to know some of these faces from the newspapers. Was that Gordon Richards, for example? She did know Gordon Richards had never yet ridden a Derby winner.

Before she sat down? But where was there to sit? She could hear Ray rattling about in the kitchen at the back. And there was a coffee table already laid with a neat white cloth, almost as if she had been expected; except that there was the lightest coat of dust on the black cups and on their green saucers—as if these were permanently set out in case of unexpected visitors but had not been recently used. There were three heavy upright chairs, but those were covered with files of loose papers. There was a writing desk in the corner with a telephone on it. The two individual armchairs in the three-piece suite were similarly cluttered, so the sofa with its three square slab seats, three soft ample embroidered cushions, and arms at each end with small round metal ashtrays set in imitation leather straps was the only available surface to sit on.

But first she went over to the window with its dull, darkish, flower-patterned curtains and looked out through the accompanying lace curtains to the sunlit silence of Witham Grove, for an assurance that she could somehow escape to it if she wanted to. Then, after a few moments thinking about that, she turned back to the room and sat down at the end of the sofa, letting her arm drop over the side and touch the hollow rexine surface. Immediately the action brought back a memory of Jack when he was about ten years old and there was regular military band music on Saturday mornings on BBC National radio. Jack liked to sit in one of their armchairs at home and bang on the side with the flat of his little hand—or with a tablespoon—in time with the thudding percussion and bellowing brass of the bands, until she told him to stop in case he damaged it.

All at once she felt very bad and uncomfortable about being here. What was she doing? The liberty Patsy believed in, the freedom to do what she liked—as long as it didn't harm anyone else—was one thing. The risk of scandal, and consequences far worse than scandal in the case of Spillar (although that all happened in the Rio and she believed no one else found out) was another thing. And there was a third; what all this made *her*. Maureen Hollard. She was not a fallen woman, but she had stumbled once, and now...After the miscarriage, she decided to put all that entirely behind her. She and Perce hadn't started having relations again yet, but there were signs that he wouldn't mind, Perce had become more cheerful and optimistic lately, that promotion coming soon and unexpectedly, and this cricket-playing, was part of it. The nurse at the doctor's had said on her visit soon after, without Maureen asking, that she could begin relations again as soon as she liked, though perhaps to leave it a couple more weeks. What if relations happened with another man again, not Perce? She moved to the other end of the sofa to be nearer the door.

Ray came back with a tray, on it a coffee pot and a jug of milk and sugar lumps in a bowl, with tongs. There was an unlit cigarette in his mouth while he spoke.

'What *am* I doing,' he said, eerily echoing the thoughts passing through Maureen's mind. 'Not offering *you* one.'

He put the coffee tray down and took a stained silver cigarette case from his pocket, springing it open, offering her a Craven A, of which there were four. Maureen prised one out from under the strip of elastic in the case. She thought to herself, he was smoking Navy Cut when we were in the Black Horse two hours ago with Patsy and Cedric, and I accepted a Craven A from Cedric and not a Navy Cut, and Ray must have noticed that and found a cigarette in the house I would be happy with, though I am not a regular smoker at all. He lighted it for her, and the moment of breathing out the smoke left her feeling complicit in—in she didn't know what.

Having poured the coffee into the dusty cups, and before sitting down himself next to her—there was nowhere else to sit, but it was a three-seat sofa and they had space between them—Ray Naughton said, 'I'd like to show you something.' From a drawer in the desk in the corner he took out a bulging scrapbook. It was a combined collection of print cuttings and newspaper photographs and personal snaps, all to do with his turf accountant's life. The only way of showing it to Maureen was to edge a little closer on the shiny cool sofa, and open the large pages partly on her lap. Plainly this book meant a lot to Ray, she thought, these were precious mementoes. They were assembled with that scanty section in the middle reflecting the interruption most careers and occupations had suffered during the years of war.

'What happened to you in the war?' she had to ask him, when he turned a page from cheerful, obviously pre-war images and columns of print into a short sequence of pages where time moved much more quickly and much less went on—and they were soon into a post-war section, where things were starting up again but the faces were older, and there was a more austere look about everything. Turning these pages for her gave him time to answer that question.

'Oh. I was in an office,' he said eventually. After a pause, an indrawn breath. 'I was too old for service—I firewatched, of course.' It placed Ray in much the same age group as Perce; surprising, because he looked younger and Maureen expected some account of the army or the RAF. On the other hand he had not mentioned the forces the first time they met, or today, and men who had been in the forces usually did, at the first opportunity. Cedric had. Ray did not say what sort of office or where. So she did not ask him.

'Here we are again, then.' Picking up the threads after the war, caught in a back page photograph with his bookmaker's stand and its blackboard for chalking up the changing odds, a duster and chalk in his hand, a broad grin on his face, and a slogan painted on the stand the way he liked it:

ReIY on RaY

In another picture, this time someone's grainy box-camera effort, he was posed with the same stand and smile alongside a huge Negro, robed and feathered and brandishing slips of paper, Prince Monolulu, most famous of all racing tipsters. 'The man himself,' Ray said. Again in these pages there were famous horses and jockeys and trainers. 'Now that's—Now that's—' Ray was pointing out, giving names, telling stories, invoking patronyms and legends of which Maureen Hollard had no knowledge or recollection, but did show an interest that was more than just polite, if it stopped short of fascination. She was finding it interesting, yes, but to say she was really absorbed in it would have been going too far.

Yet she did not feel she could just sit there and say nothing. He didn't ask her anything, he was just going on telling her about himself and the courses he worked at, and the famous people he met. She had to think of a question to ask because it could appear uninterested, and ungrateful for the lift and the coffee if she didn't. So she asked him a plain, discarnate question: 'What's it really like to work as a bookie?'

Used to it, even though it was a question he had been asked less than he might have expected, Ray had an answer prepared.

'You have to have a quick mind and be pretty good at mental arithmetic. Both of which is true in my case, naturally!' The self-deprecating smile, the chuckle. 'You have to keep your wits about you every minute of the day. And have eyes in the back of your head. You have to know your horses and courses and which goes with which. And their trainers, because a born winner has got to be trained to realise he is...Or *she* is.'

His voice began to tail off somewhat as he unfolded this rehearsed speech. Then he turned another page of the scrap-book, and well before the end there were no more pictures, only a thickness of blank, grey pages. So he closed the book and turned towards Maureen with a peculiar smile.

'But mainly you're on your own against the world,' he began again suddenly. 'You're on your own and—just lonely.'

He said it with a serious kind of emphasis, as if it was important for Maureen to believe him; the smile having gone.

'Especially nowadays,' he added. 'The way things are, Maureen—I'm so bloody lonely.'

Maureen had not ever found herself in such a situation, or anything approaching it, for twenty-five years at least. It reminded her faintly of emotional pressures from boyfriends she had met before she met Perce, but this was so different, the misery of a stranded middle-aged man who had played the charmer quite hard, but turned out to be sensitive under the surface. And kind of lost.

So she could only feel sympathy, and listen, because she sensed that Ray wanted to go on talking. And to help him, as he started to describe just how awful his divorce had been—but with a strong resolve not to let things go any farther—she closed her right hand over his left hand to still it. Because it patted the closed scrapbook restlessly as he spoke.

23

Meanwhile, at more or less this time of day, but over two weeks later—

Pierre-Henri delayed returning to Mrs Orlop's. He had begun to do this as a precaution, even though there had been no more letters, no sign (that he could detect) of anyone following him in the street.

But one particular precaution was to have a suitcase ready; just in case he had to make a rapid departure of the kind that had brought him here from La Tignelle in the first place. His obligations of teaching and examining would soon be all but ended for the summer—though some of his pupils and some of their siblings were already booked for private lessons for the autumn. But he needed to balance his need for money still owed to him against an instinct to get away from here if any further threat arrived in the post.

He had developed the habit of taking a look behind him whenever he finished walking a stretch of a street—and staring hard into the next street whenever he turned a corner. Once or twice he entered a shop or turned a corner when he saw approaching him a figure or figures that might have been French, or at any rate not English. But this was rare. It had not been common, even in the later days of the war, to see many foreigners in so obscure and uninteresting a suburb.

Thus Pierre-Henri alighted from a bus with a long look in both directions, gazed hard down the first innocuous sidestreet into which he turned off the main road, looked behind him, and looked ahead when he reached the next corner. He did the same as he turned into Benford Street, paying no attention to a clearly English boy or young man, Jack Hollard. On his way home from a strange and exciting afternoon in Soho, Jack was making a detour in order to pass Sylvia's home.

There ahead of him, no one else in the street at all, was Lettie Orlop at her garden gate, two yards outside her front door. It was a darkening summer evening by now, and the scent of the flowers in the trim front gardens was strong as he approached her and smiled.

'You've just missed them,' Mrs Orlop informed him.

'Who?'

'The two French gentlemen who came to call on you. Wanting to see you. They were so polite. Are they friends from France?'

'Did they—? Did they leave their names? Did they say where they came from?'

Why did Mr Mollie-Knot seem so agitated?

'Well no—they didn't. I didn't ask them. But they said they'd call again in a few days—or meet you somewhere else. I think that's what they meant. They didn't speak English very well.'

'And they left no names?'

'None at all...Oh dear, I should have asked.'

Upstairs he opened Mrs Orlop's heavy wardrobe door, looked at the green coat, closed the door again. He had never done anything about disposing of this, the property of a man he had betrayed, because he assumed it was well concealed in a wardrobe four hundred miles from La Tignelle. At any time in the bitter winter he might have parcelled it up, smuggled it out of the house at night when Mrs Orlop was not looking, taken a bus somewhere, and dumped it on a bomb site. But it was summer now, the longest days, and people were out in the streets enjoying the sunny evenings.

Someone was, or some people were, threatening to meet with Pierre-Henri Mallinot because he had done something wrong and they wanted to discuss 'matters of common interest'. He had now received four letters. The last had come direct to him from Paris to this address—would it now be necessary for him to leave? He knew he had to ask himself that. He had certainly thought about leaving when his commitments for this year had been fulfilled…

But the threats could be empty threats. If they were genuine, and he was visited here by people on a revenge mission after these many months, the absence of an incriminating green overcoat would not make any difference. There was no point in getting rid of it now. He would stay here and hope all this came to nothing; or move when his life proved to be in actual danger. Out of doors they could do nothing. At Mrs Orlop's, the observant Lettie herself would be a protection. But he revised this view as the evening went on. Two strangers had come to see him…

The day Marcelle Levine left La Tignelle on the long and hazardous train journey from the Marshal's observant France to the neutral Geneva, Pierre-Henri simply had to trust that she was in fact gone and was safely on her way to the arranged destination. This was a fortnight after his violent disclosure of his knowledge of her love affair with a man who was identified as 'René Picquart', and she had been to see him on three later occasions. There had been—in these dangerous circumstances there had to be—a reconciliation if he was to help Marcelle. And he loved her, still; so they had made love on the last of these evenings (and what has to be the last time is never the best). But it was on the second occasion that he produced what she had challenged him about, covertly removing it from a file in the mairie overnight: the list of the small number of Jews resident in the town, and the annexe consisting of the names of all persons recently moved to La Tignelle whose origins had not been clarified. It came to no more than fifteen or so, and presented no great burden for officials if they were summoned to the office and questioned. It was all the more dangerous to Marcelle.

'Who put me on this list?' she asked him in horror when she held the neatly handwritten sheet in her hand? She knew that it was not Pierre-Henri's own writing. But he could have reported her after he had found out that she—couldn't he? No—that was not likely. The handwriting was not as new as that, her name had not been recently added; and he was promising to convey her to safety in Switzerland.

'You don't know him.'

It was a colleague compiling the list from information given by people who knew about incomers and their current addresses: the café *patron*, the schoolteacher who received new children, the doctor, certainly; all of these were obliged to supply names.

'And this means that—one day—I can expect to be summoned to your office and questioned?'

'To the mairie, yes. Not to my office.'

It was clear to Marcelle that her lover—this one of her two lovers—was not saying that he would be able to protect her in that event, that he was standing apart from the terrible process which might come into action if she remained in La Tignelle. It was likely, perhaps very likely, that it would happen soon. Therefore he had arranged his life-saving strategy for her. She would be met from the train in Geneva by his French-speaking contacts, who would have to know that she was a close friend of his (by implication a lover), in danger from political enemies. Right-wing friends, they would believe Marcelle Grenier was marked down for vengeance by the resistance. She was not, in any circumstances, to divulge or hint that she was a Jew. These people would lodge her in an address (to be arranged) which she would not know in advance—she might tell Picquart if she did—and which even Pierre-Henri would not know until she was there and he could contact her by telephone.

There was such an alarming mixture of motives involved in Pierre-Henri Mallinot making this arrangement. First, he still loved Marcelle, the woman who had come secretly to his house in this backstreet of La Tignelle and been his frank and naked lover for so long, with a love he would have so much preferred (as long as she was Marcelle Grenier) to render open and acknowledged—but which she insisted (because of Picquart?) must remain secret and discreet. All they ever did in public together was to take rare meals—well, two or three at the most—in the one decent town restaurant, where he could trust the proprietor not to gossip. If it was found out that she was from Paris, of all places, and a Jew, and making love to a right-wing bureaucrat who once had extreme right-wing connections elsewhere, there would be so much to explain and justify...He would send her to a safe place where he would be able to join her later.

That would serve the purpose of removing her from Picquart—who would surely not be able to pursue her to Geneva and put himself in desperate danger by doing that? Marcelle had assured Pierre-Henri that René Picquart did not know, and would not know, that she had a lover in the mairie; that she had another lover at all.

Pierre-Henri Mallinot assumed that Marcelle would communicate with Picquart about her urgent departure, perhaps even see him to do that (though not in the hotel?) and promise to be in touch again to let him know where she was. Therefore there lay at the back of Pierre-Henri's mind a hard and horrible thought: that Picquart, whom he had never met, whom he had only ever seen indistinctly by moonlight in the back yard of a hotel, might himself be dealt with in some way when Marcelle was gone.

He did not really intend to put any violent move against Picquart into action. Or at first he didn't. But what he did not bargain for was the appearance of René Picquart in his own life, on his own initiative and following enquiries around the town. He came into Pierre-Henri Mallinot's life after Marcelle's departure at some risk—or so Pierre-Henri assumed—ignorant of Marcelle's simultaneous affair and completely determined to track her down. Picquart had not heard from Marcelle, he discovered. But then neither had he, Pierre-Henri Mallinot, heard from her himself. Marcelle Grenier/Levine had conceivably made a new and safer life separate from both…

With Marcelle two weeks gone, Picquart went first to Dr Villeneuve's surgery. The doctor knew of course that Marcelle had left La Tignelle for her own safety, and would be taking refuge abroad. But he did not ask her where. It was well not to possess information of that kind. He did not in the least connect her vanishing with Pierre-Henri Mallinot, because he did not know of the affair. When Picquart approached him he advised him against asking questions around the town. But Picquart had to ask questions. And in this quest his appearances in the town became more venturesome, even risky.

He believed that café *patrons* and barmen were good at noticing people and remembering them. There was a small central restaurant with a bar between the doctor's house and the mairie. Marcelle had spoken of occasional visits to it in her midday break while the doctor was out seeing patients and her reception desk was closed. In three early evening trips to it when there were few or no customers René established a sort of rapport with the owner, an alert little man with thin portions of moustache on either side of his upper lip. When would it be safe to pose questions to him about particular individuals, rather than general questions? Not too soon, he guessed. Nowadays people clammed up very quickly if they suspected your intentions. He would wait until there was no one else on the premises.

But there was always someone. One day this lean man, of about his own age, in a characteristically official-looking brown suit, was leaving as he arrived and stood aside at the door to let him in. He nodded thanks to Pierre-Henri, whom he did not recognise any more than Pierre-Henri recognised him. The place was now empty with this person gone. He took a seat, took a coffee.

'Do you pick up much custom by being so near the mairie?' he wondered. Starting with an innocent question.

'The gentleman who left as you came in is a lunchtime regular. Otherwise not that many. Well, there are some. But they're intermittent. They don't generally come after work—they go home. He drops in sometimes after work. I think he's a bachelor living alone. He doesn't have anyone to report to.'

What harm was there in saying that much to a stranger? No names were involved. But René thought the man had opened up enough for him to risk his next question.

'There's a young woman who works in the mairie—I think—whom I've seen dropping in.' To start with he was concealing his knowledge of where Marcelle really worked.

'Have you?' René at once feared the man might have realised he himself had only very rarely dropped in, and that only recently. But the boss was not cutting René short. 'I'd be surprised if you had. There's not much youth about the people at the mairie,' he said.

'I'm thinking of a rather tall, quiet young lady. Late twenties I'd say, with rather striking pale features. She sometimes spoke to pass the time of day. But we were never friends.'

This was going too far, the *patron* might start to wonder. But he did not clam up yet, because there was no harm in retailing small ordinary facts.

'You may be thinking of Dr Villeneuve's receptionist.'

'Yes—it could be! Come to think of it, I did see her come out of the doctor's once. It doesn't really matter, but—but I wondered where she'd got to.'

'I couldn't tell you. Except…' The boss was slowly sensing that the questioning suggested a modest payment for modest answers. Nothing so blatant as a banknote folded and pressed into his hand here and now, but perhaps a reasonable extra tip. And this was such mundane information he was passing on. Nothing confidential. Why shouldn't he go to the limit of what he knew, which was extremely little? 'Except,' he went on, 'the official from the mairie here ten minutes ago exchanged words with her sometimes. He probably knew her from Dr Villeneuve's.'

This was safe, it was public, other people would have seen them on his premises. He was not going to mention what he now recalled, that those two had been known—if infrequently—to dine together in his establishment and talk in low tones that suggested they might have been rather close. In fact he was now going to abandon the whole subject, just in case this amiable individual had some concealed reason for finding out about the tall, deeply pale girl.

'If you ask me,' he said generally, 'the mairie knows everything about people's comings and goings in this town, and that guy, being from the mairie, might be the one to ask. I can't help you further than that.'

The moment these words were out of his mouth he regretted them. Far from killing the topic, they might have sent his customer, who was obviously interested in the girl in the way a healthy, eager young man would be, might have sent him straight along to another man who would reveal nothing—because he might well be her lover.

It took René Picquart three further visits, all of them spent in silence reading a newspaper, before he ran into the tense and reticent-looking official again. On this decisive occasion they actually arrived together, the little *patron* greeting both of them at once, not forgetting the conversation with Picquart two weeks earlier, not sure whom he should serve first. René looked hard at Pierre-Henri and knew who he was immediately. He nodded to him as a stranger as they sat down at different tables; and Pierre-Henri nodded back rather formally. This time neither had brought a book or newspaper to read.

They had acknowledged each other's presence. The ground was laid for a conversation. Pierre-Henri Mallinot was about to see the opportunity to fix René Picquart, as he very soon knew him to be, in his sights—if he wished to take it.

Picquart was driven by love—and by desperate anxiety. That Marcelle had to leave he had no doubt. But when the weeks passed and there was no message, his desires and his fears began to override his common sense. It was not sensible to believe that in approaching Pierre-Henri Mallinot and, with his consent, moving over to his table, he was merely conducting a casual exchange with a bureaucratic nonentity; but today he went ahead and dismissed the risks. They exchanged relaxed commonplaces quite easily for the duration of a coffee. And a second coffee. Neither was in a hurry, so they graduated to have 'just one' small glass of wine. They talked sport, agreed that there was no real entertainment in this neck of the woods. For that you had to go into Périgueux or even Angoulême, on trains or buses freezing in winter and stiflingly hot in summer.

They both acknowledged they had not lived in La Tignelle for very long, and had chosen it for its charm, and for the peacefulness of this forest region, and yet...Implicitly they were agreeing that for men of their age (each rightly guessed the other to be in his early thirties) there was not enough 'life' here. Social life of a sort, if you cultivated that; but no night life. They laughed. They were getting on quite well. The proprietor was relieved to see and hear them talking openly and unsuspiciously. He mopped the tabletop around their almost-empty wine glasses.

'Another for you?' René asked, suggesting by voice and gesture that he would be paying for it, having made the suggestion.

'Absolutely the last,' Pierre-Henri agreed, with a lean smile. After the first drink, and with new glasses now on the table, René Picquart suddenly and fatally felt able to come out with what he wanted to know. First he lit a cigarette. Pierre-Henri declined one.

'I've spoken in the past to a very intelligent young woman who used to visit here with the lunchtime lot. I haven't seen her lately, and this is a small place—I wonder if you would know who I mean?'

Pierre-Henri held his full glass on the table between the thumb and the middle finger of his right hand, and stared at it without raising it. He could have been thinking hard in the effort to help René with an answer to his casual enquiry. But he was not. He was trying to control his astonishment, his embarrassment—if it could be that René was actually asking about Marcelle. Was it conceivable that this was the man named by her in their brutal confrontation on that night? The figure seen indistinctly in the moonlight below that window, wheeling away a bicycle in that hotel yard? Could this René Picquart actually have found his way to Pierre-Henri to ask for information about Marcelle's whereabouts?

Without raising his eyes to look at Picquart he pressed his features into a frown to win time, and to suggest it required serious effort to remember such a woman. He could have replied, after a while, in a way that left the man clear he was not a suitable person to ask—'I think I know who you mean, she's a close—a very close—friend of mine,' giving a strongly hinting smile. But he did not do that. He merely affirmed with a nod that he did know who René meant.

'You don't know a name?' Pierre-Henri asked.

After a perceptible second of hesitation he said, rather hoarsely, 'I don't know—it may be Monique, or Marcelle, or something like that.'

'No surname?'

'I don't know a surname.' He did, but was not so foolhardy as to give it quite so soon.

'Can you describe her a bit more?'

Trying to seem offhand, René spoke about Marcelle Grenier in a general way, pretending he could not describe her in detail, and that it was not so very important to him to know whether she had left the area, he was just curious. Pierre-Henri still played ignorant and shook his head.

'If you had any idea about a surname, an address, a place of work—I dare say I might be of assistance...Why do you want to know?'

Pierre-Henri smiled knowingly in saying that, but René did not match the smile with one of his own.

'Not what you're thinking,' he replied, granting the implication but wishing to give the impression of denying it. 'She was simply someone I spoke to—in a place where I don't know many people. A quiet place, as we were saying. I was just curious.'

An avowal of passionate commitment to Marcelle might, Pierre-Henri thought, have been a better response: he could have respected the challenge. This discreet deviousness, suggesting a man who could be both determined and subtle, played into his hands.

In fact it helped him to form the dark plan of which he now proposed the first stage. But he left himself the opportunity of drawing back at all the subsequent stages.

'Listen—if you're really wanting to know about the movements of people in a little township like this you've come to the right man. I work in the mairie.'

'You do?' He knew that; but he achieved a look of surprise.

'Yes. And I have access to records that might—I only say might—help someone anxious to trace a relative or a friend. But I can't help officially without an application which the mayor might be able to consider. On the other hand I might be able to find out one or two things *un*officially.'

Why was René not forewarned by this apparent readiness, after no more than fifteen minutes' acquaintance, of an official in a local government office—a kind of institution notorious for its bureaucracy and secrecy, especially in the atmosphere of the Marshal's France—to pass on semi-confidential information?

Because he could not conceive that the man would know anything about him; and because he was driven by love.

'We could not meet here if it happens I can be of help to you. Or even if I can't.' That was not true; a slip of paper with an address on it could be passed across when no one was looking, in any place. He heard the lie he was telling and thought the man would detect it; but he did not. 'As I say, I can guarantee nothing because we have so little to go on. But I can ask around in the office. If you wanted to call round at my place—I don't really suggest you telephone—in about a week's time—I can offer you a glass of wine in return for today's kindness.' The full second glasses were already in front of them, and René was paying the proprietor. 'We can continue the conversation, in any case.'

Why *was* René Picquart not forewarned? Why, above all, was he encouraged by this hospitable proposal to come out with the surname he knew perfectly well? The way he said it was, 'I don't know—but perhaps something like Grenier, or Grandet, might be the name. I am Picquart, by the way. René Picquart.'

Pierre-Henri did not ask him to repeat or spell the name which had echoed round in his head by day and by night ever since he had heard it from Marcelle's lips.

'Derrichet—Claude Derrichet.' Which he did then spell out. 'Nine o'clock, say? Nine-thirty? The early evening can be difficult for me.' And he gave René his address.

Nine-thirty in the darkness of a cold February night. The maquisard, as Pierre-Henri believed him to be, the resistance fighter, the man in the symbolic green coat which was a public avowal of support for the Marshal's enemies that you could not be arrested for (there being many green coats around if you looked for them), the lover Marcelle Levine admitted she had—though without betraying anything of what Pierre-Henri suspected about the man's activities—was agreeing to enter his rival's own home for what he supposed would be half an hour of sociable chat and the passing on of a piece of harmless information.

And now René's hopes rose very high indeed because Pierre-Henri calculatedly encouraged him before they parted by saying that, now he thought about it, he did have a distant recollection of someone at work speaking about a local woman who had left to stay for a while in Switzerland. He didn't want Picquart to get cold feet and miss the appointment with him, did he! He wanted him to be there at the hour in case he arranged that certain other visitors should arrive. He described it as 'in case' because he was not sure that he would do it, not sure that this plan should advance through further stages to the point where...

And if Picquart came, what if he did not arrive alone? But came accompanied, guarded, for this step onto the private territory of an official enemy? Before Pierre-Henri provisionally decided on his plan he had to consider whether it would be worth carrying it out if Picquart brought friends. If he really thought there was any danger of a violent encounter, gunshots, deaths, that might be different. He therefore provided himself with a way of abandoning the entire scheme if for any reason at all he wanted to change his mind.

It ran like this, and was very simple. Picquart was due at nine-thirty. At nine-fifteen Pierre-Henri would remove the receiver of his telephone in the next room. If it remained off, and the militia heard an engaged tone when they phoned at ten, they would not come. They would assume he had a reason for cancelling the plan. But if they rang and it went unanswered for three rings they would at once put their own phone down and set out for Pierre-Henri's house. Pierre-Henri would complain to Picquart about the idiosyncrasies of telephones, and they would forget about it. In his own mind he was going to keep the telephone off its hook if either he himself thought better of the plan or Picquart came with other people, and there was a prospect of a bloody encounter with the militia. A quiet, peaceful and unknown arrest of this suspect would be different. It could be that Picquart arriving by himself would mean that none of his likely colleagues knew about his risky enterprise, which was undertaken, after all, for personal reasons of love or lust.

At nine-ten, though this was not according to plan, there was a knock. No, it was an imagined knock, there was a wind rattling windows and shutters and it was possible to hear all kinds of sound. Pierre-Henri went into the adjoining room, a kind of study, and removed the receiver in case Picquart did arrive early. Then he went out and checked again that he had set out the wine bottle and their two glasses on a table, and that there were cigarettes for Picquart in the wooden box if he wanted one. Then there came a real knock; unmistakably real, a hammering so as to be heard on a gusty night.

Out in the dark a real man stood, in a thick green coat, Picquart, shivering a little. He was by himself—at least, Pierre-Henri could not hear or see any other figure out in the street, even when he stared out over Picquart's shoulders into the shadows.

'I came on a bicycle. May I leave it round the side of the house?'

'Of course.'

It gave Pierre-Henri the chance to go out with him and look more carefully up and down, and listen for sounds that were not the wind or caused by the wind. There was no sign of anyone else at all. No other bicycles, for example. He was sure that Picquart had arrived alone.

'It will be safe here?' said Picquart, about leaving his bicycle propped against the wall of the house.

'Of course. Yes.' Yes, the bicycle at least would be safe. 'Do please come in. Sit down. As you see, I have a bottle of the wine we had last week—which I thought very pleasant? Oh, please take your coat off.'

Picquart had sat down without taking his coat off, in the chair where Marcelle had always sat. He did not rise again but just withdrew from it and let it lie behind him in this spacious chair. It retained the impression of his body, the heavy sleeves of the garment hanging down over the arms. The stained, weary lining shone in the lifeless light of the forty-watt bulb low above the small table of bottle and glasses.

Pierre-Henri opened the bottle, chatted as the wine breathed, then poured two moderate-sized drinks, waited for them to accustom themselves to the temperature of the room, fell silent, and could not look at his guest. When he thought it was time to push one of the glasses towards Picquart across the table he wondered who or what it would be appropriate to toast. He could not betray the man so far as to propose his health, or even 'Our health!' He thought it safe just to announce 'The Republic!'

But that left René Picquart uncertain. Responding to a toast to this Republic, Marshal Pétain's Republic, did not come naturally to him. His face showed it.

'To France!' he replied; each drank to his private definition of the nation in which they sat. For the next few minutes they talked inconsequentially, as they had in front of the *patron* of the restaurant. Then Pierre-Henri noticed that nearly twenty minutes had gone by. In just over ten minutes he had to decide whether to rise and enter the next room to replace his telephone receiver on its cradle. At this moment he felt he had no justification for doing that. Or did he just lack the courage of his darker convictions? He could tell Picquart something—give him an address that would tell him nothing because it would look convincing but be a false address from which letters would be returned—and let him depart. And the militia would stay at home. An easy, bloodless, guilt-free solution.

How often in life did a man hold such power as this over a rival in love who was possibly a genuine enemy? In this case a dangerous man, supporting a cause he despised? An enemy of the Republic who deserved to be apprehended and questioned for wholly legitimate reasons?

'You have gone to some trouble to help me with a relatively small concern,' René Picquart said at nine fifty-one. 'Has it borne fruit?'

'It may have done,' Pierre-Henri assured him. 'Or it may not. I found the name Grenier—Marcelle Grenier—the only woman whose Christian name began with an M. And she appears to have left La Tignelle—to have left France. She went from La Tignelle in the last few weeks. And was bound for Switzerland. Apparently she was working at the surgery of Dr Villeneuve in rue de La Fontaine.'

'I see…'

'Is it interesting to you to know that?' The wine had drawn this degrading, this lubricious question out of Pierre-Henri Mallinot with a hard, hollow smile. He wanted to have Picquart implicitly confessing what he already knew, that he had shared Marcelle's naked body and her deep cries with his host. The wine drew out of René Picquart some vulnerable, stupidly trusting words, spoken with a smile of embarrassment.

'It is just that—just that I believed I had fallen in love with Mlle Grenier.'

'And you're sure this is the same person?'

'Yes…It must be.'

Pierre-Henri stayed silent, waiting for further revelation, indiscretion—detail. What a chance he had! Could he let René Picquart out of this?

Yes, he could let him out of his grasp. There were such things as honour, and mercy, and ordinary decency. He decided now that he would not, with six minutes remaining, make that decisive trip into the next room and restore the telephone to its cradle and receive those fateful three rings which he would ignore. He would pour Picquart more wine, let him talk, go past the hour and then bring out the slip of paper from the escritoire on which the telephone rested. Which would not help him at all.

He had his hand on the bottle again to replenish Picquart's glass when René suddenly decided to trust his obliging host completely and come out with the entire truth.

'I am sure you can understand why I am asking,' he said, speaking more urgently now. 'I simply have to know where she is. To know if she's safe. These are not normal times, everyone's life is in danger. If you have any knowledge of where she is in Switzerland—I believe I could contrive a means of seeing her. Or if she's still in France, and Switzerland is a false trail...'

So Picquart would be able to cross over to Geneva if he knew Marcelle was there? Geneva was a considerable city but he might trace her. That was not what Pierre-Henri had expected. All the same, he had decided he would spare the man his capture by the militia. Hadn't he? Magnanimity to a rival in love, nothing would be nobler than that. Except...Except that if he did not betray him it might be partly out of a fear of what might happen to himself if he did.

Yes, he knew now, he had made the decision to spare Picquart.

'I can't guarantee it will give you what you are seeking—but I have traced an address we have for this young woman's first destination when she left. It's in Geneva. You will realise that I should not, for any reason whatsoever, be giving you this information.'

It was almost ten by the clock on the wall behind Picquart, who was about to be saved from any danger Pierre-Henri might bring down on him; and the latter did feel he was doing right by getting up now and going straight to the escritoire in the next room; and ignoring, on top of it, the receiver of the phone at the end of its flex. The front of this escritoire opened, and you pulled out two wooden supports, lined with green baize to muffle the sound of wood rested on wood, and dropped the front down onto them. The inner side of this front would serve as a steady table on which you could work, and inside at the back was a row of small compartments with closed doors. One of these did not have a handle on it, it did not appear to be a compartment at all. But there was a secret button to press and a panel flipped open. In it Pierre-Henri kept the scarce contraceptives he contrived to find in the only shop in Périgueux that stocked them; which were used when Marcelle visited and after supper stood up beside the chair opposite him and came to him naked when they had looked at each other long enough and could no longer wait.

Irony of ironies. Pierre-Henri remembered he had actually used the opportunity of his visit to Périgueux on the day he had been compelled to stay in the town overnight, when his train had broken down, to purchase a further supply of contraceptives during the afternoon. Under this same packet he had slipped the piece of paper with Marcelle's spurious Geneva address. The contraceptives left her safe from impregnation by Pierre-Henri, the address would leave her safe from a visit by René Picquart for the time being, perhaps always. But if Picquart managed to get to Geneva…

Pierre-Henri turned and reached the door of the room before a thought occurred to him. Why had he not had this thought before? Had Picquart visited the same shop in Périgueux for the same purpose? Taken the same measures? He trembled for a moment, with revulsion, and with loathing of the man back there in the room, four weeks ago in the Hotel Moulin Blanc coaxing Marcelle to those deepening sounds from behind that bedroom wall. Hesitate he did, nevertheless, his free hand wavering in mid-air for endless seconds above the fateful instrument. But then he closed his fingers over the bakelite receiver and put it back on its rest.

He had hardly resumed his chair before the telephone rang. Pierre-Henri Mallinot got up again with a snort of annoyance and an apology and went to answer it. But it stopped again, after only three rings.

'It does that sometimes,' he said.

René Picquart sat looking very closely at the slip of paper in his hand, his green coat spread out on the chair behind him.

24

France was in the minds of other people.

All six members of Sixth Arts had been exercised about what passage to read aloud to the visiting examiner in the French oral for Highers, the very last exam they faced. It might impress him if they chose with enterprise and imagination—perhaps it could be something they had found in their own reading. Preferably they should not just fall back on works they had studied for the syllabus. Clive Garner had gone boldly for a short passage from a Molière play they had not studied, involving two different voices. Arkley had uncharacteristically opted for a rather grave paragraph from a Balzac novel. Jack was undecided.

Taking the train into town very occasionally, and browsing the bookshops alone—even when he had virtually no money for buying books—had been a pleasure of Jack's for a few months now. On the Saturday afternoon before the last couple of exams, with no cricket claiming him, he awarded himself that much of a respite from revision; but he justified it by thinking that he might hit upon an interesting item of French literature he could use in that final test.

The Parents v. School match, on the afternoon of next Wednesday, the day the French examiner came in the morning, would be a test of a different sort. After a little hesitation—Perce had further strained his right wrist when turning out for Mr Garner's side in the park—his father was now definitely playing. Son and father had kept off the subject at home, except for the occasional grin exchanged between them. What if he found himself facing his father's bowling? Would he want to be able to make hay with it, knocking fours or sixes? On the other hand, was his father likely to be better than he imagined (as part of him hoped)? Outright success for either father or son in a direct confrontation would be embarrassing, perhaps even painful.

He wandered slowly up Charing Cross Road past the library, the Garrick Theatre, the Leicester Square underground station. In the next parade of shops he stopped to stroke a cat belonging to a grocer's; it sat precariously asleep with its side against the glass, front and back right paws on the window frame, the two left paws on the ledge an inch below it. 'You are truly a good cat,' he murmured in French, for practice, and strolled on. He had a growing feeling that the French oral mattered, because a good mark might lift him from credit to distinction, and equally a poor showing would keep him down. His written French was good, his spoken French...That brief trip to Le Havre had not made a significant difference; he had been lodged with a family where the parents were too proud of their English to give him the practice he had come for.

He tired of the crowds on the pavements and turned left at Cambridge Circus before he had come to the bookshops in the higher reaches of the street. But this part of Shaftesbury Avenue was also busy, and had no shops worth a call. He turned off right into one of the longer, narrower streets of Soho. Unaware at first that it was actually the Soho area he was entering, he soon enough realised where he was from the open, frank stares and smiles he was getting from women who could not possibly have believed they recognised him. There was a menacing seediness about all the shopfronts and entrances here, the small, dark, weary-looking restaurants with foreign names and soiled menus in the windows. But he was not afraid, in fact he walked on feeling a kind of daring curiosity. This was not a place he wished to explore for more than a minute or two; but it was interesting to take a first proper look at it.

Then he had a brainwave which delighted him. He had already passed a shop with a pavement display of foreign newspapers on a rack: Greek, Italian, Spanish. Perhaps he could provide himself with an up-to-date French newspaper and read out an extract from that in the French oral exam? If or when he paused in his walk he thought he would need to look out for any woman, young, or middle-aged, or even old, who might approach him. If any did speak to him, Jack was firmly resolved to turn his face away and not respond.

Here was a small tobacconist's with a prominent rack of magazines attached to the wall in the shade of a grey sunblind. The contents of the window—cigarettes, cheap cigars, pipes, tobacco jars, empty faded boxes that had once, before the war, contained chocolates—suggested a degree of respectability and safety; nothing improper that Jack could see. He was similarly reassured by a glance into the interior, where a white-coated man with a neatly trimmed moustache, respectable-looking for the area, stood behind a well-used bare counter. Jack began to look at the newspapers.

Most of them, whether dailies or periodicals, were at least a week old, some older, many yellowed by the sun and already showing rust stains where they had been stiffly wedged into the wire tiers of the rack. Each price had been marked meticulously in pencil in the top right-hand corner of the front page, and the papers were expensive considering they were out-of-date. Did his plan justify spending fourpence on a much-faded copy of *Le Figaro* which would not necessarily deliver him a suitable passage to read from in the exam? He suddenly decided that it might be worth paying that, which would not leave him short of cash, thinking that reading some modern French would in any case be a good idea.

'But you are *here*?'

A girl, a small girl, was standing beside him, a lively, smiling expression on her rosy face. She wore a long dress, blue and flowery, that reached to her ankles. Preoccupied with the newspaper display, he had not seen or heard anyone approaching him. Her accent sounded French.

'I am Renée? You not remember Renée?' Quite a strong, forceful contralto voice, full of loud surprise.

'Er—no.'

'Really you not remember?'

The girl's name was French, the girl must be French.

'I don't think I know you,' Jack said.

'I am looking also for a newspaper,' she declared. 'And I meet you here in London—and I remember you, but I not remember your name!' All of this in appealing English.

'My name is Jack.'

'Absolument! Jacques—Jacques!'

It was convincing. But the confidence and the rehearsed charm gave her away.

'Alors,' Renée said. 'I come to buy a French newspaper. And you also. And then you buy me an English cup of tea.'

'No,' Jack said.

'Mais oui, Jacques,' she said, taking his arm. Gently he disengaged, and at this point nearly walked away without saying anything more at all. But he was frightened of reproaches, even loud accusations, or curses. And in the coaxing contralto of Renée's last request was a kind of pleading tone; there was also a trace of almost agonised disappointment in her eyes, though she was waiting for his answer with a smile. Then he was thinking that he had never bought Sylvia as much as an English cup of tea.

When he hesitated before denying her again, Renée leapt into the one-second silence.

'What is the newspaper you are wanting?' she asked.

For the sake of replying he named *Le Figaro*, in front of his eyes at this moment. She laughed.

'I tell you a better newspaper. Do they have it? Yes. Here it is. Voila! *Les Vérités de la Paix.*'

Jack Hollard had not seen it, never heard of it. Renée bent over and pulled it out of a low section of the rack; not the copy on the top, but a cleaner one from underneath.

'Is this a daily? Does it appear every day in France?'

'It appears every week in Paris,' she said. 'This one—' she looked at it with an eagerness he found enticing, starting to credit this dubious young stranger with intelligence as well as attractiveness, 'this one is from last week. Almost new. It is good, yes? I say to you this is a good newspaper, it says you the truth about France after the war.'

Jack Hollard. What am I doing? He would have to break into the ten-shilling note he had, he had no change. Perhaps that would be difficult for the man in the shop. Renée went with him into the dim interior; because she had persuaded Jack to purchase *Les Vérités*.

'It is all you have?' she asked him quietly when he produced the note, folded carefully into four, from the inner compartment of his birthday wallet. He interpreted Renée's remark as expressing decent concern on behalf of the shopkeeper, that Jack would trouble him for change of ten shillings. Looked at more closely, the man was austere, grim-faced, imposing. Jack felt himself to be the youngest, the least experienced, the callowest of the trio in this unsafe setting, this haunted little premises in a dangerous region. The man looked pointedly from him to the girl. Did he acknowledge her with his look? With that smallest of nods and a momentary pressing together of his closed lips that did not make a smile? Could it be that he knew her? Then he looked back at Jack fumbling to unfold the note.

A dog barked in the back of the shop. What if the man found some reason to charge not sixpence but nine shillings and sixpence? The girl would have backed up the man, the note would have gone across the wide counter, Jack might not have had the courage to change his mind about the purchase and claim it back, he would have walked out and run all the way back to Charing Cross Station where he would at least have the return half of his train ticket to get him home.

But the wordless proprietor merely took *Les Vérités*, looked hard at his pencilled price, put the paper back into Jack's hand, and counted out the change in heavy and reassuring silver pieces and coppers. Outside again Renée was repeating, though not so insistently, 'I think you have the money to buy me some tea? There is a nice little café near here.' (How did she know?) Surprised at himself, shocked even, Jack agreed. The earlier sense of daring returned. Part of it was relief at coming out of that sinister tobacconist's unharmed and uncompromised, and with his change from the ten-shilling note.

They went into the café, a tiny, cramped, exotic place, itself French despite serving English tea in a plain china pot. Renée removed the lid, looked inside, raised her eyebrows, stirred the tea with a spoon, put back the lid, smiled at Jack, poured a little into her own cup and then filled Jack's. He wondered if he himself should have done all that, but Renée was a woman and he thought she perhaps expected to. Even if he was buying it.

'So what is your job?'

'I am a student.' He concealed the fact that he was still in his last stage at school and would not know until next year, after even more exams, whether he was going to university and would claim to be 'a student'. He was suddenly so nervous again that he gazed down at the table, the teapot, the cups, unable to look round at other customers, even out of the window where they sat at this first-floor table. Was Renée enjoying his shyness? Because she was laughing, and touching him on the hand.

'So you are eighteen?'

'Yes.' But you did not ask girls or women their age.

'I was happy when I was eighteen. I will not be eighteen again. I am twenty-three.'

He had this immediate surge of powerful, extraordinary fascination with what was happening to him. Jack Hollard was taking a mature, sophisticated, physically attractive foreign woman out to tea. She had sought his acquaintance on false pretences in this risky corner of the city. But you did not ask girls or women what they did, and nothing really wrong had so far happened. Had it?

'I have been a performer on the stage,' she said, without his asking. And then she revealed things he knew at once would be worth telling Ronnie Walston about. Ronnie had never been unfriendly, but he had been underestimating Jack, patronising him, for years. Yes, he now had something worth relating to Walston. And Renée's information had startled and amazed him, because he realised he had seen her before, even if they had not—as she had pretended (though she had abandoned the pretence)—ever met before, anywhere.

'Can I have a cake?' Renée asked. He did not want one himself but believed it would be wrong not to join her. She ordered them herself, addressing the middle-aged waitress in French. 'These are their special cakes,' she said when the woman brought them. 'Now what about your newspaper?' She was more eager to look at it than Jack was, turning the pages with sighs of approval, or shock, or disgust at what she rapidly read. 'It is a very good newspaper,' she reaffirmed. He did not tell her why he had bought it, but it was helpful to him to have her remarks about it, her description of its policies and its purpose.

She stopped chewing the cake she had chosen, suddenly; and put the paper down.

'Sometimes I read this, because...Because my brother—' She shook her head, and stopped, but eventually managed to say a little more. 'My brother we think was killed by these people in the war.' Jack must have looked bewildered, because she explained. 'These people this newspaper wants to find—and punish. The militia. He was accused of being in the maquis—but he was not, he worked in the forest, it was good to be in the maquis for getting girls—you know what was the maquis? Very bad people, violent—useless. He had a girl who was a Jew—and because of the girl, and saying to her he was in the maquis, he was arrested by the militia. You know the militia?' Jack did not know, but he made assumptions. 'We have never seen him since. For four—four years! He was called René, also.'

'What happened to the girl?' Jack asked politely.

'She was not arrested. She escaped. She was in Switzerland. My poor brother René…I was a long time born after him, when I came, I resembled him so much they called me "the second little René". So I am Ren*ée*.' She actually produced a smile at this moment. But the next moment it had become real tears, and Jack Hollard had no idea whether he should console her or not. Indirectly he had made a girl cry. No, a woman. Half an hour had given him vast expanses of life to consider.

In the end he just sat there uncomfortably, and let the tears subside unconsoled. When they had, Renée ate a third cake.

Was he willing Ronnie Walston to manifest himself again, so that he could tell him? Because he ran into him an hour later on the station approach when he alighted from his own train on the way home—Ronnie destined perhaps (it would be in character) for a night out on the town from which Jack had just returned? Jack launched at once into what had happened to him that afternoon—colourful and hazardous happenings—with a deal of naive pride. Ronnie smiled and nodded and approved, but took it matter-of-factly, watching the station clock for when he would need to show his ticket to the man at the barrier and leap onto his train.

'It figures, doesn't it? Smart young woman. Promising young lad.' Jack was pleased with this generous description, provided in a joking way but without mockery—and perhaps with a hint of envy? 'She spots him browsing French newspapers in Frith Street, thinks 'obviously not French', nicely-dressed, I'll give it a try. You lose nothing. Probably a few bob in his pocket. Likely to have met a bit of totty in France if he's been there. Won't remember all the totty he's met, shop assistants, waitresses etc, who might recognise him. She can discover more if she gets talking with him. What then?'

'I haven't told you half of this! She turns out to be—you won't believe this—working last winter in a company of girls doing nude shows on the stage! Last winter my dad took my mother and me to this show at the Empire which had this troupe of women standing in the nude posing as works of art—'

'Your dad's a dark horse!'

'And this girl turns out to be one of them—a very little girl doing cupids and things.'

'You don't say.'

'Yes! And I must have seen her on the stage with nothing on—and I'm treating her to tea in Soho six months later.'

'Re-mark-able.'

'I thought so.'

'Here's the train. Did you get her telephone number?'

'I did! She gave it to me.'

'Has she got yours?'

'No.'

'Very wise of you.'

Jack laughed. It was a compliment; and he valued compliments; of whatever kind; given for whatever reason; and originating from whatever source. Jack Hollard's essential innocence never left him, all his life.

It did not always prove an asset.

25

Oh dear!—

Mrs Laidlaw was beckoning Sylvia Freeman into the little grubby kitchen area behind the staff door.

'Now don't get me wrong on this,' she said, looking Sylvia straight in the eye. If Sylvia looked away, and then looked back again, Mrs Laidlaw was still gazing at her fiercely. 'I'm speaking to everyone in the shop because it has to be found. It was all in a silver teapot at the back of this cupboard. The pot has gone. The money has gone.' Sylvia said nothing, she knew all of this by now. 'I'm asking everyone if they saw anything suspicious at any time they were passing this kitchen. It was there last Thursday night when I left money I'd collected during the day. But it was gone when I went to leave some more at Friday lunchtime.'

Yes, she had been speaking systematically to everyone, Sylvia had seen her conducting short serious conversations in corners. But Sylvia believed that Mrs Laidlaw's manner was harder with her, the interrogation more destructive of her pride and feelings.

'Did you come in here—and see anybody—any time between Thursday night and Friday lunchtime? Who was in the shop when you left on Thursday?' The phrase 'and see anybody' just about absolved Mrs Laidlaw of any implication that she, Sylvia, was the only person (apart from Mr Baxton) given to frequent use of this dingy corner to brew up tea.

'No, Mrs Laidlaw.'

'Do you remember the last time you did come in here around then?'

'I don't know, Mrs Laidlaw.'

'Did you know what the bag with the money was put in, and where it was kept?'

'The teapot? I never saw a teapot, Mrs Laidlaw.'

Sylvia heard herself denying it as if she was denying an accusation back at school. But she had never been questioned like this about anything at school, only listened to other people going through it.

'Did you ever have to go—did you ever see anybody else who had to go—to this shelf of the cupboard for anything to make tea with?'

Sylvia now believed she was trying to get her to incriminate Mr Baxton.

'Never, Mrs Laidlaw. No one needed to open that cupboard.'

'Did anyone ever speak to you about knowing where the money was kept?'

'No. I don't know anybody who knew. Maybe Mr Dindswell knew.'

She thought she should not have said that, because it was only Cyril's guess that Mr Dindswell as manager would have to know where a sum of money which did not pass through the tills was being stored on the premises; except that it was all supposed to be a secret kept from him, it being his collection. Mrs Laidlaw ignored the remark as irrevelant to her enquiries.

'Who was the last person in the shop at half-past five on Thursday? It can't have been you, can it?' The last phrase, like so much else in Mrs Laidlaw's approach, was almost accusatory.

'No. I left earlier, the same time as Mr Baxton.'

And of course, her questioner knew this, it would never have been Sylvia because someone much more senior and responsible was always the final person to see that the place was locked up, that the doors were safely closed. Mr Dindswell and Mrs Laidlaw had keys, and Mrs Laidlaw had not been the last to leave on Thursday. Which left...

Sylvia felt unhappy in using the word 'earlier' about Mr Baxton because Cyril did very much like to get away early if nobody was looking. And he would conceal his lateness at lunchtime by suddenly appearing from behind an array of raincoats as if he had not just come back into the shop from the pub. The way Mrs Laidlaw had cornered her left Sylvia feeling accused, upset, and weak. This seemed to her to continue with every look that Mrs Laidlaw and the older women sent in her direction when she walked past them. They were hard, suspicious looks. It was as if they wanted to catch her out appearing guilty, or doing something that betrayed tension or fear. If she strayed near the kitchen, which she was not going to re-enter, she imagined that everyone in the Ladies' Department had their eyes on her. Only Cyril showed her any warmth and kindness.

On this later afternoon it was raining, very hard. The only people who came near the shop were standing under the porches for shelter, waiting in vain for the downpour to stop. Baxton wandered over to the archway, could not see Mrs Laidlaw anywhere, caught Sylvia's eye, and made a tiny welcoming movement with his left hand to bring her over. She saw no harm in going.

'You mustn't worry about all this.'

'I'm worried stiff,' she said.

'Well honestly, you mustn't be.'

'They're making me almost think I *did* take it.'

'It's more likely that Laura took it herself.'

'Ooh—you don't think that?'

'No, I don't think that. I am saying it's more likely her than you.'

'Maybe they'll never find it. And we'll never know. Maybe it was a customer.'

'And maybe it will turn up somewhere and we'll never know who had it.'

'Why should it do that? If anyone's taken it in the first place, why should they bring it back?'

Next morning was the morning of the day when Mr Dindswell was to have been presented with his parting gift after work. But how could they do that if there was nothing to hand over? A small drink and a speech was no good by itself as a farewell. Mrs Laidlaw was supposed to have bought a card out of the money donated, and taken it round secretly for everyone to sign. But the shock of finding that the teapot and the money had disappeared, and the effort put into investigating that, had left no time. It now seemed that Dindswell might depart without any ceremony at all, no card, no farewell address, no present from his staff, no brand-new angler's stool to unfold and balance himself on at the reservoir.

Halfway through this morning in the shop Mrs Laidlaw went into the little kitchen to do again what she had done several times already: check whether she could have been mistaken, and find the lost article had been there all the time after all. The kitchen altogether was nothing to write home about, but what a mess this cupboard was! The shelf was a confusion of old dusters made from cut-up squares of material, pieces of wire, chipped crockery, a defective iron with a threadbare flex ending in a spray of wires, several fifteen-amp three-point electric plugs, string, a couple of cheap glass vases, all of it lodged in a sea of used wrapping paper, brown or flower-decorated, screwed up paper bags containing nails, or tacks, or rawlplugs, or nothing at all. It deserved a good clearout. In fact, here was a small empty wastepaper basket and she would make a start herself, take it round to the dustbins at the back; when she had time.

But in the middle of her foraging, towards the centre of the shelf at the back, hidden in this chaos, she found the teapot; with its full bag, bank notes, coins, the lot.

It was not—she knew that very well from her several visits to leave cash in it—on the part of the shelf where it had been originally kept. Someone had moved it. Or removed it and returned it. She stood there amazed at the discovery. Trembling with relief. Trying out every suspicious theory that came into her mind, every imaginable version of what could have happened.

Had she herself hurriedly put it back one day in a different place? Had anyone else been to this shelf not knowing what was hidden here, and shuffled the contents around in search of something? Not impossible. But her strongest conviction was that someone had taken the teapot out, made off with it, then responded to her enquiries with a stirred conscience and put it back again. In the wrong place. Perhaps some of the money had been taken? She would check; and not to be seen checking it here, she removed the pot, wrapped in a duster, to the ladies' washroom at the end of the corridor. Where an extraordinary circumstance became apparent.

How to inform people that it had been found? It was the least of her problems. The good news would spread like wildfire, she said to herself; tell one, and everybody would know within seconds. There were other things to do now, a card to be bought and taken round for signature, an extra envelope to be found for the gift, which ought to be converted into a tidy, round figure. No time to bank it and arrange for it to be presented as a cheque, but a round sum in paper money would be perfectly suitable. Today's five-thirty ceremony would go ahead. She would keep the money with her today wherever she went, patting a pocket to be certain it was still there when no one was looking, opening her handbag—carried everywhere if she transferred it to that—to confirm that it was safe. In the end she told several people, not just one, that the money was back; and she forbade them with a stern finger at her lips to raise the subject again. She would explain in due course. Except that there was one thing about this affair for which she had no explanation. When she told Baxton that the money was safe, he immediately wanted to know exactly what it amounted to, and smiled very strangely when he learnt from Mrs Laidlaw that it came to more, much more, than she had honestly believed to be there.

She made an excuse to go out and buy two dozen cheap glasses from an ironmonger's for the two bottles of sherry, sweet and dry, which Baxton was easily persuaded to go out to bring in from an off licence; then she went out again a second time for an appropriate card.

The rain had stopped and the sun was shining, and as she turned to enter the best prospect, a large newsagent's two minutes away, Maureen Hollard and Ray Naughton, whom 'Laura' Laidlaw had no reason to know, slowed their steady walk together along the pavement to let this hurrying woman in the required smart clothes of an assistant manageress go into the shop. The range of cards was very small. You could buy children's birthday cards, any age from one to seven, yes. Twenty-first birthday cards, father, mother, grandfather, grandmother, uncle, aunt, engagement, wedding, wedding anniversary, condolence, return of thanks cards. But nothing at all for retirement, what a nuisance. Wouldn't you think that in this day and age there would be cards for anything? In the end she bought one not devoted to any special occasion, one in which you could write your own words. But the choice of those was very limited. The only one of the three or four that wasn't jazzy or silly was a picture of a quiet green field with a donkey looking over a five-bar gate.

Out in the street again she realised with horror that she would have to make a formal speech when Mr Dindswell was thanked and the money was presented. Then she remembered something else driven out of her mind altogether by the temporary disappearance of the cash. There had been later talk of someone coming down from head office to do that honour; though nothing had been confirmed to her, because as the mere boss of the Ladies' Department she did not count. She must find out. She could ask Mr Dindswell himself, as there was now nothing secret about the ceremony, he would know about it and would have to be there.

She dropped the glasses and the card in the kitchen, and strode through the Gentlemen's to find Dindswell in his cubby-hole at the far end.

'Mr Dindswell'—she said it rather abruptly—'we are all set for this evening. But do you know if we are to have any kind of visitor from head office?'

'Mrs Laidlaw,' he replied, 'I do know we are to have one kind of visitor from head office. Sir Roderick is dropping in.'

'Sir Roderick is?'

'Yes, Sir Roderick is!'

'Well—' She was about to say, 'Well, I do think I might have been informed.' But she held back on this, thinking it was too late to say it now and it might come out as sounding mean and touchy. What she did say was, 'Well—that will be very nice.'

'It will be very nice Mrs Laidlaw. But would we honestly have expected anything less?' He told her that he would handle the welcome himself, and conduct Sir Roderick to his 'office' for a few words. All members of the staff from both sides of the shop should stand by their displays looking natural, as the chief would be offered a tour of inspection. Sir Roderick Mandelston Bt was the chairman of the company, heir to Sir Leonard Mandelston, his uncle and its founder. It was said that he only honoured with his presence at their retirement servants of the firm who had given over twenty years of their life to it. Doubts remained as to whether Dindswell had actually served that long, although claiming much longer. But they appeared to have been resolved if Sir Roderick was making an appearance.

'Who is Sir Roderick?' Sylvia asked Cyril.

'He's not just a Very Important Person.'

'He's not—?'

'He's the *Most* Important Person! He's the chairman of Mandelston's.'

It gave Sylvia a frightening sense of impending occasion.

'Will he speak to me?'

'He might. We'll have to see what we can do about that.'

'What do I call him if he does?'

'Sir Roderick.'

'But I don't know him.' She said it with a little moan of horror and then a laugh.

'If he speaks to you, you *will* know him.'

'But it sounds—cheeky. "Sir Mandelston" is better.'

'That would sound rude. "Sir Roderick" is polite.'

'Go on! You're trying to get me to be familiar with him.'

'I swear I am not. I am just telling you the correct way of addressing the chairman.'

'"Hello, Sir Roderick, how are you"?'

'"Hello, Sylvia, I've heard about you from my good friend Cyril."'

'"What's he told you about me?"'

'"That you are the most charming and beautiful assistant in the shop. In any of my shops."'

When he said that, Sylvia punched Cyril lightly on the arm. They were getting on well with each other. The men staff wondered how he did it, while the women reiterated their sheer puzzlement about what it was girls found in *him*. Mind you, it never lasted very long.

Time had to be allowed for final customers to leave—it was a company rule that they should never be hurried—so it was five forty-five before the highly washed and polished, enormously large grey car drew up outside the store and parked there. A uniformed chauffeur left the wheel and stepped out. He walked round to the nearside passenger door and opened it. And stood to attention. Sir Roderick Mandelston alighted and ignored him. Mr Dindswell and Mr Hobhouse were already on the pavement outside the shop. The youngest man on the staff held the shop door open. Sir Roderick went in with a general, beaming smile.

The 'tour of inspection' amounted to a leisurely, absent-minded stroll around the Gentlemen's Department, and then a very quick look at the Ladies'. Sir Roderick listened, nodded and joked by the men's raincoats and trousers, then asked Mr Hobhouse a question which no one else heard; and they both laughed. He chatted to Cyril Baxton and asked how long he had worked there. He was introduced to the younger men and told them to keep up the good work and enjoy themselves. He was then guided smiling through the archway into the Ladies' by Dindswell, and arrived with something of a sigh. Arrived beside a row of very special summer dresses where Mrs Laidlaw had positioned herself prominently,

'Mrs Laidlaw is in charge in this region,' Dindswell explained, introducing her. And oh yes, she felt the humiliation of being relegated to the status of a head of a department in which Sir Roderick had little interest, instead of walking round with him as the second-in-command of the entire branch. It was, as she recited later to Mr Laidlaw at home, 'disgraceful, utterly disgraceful'. She had worked all the hours God gave her for coming up to eight years, worked to ensure the Ladies' Department was attractive. She had kept it going through the war damage and the shortages. And her only reward was to be more or less ignored. Mind you, she was not alone in being treated like that. Everyone knew that Sir Roderick had not agreed with his late uncle's idea in 1939 that the future of the company lay with stores that catered for both sexes. Not 'Mandelston's: Gentlemen's Tailors' but 'Mandelston's: Men's and Women's Tailors'. Sir Roderick was saddled with this change. But because of women like her, Mandelston's branches all over the country had done very well with women's fashions. And all she had now was a quick handshake from Sir Roderick as she pointedly went up to this little quartet of men—Sir Roderick, Mr Dindswell, Mr Hobhouse—and Cyril Baxton, of all people—wanting to be greeted and properly acknowledged.

She noted that Sir Roderick wore a suit that would never have been found on a rail in a Mandelston's store, it had a Savile

Row look about it. And here he was, with a similarly expensive white shirt, and regimental tie, and his upper-class haircut, looking ridiculous, brushing her off and—and walking straight over to young Sylvia Freeman. Necessarily Mrs Laidlaw followed, she was not going to be left like a lemon while the chief flirted with her juniors.

When she saw him coming slowly but definitely towards her, Sylvia at first could not believe it. When she saw his smile as he made in her direction, and was only three yards away, she raised a sudden hand to her opening mouth and gave a half-giggle of the purest fright.

'I'm told you have come straight from school to work for us,' he said. Sylvia's paleness became so wide a blush that it spread to other junior staff nearby, terrified in case Sir Roderick would also speak to *them*.

'Yes, I—I have. Sir chairman.'

Sir Roderick chuckled, charmed by the mistake.

'It's all very new to you, then?'

'Yes. Sir.'

'And do you like the work?'

'Yes.'

'Well I'm jolly glad to hear it.'

Sir Roderick did not go on to ask Sylvia his standard misogynistic question when touring the branches, posed so as to get a laugh when he asked it; and another laugh when his female respondent replied. The question was 'What do you like selling best?' He would then get either a non-committal reply—'the new summer twin-sets, sir'—or be given a truth such as 'the flowered petticoats, sir.' The man could be unsubtly unpleasant, but not with the very young new assistants. What he actually said was really rather nice, and Sylvia reported it to people for days.

'Well, I hope you go on enjoying it with us, it's been very good to meet you.'

He shook her hand warmly.

Then something altogether unexpected happened, surprising for most people but intensely disconcerting for Sylvia: there was this flash. They all jumped, then settled down again. With their eyes on Sir Roderick and Sylvia no one had noticed Mr Hobhouse's appearance from out of the group of men with an elaborate flashlight camera in his hands, as big as one of those electric bowl fires. Or noticed as Sir Roderick spoke to Sylvia that Hobhouse had raised this instrument and was focusing on the two of them. It needed a few seconds to get things right, but the chairman's affable chat with Sylvia provided just enough time. The flash came and dazzled everyone, the handshake ended. Hobhouse's effort would appear in the next issue of the company's quarterly magazine.

Now they all gathered together in a cleared space in the Gentlemen's Department. There was a table for bottles and glasses, and two envelopes on it. Hobhouse and Baxton did the honours with the dry or sweet sherry, and when everyone had an inch of liquid in his or her glass, including Sylvia, Dindswell stepped forward to commence his own ritual of leavetaking. Broad squares of late afternoon sunlight, because the weather had changed drastically since yesterday, fell across the long counters, across the summer light-jacket displays in front of them, across the faces of the people assembled together as one staff as rarely before. They looked at each other, the women collectively come into the men's space, the men aware of the press of women on their own ground. Dindswell looked at the sunshine and stood himself just outside one ray of it because it was bright enough to dazzle, and he wanted to be able to see his tiny slip of paper with all his prepared words written down on it. The upward curl at the corners of his lips seemed more pronounced at this moment, Mrs Laidlaw thought, as if he was actually intending a smile, the perennial cunning look reinforced by the show of amiability. As well as that, Mrs Laidlaw was thinking that she had never seen him before in what he was wearing today: a Mandelston's Town Gentleman suit.

'Ladies and Gentlemen,' he called out suddenly, 'we are greatly honoured by Sir Roderick visiting us this evening—I haven't the faintest idea *why* he is honouring us.' The sally of false modesty raised a small laugh among the men staff, and Sir Roderick, propped against a wall, a tall gangling man in his suit from a superior tailor's, gave a heaving guffaw quietly at this introduction. 'Whatever the reason, we are honoured to have him in our humble abode, where we'—here, a quick, serious look—'have made our own contribution to the success of Mandelston's in some not-very-easy post-war months. Now! I am not proposing to test your patience and my speech-making talents with a long address. (What? You aren't cheering?) I'm going without more ado to hand over to Sir Roderick, and let him offer, no doubt, some words of greater wisdom that I can aspire to.' Dindswell had been reading every word of this verbatim from his pencilled slip of notepad paper; but he had rewritten and practised it (down to following his own instructions like 'pause' and 'change voice') so thoroughly that it sounded impromptu. Sir Roderick Mandelston had no notes, and needed no rehearsal. 'Mr Dindswell, ladies and gentlemen. To be here today is a pleasure indeed for me. But of course it is a pleasure tinged with sadness, as I have to say good-bye on behalf of Mandelston's, and with much personal regret as well, to the loyal and long-serving manager of this branch.'

Sylvia, who had after all just shaken hands with this man and had her photograph taken with him (Baxton put the idea to Hobhouse but she didn't know that), stared in absorbed fascination as he uttered those words and the sentiments that followed. She had never before been so close in the flesh to someone who spoke like that. She heard such voices on the radio. But standing just six feet away from such a person carried her, for these few short moments, into another world. With the lost collection money found, bringing her such a relief that she could have cried, she was enthralled and proud to be working at Mandelston's. For the first time it was better than anything she had known at school.

'Walter Dindswell,' Sir Roderick went on, 'or should I say "Wally"?—because I understand he is familiarly known to you as "Wally"—has been with the company since far back before the war, starting as an energetic junior back in 1923, I believe.' Mrs Laidlaw believed differently: that no one, not even his closest male colleagues, had ever called Dindswell 'Wally'; and that he had only joined the firm some sixteen years ago, or less. Memory fades very quickly in organisations. People go and are replaced by those who know nothing about past history, accepting their superiors as more senior than they really are. Archives had been lost when head office was destroyed in the blitz. The account Sir Roderick was giving represented someone's pure invention; his uncle, Sir Leonard, was no longer alive to put the record straight. '"Wally" therefore joined this branch three years before the General Strike and helped to see it through the throes of the Depression. The 1930s were not an easy time, but far greater problems of supply and staffing arrived with our friend the Fuhrer.' Mrs Laidlaw watched Dindswell's chin drop slowly until it touched the knot of his tie, where it rested with sincerity and modesty during the solemn passages after that statement. 'It was with the calling up of Wally's predecessor, and other members of our staff in this store—some of whom, very sadly, gave their lives to preserve the freedoms we cherish—that Wally received his own call from the company, to be promoted to the role of manager, which he has performed very splendidly right up to the present. But then no one doubted he would fill the post admirably, and our own faith in him through these seven—nearly eight—years as manager has been amply justified. You will all, I know, be very sorry to lose him as he passes on to a richly deserved retirement—as all of us at head office will be sorry. Many "gentlemen" have left this shop habited much more like gentlemen than when they came in, as the result of Wally Dindswell's efforts.' Mrs Laidlaw was waiting for some reference, however brief or indirect, to the Ladies' side of the store. None came.

The idea of 'habiting' gentlemen, used by Sir Roderick on many occasions like this, went down well with the male staff, as it usually did. Baxton grinned and took a large sip of sherry. The younger men smiled broadly and proudly. The women stood straight-faced. It was as if they and their labours did not exist. 'You have combined to show your own appreciation of Wally Dindswell with a gift for him from his colleagues—which I believe is ready to be presented?' Not smiling, Mrs Laidlaw held up the envelope containing the card and the banknotes so that Sir Roderick Mandelston could see it. At which moment he dipped a hand into his wallet pocket and declared, 'In accordance with a very fine tradition of the company, I am delighted to say we are adding our own bonus to the sum you have donated. We are, by company custom, doubling the amount—for someone who has given over twenty years' faithful service to the firm.'

As Mrs Laidlaw handed her envelope to Sir Roderick, who took it in his left hand along with the cheque from head office so that he could shake Dindswell's hand with his right, she realised that it would have been necessary for someone (Hobhouse, or even Baxton?) to impart information about the exact size of their collection to head office very rapidly. She joined in the patter of applause that accompanied the handshake. But she was suddenly much too distracted by another extraordinary thought to take in any of Dindswell's brief yet fulsome speech of thanks. Mrs Laidlaw was thinking this: told by someone, Baxton perhaps, of where the collection money was concealed, Dindswell could at some point have temporarily removed the teapot, added a considerable extra sum to the total to be doubled in accordance with company custom; and put it back in the wrong place among the junk on that lower cupboard shelf.

26

Notwithstanding, on the Wednesday week after that—

Jack Hollard woke up and thought, 'Today I have these two challenges to face, the French oral exam and the School v. Parents match—and which is worse?' Until late the previous night Jack had re-read and rehearsed the rhetorical item he had chosen from *Les Vérités*, having checked any word or phrase he was unsure of. He now knew it almost by heart, but thought he should be seen to read it; a straight recitation of the passage might look arrogant.

The alphabetical order of names in Sixth Arts would be followed for the oral: Arkley, Clissold, Edwards, Elmborough, Garner, Hollard. Twenty-minute orals at thirty-minute intervals (in case they overran) would, Ferguson said, give 'time to relax and chat naturally'. But they feared running out of vocabulary. Deprived of their form room, the library, which had been made over to the examiner, they gathered apprehensively in a book-lined stockroom from which Ferguson came for Arkley as first victim. 'A rather quiet man,' he announced, 'I'd say a bit studious and correct—but nothing to fear. I gather he's from Paris, so there'll be no accent problem.' Ferguson had been unsure about the recent slang-using French assistant from Marseille. He had introduced the boys to some extremely dubious usages, and become very popular.

After twenty-five minutes Arkley returned, shrugged, and said, 'Search me! He's a dapper little character in an old suit, pretty quiet, as Ferguson says...Going through it all a bit automatically, as if *he* was shy of *me*.'

'Anything about the set books?' Elmborough.

'Victor Hugo. I said I admired Hugo because of his "grandeur" and "dignity".'

They were Ferguson's favourite words for Hugo, used very often.

'Damn! I can't say that now, can I?' Jack.

Ferguson came to collect Clissold who, after a rather shorter session with the examiner, emerged with a similar verdict on the interview.

'A furtive-looking chap—I think I coped—he's not frightening.'

There was an hour to go before Jack himself went in. He did not fancy mouldering in this dark little room for all that time, and made a proposal.

'Do you fancy a bit of time in the nets?'

Clissold, as well as an opener with Jack, was one of the school's better slow bowling prospects.

'Whyever not!'

As they made their way with a bat, a ball and pads to the one practice cricket net, by the side of the field, Clissold asked Jack, 'What does your father specialise in? As a bowler, I mean?'

'I really don't know. I really don't. Medium pace, maybe?'

Jack was disconcerted not to know about his own father... It showed the gap of ignorance—or was it indifference?—that had opened up between father and son: Perce private and remote, obsessed with keeping his dull position safe at Fitch & Armstrong after his experience of unemployment in the thirties, Jack an only child separated from his parents by the education they wanted for him. His embarrassment about his father's taking up cricket again at forty-seven was deepened unimaginably by the fear that Perce would be humiliated by the superior skill and energy of the school.

'You've never faced his bowling?'

'Only under-arms in the back garden when I was seven.'

'With one of those little toy orange bats about the size of a ruler?'

'One of those.'

'Does he play regularly?'

'No.'

As Jack hit out at the deliveries sent down by Clissold in the net he wished seriously that his father had either kept up his cricket all the time or declined the invitation. He would be an unknown quantity at best; at worst he would show he was too old, he would make a fool of himself, it was frightening.

'Is there any cricket in your ancestry?' he called out to Clissold. He knew nothing about Clissold's family, Clissold never spoke about it. About to bowl another ball to Jack, Clissold paused at this question. He breathed in very audibly, exhaled with a rueful smile, shook his head.

'Nope! As you may know—or you may not—I do not see my father. I do not know my father any more. I have no brothers or sisters. My mother...'

He ran up and bowled, and Jack smothered the spin on this slow, wily delivery. He said nothing further, picked up the ball, bowled again. Went on for several more balls in silence. He only spoke when Jack handed him the bat.

'My mother and my father were never married,' he said slowly. 'And my father took his leave when I was twelve. My mother keeps the household together with her job in an office—she's actually rather ambitious. Gets around and talks to everybody, likes to think she's got her finger on all the pulses in the company. She's rather cheerful at the moment—promoted, or something.'

He was about to ask whether, by any chance, it was Fitch & Armstrong that Clissold's mother worked for, where she kept the household together—but it was too complicated and delicate a question to ask during a cricket practice.

Back inside the building after three-quarters of an hour—'You ready, Hollard?' Ferguson called out, letting Jack see he was looking at his watch. 'You're in there in about ten minutes.' They had stayed in the nets longer than they reckoned. Where had the morning gone? Jack had reckoned on getting into the library in the break to collect the copy of *Les Vérités de la Paix* from his locker, but break had come and gone. He had no chance to collect the newspaper before he re-entered the room for his oral exam. He would have to excuse himself and leap across the room to fish it out when he went in, with no opportunity to run through the article again to refresh his memory.

So at twelve-fifteen exactly, Ferguson pushed open the left half of the library swing doors and ushered him in, calling out his name and informing the examiner in French that this was Hollard, the last of the candidates—'but by no means the least'. From the master's seat at the end of the table near the fireplace, a notepad in front of him, Pierre-Henri Mallinot looked up and rose to greet him, a courteous action mixed with a relief that his morning's task would soon be done. But he did not smile, so Jack did not. 'Good morning, sir,' he said, in French. He heard himself saying it rather too abruptly. 'Excuse me.' He gave Pierre-Henri a very direct look, which he thought it proper to do before he turned his back on him to collect the copy of *Les Vérités*. Pierre-Henri wondered why the boy stared at him suspiciously for those two seconds, appeared to think of something, darted across the room and fished a newspaper out of a locker. When he saw this candidate sit down with this particular journal his mouth opened with an expression Jack took to be disapproving. Jack felt he was off to a bad start.

Conversation began with smalltalk as recommended. It was a fine day, but somewhat too warm for comfort. Had Jack enjoyed the school trip to France the year before? What part of the

French syllabus for Higher School Certificate had most appealed to him? That question gave Pierre-Henri a bridge to the next stage of the interview. If there was an author on the syllabus—or a French author not on the syllabus whom Jack would enjoy exploring further, who would it be? With utter genuineness Jack offered 'Jean-Paul Sartre, sir.' Adding at once that Sartre was not on the syllabus. The examiner gave him a sudden, sharp, unfriendly glance.

'Why?'

'I have heard his play *Huis Clos* on the wireless. It was extremely interesting. But I have not had the opportunity to experience more of M. Sartre's work.'

It was as if this neat, cagey-looking little examiner wanted to direct Jack away from a sensitive subject. He did not follow up Jack's explanation, asking instead somewhat coolly whether Jack had any interest in any different French authors, such as Paul Claudel? Had he heard of an author called Charles Maurras? Jack told him he knew the names but not the books, which was only true in the case of Claudel. Pierre-Henri thought he had done enough by dropping the names in this bright young man's ear. Jean-Paul Sartre indeed!

'And so. You have a passage of your own choice you are going to read to me? What author have you found?'

'It's a newspaper with a topical interest, sir,' he said. 'It's an article in *Les Vérités de la Paix*.'

The examiner's look was almost fierce with apprehension. Jack wondered if he had made a blunder. Were newspaper articles forbidden in the oral? For a second he thought he should go to the French shelves here in the library and find something different—perhaps a passage of Victor Hugo? But it was too late. Besides, he believed the article to be well written, eloquent, obviously up-to-date, a clever voluntary choice when most of his colleagues had fallen back on classics they had been obliged to study anyway.

Pierre-Henri's hands had been clasped together on his diaphragm up to this point. Now he unclasped them and brought them forward, and dropped his eight fingers on the edge of the table, his thumbs gripping the underside. It suggested someone about to make a point in an argument impatiently, or wanting to end the discussion and leave the room; or needing to get a grip on his nerves or his temper. 'Very well,' was all he said to Jack, who was disconcerted by the look in the man's eyes. He compensated by doing his level best with the three paragraphs he had chosen from the end of the piece, giving them more drama than he had intended.

> It is now over three years since the nation began the recovery of its freedom (with the assistance of allies from across the nearer sea and the greater ocean beyond). And over two years since the conclusion of the wider war in Europe in which the French fighting man played so valorous a role. In that time this newspaper has been foremost in bringing to justice those few whose despicable crimes and treasons threatened to deposit a stain on the honour of our beloved France.
>
> Evil and once powerful traitors have been deservedly punished, their servants and lackeys in cities, towns and country villages have been pursued without remorse. We believe that no one of importance in the infamous betrayal of our great country has escaped our net. But the net remains spread to catch those whose little names remain on our lists because their whereabouts and subsequent careers are not yet known to us. They should not hope that fleeing to another country and disguising their identity will protect them. Our net is wide. It spreads across national boundaries. It extends over oceans. The darkest corners of foreign cities will not protect them. They cannot expect to be invisible in distant forests. Neither deserts nor wastes of snow and ice will deter their pursuers, who will see them as plainly as if they strolled a boulevard in Paris or a town square in Angoulême, or sat at an innocent desk in Périgueux or even La Tignelle.
>
> The face of Justice is stern and pure. The hand of Justice—

Jack Hollard was only that far into the last paragraph, the most rhetorical of the three, when Pierre-Henri Mallinot stopped him. When Jack lifted his eyes from the newsprint at the interruption he was astonished to see the man staring at him wildly with his mouth rigidly open, his hands now pressing down on the table as if he wanted to lift himself out of the chair.

'Who suggested that newspaper to you? That passage?' he eventually asked.

'No one...Well...No, nobody did.' Obscurely he wondered whether he might be getting Renée into trouble. 'I thought it might be interesting to have some—some more modern material.'

He could not sit here with the oral examiner in French for Higher School Certificate and say he had been persuaded into buying this newspaper by an attractive small French girl in Soho whom he believed may have been a rather young prostitute but he couldn't tell, all he knew was that she had had for a while a most unusual occupation which might lead you to speculate...She never actually said, but she promised him a most interesting time if they ever met again and he could lend her, say, three pounds. He should ring her up at the number she wrote on a small white card that smelt of scent. Meanwhile, this article on the tracking down of French collaborators with the Nazis and the Vichy government was worth reading, she said, if he could understand the French. He placed her card between other items in his new wallet and closed it, and smelt it. The sweetness of the scent came through the shiny leather, and he buried the card among the pants and socks in his bedroom drawer.

The examiner took the newspaper from him and appeared to tremble as he scanned it.

'You do not know this newspaper well? You do not know anyone connected with this newspaper?'

The man's voice was full of urgent, perplexing anxiety. It was a hot day, they had agreed. But was the examiner shivering?

'No—I had never seen it before last Saturday.'

Inexplicably, almost as if he did not want to be overheard saying this in French, the examiner went on in English,

'It's a very violent publication—not worth reading. All they want to do is make enemies...It's—it's decadent. They trade on fantasies of revenge.'

Jack was startled back into English himself. Were they abandoning the examination? He would tell the others—and go on thinking about it long after—that this was one of the most peculiar moments of his life. A formidable-looking little French examiner had had some sort of nervous breakdown while conducting his oral for Highers. This was something he could legitimately tell Renée about—if he ran into Renée again—since she had suggested the newspaper to him. None of his form-mates had seen anything odd while nattering about Marivaux, or Hugo, or Lamartine. Arkley also believed that, on the other hand, who could be blamed for going mad while trying to examine Hollard?

Pierre-Henri fought down the rising fear, the paranoia connecting this absolute coincidence with the arrival of two Frenchmen at Mrs Orlop's the night before; who had denied him most of last night's sleep. They had not reappeared. But he had brought his smaller suitcase with him to this, the last of his examining appointments. His interview with Jack Hollard overran, and Ferguson, delighted to think that Hollard had sustained a dialogue for so long, had to hurry the examiner over to lunch in the prefabricated canteen.

The short cut to the canteen went across the lawn, out of bounds for the boys, and along by the high railings separating the school from the lower end of the High Street of this suburb. Ferguson was full of sociable chitchat, interlaced with artful praises of his current group of Highers candidates. But halfway across this stretch of glistening summer grass Pierre-Henri stopped listening. Beyond the dark green railings, beside the broad pavement, a car was parked. Two men were alighting from this thoroughly unnoticeable vehicle, which was not even French, and they were looking into the school grounds—and they were unmistakably French in appearance. One of them was looking up at the school board, but dropped his gaze as Ferguson and Pierre-Henri went by, and called out, and waved.

'See you soon, Claude,' he called out in French.

When Ferguson saw this he assumed that the visiting examiner had cordial French acquaintances in the district whom he was scheduled to meet later in the day. He did momentarily think it strange, though, to see the car was still parked there with the two Frenchmen chatting beside it and looking through the railings when they adjourned to the masters' common room for coffee.

Over the coffee, Ferguson said, wondering when he could decently escort the examiner to the door (and thinking about his games staff preoccupations this afternoon)—but enjoying the chance of talking in French with a native—'It's a great sadness to me that we've never managed to interest many of the French in taking up cricket. "Fotbal", certainly and a little "Rugby", I suppose. But cricket? Alas! And you are so close to us. We could have Normandy and Brittany in the County Championship. Clubs could be crossing the Channel for weekend matches. It's a game for philosophers, cricket, and you are, after all, a nation of philosophers. One of our English philosophers said that, logically, cricket is the most exciting of all sports because there is a potential crisis in every ball.' And so on.

Pierre-Henri was hearing very little of this, just nodding, forcing a smile, picking at his mince and mashed potato and cauliflower. Only when he heard his host jovially extending an invitation to him to stay and watch the school play the parents did he listen. 'You no doubt have another port-of-call?' Ferguson asked. 'You don't? Well why not stay? You're very welcome to watch our annual match between the boys and their fathers.'

Was this, conceivably, a lifeline for Pierre-Henri? Because he was not going to leave the premises alone while those two men were there. If, by staying on, he could leave in the company of a member or members of staff, even obtain a lift (though he had seen only two cars in the drive), then there might be an opportunity of avoiding them. He would not be going back to Mrs Lettie Orlop's. All he really needed was in the bag he had brought: personal documents, addresses (the University of London Examinations Board, who would be asked to send his fees to some future destination), money, a few clothes, a book or two. Picquart's green coat could stay in the wardrobe in his bedroom in the safe keeping of Mrs Orlop; he had no intention whatsoever of reclaiming it. He would write to her, of course, and say that he had been urgently recalled to France, and send a few pounds as compensation for the abruptness of his leaving. Then he would go north and sink into the darkness of some industrial city that had an examinations board for secondary schools. And write with apologies to parents whose children he was abandoning by this departure.

Just inside the gate a trestle table had been set up, with two women, mothers, busying around it in the sunshine, laughing. 'Open to the Public', Ferguson noticed. And suddenly Pierre-Henri Mallinot said, 'Thank you. I would like to stay this afternoon. I have no other engagement today.'

'I'll find you a deckchair,' Ferguson told him. 'You deserve one after your efforts this morning.' Nothing was lost by a little cosseting and flattery of examiners. A car drew up at the gate, and the local member of parliament had arrived to pay a courtesy visit and conduct the toss.

The fathers were arriving and making their way to their changing room on the long, ample, ground floor of the pavilion, a large converted house predating the foundation of the school and now containing, upstairs, flats for both the caretaker and the groundsman. Perce Hollard went up the wooden steps onto the veranda and the front door, saw his son, and waved. 'See you out there,' was all he said to Jack, because in truth he was late and would have to hurry to change into his borrowed whites. His father's breeziness gave Jack a reassuring surge of pride, and a sudden hope that he might not end the day looking absurd or incompetent.

Was it different—worse still?—for the father and the son, Reginald and Clive Garner, who were the captains, respectively, of the Parents' and the School XIs? Jack watched them walk out from the pavilion with the umpires, together, go down the steps, cross the boundary rope to be visible to all eyes: the teams, the masters and guests, including Pierre-Henri, the ring of boys circling the field—allowed the afternoon 'off school' as long as they attended the match. Mr Garner's arm was round Clive's shoulders, they were laughing, the MP was producing a coin from his pocket, a florin with the bald head of Edward VII on it, smooth from forty years' use.

Clive Garner won the toss. Was he right to put his father's side in to bat? Clive believed it would be better for the school to have a target to face between tea at four and the supper provided in the pavilion by the mothers at six-thirty, and not present that task to the Parents. The boys' fathers would probably show signs of weariness in the field towards the end of the afternoon; or that was Clive's somewhat cruel reasoning. The School ought not to have much trouble with the Parents' total of anything up to seventy, even eighty. The only faint worry in his mind was the quality of the lst XI's bowling if any of the Parents—perhaps his father's 'secret weapon' recruit—should put it to the test. It had dogged persistence, but not much variety or inspiration.

Jack had never achieved very much as a close fielder and was happy for Clive and the bowlers to let him take today a deepish off-side position where he could cope with any rude slogging from forty- to fifty-year-old fathers; perhaps even make a catch or two. In fact, the first serious shot from the Parents' No 1 came in his direction, not a hook but a clumsily mis-timed drive without much force. All Jack had to do was to dart in five yards or so towards the wicket so as to scoop it up and prevent the batsman snatching a single. 'Never look at the spectators', was his maxim as a fielder. But as he strolled back to resume his position something distracted him, and he broke his own rule. At the boundary immediately behind where he had been standing, under a tree on two unfolded seats, were two figures, an oldish man and a girl. There was little reason why Jack in these few seconds should have recognised the man who had sold him a new jacket in Mandelston's a couple of weeks before. But the girl was Sylvia Freeman.

When the field changed at the end of this first over with no runs on the board, he briefly had a better view of this pair. The man was talking energetically to Sylvia, indicating things with his fingers, explaining the match to her. Sylvia was nodding. At one point he could see her laughing, and he swore he could hear it, Sylvia's lovely innocent laugh. Luckily a second, better-timed stroke from No 2 went well wide of Jack's fielding position and no one would have expected him to reach it. But he still had to tell himself to keep his mind strictly on the game. Which for a moment became more difficult again when he happened to glance over at the pavilion and see his mother walking up the veranda steps towards his dad, who was watching everything keenly from a deckchair.

This happened not between overs but between balls, and it was just possible that he might have caught the next shot, lofted in his direction, if he had reacted just half a second faster and covered about ten yards towards the boundary keeping his eye on it over his left shoulder. Only a few fairly alert and attentive persons believed he could have done it, but they included Clive Garner and Perce Hollard. After it landed on the rough grass of the outfield, Jack did manage to intercept the ball before it reached the boundary in front of Sylvia and Cyril Baxton; but the batsmen ran three. Unfortunately for the Parents, No 1 was clean bowled by the next ball for a duck.

Perce was now standing up on the pavilion veranda, Maureen having taken his deckchair. Three deckchairs along, someone Jack honestly believed must be this morning's French oral examiner was sitting, rigidly upright as if he might want to leap up suddenly. And he could now, yes, place the man Sylvia was with: the older assistant from Mandelston's who had helped him try on the new jacket. Her connection with him from the store was explicable, but their presence here together was puzzling in the extreme. Had they just happened to drift in on early closing day, to an event open to the public? Jack could not know that it was because Cyril received circulars about this annual event as a member of the school Old Boys' association.

Perce had urged Maureen to come and support him and Jack, but she had said she would not. She had little interest in cricket. Besides, she was thinking of looking in at the doctor's to be checked over that morning; and she had shopping to do; and she wouldn't have time. So he was very surprised to see that she had changed her mind and found her way here.

'Have you had a bat yet?' she asked Perce. It was two-twenty and the Parents had made 3 for one.

'It's only just started.'

'When will you go and bat?'

Perce made a face. He was listed in the order at No 8.

'Sooner than I want to, maybe,' he said. Maureen did not understand what he meant. She went on smiling.

No 3, a man called Brian Thackeridge, was now at the wicket, and began his appearance promisingly. He was one of the Parents' three new recruits, and everything about him suggested a player who knew what he was about. It was in the way he took guard, surveyed the field with a leisurely, superior stare, tapped his bat on his mark with stylish smartness. He sent the first ball through the covers to the boundary; ignored the second completely; prodded the third deftly through the leg-side field to collect a two.

'Vous comprenez cette spectacle, Monsieur?' Ferguson felt that, having invited the examiner to stay, he should play the sociable host, just a little.

'Pas entièrement...'

'C'est meilleur que "pas du tout"!'

Pierre-Henri was looking out across the field to the left, where two figures were pacing along very slowly behind the groups of small boys sitting on the grass, and looking in the direction of the pavilion. How had they got into the ground, he asked himself? He did not understand that if the match was open to the public they had simply paid threepence each for their tickets, or even a shilling each for the admission fee plus the supper at the end of the day.

In the next over, with Thackeridge having established some credibility for the Parents' XI, No 2 found the courage and daring to hit two twos and two fours. At 21 for one the atmosphere of the match had changed considerably in a mere ten balls. Clive Garner now brought Clissold on to bowl, thinking that the two parents at the wicket may already have demoralised his two most consistent bowlers. Nothing would be lost by a change in tactics.

With Clissold's first ball to Thackeridge, fairly rapid after his surprisingly short run, Jack thought that he heard two distinct sounds. One sound was made by a split-second glancing contact of the ball with the bat when Thackeridge made to block the delivery. The second, louder noise was caused by an undoubted connection with his pad. When the bowler appealed, a visible expression of doubt crossed the School umpire's face. But it was there for less than a second. The boy understood the need to pronounce a verdict without hesitation, and gave the batsman out l.b.w. Heads were shaken and angry sighs exhaled on the pavilion veranda, where Ferguson observed to Perce Hollard that it would have been good to have been able to film that, and watch it on a cinema screen so as to see and hear what really happened. But that was forgotten with the disaster in the next ball from Clissold, which sent No 4 back to the pavilion at once. A score of 21 for three, with all but one of the four best batsman in the Parents' side dismissed, promised catastrophe.

'Where are you going?' Maureen asked Perce as he turned away from her to re-enter the dressing room.

'To get my pads on.'

'Already?'

He did not reply.

'I've got something to tell you when you come back,' she went on. Maureen was on some determined track of her own.

Ferguson wandered along to the other end of the veranda and stopped beside Proctor.

'I see Baxton has honoured us with his presence,' he observed.

'Oh, my God. Where? Is he sober?'

'Appears to be—so far.'

'Where is he?'

'Take a look straight across to the trees. Sitting on a chair under the second—no, the third—tree.'

'You're right. Did that girl come with him?'

'My God! Looks like it.'

'Jesus! Poor little thing.'

Another wicket went, No 5 caught and bowled for a single run after playing weakly forward to the last ball of the next over. The Parents faced defeat of a humiliating kind. Now Reginald Garner came in himself, a batsman of only moderate talent and with the responsibility of producing a captain's innings when things were going very badly indeed.

He proceeded to confer with No 2 in the middle of the wicket, as much to win a little time as to offer any constructive advice. It was something that No 2 was still there, and Garner was delighted to see him send the first ball he now received down to the boundary in front of the pavilion. It suggested that there was not really very much to fear from the School's bowling—as long as the rest of the Parents kept their nerve. The poor tally (still only twenty-five runs on the board for four wickets) was the result of nervous mistakes—apart from that dreadful and crucial l.b.w. decision that had denied them their greatest hope.

Two balls later, No 2 drove a loose delivery into an empty space between the on-side fielders, without the speed to take it very far, though far enough for them to gallop a three, and reach 28 for four. This sudden brightening of the prospects encouraged Reginald Garner first to hook a short delivery for two, after that to cut a better ball through the slips for the same. Then a no-ball was called (which he might have hit harder, but merely knocked into the offside field), bringing the score to thirty-three, and suddenly the Parents seemed to Mr Garner to be slowly emerging from desperate trouble.

Quite why he behaved as rashly as he did now he couldn't later explain. An illusion of safety? An instinct to go prematurely for a triumph over what was, with the exception of a few of Clissold's unexpectedly good deliveries, an indifferent attack? Whatever the psychology of it, Reginald Garner went down the wicket and hooked the short ball high into the air above mid-off. Positioned farther out after this brief spell of fierce hitting and scoring, Jack saw that Clive's father had too courageously gone for what was called in school cricket 'a six over the trees'.

Jack also saw that the ball was not going to make it quite that far. It might drop onto the grass just short of the boundary rope. With speed and luck he could possibly prevent it falling anywhere at all except into his outstretched hands. Coming down from that height it brought Jack almost to his knees in catching it. But catch it he did, and held it safely, and realised to his delight that Sylvia sitting under that tree would have seen him do it. The Parents' captain was thus out for four runs, plunging his side back into crisis with, to follow, two members of his side who were new and completely untested performers.

One of them was walking out to the wicket now, a small, stocky, red-faced man with bristly red hair. He would not face the bowling immediately, No 2 would do that. Much depended on No 2, who was well-set and looked confident after having made nineteen runs of the Parents' total. He told the incoming batsman that he intended to play cautiously for most of the over, but try to keep the bowling for the next one by taking a single towards the end of it. But he did not enquire whether the small newcomer would feel the need of this protection.

Protection was not to be provided. Advancing to hit the last ball of the over, from which he hoped to snatch that one run, No 2 unaccountably missed it altogether, whirled round and shoved his bat towards the crease a second too late. He had already been stumped. Thirty-three for six.

So it was now the turn of the second of the two wholly unknown quantities to bat, the little red-haired man—with Perce Hollard as his partner.

'Are you on now?' Maureen asked Perce as No 2 began to make his rueful way towards them, back to the pavilion and half an hour of blaming and cursing himself for his folly...

'Yes, I am.'

'Well, I'll tell you before you go, then.'

'Tell me? Tell me what?'

'I'm a month late, and the doctor says it's quite likely I'm expecting again.'

What Perce said, not unkindly, but thrown by the news and smiling with exasperation, was 'Well, you do choose your moment, don't you!'

Before picking up his bat and bracing himself to go out to the wicket he pressed with his gloved hand Maureen's two hands, which were clasped in her lap in the deckchair. He did not feel it was enough in the circumstances, but...

What Jack was thinking as his father walked slowly out to the wicket was: 'I'm very glad it was Clive's dad I caught on the boundary.' Jack hoped he would not have the kind of opportunity Mr Garner had given him. Not that he could imagine Dad striding down the wicket and attempting a majestic clout of that sort...Other thoughts, too, went with that. This man coming out to bat, his father, Perce, had become a stranger. The woman he had left on the pavilion veranda, his mother, was a stranger. He had merely assumed that he knew them, that he understood what they were all about. He didn't.

With the new over beginning, the other new batsman, and not Perce, would have to face the first ball. The man was really very short, surely no more than five feet tall, stocky, and angry-looking with a straggly, greying red moustache and that wiry red hair. He walked slowly towards Perce from the wicket to have a permitted word or two before play resumed.

'I'm Osric Evans,' he said. 'Father of Achilles Evans in Form 2C.' In a rich, gruff, Welsh voice. And before Perce could give his own name, he continued quietly, 'To my mind, in this situation, there will be no merit in caution? Right, then. I hope he's not your son, is he? Good! I've watched him, that little bugger'—this about the current bowler, not Clissold, who was nearby but out of earshot and looping the ball from one hand to another with a happy smile while waiting—'I've been watching him particularly, and he thinks he's God's gift to bloody cricket. We'll see, won't we now! Good luck.'

Evans positioned his bat vertically in front of the least likely stump and loudly asked for 'Leg!' This was so weird a request that the closer fielders wondered whether he was mad, or mocking, or had some eccentric tactic in mind. Given guidance by the umpire, he took a very long time indeed to assess the positions of the fielders. When he bent over his bat, in a posture of furious concentration, he seemed no higher than his wicket—but suddenly he straightened himself up again as the bowler started his run. 'No!' he called out. 'STOP!' This he did so loudly that even people preparing the tea inside the pavilion heard the shout. 'There's people moving, look you. Behind his arm. In front of the sight screen!'

'Huh!' Ferguson exclaimed, a huge gasp, a bark of furious impatience from the back of his throat. 'Who might *they* be?'

'Frenchmen,' said Proctor. 'I saw them pay to come in at the gate.'

'I think they've got some sort of connection with our oral examiner—who's still with us, I see.'

Pierre-Henri Mallinot was indeed still with them, aware that the two strangers had seen him and were repeatedly casting looks in his direction. Did he have the choice of making a run for it? That was doubtful. He would need to collect his suitcase from the masters' common room, and if they spotted him leaving there was no chance of making a rapid unseen departure with that burden. He decided to stay put, in the hope of obtaining protection in the middle of a group when everybody left.

'I don't think these matches should automatically be open to the public,' Ferguson said. 'We'll be getting any Tom, Dick or Harry turning up.'

'Those characters didn't buy any jam, either,' Proctor complained.

'Well, that's another thing. Some people would turn this into a WVS fete,' Ferguson remarked, thinking of the volunteer mothers at the gate selling pots of home-made preserves as well as knitted pullovers and a few second-hand books.

Osric Evans crouched again to face his first ball with the whole of the white sight screen now clear behind the bowler's arm. As the first slow delivery reached him, his crouch appeared to intensify; for a tenth of a second he seemed to stare down at the approaching ball almost myopically. Then, with a decisive clip, he had sent it off at high speed two yards wide of square leg down to the boundary between the pavilion and the trees. It happened too unexpectedly for Perce even to think of shouting for a run.

At square leg Clive Garner shifted a little in case this batsman had only the one stroke, and tried it again. But this time Osric Evans hammered the ball precisely through the space left by Clive's moving, and he and Perce Hollard took two runs. He blocked the third and fourth balls, slammed the fifth through the covers for four, and shouted 'Stay there!' to Perce after they had run a single for the sixth, obtained with a defiant drive for which they could have taken another couple. The score now stood at 44 for six.

A no-ball was called for the first delivery Perce faced; and in response to a loud call from Osric Evans they galloped a single. Perce suddenly thought, I have survived my first ball without realising…Next, after two balls which he ignored, Evans's six landed among the trees instead of sailing over them. His elation at the achievement encouraged him to look for too much from his next square cut, because Perce had to send him back firmly when he turned for a second run. This meant that Perce would face the two remaining deliveries of the over.

'Why on earth did I agree to do this?' he wondered, as the bowler began his run. 'In those two matches I played for Reg Garner's scratch side last month I did not have to bat. I've had nothing you could call serious practice. Except for a couple of sessions in the nets, I have not faced a cricket ball bowled in anger for twenty-two years. I have the new post at Fitch & Armstrong coming up. I'm told once more I might be a father all over again. There's Dora Parsons…Am I thinking this is my second youth? Where are the younger men?'

Many had been killed or maimed in the war, or were too young to have fathered boys old enough to be attending the school.

Perce took in the sight of Osric Evans—now how old was he?—taking short, resolute strides forward, backing up ready to run as the bowler reached the crease; the man's faith in Perce's batting was heartening. Perce swung hopefully at this first ball, but failed to connect. With the second, the last of the over, he took a similar chance—and actually hit it. It was a clumsy, primitive shot of the kind known as 'a tennis stroke'. But did it really matter how runs came? In fact two runs came of it, and he was off the mark. Yet he did notice that the long-unfamiliar sensation of hitting ball with bat jarred the wrist he had strained in helping lift some of that office furniture several weeks ago.

It was a relief that Evans would have the bowling again. Before that they met for a third time midway between the wickets, and the Welshman complimented him.

'Very good shot that!' he said. 'But where are we up to? I'm too bloody blind to make out the total. Can you see the telegraph?'

Perce could not believe in this shortsightedness after the accuracy of the man's stroke-play; but he looked across to the contraption which 'telegraphed' the up-to-date score to players and spectators as long as someone slotted into it the tally of runs made and wickets taken, using numbers painted in white on black tin sheets. '53 for six,' he told him.

'Well, now. That's not bad, is it! Definitely not bad at all, considering how things started. But now we should play it a bit safe, should we not?' As if Perce had been playing dangerously. 'Otherwise we might start enjoying ourselves, which would be very foolhardy. Remember those words from the good book on every packet of three: "Better safe than sorry", Revelations 69.'

Nevertheless he saw a loose delivery coming towards him to start the next over, and successfully lofted it above the heads of two on-side fielders for a further four. The ball crossed the boundary immediately in front of Sylvia and Cyril, Cyril leaping up agilely from his chair to pick it up and fling it to the boy who had chased it in vain.

But suddenly Cyril heard French being spoken, and after his education in that language in this very place, mainly under Ferguson when he was new and young on the staff, he had been proud of his knowledge. These days he could even use his currency allowance to practise it occasionally in France itself.

'I do not comprehend in the least this game they are playing. When does it finish?' one of the two Frenchmen was saying. 'Why did they tell us to move? And then to stand still?'

They had strolled on from the sight screen to continue their slow circuit of the boundary with Pierre-Henri still in full view, sitting fixedly in his deckchair on the veranda over there where a large group of players in white shirts and trousers, and some well-dressed spectators, were gathered. Here was a chance for Cyril Baxton to impress Sylvia Freeman with his expertise in their tongue. So he stopped the two men as they went past, and attempted a friendly dialogue. He found, as they put it, that they were 'holiday visitors'. Unfortunately he had no more skill than Ferguson would have mustered in describing to them why movement behind the bowler's arm in front of, or even near to, that large, rickety white board should not be allowed. They listened, still puzzled, and walked on.

'This ticket entitles us to a cup of tea soon, and a full stand-up supper later,' he said to Sylvia on returning. She held his hand now, but still very lightly; not threading her fingers between his. 'We had a lovely supper last year. You wouldn't have believed we lived in a time of rationing and shortages. New bread with butter and home-made preserves. Slices of ham. Salad. Cake. The lot.'

Cyril Baxton was proud and eager to show off Crofton County Grammar School to Sylvia, even if he sometimes felt he was being treated as something of a black sheep by young staff who had never known him as a boy. But at tea and at supper he would be recognised and greeted (they would raise their eyes to heaven behind his back) and today he would show Sylvia off to *them*.

Loud shouts of 'Yes!' or 'Come On, then!' continued out at the wicket. Suddenly the telegraph stood at 84 for six. Perce had four runs to his credit.

'You told me you didn't know anything about batting,' Reginald Garner said to Osric Evans as they drank their tea in the interval.

'No more do I,' Evans maintained. 'Can you call it "batting"? I'd call it brute force and bloody ignorance—and a lot of luck. I'm as blind as a bat. If I can't see the ball, I have a go—in case it's there. But I reckon we can beat them if we try.'

'Well, Osric, go on trying!' Reginald Garner encouraged him, 'You've made all the difference.' And more quietly, 'I'll tell you what my plan is. I'm going to give the side two overs after tea—you hit everything as hard as you can, and I'll declare if you've put on a few more. Then you can show us what you can do keeping wicket.'

His declaration duly came at 102 for six, with Osric Evans not out with 67 and Perce Hollard not out with four. It left Clive Garner, as captain of the School 1st XI, with a dilemma. A steady game taking few risks might gain a draw, but make for a dull ending. He considered that, but decided to tell his batsmen to be bold and resolute. Especially Bert Furnell.

With Jack at the other end, Clissold now faced the Parents' opening bowler. He expected bowling of no more than the Parents' usual standard, although he was impressed by the length and vigour of Mr Thackeridge's run. He hardly saw the first fast ball, which he was lifting his bat to block when it was already well past his off stump. The second, somewhat slower delivery Clissold did see; but it was still too rapid for him to do more than set his bat in front of it and let it bounce off onto the grass about four feet in front of him. Silly mid-off scooped it up, and returned it to the bowler with a cheery smile. But the third delivery was faster, and Clissold could do no more than react with the reflex action of lifting his bat a few inches off the ground into a vertical position; from which the ball rebounded easily into silly mid-off's cupped hands.

Clive Garner came in, determined to look confident, but full of fear. He knew from his father's hints that this near-professional parent of a boy in the first year was likely to be very difficult to play. But he hadn't foreseen the arrogant speed with which the man would get rid of the School's No 1. Would he himself—or Hollard, waiting out at the wicket—be able to do any better? There didn't seem any point in going to speak to Jack, as nothing had happened they could seriously confer about. The School faced disaster. It looked as if this Parent could take all the 1st XI wickets in about three of his overs. Surely his father, as captain, would have mercy on the School? It would serve the interests of the match better if the boys were given a chance. It would be thinking of the spectators and the scheduled time for supper. It would be sporting. It would be cricket.

Clive did see the three hurtling deliveries he had to play, and survived them. The last one he even managed to strike safely out to deep mid-wicket, where Perce Hollard fielded it, no run being taken. At the end of the over, with Jack preparing to face his first ball, Reginald Garner decided to be ingenious. He gave the bowling to Perce Hollard, knowing from Clive that this father and son were not even accustomed to knocking a ball about together in the park, let alone playing against each other in matches.

Jack saw his father catch the ball lobbed to him by Mr Garner, look down the wicket at him, smile, and wink. And what came weirdly to mind for both of them was the back garden as it had been before the war, long before the Anderson shelter was installed under the trees halfway down, destroying the narrow, crazy-paved concrete path along which Perce had pitched a worn tennis ball, under arm, to Jack when he was seven years old. 'Hit it, lad!' he said. Jack obeyed on the occasion he remembered best, and clumped the first ball into his mother's favourite flower-bed. 'Forward strokes, straight bat—Good! Again!...Good!... This time—Good!' But the fourth forward stroke had given Perce an easy catch; and given Jack a lesson in how to expect reverses which came not out of ill-fortune but from not knowing certain rules by which life was played. 'You're out,' Perce declared. 'Give me the bat.' 'I'm *not* out'. 'Yes you are, I caught you, you're out.' 'That's not how they play in test matches,' the seven-year-old protested, unconsoled tears beginning. 'Oh yes it is. Now you try to catch me.' Another lesson in that: Perce clouted his son's first ball over the fence and on to Harry Foster's lawn next door. Jack's bowling, as well as his batting, would be chastised by superior forces, his father suddenly becoming a horrible, hated being whom he wanted dead. That game had ended there, Jack in tears. 'Rain stopped play,' his father joked.

Jack stabbed the first ball a bit awkwardly in square leg's direction, saw it to his surprise nip past the fielder and be collected by someone deeper running in, but not before two runs could be taken, Clive bellowing at him from the other end for the second. It crossed Jack's mind that his father might be still warming up; but if much of his bowling was as mild as this...But Perce was in fact planning to give Jack his faster delivery now, having seen his son open the scoring for the School...Provided that this wretched wrist was not going to let him down.

The faster ball beat Jack, but failed to bowl him. And it was the first and last quick delivery Perce tried, because he knew at once that his wrist would take no more attempts to bowl at this speed. He would have to go back to the slower balls. The next of these Jack hit for a two, very easily. The fourth was not exactly wide, but it was a loose ball coming at Jack quite slowly, and well away from his leg stump. The umpire was silent. It was ripe for hitting hard and Jack resolved to do so—but then changed his mind, and pushed the ball rather gently and considerately away through the leg field once again.

He had not tried to belt this ball hard because he hadn't wanted to take a boundary off his dad's bowling, which was getting easier. It came to that. Let someone else do it. Jack preferred not to do it himself. He and Clive had already run a single off this shot, and Clive was wanting to go for a second—and then Jack tried to make him go back. But Clive was already halfway down the wicket and a fielder at deep fine leg had picked up the ball with surprising swiftness. So Jack altered his resolve a second time, resumed his run, crossed with Clive—who gained safety behind him—saw a quick return land in the little wicketkeeper's gloves, saw the bails swept off the stumps to run him out.

'You were not out there for long,' his mother said sympathetically as he passed her in her deckchair on his return to the pavilion. He went straight into the changing room ignoring the remark, not desiring to speak because there was no one to whom he could explain the sensitivities that had brought about his downfall. They were too delicate for even his closest friends to understand. He sat on a narrow locker seat clutching his bat for a full five minutes, trying to comprehend himself and failing. There was noise outside, exclamations of shock or anger on the veranda, patters of applause. Then when he went out again he realised the reason for that—his father had taken a wicket while he had not been watching. Thackeridge had taken two. The School stood at a dismal 13 for five and Reginald Garner was going to have to save the match as a spectacle by taking his fastest bowler off and giving the School a chance.

'This is going to be over in no time,' Cyril Baxton observed to Sylvia. 'Then we shall be able to have our supper.' He felt in his pocket for the two tickets valid for both admission and meal, costing a shilling each at the gate. 'You can meet one or two of the masters who taught me.' Cyril hoped that would stress his comparative youth, the masters still being there, and be of interest to a very young girl who had just left school. How completely elated he felt in view of the marvellous way things had turned out between him and Sylvia. At the end of the rainbow was genuine gold, there are gold coins trickling through my fingers.

But Sylvia: she was amazed to think she would be meeting people who had taught someone so much older than herself—they must be very old indeed. Cyril, whom she had really come to like soon after they first met, was young by comparison with them, she supposed. On this hot afternoon, watching a game she had never understood, she felt that everything had changed in her life. It began with Cyril allowing her to borrow clothes from the store so as to dress properly for Mum's funeral. It continued with her leaving school and getting a job at Mandelston's. She had grown up, though no one had told her she had. Cyril just assumed she had, he never criticised her or talked down to her. She had overtaken her older sister Eileen, who had never had a boyfriend and now she, Sylvia, had had *two*. Not that she had told Eileen or her dad about her going to Cyril's house in Witham Grove, or indeed that Cyril existed at all yet; but she would do it soon. She felt muddled about most of this, but happy about it. Cyril was such a funny and kind man. And over there was Jack Hollard, her first boyfriend, playing in the cricket match, what a coincidence! She wondered if he was going to wave to her when he ran over to collect a ball, but he didn't seem even to have seen her.

With the Parents' dangerous bowler taken off, the School settled down to a slow improvement on its score. Slowly they went through the twenties, thirties, forties, losing wickets at perfectly decent intervals (though not to Perce Hollard, who had asked to be rested without explaining why). The School tail wagged, in singles and twos. No-balls were called, and clouted. Harmless shots were misfielded. The fathers' total of 102 looked far away still. But suddenly the score was 76 for seven. Reginald Garner reckoned it was now time to bring back his best bowlers, with two middle-order School batsmen well settled in, on 26 and 28. Perce Hollard did now agree to bowl again; though he felt some reluctance because of this undisclosed pain in his wrist.

Perce managed two deliveries which foxed the batsman who had made as many as 28, but the boy took a lucky two off the third, edged through the slips. His partner, on 26, then slogged a four, and a two. Had Perce lost his touch, and were the fathers tiring in the field? The batsmen actually ran five off the last ball of the over, after a wild overthrow in an attempt to obtain another run out. So was there really now a threat to the Parents' total of 102? Thackeridge must come back at once, no question about that.

The boy who had punished Perce's bowling he dismissed with his first ball, for an applauded 37. But the School's No 9 was Bert Furnell, a huge and carefree third-year sixth former retained in the side for respectable bowling and an ability to show disrespect for superior talents with the bat, provided he didn't try too hard. In truth, Thackeridge himself was tiring a bit by now. All the same, Furnell failed to see his first delivery. Neither did Osric Evans see it, keeping wicket. The ball raced some way towards the boundary without having been hit, and the batsmen took two runs to which they were completely entitled. Furnell saw the next ball, swiped at it, and off the edge of his bat it sped through the slips and added a further three. But Thackeridge made sure of the other batsman with the last ball of the over. It was now 93 for nine, with ten to make and the last man in.

Clive Garner cheered himself with the thought that, with Furnell at the wicket, anything could happen yet. Hadn't he contrived a lucky five runs off Thackeridge's bowling? On the pavilion veranda Ferguson was delighted at the thought that all his theories about cricket were again proving correct. The match was building up to a climax of considerable excitement. What could Mr Garner do other than keep Perce Hollard on at this end, with Thackeridge's over finished, to dispose of the final wicket? Was he not precisely the kind of artful bowler against whom the brash Furnell would make a crucial error?

Yet it did not look as if he would. Perce's first ball he hammered through the covers for a two, 95 for nine. They were seven runs short of the Parents' total, and eight short of—short of victory! With the second ball, Furnell was late in smothering the spin, it was not at all a confident shot; but he was not in danger. When the third, definitely loose-looking, delivery came, Furnell risked everything in a gigantic hook shot—and it worked. Coming in at No 9, Bertram Furnell was the first School batsman in the post-war years to achieve a coveted 'six over the trees'. Off Perce Hollard's bowling.

'Why are they clapping?' Sylvia asked Cyril.

'The hundred is up. A hundred and one. They want just two more to win. And that just now was a six!' She did not understand Cyril's sudden absorption in the game, and the tension he showed. But she was willing to try.

Perce knew, as he ran up to send his next ball down to Furnell, that he was virtually incapable of dispatching it towards him unless he tried, as they say, to push himself through the pain. His forearm and wrist had almost seized up in agony, he would have little or no control over what the ball did and where it would go when it left his hand. Perhaps a short ball that bounced high and did not let the batsman score was the best hope. Then another, and another—and then it would be the end of his over and Thackeridge would be on again.

This ball left his tormented hand and landed no more than halfway down the wicket among a chorus of gasps from the fielders. It was travelling on towards the crease, but only rather slowly... Would it have enough velocity to reach the batsman? No one was ever to know. Furnell, smiling very broadly, walked towards it bat in hand, picked it up contemptuously, and pitched it back to Perce.

It was Osric Evans behind the wicket who appealed, bellowing 'How is that?' And the School umpire, proud of his recent re-reading of the laws, raised his finger.

'What on earth—?' Furnell exclaimed.

'Out. Handled ball,' Evans shouted. Furnell turned to the umpire in bewilderment.

'Out handled ball,' the umpire insisted, again raising a finger.

'But heck—!' Furnell called out in astonishment.

'Quite definitely out,' the Parents' umpire agreed, proud to be able to interpret this little-known law so severely. The match was over. The Parents had beaten the School by one run.

Pierre-Henri Mallinot understood less than anyone why the game had suddenly ended merely because a player had picked up the ball. But then, in his bleak terror, he had been paying no attention and seeking no elucidation. As the last two school batsmen came off the field, followed by the rest of the participants, the two French strangers approached the veranda and stood looking at him so that he would see them, incongruous but unobserved among a loose crowd of spectators and players. Pierre-Henri was directed by someone into the pavilion, if he was staying for supper—Ferguson noticed, and thought 'Well, he's certainly making the most of it!' Inside he heard busy middle-aged women's voices calling people to form a queue for drinks—but 'Give the teams priority.'

The tea came in twisting jets from an urn managed by the two mothers who had been on the gate. Pierre-Henri joined this over-sociable line as soon as he could, waiting behind the final players to be served, still in their whites because a photograph was going to be taken between the main plate and the dessert. The people immediately in front of Pierre-Henri were in fact Perce and Jack Hollard, Maureen Hollard with them—inscrutably smiling. Jack recognised the examiner. Behind them, equally anxious for refreshment, stood Cyril Baxton and Sylvia Freeman, a combination which left Jack in confusion now that the match (and its own emotional turbulence) was over. The two other French spectators were next, behind that unlikely couple.

Pierre-Henri Mallinot. Sylvia Freeman. Perce Hollard. Jack Hollard. Maureen Hollard. It was the order in which they had sat in the Stalls seats in the Empire in January to see the show which included the nude presentations of famous paintings. While Cyril Baxton had remained in the Black Horse and Harrow.

'Run out!' Perce was observing to Jack; genially, because he felt that he himself had done rather well. Even his damaged wrist, which still hurt, had resulted in a last, vital wicket tumbling in the most unconventional manner. 'You couldn't make your mind up, could you!' Perce challenged. 'Yes I could,' Jack responded. 'I made it up *twice*! To stop—and then to go on.' This was Arkley's joke, but he did not acknowledge him.

'He taught me French,' Cyril Baxton was saying to Sylvia Freeman, pointing a conspicuous finger at Ferguson, who was fortuitously crossing the room in their direction. 'Would you like to meet him?' Ferguson, after being introduced, was shaking hands with Jack's father, and could hardly not reply to Baxton's greeting.

'What ho!' he said. Often Ferguson's expression on encountering someone with whom he was ill-at-ease.

'This is old Tommy Ferguson, who taught me all the French I can command,' Cyril explained to Sylvia.

'Hullo, sir,' Sylvia said to Ferguson, immediately wondering if she had said the wrong thing again, as she had with Sir Roderick Mandelston.

'I remember you well,' Ferguson said; a greeting with more implications than Sylvia could pick up. 'So...What are you up to these days?'

'Earning an honest copper,' Baxton replied. Ferguson did not press him as to where, and how, and how much. 'How fares it at school?'

'Oh, pretty fair.' Ferguson was merely bored and embarrassed, not intentionally playing on words. He glanced at Sylvia, wondered whether he should ask her or Baxton what she was—

niece, daughter?—and then decided it was safer not to. He excused himself from their company.

Ferguson was about to resume his host's role wearily with the oral examiner when he noticed that the man was suddenly engaged with the two French people who had parked their car on the road outside at lunchtime, then come in to watch the cricket and held up the match by walking in front of the sight screen. He was relieved that he did not have to go on entertaining him. Pierre-Henri had taken a cup of tea, and a plate of food he had not begun to eat, to a corner, and was giving Ferguson expectant glances; but in the next moment the examiner's two countrymen had blocked his view. They had heavy cups of strong tea in their hands as well. All right, in due course Ferguson would content himself with a polite good-bye to all three.

Had Tommy Ferguson been able to hear, he would have caught one of the two men saying to the examiner, 'We believe you are Claude Derrichet, more recently known as "Pierre-Henri Mallinot" of La Tignelle in the Department of Charente.'

'We *know* you are Claude Derrichet,' said the other, taking a sip of the tea and pulling a face.

'Aren't you pleased?' Maureen asked Perce when she managed to have a word with him out of Jack's hearing. Just in time, he realised that she was not referring to the Parents' victory in the match but to her new pregnancy. Afterwards he thought that he should have embraced her at this moment, putting the matter to rest until there was a good time and place to congratulate her properly. Congratulate himself, come to that… But there was nowhere to put down his cup and saucer and plate.

'Yes, of course I'm pleased.'

'But you don't seem very pleased.'

'I am pleased. Oh yes—I am. It was just—a bit unexpected.' Luckily he did not say that his mind was on the cricket; which would have been true, but a bad blunder.

Sylvia had been avoiding Jack's eyes. But when they accidentally met—there being food in their hands and Cyril not looking—they did actually exchange hullos. When Cyril heard them he shuffled up beside Sylvia. Jack wondered why on earth Sylvia had come here with this old man from the shop. His clothes, and his manners, and his outdated heartiness, were from another age. When Sylvia said, 'This is Cyril,' Jack did at least try to produce a free hand to shake Cyril's because Cyril was extending a hand in greeting and he could not ignore it.

'I gather you're in the sixth form and will be going up to varsity? I never made it into the sixth myself...Afraid I missed the boat.'

Before Jack could make any kind of reply Sylvia thought she needed to explain. She was sixteen now and all the changes in her life had given her the required confidence.

'Cyril and I are going to be engaged,' she said. Cyril nodded, and laughed a laugh of embarrassed pleasure.

At this moment Sylvia seemed to Jack Hollard far taller than she had ever been, and older, and more mature, and farther away, and absolutely unattainable. This was not the girl who had taken frozen walks with him in the streets and parks of the winter. She was taller because of high heels, yes...But she was just utterly different because of everything else. Sylvia Freeman, he thought (that magic, resonant name) is sixteen—I am eighteen—and she has raced beyond me. She has actually planned *marriage* with a man who, for all his oddity, his air of fraudulence, his indeterminate age (but he must be over forty), represented maturity, the world of life-fixing decisions, work—marriage—home—children?

The raised voice of Ferguson was suddenly heard, claiming everyone's attention for what was happening next. Jack saw Sylvia's hand feel for Cyril's at his side and clutch it, intimately. It was one of the most—'formative' would be the later word?—moments of Jack Hollard's life.

'Ladies and gentlemen—I have an announcement to make. Ladies and gentlemen, please! We are going to resume an old tradition now, if we can manage to do it.' They were quietening down and listening. 'Thank you. Ladies and gentlemen, this fixture in the calendar of the 1st XI goes back, if you can believe it, to the 1920s. Every year up to 1939 a photograph of teams and spectators was taken at the end of the match.' ('I was in two of them,' Cyril Baxton said to Sylvia.) 'The fixture went by the board during the war, and so this photograph Dr Proctor is about to take will be the first of its kind since 1939—we didn't have the facilities to take one last year, or the year before. So. In a moment we shall ask everyone if they would kindly move outside onto the grass just below the veranda, where we are arranging the benches for the two teams—and we'll ask you to be so good as to fill up any empty spaces and stand around, and behind, and close to, the players.'

The younger boys required to watch the match until the end of the school day had disappeared over two hours before this, unless they were related to the teams. So there was a chance of the entire supper party being fitted in, including any members of the public who had paid their entrance fee—like the two visitors from France. And guests like Maureen Hollard. And Pierre-Henri Mallinot, really Claude Derrichet. And Cyril Baxton, with his own guest, his fiancée Sylvia Freeman.

There was a very great deal of positioning and re-positioning of benches and chairs, of instructing the taller to stand behind the shorter, of getting the two untidy ends of this group of some fifty people to cluster together, stand in close a bit, and get within the span of the camera Dr Proctor had poised on a tripod. Reginald Garner and Clive Garner, father and son and the two captains, had to be in the middle. Jack Hollard sat next to Clive with Maureen behind him. Next to her was one of the two French strangers, who stood one on each side of Pierre-Henri Mallinot.

Each of these posed with a mind fixed on a future which this last six months, from appalling winter to sweltering summer, had set on an entirely different track. Jack was in his first youth, his future probably the least decided of the five. He assumed he would make it to university, but there was no telling which. (He was correct in that. He would go to the University College of Exeter.) He would leave school after obtaining a scholarship or place, and suffer many months of military service. It would mean that neither he nor his father would qualify to play in this match again. It was their first and last time. Jack was thankful for that.

Perce was about to take up the new post created for him by the unanticipated beneficence of communist comrade Jedleigh (and Carstairs?), a promotion which would establish him as senior to Luddon, or to Luddon's successor if Luddon left the firm in disillusion. Perce had taken a wicket—or in a sense, two wickets—and made four runs. He fancied stepping into Garner's modest Saturday park team again if he was asked. Dora had been to watch it once. Maureen was expecting again. It was like a second youth for her as well, with all these romantic attentions in her mid-forties. Sylvia still held Cyril's hand, out of sight of the camera, and was amazed to think what her future was turning into. She thought Cyril was terrific, being thirty-six didn't matter, in fact it made him much more interesting than boys of eighteen (she did not do the arithmetic and see that this was a modest estimate of his age). Who could she ask about the first night of a honeymoon? There was the older cousin who had come to her mum's funeral, but she lived a long way away, Bishop's Stortford or somewhere. She might have asked her mother, had she been alive—she heard girls did—but she would have felt dreadfully shy about it. As to babies, if you didn't want one every year, the Spanish Maria at school, a Catholic, said, 'You have to read by the moon.' What did that mean?

These five people had been as close together as this in the depths of winter watching eight utterly naked performers including Renée, all of them motionless except for shivering in a time of frosts and snows in the enclosed space of a theatre. Now they were reunited without knowing it, having watched clothed performers running around in a field in the middle of a heat wave. They would never come together again in this kind of accidental group.

'Really still, please. Really still,' Proctor called out from under his black hood. 'Still as corpses.' Everyone obeyed. 'Just one more. Hold it. Thank you. Excellent. Excellent. You may return to your regiments.'

'Did you enjoy the match?' Ferguson asked the examiner. And since there was no point in getting into an explanatory discussion of what had happened he went straight on and said in French, 'I could offer you a lift somewhere myself, but I think your friends have a car?'

'We shall be able to give him a lift,' said the taller of the two French strangers before Pierre-Henri could reply to Ferguson and accept his grudging offer. Relieved, Ferguson thanked him, a little abruptly, for coming, and for staying so long. And for interesting his two friends in attending.

'I have to collect my suitcase,' Pierre-Henri told Ferguson, hoping the man might still escort him courteously to the masters' common room, unknowingly protecting him. But Ferguson did not hear, having already turned away.

Pierre-Henri had been looking at someone during the stand-up supper, a man whose face was familiar but whom he simply could not place. It was not a recent familiarity. The face suggested someone met some time before this. It had English associations, obviously, but he thought he had seen it in another place. Not England. And yet not France—

Suddenly he knew where he had seen Cyril Baxton before. It was in neither country, but on the sea between them, on the boat between Calais and Dover, in the dismal bar, the man who had bored him with talk of Lawrence and Virginia Woolf and...This was one last lifeline, if only he could grab hold of it.

Briefly a vista of vain hope opened up. He might be able to claim acquaintance with this man, walk away with him and escape his enemies if the fellow only remembered that profound, philosophical (and utterly shallow) dialogue they had had in the lurching bar on that bright day on the English Channel. He pushed through the dispersing crowd and made his way towards Cyril Baxton. Cyril was surprised—more than that, he was thoroughly perplexed—to be greeted by this French stranger, not one of the two he had tried to conduct a conversation with earlier. Had the place been *invaded* by Frenchmen?

'You are *here*?' Pierre-Henri asked him. In French. Because he recalled the man's very capable French. He was back in the bar, discussing fate and rainbows.

Cyril looked taken aback. He himself was not back in the cross-channel ferry bar. Pierre-Henri smiled at Sylvia in a way he thought courteous, but Cyril suspected the man of wanting to make a pass at his new fiancée.

'You don't remember me? From the boat last year?' Pierre-Henri tried.

'Er—no. The boat?' Deepening suspicion of the man's motives, especially as he now gave Sylvia another uncomfortably ingratiating smile.

'I don't think I know you,' said Cyril. Pierre-Henri tried again, in near-desperation.

'We were talking together on the ferry between Calais and Dover—talking about literature.'

'Talking about literature?' Cyril shook his head and moved closer to Sylvia to assert his ownership in case the man attempted anything; although his puzzling questions were not addressed to her. Faint memories were stirring in him, though. And a few days after this he did recall the boat encounter—when, after all, he had taken a few drinks. That was too late to make any difference to Pierre-Henri Mallinot. For whom this evening a rainbow of hope was now fading fast.

'Excuse us,' said Cyril, putting an arm round the tall Sylvia's shoulders and moving her aside. 'We have to go and speak to someone.' Not true. He just wanted to guide her away.

The action created space for two other persons to move in.

'You have a suitcase ready?'

One of his two French pursuers was saying that, having overheard what Pierre-Henri had not long ago said to Ferguson. The trio of them walked slowly over to the back entrance of the school, Pierre-Henri passively leading the way and still hoping there would be some acceptable device by which he could evade these two unidentified countrymen who had followed him to Benford Street and this school on their mission of retribution. He went on insisting, up the back stairs, that this was a case of mistaken identity, that he was Pierre-Henri Mallinot and no one else, that he had never been Claude Derrichet, he had never owned or even heard of such a name.

'I lived in this country most of the war,' he protested. 'I lived in La Tignelle and I left with the forces that went to North Africa to continue the fight. I was with the Free French. I have a brother in La Tignelle who will testify for me.' All lies.

'We shall be interested to see if you have any documents in your suitcase to prove any of that,' François said.

Then a momentary fantasy possessed Pierre-Henri, of reaching the cloakroom where he had left his suitcase and running into one of the lavatory cubicles, locking himself in until a suspicious caretaker cleared his pursuers off the premises and he could let himself out and escape in the morning. Not possible. The caretaker would examine the locked door, and these two would be waiting for him to emerge from the building.

Therefore, allowed by François and Julien to go into one of the WCs, he performed his function and came out again; and retrieved his suitcase from where it stood among a jumble of boxes and rags and broken umbrellas. They then walked along the corridor and down the main staircase towards the front door, meeting no one but still catching the distant sound from the field of voices and laughter, and one small cheer for some reason.

Maureen's main thought at exactly this moment was that she needed to find a lavatory. She had not been drinking much tea or anything today, but she believed that this need had something to do with her pregnancy, early days though it was. Once more the future was going to be different, she had been saying to herself. Father and son had changed out of their whites and were ready to leave when Maureen exclaimed, 'Will you wait for me? I've got to find the you-know-what.'

'We'll wait here.'

She remembered that there had been the word 'Ladies' on a large piece of card on the wall in the room where they stood to eat the supper. And 'Gentlemen', pointing in a different direction. Both were upstairs. But the cards had already been taken down by the mother clearing up. When Maureen asked, one of the mothers advised her to go upstairs and follow the corridor round to the left. There was a white door at the far end.

It turned out to be a long, narrow flight of stairs, and the landing at the top was also the destination of a second, broader flight. The Ladies', behind the white door she eventually reached, was the groundsman's bathroom, allocated to the women because today there was a mixed audience of spectators. As she approached the door, which she now needed to reach very badly, she was conscious of someone else, a man, judging by the footsteps, coming up the other stairs with a similar intention.

Baxton had helped Ferguson and some of the parents and boys by taking back a chair or two from the grass into the pavilion. 'I'm surprised you don't put on a bar for this match,' he observed to Ferguson. Ferguson ignored the remark but relayed it to Proctor later. 'The only bar I'd favour is a bar on Baxton's attendance,' Proctor said. For the moment, though, Cyril had vanished on a necessary errand leaving his young escort—well, his fiancée—alone at the foot of the pavilion steps.

Waiting for Maureen, Perce and Jack exchanged comments on the match which of course stopped well short of any further mention of each other's role in it. They were tired. Perce knew as well as his son that they were unlikely ever to meet on opposing sides on a cricket pitch again. But neither said so. They then stood in silence hoping that Mum would not be very long.

Sylvia walked idly away from them along the veranda. Her high-heeled shoes clacked out a message of unattainability; the place having gradually cleared, sounds like that were audible. The sunlight of early evening began to get that deep, matured quality that shows in late July and completely possesses a warm August. Jack was conscious of Sylvia's every move, and considered whether he might be expected to go and say something to her at this point. He decided he could not, because it would not look right for the two of them to be seen together when her companion rejoined her. And there was really nothing to say.

All he did when she casually retraced her steps and came back towards them was to smile. She smiled noncommitally back; but no word passed between them.

'Do you know that girl?' Perce asked him, for something to say.

'Not really.'

That evening Jack Hollard went out to a telephone kiosk and rang Renée.

Epilogue

When a woman enters a room for the very first time, with a man following her, there is a rule that she goes straight over to the window. She is curious about the view, but she is also seeking some reassurance that she could escape to freedom if she needed to.

Today the rule was not immediately tested and proved, as it had been in Spillar's rest room and, a while before this time, at Ray Naughton's in Witham Grove. And Cyril Baxton was not accompanying Maureen Hollard. He was just happening to be behind her, arriving by different stairs in the search for a lavatory, and not at all aware that they might be looking for the same thing. Surely he might have guessed that?

When Maureen reached the longed-for door he wrongly assumed that she would be passing through it, for some reason, into an extension of the same corridor; he had never been upstairs in this house before. So he did a little run to prevent her letting the door close in his face, because he thought she hadn't seen him. Maureen saw, when she looked into the room, that she had located what she needed; and thus had the impression that Cyril Baxton, though she did not know him or his name, was trying to force his way into the bathroom with her.

'No!' she exclaimed. With some consternation, ramming the door shut. She looked round in vain inside for a lock, or a bolt. But now Cyril did realise; and on the other side of the door he called out elaborate apologies. 'Sorry—came to the wrong place by mistake. What was I thinking? Really, am most frightfully sorry, do forgive me!' A lot of which was fibbing, because Cyril had fully intended to find a lavatory to himself, even if he had to use the Ladies'.

Maureen found a chair in the bathroom to prop up under the door handle, and a small stool to stand on the chair as an extra protection. She supposed that if she made sufficient noise dropping the chair and stool into place, pulling the chain to start with, turning on taps, etc, it would deter anyone else from trying to enter. Why on earth wasn't there a lock on this door? She couldn't spend much more time pondering that deficiency, and proceeded to enact what she came for. When that was achieved, to her considerable relief, she went and washed her hands. And then, finally, she paced over to the window, parted the wooden slats of the blind, and gazed out onto the free summer air of the field.

The action of prising those wooden Venetian blind slats apart to look out reminded her, with inexplicable vividness, of doing the same thing somewhere else not that long ago. Or had the action broken a dream? Maureen did not recall a particular dream. But then, yes, she did remember—not a dream, but a nightmare, if you like: Spillar's 'rest room', and the street below, last year. On the same kind of very hot day in July. And all the consequences that had followed.

It was odd that the most important parts of life, she thought, the things that changed you for ever, went on in the midst of so much ordinariness, so many trivial things. Put it all on a stage with grand music, in an opera, and it made much more sense because all the dull, foolish little matters had been cut out, and life and death had romance and grandeur and dignity. If only you could live life like that! Standing there, incontestably some weeks pregnant again, with no more certainty than last time about one thing, Maureen Hollard knew she was having profound thoughts about life—and she was not a profound person. It was not possible to turn it into wonderful operatic shapes, and yet that was the only way life was worth living. For people like her, poor really, dropped into a tedious existence that was unworthy of her dreams, it was a muddle. She washed her hands, and in the mirror above the basin rearranged her hair a little. Twenty-five minutes before this Sylvia Freeman had found the same mirror in the same bathroom. She had given herself a good long look and been content with the beauty and the crazy happiness she saw in her face. Maureen saw a middle-aged woman who had kept her looks but did not know whether to be happy or just confused by the route her life had taken. For a second time, she didn't know why, she went back to the window and the blind.

Through the slats she saw such ordinary sights. There was Perce, and Jack, immediately below. And then the man she had caught a glimpse of following her in the corridor and trying to enter the bathroom (had she seen him somewhere else before this? He seemed familiar)—this man walking off with a very young, tall girl, their arms round each other. The two walked in step, though the shorter man had to take longer strides to keep up with the taller teenager. A few last white-shirted figures were drifting towards the gate. And over in that direction Maureen saw three foreign-looking men, one carrying a suitcase which appeared to be quite heavy, leaving via the gate and entering a car together.

On the other side of the field, to the side, she could see near the place where—as had been explained to her an hour before—the ball had landed to score a six, one of the groundsman's most expensive and prized possessions. It was (with the exception of Pierre-Henri Mallinot, who would soon realise that he had nothing further to hope for) the only being in sight whose achievements were entirely in the past. It was the retired race-horse on which the School groundsman, Henry Spillar, estranged brother of family black sheep Bob Spillar, would occasionally take a very light canter.

Whether the pale full daylight moon set incongruously in this amazing blue sky had anything to tell her, or anybody she knew, anything at all, was not a question she addressed at this moment.